ON THE LOOKOUT

BOOK 10 IN THE RYAN KAINE SERIES

KERRY DONOVAN

CHAPTER 1

Monday 22nd May – Early Morning

Cardiff Airport, South Wales, UK

Kaine settled his Bergen more comfortably on one shoulder, descended the steps of the ESAPP Gulfstream G550, and stepped out onto the blustery apron of Cardiff Airport's private runway. He hooked his long hair behind his ears to prevent the breeze blowing the curly strands into his unprotected eyes.

A trim fifty-something man wearing steel-rimmed glasses, a full peppered beard, and a smart UK Border Force uniform complete with its peaked cap, awaited him in the shadow of the airport building. The epaulettes on his dark blue dress shirt sported three silver pips, and he had the straight-backed, stiff-shouldered bearing of a military man.

Kaine braced himself, scanned the area, but found little to concern him unduly. Little apart from the prominently placed surveillance cameras and the border guard himself.

Take it easy. Nothing to worry about here.

He'd crossed country borders often enough since the nightmare began. No reason to worry unnecessarily.

"Welcome to Cardiff, Major Griffin," the man said, his flat accent marking him as hailing from the West Midlands rather than South Wales. "I'm Senior Officer Greenly. Do you have any baggage, sir?"

"Just this," Kaine answered, patting the Bergen's webbing strap, trying his best to adopt the aloof detachment of the well-heeled international jetsetter.

"I like to travel light," he added.

Greenly eased out a thin, patient smile. "Very good, sir. If you'll follow me to the private lounge, we can expedite your entry into the UK."

"Thank you. Has my wife arrived?"

The border guard nodded. "Mrs Griffin and your driver are waiting in the arrivals lounge, sir."

"Excellent," Kaine said, nodding absently, but surprised by the nervous anticipation rippling through his gut.

How would Lara greet him after he dumped her in Paris? He'd find out soon enough.

Deep breath, Kaine.

Greenly turned and led Kaine towards the shiny glass automatic doors marked, *Private – Arrivals.*

"You do have your passport handy, sir?"

"Of course."

Not even multimillionaires with access to private jets could cross oceans and enter new countries without the correct paperwork. Fortunately, Kaine had landed in the UK with the best forged documentation money could buy. The passport he carried gave his name as William Griffin, a retired Major in the Royal Marines, and the platinum credit cards in his wallet suggested he could buy anything he wanted, no matter the cost. Who needed luggage when they could walk into any clothing store in the country and empty its shelves? His documentation had already passed muster at borders a number of times, but this would be the last time Kaine would use the Griffin persona. It was time to drop the middle-aged former marine perma-nently. This particular legend had outlived its usefulness.

Greenly stepped aside, gestured with an open hand, and allowed Kaine to enter the comfortably warm and pleasantly quiet confines of the private customs area first. No bullet-resistant screens required to protect the border guards in such rarefied and deep-pile-carpeted domain. A waft of scented air tickled his nose—sandalwood and spice—relaxing, calming. Subtle.

How the top one percent live.

Kaine's guide marched to the far side of a polished-marble-topped counter and smiled almost apologetically. He held out a hand, adopting the pose of a waiter requesting a tip.

Simulating bored disinterest but keeping his senses primed, Kaine removed the passport from the inner pocket of his crushed, faded denim jacket and passed it over the counter. Greenly opened the booklet to the picture page, studied the photo carefully and narrowed his eyes to peer directly at Kaine. Without taking his eyes from Kaine, he angled his head to one side and frowned, in what? Recognition?

Hell.

He'd become too blasé.

Kaine's heart leapt, his mouth dried, and the world closed in around him. His hand reached up to the strap of his Bergen, making ready to drop it and lighten his load if he had to take off. Slowly, without making it obvious, he glanced around the open space, searching for the fastest route of egress.

To his right, automatic sliding glass doors led through to a thinly populated departures lounge and, eventually, to the sunny outside. Possible, but he'd have to run the gauntlet of airport security. *Armed* airport security.

Directly behind Greenly, a single unmarked door would lead into the bowels of the building, probably an office complex.

No escape there.

Turning back the way they'd entered would take him out onto the apron and the runway. He might be able to find a hiding place in the storerooms and hangars, but how long would it take an experienced search team to find him? And, at an airport, how many doors would be unsecured and unalarmed?

Precious few.

Bluff it out, Kaine. He doesn't recognise you. He can't.

"Is there a problem, Officer Greenly?" Kaine asked, allowing impatience and a little anger to rumble through the words. Well-heeled travellers weren't prepared to wait for anyone. Let alone a jumped-up jobsworth.

"Not at all, Major Griffin," Greenly said, taking his time to answer. "It's just that your photo—"

"Yes, yes. It's different, I know," Kaine interrupted, scowling, and raking his fingers though the unruly mop. "I've been out of the country for a while, and I don't let anyone touch my hair except for Nicky."

Greenly lifted an eyebrow. "Nicky?"

"Oh dear, really?" Kaine snapped, allowing exasperation to bleed into his voice. "'Nicky'. As in, 'Nicky C'. The man who happens to be the best hair stylist in the UK. Bar none."

"Is he, sir?"

"Yes. The very best. I wouldn't let anyone else near my hair with a pair of scissors."

"And your beard, sir?" Greenly fingered his well-maintained facial hair.

Kaine scratched the fur on his chin. "A newly acquired fashion statement I intend to ask Nicky to tidy up the moment I reach London." He raised an arm, tugged back the cuff of his jacket, and scowled at his watch.

Steady, Kaine. Don't overdo it.

Again, Greenly took his time to do his thing. Kaine relaxed a little. The man hadn't recognised him. Greenly simply relished his role as defender of the gates of the principality. He was the voice of the poor and the oppressed, doing what he could to rail against the rich and the self-absorbed.

Let him.

Greenly studied the passport photo again.

"Officer Greenly," Kaine said, teeth clenched. "Do I really need to buy a pair of scissors and head for the restroom?"

Greenly showed Kaine a mirthless smile. "No, sir. Of course not, sir. That won't be necessary. And it's *Senior* Officer Greenly, sir." He tapped the pips on his epaulettes with an index finger, wrinkled his nose, and held the passport under a scanner far longer than strictly necessary before handing it back. "Everything's in order, sir."

"Yes, I know it is," Kaine grumbled. "Which way out?"

"That way, sir." The rail-thin jobsworth pointed to Kaine's right.

"Thank you, *Senior* Officer Greenly," Kaine said, gracing the officious border guard with a forced smile. "Thank you very much."

Dial it back, man.

Kaine turned towards the exit and released a pent-up breath. He stepped through the sliding doors and the nerves struck again. Unease rippled through his stomach. Not the unease driven by bureaucratic border guards, but something entirely different.

Pack it in, Kaine. You are an idiot!

In his time, he'd faced hordes of angry, evil men hell-bent on doing him nothing but mischief. He'd survived most encounters relatively unscathed, yet there he stood in the comfortable and fragrant customs office, quailing at the prospect of facing an auburn-haired woman who barely tipped the scales at fifty kilos. Although, this particular woman could slice open his innards and stop his heart with the merest hint of a disappointed frown.

What sort of reception would he receive? His last conversation with Lara—the video call aboard the Gulfstream high over a raging north Atlantic—had ended badly. She'd cut him off mid-apology and had refused to answer his repeated attempts to reconnect. She'd also failed to accept any of his ensuing satellite phone calls. It had been the first serious fight in their eight-month relationship, and he hated it. It left his world unbalanced. Yes, the blame for their quarrel lay firmly at his door. He'd ditched her in Paris under the protection of his longest-serving friend, Rollo, and had flown to Arizona without her, and without warning. In his defence, his only motivation had been her safety.

During their curtailed video conference, she'd objected to his decision and called him out on it. He could see her point, though. He really could, but should a similar situation arise, he'd make the same decision again. If Lara couldn't get past his need to protect her, where did it leave them? She needed to understand that he only had her safety in mind. He'd dragged her kicking and screaming into his world of hurt and danger, and he would forever be responsible for her. If anyone ever deliberately hurt her, it would kill him—and he would kill the person responsible. No qualms. No second thoughts. Instant retribution.

Kaine strolled forwards, following the arrows. The double doors slid silently open to reveal a smartly appointed lounge and bar that wouldn't have disgraced the foyer of a five-star London hotel. After a brief scan of the few people sitting in the heavily upholstered chairs revealed nothing to raise his hackles, he spotted his two-person welcoming committee on the far side of the room. Neither smiled.

Uh-oh.

Rollo, playing the role of the paid employee, stood dutifully behind a po-faced Lara. She, in a smart, navy blue business skirt suit, stepped forwards to greet him.

"Good flight?" she asked, ice cool, emotionless.

"Very good, thank you," he answered, matching her aloof manner. If necessary, he could play it cool, too.

She offered her cheek, which Kaine duly pecked. When he reached out to pull her into a gentle hug, she stiffened and backed away. How much of the display was an act for public consumption and how much a legacy of their ongoing fight, only time would show.

"Let's go," he said.

She nodded, turned back the way she'd come, and he strode after her. Once alongside, he crooked an arm for her to grasp, but she ignored it.

Not an act, a legacy.

Kaine sighed. So many fences to mend.

Rollo led the way through to the car—a top-of-the-range BMW 7 Series with a cherished plate, E5APP—which he'd parked in one of a few spots reserved for VIPs. He pointed the key fob at the car and pressed a button. The central locking double-clicked, and the indicators flashed. He pressed another button and the boot lid powered open. Rollo stepped forwards and opened the nearside rear door. Lara slipped inside, ignoring Kaine's outstretched arm and offer of support.

Kaine shook his head sadly, slipped the Bergen from his shoulder, and headed for the far side of the car. He paused long enough to lob the Bergen into the open boot, before carrying on to the offside passenger door. He opened the door all by himself and climbed inside.

"That's a demarcation issue, that is," Rollo grumbled, barely able to stifle his smile.

"What is?"

"It's *my* job to open and close doors for you, *sir*," he explained, sounding hurt, but adding a sneaky wink.

"Cut that out, Colour Sergeant," Kaine snapped. "I've had a long flight."

Rollo cracked the driver's door and slid behind the leather-clad steering wheel. He pressed a button on the dashboard. The boot lid lowered, and the lock clicked.

"A long flight in the lap of luxury," Rollo said, staring through the rear-view mirror, and staring hard. "We should all suffer such privations. How was the king-sized bed in the Gulfstream, by the way?"

Kaine grinned. He could always rely on Rollo to cut him no slack.

"An absolute delight, thanks."

"Egyptian cotton sheets?"

"Eight hundred thread count at least."

Kaine shot a sideways glance at Lara, but she kept her head turned away, apparently staring through the passenger window and studying the shadows of the clouds sliding over the distant runway.

"Nice," Rollo said, continuing the conversation. "Beats the heck out of a military sleeping bag, eh?"

"Yep, they had a thread count of about twenty—and each one static-charged nylon."

"Decent galley?" Rollo asked, still pushing.

"Better than the usual airline food, thanks. Although I did have to serve myself."

"Oh dear. Poor you."

"I'll survive."

Rollo pressed the ignition button on the dash and the big diesel engine whispered into life. He lowered all four windows before rolling slowly out of the parking spot and heading for the exit road.

"What's with the windows?" Kaine asked.

"Doctor's orders." Rollo jerked a thumb towards Lara, who finally turned to face them.

"Any symptoms?" she asked, referring to the short time he'd spent in the Doomsday Creed's infirmary, and to his brief but potentially dangerous exposure to an exceptionally virulent form of typhoid.

"None. I'm good, thanks."

"Raised temperature?"

"None so far." He smiled and double hitched his eyebrows. "Although being this close to you has ..."

She scowled and he let the remains of the trite sentence fade into oblivion.

Still scowling, Lara tugged a medical bag from her footwell and rested it on the seat between them, using it as a barrier to keep them apart. She opened the bag, removed an infrared thermometer, and pointed it at his forehead.

"Hold still."

"Anything for you, my guardian angel."

In the front, Rollo snorted. He waited for an automatic barrier to rise before gunning the Beemer's engine and filtering his way into heavy exit traffic. They tucked in behind a white panel van and ahead of a compact Fiat. The Fiat driver—a long-haired youngster smoking a cigarette—blared his horn. Rollo stuck an arm through the open window and waved in apology and thanks. Shaggy blared the horn again and closed the gap to danger levels.

"Bloke's an idiot," Rollo said. "There was plenty of room."

Kaine nodded. "Doesn't know who he's messing with."

"I told you to keep still," Lara snapped.

"Sorry, boss."

"You will be."

No doubt.

Seconds later, the thermometer bleeped. Lara read the temperature displayed and returned the device to her bag.

"Normal?" he asked.

"So far," she answered.

Noncommittal. The way of all medics.

She fished around inside the bag and removed a blister pack from one of the internal pockets. "Take these with plenty of fluids. You need to stay fully hydrated."

She handed him two tablets and a one-litre bottle of still water.

"What are they?"

"Antibiotics. Five hundred milligrams of *ciprofloxacin*. You'll take them twice a day for the next five days. It that clear?"

"Yes, doctor," he answered in his most serious voice.

To confirm his promise, he popped the pills into his mouth and eased them down with half the bottle in three long pulls.

"Where are we heading?" Kaine asked, still looking at Lara.

"A place called Glyn Coes," Lara answered.

"Hmm," he said, nodding. "What's at Glyn Coes?"

"Becky and Gwynfor Cadwallader, and their two children, Dewi and Myfanwy."

Cadwallader?

The surname didn't ring any bells.

"Members of The 83?" Kaine asked and she nodded. "I don't recall seeing a Cadwallader on the list. I'd have remembered a name that distinctive."

"Gwyn's widowed sister, Sharon, was ... on the plane," Lara said, finally making eye contact. "Her surname was Pierce."

Lara's voice softened in deference to the sensitive nature of the subject matter. They were, after all, talking about the eighty-three innocent people who had lost their lives on Flight BE1555. The eighty-three innocent souls Kaine had killed.

"I see," he said, forcing out the words. "And the Cadwalladers are Sharon Pierce's nearest next of kin?"

Lara glanced at Rollo through the rear-view mirror. Something passed between them. Something Kaine couldn't read and didn't understand. They were holding out on him.

Unwilling to interrogate either the woman he loved or his longest-serving friend, he let it pass. They'd tell him what he needed to know, and when he needed to know it.

"What's the issue?" he asked.

"Sheep rustling," Rollo said. "Amongst other things."

"Sheep rustling?" Kaine asked, again looking at Lara, trying not to appear dismissive.

"There's more to it than that, Ryan. Much more."

"Rollo, how long before we reach Glyn Coes?"

"About ninety minutes."

"But we are breaking the journey, right?"

"Of course." Rollo indicated right and made the turn. "Services on the M4, Junction 33. We'll do without the coffee."

"How long?"

"Thirty minutes in this traffic."

"Okay, that should be long enough to make a start on the briefing. Fire away, Lara."

"Oh no," she said, shaking her head. "From now on, I'm Annabelle Hallam. Annie. Rollo is Adrian Bennett, my older brother. I'll give you our full bios later."

"Okay, Mrs Hallam. And who am I?"

"You are Peter Sidings."

"Sidings again? Got it," he said, trying not to smile. He did push out an extended sigh, though. "How the mighty fall."

"Sorry?" she asked.

"An instant demotion. *Major* Bill Griffin one minute, *Staff Sergeant* Peter Sidings the next."

"No more than you deserve, sir," Rollo announced from his perch in the driving seat. Forever sniping.

Rollo eased the Beemer into the outside lane and added more pressure to the throttle. The big saloon's rapid acceleration forced Kaine deeper into his plush leather seat. Within seconds, the Fiat and its floppy-haired tailgater had faded into the distance, unable to match the 7 Series' superior performance.

Staff Sergeant Peter Sidings.

Kaine ran through the bio in his head. Having used the Sidings legend many times before and since the disaster that changed his life forever, he didn't have to work too hard.

Staff Sergeant Peter Sidings. Retired 2 PARA veteran of two Gulf Wars, registered bodyguard, advanced driver, and long-serving employee of *Conqueror Security Services*, one of the largest and most well-respected private defence consultancies in the UK. Physical characteristics: dark hair, blue eyes, badly broken nose.

Uh-oh.

Becoming Peter Sidings required a couple of cosmetic props.

"I'll need blue contacts and something for the schnozz."

Lara reached into her capacious bag, pulled out a contact lens case, and handed it across.

"Thanks, love. I'll wait until we stop. Last time I tried fitting contacts in a moving car I nearly poked my eye out." He tried a cheery grin, but again, she dismissed his attempt at levity.

"No need for the putty, though," Rollo announced. "Staff Sergeant Sidings recently went under the knife. Cosmetic surgery. The doctors rebuilt his nasal bone. Straightened his nose up a treat, apparently."

"You updated his bio?"

Rollo dipped his head in a nod but kept his eyes on the road. "Sure did. At least, Corky did. The doc asked him to work his magic last night. She thought you'd find sticking a tissue up your nose for days on end a little uncomfortable. Isn't that right, Doc?"

She does *still care.*

He turned to face her. "Thanks, Lara. I appreciate it."

"It's 'Annie Hallam', remember." Another frown furrowed her forehead, this one less defined, less severe. Signs of a thaw?

Kaine's shoulders relaxed and the tension in his stomach eased.

"Okay, Annie. Why not spend the time telling me all about Glyn Coes and the Cadwalladers."

"Okay," she said. "Pin your ears back. I don't want to repeat myself."

Uh-oh. The ice is still crackling.

CHAPTER 2

Monday 22nd May – Senior Officer Greenly

Cardiff Airport, South Wales, UK

Senior Officer Percival "Perce" Greenly studied Griffin's receding back. Something didn't seem right about the long-haired "Major" Griffin. The bugger had been too damned patient. Too restrained. Nowhere near arrogant enough. The number of jumped-up privileged arseholes Perce dealt with over the years had polished his view on the well-to-do. Arrogant pricks, the lot of them.

Griffin hadn't even overreacted when Perce had intentionally wound up with the question over the passport photo. And all that nonsense with "Nicky C", as though name-dropping a celeb barber would impress Perce. What the hell was that all about?

Nah, something was up with the scraggy-haired Major Griffin.

Most of the rich pricks he had to suffer every day didn't bother to look him in the eye. To them, Perce was nothing but the hired help. An insect to be endured. They didn't care that he was a thirty-year veteran of the UK's Border Force. Although it hadn't always been called that. UK Border Force. UK Border Agency. Border and Immigration Agency. Whatever next, Border Patrol?

Bugger it. What's in a name?

Nah, Griffin didn't fit the bill. He was different. His brown eyes never stayed still, never stopped searching his surroundings. Like he was on guard. Although he tried hard not to let it show, the man was too defensive.

Most of the rich buggers who stepped off a private jet oozed money and privilege. They wore wealth like their well-tailored suits. Even the youngsters who dressed down, protesting against Mummy and Daddy's riches, wore designer rags costing as much as a week's pay for the average worker. On them, everything matched, even when it wasn't supposed to. They all used personal shoppers even during their short-lived rebellious stage. The pricks didn't know any better.

Rich bastards, the lot of them.

Most of Perce's "customers" were pudgy, pretentious, privileged arseholes who could barely climb down the aircraft steps without help. As for carrying their own luggage? Not a chance. Such a thing was beneath them. And making eye contact? It rarely happened. Except when they were complaining and delivering a bollocking, the rich looked *through* working stiffs like Perce, not *at* them. No, working stiffs didn't count. They didn't matter.

Griffin, though. He was different. Lean, fit-looking, composed. The minute he entered the building, he scouted the place, looking for exits and trying not to make it obvious.

And there he was, in the lounge, meeting his wife and their huge lackey. The stiff way the Griffins greeted each other seemed genuine enough, but ... Mrs Griffin. No airhead eye-candy that one. What a creature. Beautiful without needing to flaunt it. Slim, elegant. Nice clothes that fit well but didn't expose too much in the way of curves or flesh. Stunning. The way Perce liked his women.

Something was wrong with the picture.

The picture.

Perce pressed a button on the desk scanner and rolled the screen back to the most recent status check. Major William Griffin's passport information page appeared on the screen, including its photo, greyscale, 35x45 millimetres.

Too small.

He enlarged the picture to the maximum available without deterioration of the image, without pixilation: 75x95 millimetres.

A rugged but handsome face stared out at him. Brown eyes, dark hair with feathers of grey at the temples. A shaggy beard hid what was probably a strong jawline. The date of birth showed him as forty-seven, but Griffin could have easily passed for a much younger man. Thirty-nine, maybe.

Perce rubbed the edge of his thumbnail across his lower lip. "What is it about you, Griffin?" he asked the silent screen. "Why've you tweaked my Spidey sense?"

Perce swivelled his chair to face the CCTV monitor to the left of the scanner. He dialled up the main camera and watched Griffin and his two-person entourage approach a dark blue, late-model BMW. The driver, an enormous man wearing a smart suit and carrying not a spare ounce of fat on him, opened the passenger door for the beauty. More bodyguard than simple driver, that one.

And as for Mrs Griffin, she ignored the major's outstretched arm. No love lost there. Interesting. Griffin said he'd been away a long while, but they acted like strangers.

What's that all about?

Window dressing?

Griffin made his way around the back of the Beemer, threw his backpack into the boot, and dived into the passenger's seat on the far side of the car.

"Okay, Major Griffin, let's see who you really are."

Perce paused the livestream feed and zoomed in on the car. He captured a screenshot, hit the "print" button, released the pause, and followed the car all the way out of shot.

"Okay, the gloves are off."

Perce grabbed the handset of the desk phone and dialled an internal number. She answered on the second ring.

"Hi, Percival," Patty Lewis said in her sing-song Welsh accent, even though she knew he hated his full name. She ought to know, he'd told her often enough.

"That's Senior Officer Greenly to you, Officer Lewis."

"Oh cut the bull, Perce. There's only the two of us on shift, mun. No one to impress but me, and it takes a lot to impress little ol' me. What's up, now?"

Perce grinned. Patty always could put him in his place. They'd worked together for six years, and each knew how to press the other's buttons.

"Can you cover the front desk? I want to check the Home Office notices and the DVLA records. I might even raise a query with the ANPR cameras. I'd like to know where our latest passenger's headed."

"That long nose of yours caught a whiff of something iffy?"

Perce winced, not that Patty could see it down the phone line. "Long nose? Me? You looked in the mirror recently, Nellie?"

"Ha. Touché, boy. Well, is there anything pungent in the air?"

"Not sure yet. We just had a private land and the guy who disembarked, Major Griffin ... well, something didn't feel right."

"Is he still there? Want me to book him into a holding cell?"

"Nah, I didn't have any real reason to detain him."

"Never stopped you before."

"True enough, but after the last time—"

"Yeah, mun." Her light chuckle tinkled down the line. "You really stepped into the doo-doo that time, didn't you. Fancy thinking the captain of the Welsh rugby team was smuggling drugs. Bloody daft, mun."

"Why would I know anything about Welsh rugby? Bloody stupid game with a wonky ball that bounces all over the place and you have to pass back to move forwards. And anyway, the bloke looked weird. As for Major Griffin, he flew in on a Gulfstream registered to ESAPP, the French firm. I didn't want to hold him up and start an international incident without due cause."

"Again, when has that ever stopped you? And what's ESAPP when it's at home?"

Despite her many assets, Patty didn't always keep abreast of the movers and shakers in the world of international air travel. She usually just showed the VIPs a set of perfectly straight, whitened teeth, and let them through with barely a glance at their credentials. Perce Greenly, on the other hand, didn't give an inch. Made of much sterner stuff, was old Perce.

"ESAPP," Perce said, through a deep sigh, "is European Small Arms and Personal Protection, A/S."

"Weapons manufacturers?"

"That's right. Buggers who grow rich on the suffering of others. Bloody warmongers, the lot of them."

"That why you've got the hots for this Griffith bloke?"

"Griffin, Patty. His name's Griffin. At least that's the name on his passport."

"Any reason to think it's not his real name?"

"None. The passport was genuine, passed all the tests, but like I said—"

"He 'didn't seem right'," she said. He could almost sense the woman rolling her eyes. "Okay, I get the message. When's the next arrival?"

"Nothing due in or out for an hour or so."

"In that case, why not come through and make me a cuppa. I'll search the DVLA database while you trawl through the warning notices. We can alert the police and the ANPR centre if anything stands out. Right?"

"Okay, girl. You're on."

Perce grabbed the keys from the top drawer of his desk. He locked both the exit door to the airside apron and the door to the departure lounge and set the alarm. No one could ever accuse Perce Greenly of lax security.

After a final glance at the CCTV multiscreen, he pushed through the back-office door and entered the cluttered and dingy cupboard the bosses laughably named the Security Operations Hub.

CHAPTER 3

Monday 22nd May – Senior Officer Greenly

Cardiff Airport, South Wales, UK

Perce slurped his coffee and hit return on the keyboard for what must have been the fiftieth time. The National Crime Agency database—a crock of shite software that hadn't been upgraded in a decade—took three seconds to flip to the next record.

Three full seconds! I bloody ask you!

No wonder the UK borders leaked like a chuffing colander.

The mugshot staring out from the screen shook Perce to the core.

"Bugger me! Bloody bugger me!"

Blood drained from his face and bile rose from the pit of his stomach. He lowered the mug to the desk so fast, the cold dregs splashed over his fingers.

"No thanks," Patty said, sitting so close they almost rubbed shoulders. "You're not my type."

"Ryan Kaine! The bugger's Ryan-bloody-Kaine."

"Huh? What was that?"

"William Griffin is Ryan Kaine, the mass murderer. The terrorist." He turned to face Patty. Her jaw dropped open. Even she recognised the name of the UK's most notorious home-grown terrorist.

"Bugger me!" she gasped.

"Yes. That's what I said."

"Are you certain?"

"It's him, look." Perce reached for the hard copy of Griffin's passport ID and held it up to the NCA's record on the screen.

Perce swallowed hard. He'd been within arm's reach of a man wanted for murdering eighty-odd people. A man who'd snuffed out all those innocent lives without compunction, without a second thought. A man who could kill with his bare hands. Perce shuddered.

How close had he been to death?

Patty compared the two images, her frown deepening in concentration.

"I dunno. Could be him, I suppose."

"The hair's longer, and the mugshot pic doesn't show such a heavy beard, but look at his eyes. It's him, I tell you. It's Ryan Kaine!"

"I dunno," Patty said. "You could be right. If so, he was right here. We could have had him!"

"I knew he was a wrong'un. I just knew it."

"Jesus. We could have had him in cuffs. Think of the reward. Half a million quid, last I heard. If only—"

"Don't be stupid, girl." Perce rounded on her again. "If we'd tried anything, the sod would have torn us apart. Read his bio. He's former SBS. Black ops. A trained killer. We wouldn't have stood a chance. Don't know about you, but I enjoy breathing. I like going home of an evening." Perce swallowed hard and again he shuddered.

So bloody close.

"No, lass," he muttered. "I'm glad he's miles away by now. Leave him for the specialists. The specialists with the fancy guns."

Perce picked up the handset on his desk phone. His fingers trembled so much, he struggled to hit the right numbers. He sucked in a deep breath and tried to calm himself.

"Are you calling the Assistant Director?"

"No, that useless bugger can wait. How far could that Beemer have travelled by now? I'm going to call in the big guns."

"GCHQ? The spooks?"

Perce nodded. "Assuming my fingers stop shaking long enough to dial right." He ran his eyes down the list of emergency contacts pinned to the noticeboard on the wall in front of the desk. He'd never called the number before. Scary stuff.

"Want me to contact ANPR?"

He nodded. "Yes please. The Beemer can't have gotten very far. Thirty miles, depending on how fast he was driving."

She raised a shoulder. "If that is Ryan Kaine, he'd be wanting to keep to the speed limits, I imagine. Stay below the radar."

"What d'you mean, 'if'? It's Kaine. It's Ryan bloody Kaine."

Perce misdialled and had to start over.

Shit. Why's this so bloody difficult?

Patty grabbed her phone and dialled the numbers, making a better fist of it than he was.

He punched in the eleventh number and waited.

"GCHQ, how can I direct your call?" A man's voice, clipped, efficient.

"Blimey, that was quick. I expected to be put on—"

"This is GCHQ, how can I direct your call?" the voice repeated, more insistent.

"Sorry, sorry." Perce swallowed. "I'm reporting a sighting."

"Who are you, and who have you seen?"

"Oh yes, sorry again. I'm SO Greenly, UK Border Force, Cardiff International Airport." He quoted the airport's ID reference and his badge number. "I've seen Ryan Kaine."

"Ryan Kaine?" The voice maintained its even cadence as though the man attached to it couldn't raise any interest.

"Yes, sir. Captain Ryan Kaine, Flight BE1555! The North Sea. Eighty-three dead. That Ryan Kaine."

"How certain are you?" The voice increased in speed and volume.

More emotion. Keys tapped on the other end of the line. The rapid taps of a proficient typist.

"One hundred percent. It's him, I tell you."

"Arrivals or departures?"

"Er, arrivals. He landed about forty-five minutes ago. He disembarked from a private jet. A jet owned by ESAPP, the French arms manufacturer."

"I see. Is Kaine in custody?"

Greenly swallowed past a dry throat.

"Er, no. I-I didn't make the identification until *after* he'd gone. His papers ... passport, I mean. His passport was ... perfect."

"One moment," the dry voice said.

The silence dragged on for a full minute. Perce counted off the seconds on the wall clock. What the hell was happening?

"Hello? Are you still there?" Perce asked.

More silence.

Perce tried again.

"Okay, we hear you," the voice said, and the keyboard tapping started up again. "We have this."

"He, Ryan Kaine, left with two others in a BMW. The car's registration number is—"

"Senior Officer Greenly, we know."

"What? How?"

"We have access to your surveillance systems and the data on your passport scanner."

Bloody hell. So fast?

"You do?"

"We do." More tapping. "Facial recognition suggests an eighty-six-point-five-percent match between the two images. Not close enough for a positive identification. Thank you for contacting us."

Against his dentist's recommendations, Perce ground his dentures.

The useless bugger didn't believe him.

Fuck's sake.

"I don't care what the bloody computer says. It's him, I tell you. It's Ryan Kaine. What are you going to do?"

"We'll add it to our list of suspected sightings. Thank you for contacting us."

"But it's Ryan Kaine, I tell you. I'm certain of it."

"In that case, you should follow your internal protocols."

"You mean call in the local police? Aren't you going to do anything? Aren't you going to coordinate the search?"

"That's not our role, Mr Greenly. We're an information gathering facility."

"What the bloody—I've given you vital information on the current location of a mass murderer, and you're just going to sit on your hands? What's your name?"

"I'm not prepared to give you that information, sir. Adjust your tone."

"No, I won't adjust my bloody tone. What are you going to do?"

"I've already told you what we'll do. Good day to you, Mr Greenly." The phone line clicked into silence.

Greenly pulled the handset from his ear and glowered at the lifeless device. What the hell just happened?

"...I'll leave it with you, then," Patty said, ending her call. She replaced the phone and swivelled her chair to face him. "What's up? You look a little peeved."

"No, not peeved at all." He shook his head. "I'm bloody livid. Pissed off. Big time."

"What happened?"

He told her.

"For God's sake. Eighty-six percent's not a good enough match? Bloody computers."

"Yeah. That's pretty much what I said. What happened with the ANPR?"

"I got hold of your drinking buddy, Blue—"

"That's Superintendent Jefferson to you, Officer Lewis," Greenly snapped, still scowling deeply.

"Yeah, yeah." She flapped her hand, dismissing his gentle scolding.

"And did Blue do his thing?"

"Yep. Since it was Ryan Kaine, he's happy to accept your ident at face value. He got straight on to the ANPR centre in Hendon. Let me listen in to the call, too. Unfortunately, there's a five-minute lag on the system today. Heavy usage. He's gonna get back to me if and when they locate the BMW."

Perce puffed out his cheeks and ran his fingers through his hair. At least someone was doing their job.

"That's it for us," he said. "Nothing more we can do. Hope they catch the murdering bastard."

"Uh-uh," she said, wincing.

"What d'you mean, 'uh-uh'?"

"One of us has to call Assistant Director Raymond, and since you're the Senior Officer ..." She double hitched her eyebrows.

"After the last time with the rugby player?" Greenly shook his head again. "No chance. Be much better coming from you. I'll liaise with the police. At least Blue and I are on speaking terms."

"Okay, I'll call Raymond, but you're buying lunch."

"It's a deal."

Perce reached for the desk phone again, delighted to be stepping aside and letting someone else—anyone else—handle the search for Ryan Kaine.

He glanced down. The image on the printout stared up at him from the desk, taunting. The terrorist's cold, hard eyes glowered out from the paper, threatening. They would haunt him forever. Perce Greenly had never felt closer to death.

CHAPTER 4

Monday 22nd May – Superintendent Jefferson

South Wales Police HQ, Bridgend, South Wales, UK

Superintendent Christopher "Blue" Jefferson hated the waiting. It had to be the very worst part of his job. He'd rather face down an angry, baying mob than sit behind his desk while his officers hit the roads and raced into action without him. No use crying about it, though. He'd accepted the promotion, the desk job, the added responsibility, and the increased salary that went with it. The alternative—early retirement on health grounds—didn't even bear consideration.

Still, the waiting didn't stop being a stone-cold nightmare.

Blue leant forwards in his chair and winced as the stabbing pain shot through his lower back. The bloody car crash had crushed two lumbar vertebrae, which the surgeons had fused together for support. The resultant loss of mobility had threatened his career, and the constant pain threatened his sanity.

Suck it up, Blue-boy. Nobody said life would be easy.

He read the bio on the screen for a third time.

It didn't make good reading.

Ryan Kaine. Captain in the Royal Marines. Special Boat Service team leader. Exceptional shot. World class sniper. Rated as an expert in hand-to-hand combat. Mass murderer. Terrorist. Not a man to take lightly.

This could turn into a national incident.

Jefferson tugged the "ready readers" from his nose and rubbed his eyes. The cheap specs didn't help much. Little short of bloody useless. He'd bought them from a local chemist. Should have gone to the optician, but who had time to visit a bloody eye doctor these days?

He hit the "CTRL" key and scrolled the mouse wheel to enlarge the text. It helped, but the latest review of the transcript didn't improve the contents.

Jefferson chewed on the skin inside his lower lip and gave up a silent prayer.

Please let this go down easy and safe.

Ten minutes earlier, he'd scrambled the best Armed Response Unit available. Over the phone, they'd cobbled together an instant game plan—*Operation Contain and Control.* Fifteen minutes later, Inspector Odawa and his team of six headed out, together with every police interceptor available—twelve vehicles in total. Even now, they approached Junction 33 of the M4 and the Cardiff West Services.

The ANPR cameras—some of the very best tech available to modern policing—had turned up trumps. The BMW 7 Series they'd been searching for had pinged the cameras all the way from Cardiff Airport but none beyond Junction 33. Then, the vigilant eyes in the Force's Command and Control Centre, had spotted the car in question, parked in a bay outside one of the many coffee shops in the service station.

What was it with fancy coffee anyway? What the hell was wrong with instant? Or tea, for pity's sake? And as for the need for a "Drive Thru", why couldn't people walk twenty metres to fetch their own bloody drinks? The slippery slope down the road to American consumerism had become a blooming Cresta Run.

May the Good Lord save us all.

The phone on his desk buzzed. An external call. He leant forwards and reached for the handset, trying not to grunt with the effort.

Bloody back.

"Superintendent Jefferson," he said, disappointed at how lacklustre he sounded.

"What's up, Blue? How's it hanging?"

Jefferson collapsed into his chair's backrest, wincing as another lance of fire shot through his lower back. Getting worse all the time. How long before it seized up on him completely?

"Not a good time, Perce."

"Busy?"

"'Course I'm busy. You drop a steaming hot dog turd in my lap and leave me to it, why wouldn't I be busy?"

Perce's chuckle rippled down the phone line.

"Any sign of the BMW?"

"Yes."

"Crikey. You've found it already? You caught the beggar?"

Oh, the naïvety of the man.

"Not yet, Perce. But we know where he is."

At least we know where the car is.

"Where's that, then?"

Jefferson gave him the management summary, only leaving out the location. He wouldn't put it past Perce Greenly to head for the service station just to watch the show he'd initiated. He might even be keen to claim the reward on Kaine's head.

"I've sent armed units to apprehend him. Shouldn't be long now."

Fingers crossed.

"Bloody hell, Blue. You've told your people who they're dealing with? Kaine's a killer, you know."

"Yes, I know. I'm reading his profile right now. Highly skilled, deadly. My people have skills, too. They know what they're doing."

"But—"

"No 'buts', Perce. I'm hanging up now. The first units are approaching the target's location as we speak. I'll give you the full rundown over a pint at the weekend. My shout."

"Okay, Blue. Give the murdering scumbag hell."

"Will do, Perce. Will do."

Jefferson replaced the handset and uncrossed his fingers. The moment he ended the call, the phone rang again. This time the double chirrup of an internal call. He snapped up the handset again.

"Superintendent Jefferson."

"Sir, it's Gene Hunter. We're ready."

"The live feed's set up?"

"Yes, sir. The first units have eyes on the target's car. Would you like to see the action on the big screen?"

Try keeping me away.

"Thanks, Gene. I'll be right across."

Carefully, Blue eased himself out of his comfortable chair and sidestepped around the desk. He sneered at the walking stick dangling from the hook screwed into the back of the door and shook his head. He could do without the damn crutch for one morning.

BLUE PUSHED OPEN THE DOOR TO THE SOUTH WALES POLICE'S Operations Hub and stepped inside, trying to minimise his shuffle-limp. A hush fell over the brightly lit room, and a dozen heads turned in his direction. The heads belonged to the control staff. Each wore a set of headphones with an attached boom mic and sat behind a pair of split-screen monitors, their faces bathed in a blue-grey light.

He waved a dismissive hand and the heads faced forwards, once again concentrating on their screens. The hush disintegrated, and the noise levels increased to a dull thrum.

"Morning, sir," Gene Hunter said, her brown eyes sparkling in a dark and attractive face.

The woman, mid-thirties and tall, looked smart in her police uniform. She filled one out really well, too.

Stop it, Blue. Eyes up.

"What do you have for me, Inspector?"

She pointed to the big screen in the centre of a bank of smaller, satellite screens on the wall opposite. "As you can see, sir, the BMW is parked in front of Centre Coffee. It's empty, sir."

Blue peered at the large screen. The picture showed a row of parked cars, the first in line being the midnight blue Beemer the man suspected as being Ryan Kaine and his two companions had driven away from Cardiff Airport that morning.

"Any sign of the targets?"

"No, sir. The service station operators were more than happy to grant us remote access to their internal surveillance system. We have footage of the suspects parking and exiting the vehicle. Would you like to see it, sir?"

"I would." Blue eased himself closer to her desk and perched one arse cheek on its edge. The pain in his back eased a fraction.

Hunter grimaced in support of his condition. The whole force knew about his injury in the line of duty, and none would begrudge him taking liberties with their desks.

Hunter turned to the heavyset man sitting at the closest desk and nodded. "Boyd. Show the film."

A couple of keystrokes later, a window opened in the bottom right-hand corner of the large screen. The timestamp running along the top of the window inset confirmed the target car had arrived twenty-three minutes earlier. The driver's door opened, and a large individual unfolded himself from the car. He stood tall and his head swivelled, eyes taking in the scene. His lips moved and he said something inaudible. A second later, the two rear doors opened. A woman slid out of the nearside of the vehicle, slim, taller than average, long dark hair tied back in a loose ponytail. She carried what looked like a make-up case and kept her back to the camera, her face hidden. The final occupant—the man Perce Greenly had identified as Ryan Kaine—climbed from the offside passenger seat, collected a camouflaged backpack from the boot, and stood behind the large driver. Wavy brown and grey hair, worn long and loose, heavy beard. Dark aviator shades hid his eyes and most of his face. Impossible to make an identification from such a distance. It could be Ryan Kaine. Then again, it could have been Ryan Giggs, the Welsh footballer. Their statures weren't dissimilar. Both Kaine, the prime target, and Giggs, the ex-professional footballer, had wiry builds and were no more than average height. The man-mountain of a driver dwarfed the prime target, who looked weedy by comparison.

Ryan Kaine—if the suspect was indeed Ryan Kaine—didn't look powerful enough to be an expert in hand-to-hand combat. Didn't look much like a mass murderer, either. Then again, what did a mass murderer look like?

Jefferson shook his head and followed the progress of the trio as they met up at the front of the car, grouped close, and headed into the coffee shop. The woman and the prime target stood on the far side of the driver, who acted as a screen. At no time did her face turn towards the camera.

"Is this the only angle we have?" Jefferson asked.

Again, Hunter winced. "No, sir, there are others, but this is the best shot. The other cameras are too far away or don't have a clear line of view to be of any use."

"Any idea of who the other two might be?"

"Not yet, sir. The driver could be a bodyguard—"

"Brick outhouse more like," Boyd suggested, but lowered his head at Blue's silent frown of rebuke.

"As for the woman," Hunter continued, "we have no intelligence on her, either. She could be a blind. Window dressing. Who knows? For the operation, we've designated the target as Romeo, the woman as Juliet, and the driver as Delta."

Jefferson nodded. "Any footage from inside the concourse?"

"Yes, sir. Boyd, show sequence two, please."

The image on the window insert changed to an internal shot of the service station shopping area. The three subjects, Romeo, Juliet, and Delta, strolled along the main thoroughfare and ducked straight into the rest room facilities.

"That's all we have, sir," Hunter said.

"They're still in the loo?"

Hunter shrugged. "Not sure, sir. We lost the feed to the internal cameras right after they disappeared from shot."

"What do you mean, 'lost the feed'?"

"The surveillance systems cut out, sir. The cameras went dark."

"Suspicious?"

Hunter winced again. "Not sure, sir. We're in touch with the service station operators. They say the system just stopped working. They also claim this has never happened before. It's usually more stable.

Definitely suspicious.

"Is Inspector Odawa on scene yet?"

"Yes, sir. That's his bodycam footage on screen S1." She pointed to the monochrome image on the screen to the left of the primary monitor. It showed the parked BMW, but from a slightly different angle.

"Can I talk to him directly?"

"Yes, sir. Of course." Hunter handed him a headset.

"Is this live?"

Hunter nodded. "His team is Tango One to Tango Six. You are Control."

Jefferson cleared his dry throat. The cough reverberated through his headphones.

"Control to Tango One, can you hear me? Over."

"Tango One to Control. Reading you full strength, sir. Over."

"Sitrep, please. Over."

The image on screens S1 and S2 panned to the right and the left respectively and centred on two ARU officers in full tactical dress. S1 showed Sergeant Rick Brownlee, the ARU's second in command. S2 displayed a razor-sharp monochrome image of Tango One, Inspector Odawa, his expression serious.

"We've contained the area. Interceptors have blocked the road into the

services. We're stopping any vehicles from entering and searching all vehicles leaving. Over."

"You aren't stopping any vehicles leaving? Over."

"Can't do that, Control. It would cause a tailback and tip our hand. Over."

"What next? Over."

"We'll wait them out, sir. Can't risk entering the building. Hundreds of potential hostages in there and dozens of hiding places. When the targets leave, we'll herd them onto a spur road. We've identified a good place of containment for a TPAC. It's the safest option. Over."

"Agreed," Jefferson said, offering up another silent prayer. "We wait. Keep these comms open, Tango One. Control, out."

They'd wait. Definitely the safest option.

The second hand on the analogue wall clock above the bank of monitors jerked slowly around, counting off the time.

Bloody hell, how he hated the waiting.

CHAPTER 5

Monday 22nd May – Dwayne Odawa

Cardiff West Services, M4 Motorway, South Wales, UK

Dwayne "Dee" Odawa eased back the cuff on his Nomex jacket to expose his watch, a "pre-loved" Breitling Endurance Pro. A present from his father after his promotion to Inspector. Three minutes had passed since the last time he'd checked, and twenty minutes since they'd arrived and set up the containment area. Twenty excruciating minutes spent sweating his bollocks off inside his full tactical gear, which included the ballistic vest—all seven-point-four kilos of it.

They'd found a great spot for their obbo point, out of direct sight of the target vehicle, but under the full glare of the unseasonably hot sun. The interceptors, brightly liveried BMWs, Audis, and Škodas, had arrived running silent and without lights. They'd taken up positions upstream and downstream, out of sight of the service station's food hall, blocking entrance to the facilities, but allowing vehicles to leave.

Twenty-four minutes.

How much longer could they maintain such an expensive operation? He dreaded to think of the cost of tying up so many resources.
Not his decision. The Super earned the big bucks. He would make
the call. And good luck to him, poor bugger. The suffering he put up
with after the bastards in the getaway van deliberately rammed his
police car forever showed in his eyes—the deep blue eyes that gave
Blue his nickname.

As if it could read his thoughts, his earpiece clicked.

"Control to Tango One, can you hear me? Over."

"Tango One to Control. I hear you. Over."

"Any movement from the target's car? Over."

Don't be daft, Blue.

The Super could see the Beemer on the screens as well as the
Tango Strike Team and everyone else in the Control Centre.

"That's a negative, Control. Over."

*"The surveillance cameras inside the concourse are still offline. We don't
have eyes on. Over."*

Oh for fuck's sake.

Dee gritted his teeth. He had operational control and would
use it.

"I've had enough of this, sir. We could be out here sitting on our
hands for hours. I'm going in. Over."

*"Are you sure, Tango One? Have you carried out a risk assessment?
Over."*

Risk assessment, be buggered.

"Yes, sir. And I'm going in, sir. There's no other option. Tango
One, out."

He muted the comms unit and beckoned to Rick Brownlee.

"Are you sure, Dee?" Rick said, muting his own comms and stepping closer. "We don't have a Scooby what's going on in there, mate."

"This is one royal screwup. We've given the buggers plenty of time
to finish brunch. For all we know, he's spotted us and has fortified his
position. Taken hostages."

"Unlikely, Dee," Rick said, pointing to the gentle smattering of customers strolling out of the main exit from the food hall. "The punters hardly look panicked, eh?"

"Yeah, I know." Dee snorted and added a rueful grin. "But I have to justify my decision somehow, don't I?"

Rick shot yet another glance at the dark blue Beemer parked some fifty metres distant, the creases on his forehead deepening and his brows joining in the middle. "How could we have missed the bugger? We've had eyes on that motor since it left the airport, and we arrived here within twenty-five minutes of him parking."

"Twenty-five minutes is a long time to do a runner. Rae"—he signalled to his go-to girl—"fancy a little stroll?"

PC Rae-Anne Johns tilted her head in query. "Where to, Guv?"

"The food hall. I going to take a gander inside. I need some camouflage and you're better looking than our Rick."

"My mother's pet shih-tzu's better looking than Rick, Guv." She grinned at Rick and stepped closer.

"You got a civilian jacket in your car?" Dee asked.

"Sure have. Be right back." She turned and hurried off towards her Volvo.

Dee removed his helmet, set it carefully on the bonnet of their Vauxhall Antara, and resettled the earpiece. A welcome breeze cooled the sweat on his scalp. He unclipped his shoulder harness and tore open the Velcro straps of his ballistic vest. After removing his Glock 17 and confirming its load, he handed both vest and harness to Rick for safekeeping.

"You sure about this, Dee?"

"I've had it up to here with kicking my heels in the sun."

Rick pulled his eyes away from the car parking area and his frown deepened. "Fuck this up and the brass are gonna rip you a new one."

Dee snorted. "Blue will have my back. And if we've let Ryan Kaine slip through our fingers, the brass are going to have a lot more on their plates than me to bother about." He shrugged out of his jacket, leaving him in T-shirt and tactical trousers. The cool wind on his chest and arms felt great, refreshing.

Rick pursed his lips. "Kaine's been on the run for the best part of a year. He's either had a shitload of luck or he's had help. Maybe both."

"The evil bugger's on my turf now. He isn't getting out so easy. Not if I can help it."

Dee tugged the bottom of his trouser legs out from his military boots and let them flap free and loose.

"How do I look?"

"Like a sweaty ARU officer who's just removed his tac gear." Rick's ready smile took ten years off him.

"You got that fancy new gilet of yours in the back of the car?"

"Yeah, but it won't fit you."

"I don't have to zip it up. C'mon, hand it over."

Rick reached through the Antara's open window and reversed out, clutching a light grey quilted gilet. Dee tugged it on. He could put up with its snug fit for as long as he had to. He transferred the camera from his tac gear to the gilet's front pocket and hid everything but the lens.

Rae returned from her car, her baggy plaid jacket billowing out and hiding her assets. She'd let her hair down and the fair tresses hung loose around her shoulders, partially hiding her comms unit and camera. How could she stay so cool under full tactical gear? She looked good, but window dressing, she wasn't.

"You ready for this, Rae?"

She grinned. "I was born ready, Guv."

Rick groaned and turned his eyes up to the clear blue sky.

Dee keyed the comms. "Tango One to Control. Are our cameras still operational? Over."

"*Control to Tango One. That's an affirmative. Over.*"

"Thanks, Control. Tango One, out."

Dee turned his focus to his second-in-command. "Keep your comms unit open and come running if I call. Rae"—he shot her a grim smile—"you're on my left flank. Keep clear of my gun arm."

He held his right arm pressed tight against his side, hiding the

Glock 17 as much as possible in the folds of his baggy cargo trousers, his index finger running along the trigger guard. Rae, a leftie, did the same.

"Okay, let's go."

CHAPTER 6

Monday 22nd May – Dwayne Odawa

Cardiff West Services, M4 Motorway, South Wales, UK

Dee and Rae stepped out from behind their protective barrier of unmarked police cars and strolled towards the entrance to the food hall. She hurried forwards, gaining a lead on him.

"Take it easy, Rae. We're not in a race."

She slowed and waited for him to catch up. "Sorry, Guv. It feels like the whole world has its eyes on the back of my neck."

"Grab my hand," he said, holding out his free hand. "Pretend we're a couple heading for brunch."

She slid her cool, dry hand into his sweaty palm and smiled.

"Clammy," she whispered. "You're not as relaxed as you make out."

"Ryan Kaine's a highly trained killer. There's no telling what he'll do if he's cornered."

Rae stepped closer and their shoulders touched.

"We're trained for this, Guv."

So's Ryan Kaine.

They reached the food hall and climbed the ten steps up to the main entrance. Halfway up their ascent, the automatic doors slid apart and a family of four—parents and two pre-teen kids, one of each—burst out into the sunshine. The mother held her son's hand to stop him running towards the traffic. The father, head down, tapped something into his phone. His daughter did the same.

As they crossed on the steps, the little boy passed close to Dwayne, his eyeline level with the exposed Glock. His big eyes bugged wide, and he pointed at the gun.

"Mummy, mummy! Look."

Shit.

Dee tried to bury the Glock deeper into the folds of his trousers and tugged Rae faster up the steps.

"Billy, stop dawdling," Mummy said.

"Mummy, it's a gun. A gun! Look!"

Billy's free arm, jagged towards the Glock, the movements frantic. His mother stopped and glanced up at Dee and Rae. They turned towards the family. Rae released Dee's hand, waggled her fingers at the lad, and smiled. "What a pretty boy. Wonderful imagination, too."

Billy glared at her and stuck out his lower lip. "I'm not pretty," he shouted. "I'm a boy. Boys are handsome, not pretty."

"And so you are," Rae conceded, straightening her face and nodding in great seriousness.

Dee tried to relax his shoulders, but they didn't want to comply.

"Billy," the father shouted, finally dragging his eyes from his phone. "Leave those good people alone. Grandpa Barry promised to show you how to fly his drone, remember? We're going to be late." He threw Dee and Rae an apologetic smile and added. "Sorry about that, guys. He's a real live wire."

"That's alright, mate," Dee said, turning to make sure his left side faced the family.

"C'mon, Mummy." Billy tugged at his mother's hand, all thoughts of the Glock clearly set aside by the prospect of flying a drone.

"Bloody hell," Rae said, grasping Dwayne's hand once again.

"Nicely played, Rae." They turned and continued climbing the steps. "What made you call him 'pretty'?"

"I've got young cousins. I know how to wind them up." She grinned. She had a great smile. Warm.

"Nonetheless, it was brilliant. It gets you a gold star in my report."

"Thanks, boss."

The automatic doors slid apart to allow them entry to the shaded concourse. Dee swallowed, his senses heightened, heart pounding.

The squeaking of their rubber-soled military boots echoed throughout the near-empty food hall.

They strolled past the usual array of eateries, coffee shops, and clothes stores. The servers relaxed, cleaning surfaces, apparently making the most of the unexpected lull in trade. Grey Formica tables, red plastic chairs, mostly empty. A few stragglers sat eating or drinking or staring at mobile phone screens. None looked remotely like their targets.

"Quiet in here," Rae whispered. "Spooky quiet."

Dee nodded, head still, eyes on a swivel.

"Kaine's not blind and he's not stupid. He'll have noticed the lack of punters. We've left it too late."

He couldn't work out whether to be relieved or disappointed but kept his guard up and his eyes roving.

Further along the corridor with the shops on their left and the wall of glass on their right, the opening to the toilet block appeared between a couple of shops.

"Check the ladies," he said. "I'll scout out the gents. Don't take long. If you're not back out in sixty seconds, I'm coming in after you, gun raised."

Rae nodded. "I'll do the same for you."

"Okay. Go."

They entered the short corridor. She turned right. He turned left and stepped through the open archway. The Glock felt heavy, its textured grip the only thing preventing it slipping from his sweaty fist.

A modesty wall to his right opened into the gent's toilet and revealed two dozen urinals. Each one empty. Opposite the urinals stood a row of stalls. All but three doors stood open. As he strode towards them, Glock raised, one opened and an elderly man, grey hair, embarrassing combover, stepped out. Head down, he finished adjusting his fly and looked up. He stopped dead. His jaw dropped and he sucked in a breath in preparation for a scream.

Dee pointed the gun at the floor, raised a finger to his lips, and pulled open his gilet to expose his police badge. The man snapped his mouth closed and nodded, blinking rapidly.

Dee waved the obviously relieved man towards the exit and waited for him to clear the area before pressing on. The old boy didn't stop to wash his hands but would probably have to use the facilities again sooner than expected, judging by the dark stain spreading down his trouser leg. Excusable, though. No reason for the embarrassment he would no doubt feel.

Two more closed doors separated by three open stalls.

Heart thumping hard against his ribs, Glock lowered to chest height, Dee sidestepped to the first closed door and pushed. Empty.

Deep breath.

Two more sidesteps. He faced the final closed door, reached out a hand, and pushed. The door squeaked open to another vacant stall. Dee closed his eyes for a moment and sighed. He spun on his heel and raced from the gents. Rae waited outside, shaking her head.

"Nothing?" he asked.

"A mother changing her baby and a woman taking a dump. That's all. I've been through the disabled toilets, too. Empty. We've missed the buggers."

"Not necessarily," Dee said, lowering his Glock to his side once again. "We've still got the other half of the concourse to check."

"And there's a Travelodge on site. They might have booked in for the night."

"That'll take hours to clear."

"You reckon they've gone, don't you?"

Dee nodded. "Don't know how, but that surveillance blackout's dead suspicious."

"Agreed," she said, lowering her Glock and hiding it away. "What next?"

"We scout the rest of the concourse and report back to Control. Follow me."

They exited the toilets, turned left, and headed off again, passing a shop selling sandwiches, sweets, and soft drinks, and a darkened booth stuffed full of arcade games to prevent the punters developing the shakes from missing their fix of shoot-em-ups. After a pair of coin-operated vibrating chairs and a nail bar, they reached the final offering, *Ye Olde Coffee Shoppe*. As with every other enterprise they'd passed, the tables in the concourse opposite were sparsely populated. Here, a smartly dressed couple sat in padded chairs separated by a low table covered in mugs and the remains of a snack—plates, knives, and paper napkins. The woman, long auburn hair tucked behind her ears, touch typed into a laptop, her eyes glued to the screen. Her sandy-haired partner studied the pink pages of the *Financial Times*.

Dee's gaze found focus on an area three rows beyond the smart couple—an area near the wall of dirt-encrusted windows.

A man with wide shoulders sat at a table. He leant forwards, hunched over, his head lowered, and his broad back towards them. He barely fitted into his dark jacket.

Dee stopped dead. Rae stopped alongside him.

"It's him," Rae whispered. "The driver. Delta."

Dee nodded. "Fits the description." He held out an arm and shepherded her behind a vending machine, out of sight. They stood still, watching the giant snaffle his food.

"Eyes open, Rae. Watch out for the others." Dee tapped a button on his comms unit. "Tango One to Control, can you see this? Over."

"*Control to Tango One, yes. We see him. Over.*"

"Can you confirm the ID? Is that Target Delta? Over."

"*Sorry, Tango One. Can't tell from this angle, but it's possible. Can you get a better view? Over.*"

"Not without making it obvious. Over."

"Any sign of Romeo and Juliet? Over."

Dee and Rae eye-searched the immediate vicinity.

"That's a negative, Control. What do we do? Keep eyes on, or take him in? Over."

"You're the boots on the ground. I'll leave that decision to you."

Gee, thanks, Blue.

"Whatever you decide, I'll back you. Over."

Dee shot Rae a grim smile. He'd expect nothing else from Blue Jefferson.

"Message received, Control. Tango One, out." Dee ended the conversation but left the link open and live.

"What d'you think, Guv?" Rae asked.

"Romeo and Juliet are probably on their toes, but Delta might know where they're headed. We'll take him in. Guard my six and watch for interlopers."

"Should we call for backup? It won't take long for Rick to get here."

Without drawing his eyes from their target, Dee shook his head. "Delta will hear them coming. If we go now, we'll have the element of surprise. Ready?"

She swallowed and dipped her head.

Dee stepped out into the open and shuffled around to his right. Rae took the left flank. Both moved clear of the smartly dressed couple. He raised his gun, gripped it with both hands. He slid his index finger through the trigger guard and aimed at the middle of the broad back. Centre mass. Unmissable.

Don't twitch. Please don't twitch.

"Armed police!" he bellowed. "Armed police. Raise your hands."

CHAPTER 7

Cardiff West Services, M4 Motorway, South Wales, UK

The red-headed woman squealed. Her partner scrunched up his paper and froze, eyes wide. His lower lip trembled. Redhead slithered under the table, cowered into a tight ball, and covered her head with her hands.

The huge man in Dee's sights roared, "*Ära tulista!* I no have gun!" his voice deep and guttural. Both arms shot above his head, the trembling right hand still holding tight to his half-eaten baguette.

The world stopped.

Delta's shovel for a hand squeezed the baguette tighter. Its filling —lettuce, cheese, and a creamy white sauce—spilled out and ran slowly down his fingers.

"Stand up!" Dee shouted. "Do it slowly."

"I-I stand. I stand," the man shouted. "I-I no have gun! No shoot. No shoot."

His left hand dropped a few centimetres and he half twisted in his chair.

"Keep those hands where they are. Stand up," Dee roared, his voice booming.

Shock and awe.

Basic armed takedown procedure, drilled into Armed Response Officers from the first day of training. The only way to maintain control of a tense situation. They couldn't give the target any options.

Shock and awe.

Dee breathed slow and deep. Controlled. His racing heart rate eased.

Redhead whimpered. Her partner slid from his chair and joined her under the table. He wrapped her in his arms and used his body as a shield.

Good man. That'll earn you some brownie points.

Behind Dee people screamed, their scurrying movements reflected in the wall of glass. To his left, Rae backed up against the solid end wall, finding a better defensive position. Right foot in front of left, arms up and out, her Glock held rock steady in both fists.

Slowly, his movement awkward, Delta leant forwards, closer to the table, and eased himself upright. Dee raised his Glock with Delta, maintaining his shot, aiming between the giant's shoulder blades.

The backs of Delta's knees pushed his plastic chair away. Its feet scraped on the polished tiles and caught. The chair tilted backwards, toppled over, and clattered to the floor, the noise barely rising above the screams erupting from the panicked customers and staff.

"Stay where you are!" Dee shouted. "Do not move."

"I stay. I-I stay!" Delta called, his deep voice echoing through the hall.

"Rae, do you have him?"

"Yes."

"Any sign of Romeo or Juliet?"

"No. We're still clear."

"Cover me while I approach."

"Roger that."

Without compromising his shot and leading with his left foot, Dee closed in. He took a circular route. Apart from his trembling hands and heaving chest, Delta remained still.

Gradually, as Dee approached to the side, the man's profile appeared. Dark hair, long, uncombed, full beard, moustache covered in the same creamy sauce that still dripped from the baguette. His breath rumbled in the broad chest, the deep rattling rasp of a heavy smoker.

"Control to Tango One—"

Jesus. Not now, Blue!

"Stand down. Repeat. Stand down. He has a beard. It's not Target Delta. Repeat. That is not Target Delta! Over."

Dee jerked the Glock upwards, pointing it towards the vaulted roof space. He removed his finger from the trigger and rested it along the guard.

Jesus wept. Jesus bloody wept.

"I no move! Please no shoot," the giant wailed.

"Easy, sir," Dee called, trying for soothing, but sounding more frightened than relieved. "You can lower your hands and turn around."

The big man failed to move.

Rae unloaded her Glock, slid it into her trouser pocket, and rushed to close the gap between them. She stepped in front of the man who wasn't Target Delta and showed her hands—both open, both empty—and did her thing. She smiled.

The giant dropped the crushed baguette, collapsed into an empty nearby chair, and buried his face in his hands. His broad shoulders heaved in silent tears.

What a clusterfuck!

To his side, Redhead and her partner scrambled out from under the table. Eyes blazing, Redhead rounded on Dee and sucked in a deep breath.

"What on earth do you think you were doing?" she screamed. "Look at me." She pointed to a small coffee stain on the sleeve of her clearly expensive jacket. "It's ruined."

Her partner rested a hand on her forearm. "It's nothing, love. It'll clean out."

She snatched her arm away.

"Take your hands of me, you idiot," she snapped. "You nearly crushed me under that table."

"But, darling—"

"Don't you 'darling' me, you big lump."

Dee smirked. So much for earning brownie points. He turned away and stepped closer to Rae and the distraught giant.

"Did you see that, Dominic? He's smiling at me. That's just—"

"Darling," Dominic soothed, "let the man do his job. He's busy."

"Don't talk to me like—"

"That's enough!" he snapped, finding a backbone. "Just be grateful it ended without shooting or bloodshed."

"Get that officer's name and badge number," Redhead said, pointing at Dee. "I'm going to call Nigel."

"Don't be silly. He can't do anything."

"Nigel's a solicitor—"

"He's a conveyancer. A different thing entirely."

"But—"

"No 'buts', love," Dominic said, easing his tone. "Grab your laptop and let's go. We're already running late ..."

Dee left the pair to it and approached the sobbing man. Rae had her hand on the giant's shoulder, her comforting voice bringing him down from the edge of hysteria.

"*Control to Tango One. Stand down. I'm sending some uniforms in to smooth the waves. Over.*"

"Roger that, Control. Constable Johns and I will stay here until they arrive. Over."

"*I'll need a debrief the moment you return to base. Over.*"

'*Course you will.*

"Any news on the service station's surveillance equipment, sir? Over."

"*It's just this moment come back online. Our operators are searching for any stored data. Over.*"

"There won't be any, sir. Romeo's smarter than we gave him credit for. Over."

"You're probably correct in your reading of the situation, Tango One. Control, out."

"I know I'm right, Blue," Dee mumbled into a dead mic.

He'd never heard the Super sound so glum, so disappointed. Not even when he'd suffered his accident. Dee felt the same way. Ryan Kaine had slipped through the net again. Sooner or later, his luck would run out. It had to. Dee sent up a silent prayer that he'd be there during the takedown.

He unloaded the Glock before slipping it into his trouser pocket.

"Rae?" he said—the big man jerked at Dee's voice. "Everything okay here?"

She looked up from comforting the giant and smiled. "I'm explaining the situation to Mr Saar. He's Estonian, by the way, and he has a heart condition. I've called for the paramedics. They won't be long."

A heart condition, now?

Bloody hell.

Dee took in the way Saar's sizeable midriff stretched the material of his dark blue sweatshirt, and he noted the three empty beefburger wrappers littering the tabletop. A cardiac arrest waiting to explode through his chest, and Dee had pointed a loaded weapon at the man's back.

The phrase "dodged the bullet" snapped into Dee's head, and it didn't relate to the overweight Estonian.

He pulled in a full, cleansing breath and let it out slowly, trying to decompress after the hour's tension.

The post-adrenaline aftermath washed through his system, leaving him tired, trembling, and sick to his stomach.

What a God-awful day.

CHAPTER 8

Monday 22nd May – Superintendent Jefferson

South Wales Police HQ, Bridgend, South Wales, UK

Blue Jefferson's mobile vibrated in the pocket of his uniform jacket.

Who's this now?

He unbuttoned the flap and tugged out the device. The caller ID read *Unknown*. Blue declined the call and replaced the phone in the same pocket. Before he could refasten the flap, the phone vibrated again. And again, it showed the same caller ID. Blue rejected the second call and waited. Seconds later, the mobile pulsed again.

Persistent bugger, whoever you are.

He glanced up at the wall of screens. The ones that had been blank for the best part of an hour burst into life, showing various images of the Cardiff West Services. One of the older officers let out a sarcastic cheer. Others clapped. One young constable called out, "A bit bloody late," before looking about him and flushing bright red in the face. He smiled an apology at his team and hunched closer to his computer.

On the images, Dee Odawa and PC Johns seemed to be handling the situation well enough. Dee stood in the centre of a five-officer huddle, debriefing his team. PC Johns signalled to an apron-clad barista who stood in the entrance to the coffee shop. She called for something. The barista ducked into her kiosk and emerged seconds later carrying a glass of water. In the distance, near the main entrance, a couple of men in green paramedic coveralls hurried along the corridor, each carrying heavy medical bags.

The large civilian, Mr Saar, would be well looked after.

Blue's mobile pulsed again, apparently more strident. This time, he hit the green "accept" key.

"Who is this, and how did you get my phone number?"

"Superintendent Jefferson," a voice said, Home Counties accent, clipped and confident, "please move to a place where no one can hear you. Might I suggest your office?"

Who's the arrogant prick to give me instructions.

"If you don't tell me who you are, I'm ending this call."

"Superintendent Jefferson, my name is Commander Gregory Enderby of the National Counter Terrorism Agency. Please comply with my request."

"Your request?"

Instruction, more like.

"Yes," Enderby answered, sighing with extended patience. "Please move to a place where no one can hear this call."

Crap on a stick.

What the hell did the spooks want with him?

"Gene?" he called.

Blue waggled his phone at her and pointed towards the ceiling, suggesting he had to take a call from the top brass. She nodded her understanding.

"If you need me, I'll be in my office," he added.

He levered himself up and out of his chair and made his painful way towards the exit door.

"Thank you," Enderby said once Blue had reached his office, closed the door, and collapsed into his chair.

"For what?" Blue asked.

"For doing as I asked without kicking up too much of a fuss while you're in the middle of an operation."

"How do you know I'm in the middle—"

"Oh, come now, Superintendent. There's no need for us to dance around the ballroom. I have your record in front of me. A man in your position is *always* in the middle of something. Before we continue, I think an apology is in order."

Blue tightened his grip on the mobile and tried to squeeze the life out of the thing. "What the hell do I have to apologise for?"

"No, no, Superintendent Jefferson. Not you, me. I have to apologise to you."

"What for?"

"For interrupting you in the middle of an operation. And for that, you deserve the apology … and an explanation."

Blue eased his grip on the phone—eased it just enough to ensure its survival.

"By the way," Enderby continued, "I must congratulate you on the way your people dealt with the situation at the service station."

"Wait a minute, how do you know—"

"We know more than you'd think, Superintendent. We've been watching your team in action. Inspector Odawa showed great presence of mind. Heading into such a dangerous situation, not knowing what he faced, was the action of a brave man. An action worthy of the highest commendation."

"How did—For God's sake, you've been watching, haven't you? Were you responsible for the loss of the surveillance cameras at the services?"

"Well, yes, I'm afraid we were," Enderby answered after a momentary hesitation.

"You left us blind! Why the hell would you do that?"

"Couldn't be helped, I'm afraid. We needed to delay your team's entry."

"Why? ... Answer me, damn you," he added after another hesitation silenced the line.

"Easy, Inspector. Please lower your voice. I wouldn't want you to draw attention to yourself. Walls have ears, don't you know."

Blue squeezed his eyes tight shut and took a deep breath before returning his attention to the man on the phone—the man with the smooth, almost oily voice.

"Okay, Commander Enderby. Carry on."

"Yes, well. Here's where the apology comes in. We had to delay you long enough to give your targets, Romeo, Juliet, and Delta plenty of time to skedaddle."

Blue forced himself to stop grinding his teeth. He'd been doing that too often recently. Much more and he'd wear them down to stubs.

"And why on earth would you want to do such a thing?" he asked with enforced patience.

After another momentary pause, Enderby continued. "As you know, the NCTA falls under the joint auspices of the Home Office and the Ministry of Justice. What you may not know, is we also report directly to the Ministry of Defence and the Prime Minister."

"And?"

Blue waited for the inevitable "Official Secrets Act" bullshit.

"Suffice it to say, that whatever my agency does has the full backing of the Her Majesty's Government."

"And that gives you the authority to let a wanted terrorist go free?"

"An *alleged* terrorist, Superintendent Jefferson. As far as the law is concerned, Ryan Kaine is innocent unless and until found guilty by a jury of his peers. As a police officer, you must be aware of the legal nuances."

"You don't need to lecture me on—"

"Yes, yes. Quite so."

"Are you telling me Ryan Kaine's an innocent man?"

"No, I'm not telling you that at all. Not in so many words, but let's park that for the moment. I would have called you earlier, before you exhausted so many resources on the operation. However, it took rather longer than expected to obtain the authority. The PM was on a call with the US President. Couldn't be interrupted."

"This comes straight from the PM?"

"I couldn't possibly say." The non-committal response was instant.

"Why all the cloak and dagger? If the PM wants Ryan Kaine on the loose, why doesn't he just instruct the Home Office to remove him from the watch list?"

Enderby made a noise that sounded suspiciously like a chuckle. "That would seem to be the better option, Superintendent. However, it would raise all sorts of media scrutiny. It would also reignite the investigation into the tragedy of Flight BEI555, and that would not be in the public interest right now. The defence of the realm would be jeopardised."

"How so?"

"That, I'm afraid, falls outside the scope of this briefing, Superintendent Jefferson."

"A cover up?"

"In a manner of speaking." Enderby rattled out another irritating chuckle. "Let's just put it this way. At present, Her Majesty's Government would much rather the Ryan Kaine story fade into obscurity. The last thing anyone in government wants is for Ryan Kaine to surface and tell his side of the story. Hence my telephone call."

"And what would you like me to do?"

"Quite simple really. Draw a line under your operation and mark it down as a case of mistaken identity. A false alarm. As far as anyone else is concerned, Ryan Kaine was never in Cardiff. Can I rely on you, Superintendent?"

"How am I going to write down the costs—"

"Oh, I'm sure you'll find a way, Superintendent Jefferson. By the way, I spoke to your Chief Constable immediately before calling you. He is fully in the loop. And don't be surprised to hear that the Commissioner has been able to find a little extra in the budget for special operations in your next funding round. Good day to you, Superintendent Jefferson."

The call ended and the line fell silent.

Blue pulled the mobile away from his ear and stared at the blank screen as though it would tell him something he hadn't learnt from Enderby. Had he just heard the man correctly? On the face of it, Ryan Kaine was being protected by the highest authority in the country. Or was he?

The detective in him wanted to dive deeper into the Ryan Kaine story and learn more, but the operational leader in him—the man fighting off the calls for him to take early retirement on medical grounds—wanted to follow orders and bury it in the sandpit of expediency. The operational leader living on borrowed time won out.

Bloody coward.

On the other hand, Blue didn't know Commander Enderby from a hole in the ground. It wasn't as though he could verify the man's credentials. Enderby hadn't offered to give him any.

No harm confirming at least part of his unlikely story.

Blue dropped his mobile on his desk and snatched the landline's handset from its cradle. He dialled an internal number from memory and didn't have to wait long for the answer.

"Hello, Superintendent. How can I help you this morning?"

"Morning, Julie. Is the chief available?"

"He is, and he's expecting your call. I'll put you straight through."

Bloody hell. Enderby's legit.

"Thanks, Julie. Much obliged."

Blue only had to wait three seconds for three metallic clicks to confirm the connection.

"Christopher, how's the back this morning?" The chief constable sounded as ebullient as he'd ever heard the man.

"On the mend, sir. Improving every day."

Bloody liar.

"Excellent. Glad to hear it. I expect you're calling about our friend from the NCTA."

"I am, sir. Is he legit?"

The chief laughed. The man actually laughed.

"He is indeed. I've met him before, in person."

"You have, sir?"

"I have."

Blue wanted to ask when and where they'd met, but he bit the question back. He didn't want it to come across as an interrogation. The chief would no doubt consider it as a subordinate going at least a dozen steps too far.

"And he had the correct contact idents and came through via the official GCHQ channels. Otherwise, Julie wouldn't have put him through to me. His credentials are sound, Christopher."

"What do you make of him, sir?"

"You mean all the Secret Santa nonsense?"

Blue sighed but tried to keep it silent. It wouldn't do to sigh at his commanding officer. "Yes, sir. That's exactly what I mean."

"Par for the course with spooks like Enderby. You grow accustomed to it."

"You do, sir?" Blue asked, trying to sound interested.

"It may surprise you to learn that during the NPCC's quarterly gatherings, we just don't sit around drinking tea and eating biscuits, discussing budgets and the staffing levels, Christopher."

Sarcasm? Really?

Blue had never heard the chief constable so upbeat, or so loose-mouthed.

"You don't, sir?"

"No, we also meet with other branches of the security network, both internal and external. In fact, during our most recent get-together, we received a security briefing from the NCTA, which is where I first met Commander Enderby."

That's two questions answered.

"And was Ryan Kaine's ... situation mentioned at this briefing?"

"Actually, it wasn't, although I'm not sure you need to know the details."

That's told me.

"Might I speak freely, sir?"

"Please do, Christopher."

"Aren't you the least bit pissed off with the situation? I mean, all those wasted resources. When the bean counters start working out the costs—"

"No need to worry about that, Christopher. It won't come out of your departmental budget. I'll see to that. What's more, you can count on an inflation-beating increase in your operational expenditure in the next financial year."

Blue nodded to himself. Enderby had already sweetened the pot. No wonder the chief sounded so upbeat.

"Thank you, sir. I suppose the only thing left is to find a way to keep this under wraps."

"What do you mean by that?" A note of warning crept into the chief's voice.

"Inspector Odawa's team will want to know why we aren't launching a force-wide search for Kaine."

"Why would we do that in a case of mistaken identity? You heard Commander Enderby, Christopher. Ryan Kaine didn't fly into Cardiff Airport this morning, and as far as we know, he's never even been to the principality. I'm sure you'll be able to brief your people accordingly. Am I making myself perfectly clear, Superintendent?"

Blue sighed again. This time he didn't try to stifle it. Who cared if the chief heard him?

"Yes, sir. I understand."

"Will that be all, Christopher?"

"Yes, sir. Thanks for sparing me so much of your valuable time."

"Are you taking the mickey, Superintendent?" The officious note had returned.

"No, sir. Wouldn't dream of it, sir."

Yes, I bloody would.

A click on the line indicated an end to the call, and quite possibly an end to the amicable relationship he'd built with the chief over the years. The enforced retirement on health grounds had just drawn a little closer.

Blue tried hard not to scream in frustration.

CHAPTER 9

Monday 22nd May – Early Morning

The Road Network, South Wales, UK

At the Cardiff West Services, and without the need for advanced discussion, Kaine, Lara, and Rollo rushed through their well-rehearsed routine. After a swift dash to the toilets for a change of clothes, they left the easily recognisable and ANPR-tagged BMW 7 Series and swapped it for a pre-booked and modest silver-grey Audi A5 rental. The whole escape and evade operation had taken less than fifteen minutes.

On leaving the services, they rejoined the M4 motorway, sloughed off at Junction 32, and picked up the A470, a dual carriageway heading due north and deep into the rolling Welsh hills. Before Lara could finish her briefing, the Audi's infotainment system bleeped, and Corky's round and bearded face materialised on the screen in all its smiling glory.

"Whatcha, peeps," he announced. "How ya diddling?"

"Morning, Corky. How are you? It's been a while."

"Hi there, Mr K. Enjoy your trip to the States?"

Kaine shot a glance in Lara's direction, but she refused to meet his hopeful gaze. "Not particularly, Corky. A flying visit only."

"You're telling Corky. Thought you'd like to know that Sabrina's on the mend. The poor thing's battered and bruised, but the medics got to her before the lurgy took hold too deep. She's getting the best care US medicine can provide—so long as you can afford it. And as you know, *grand-père* Mo-Mo ain't short of a bob or two. Or three." He chuckled.

"That's a relief," Kaine said. "I assume you shut down the surveillance cameras at the service station?"

The self-styled "information acquisition specialist" winced. "Ah, now ... Erm, that's why Corky interrupted your drive through South Wales, Mr K."

Alarm bells fired off in Kaine's head. He twisted in his seat and stared through the rear window but saw nothing to cause concern. No flashing blue lights. No police interceptors. No unmarked patrol cars. Just a row of nondescript vehicles following them into the rolling hills.

"I don't like the sound of that, Corky. Are we compromised?"

Rollo eased into the inside lane and reduced speed in preparation to leave the dual carriageway if necessary.

"Corky ain't sure, Mr K."

Kaine opened his mouth to speak, but Lara jumped in with, "Please explain, Corky," before Kaine had the chance to say something he might regret. Corky volunteered his expertise free of charge, and the pocket genius could withdraw the same support on a whim.

Corky smiled in Lara's direction as though he could see her in the car's internal cameras. Knowing the man's skillset, he probably could.

"Hi, Doc. Is you okay?"

"Corky," Kaine said, "what happened at the services? Did you disable the surveillance cameras or not?"

Another wince. "Well, Corky was about to do that very thing when they fell offline all by themselves."

"An actual systems crash?"

The head on the screen shook. "Nope. That would be too much of a coincidence. Someone else broke into the system and blacked out the cameras—someone other than good ol' Corky."

"Any idea who?" Rollo asked. On full alert, he constantly scanned the road ahead and regularly used all his mirrors.

"Not yet, Mr R. Corky's gonna get onto it right away. But Corky'll tell you something for nothing. Whoever done it had skills. They didn't leave no obvious trail of digital breadcrumbs for anyone to follow. Weird. If Corky didn't know better, he'd think Sabrina were up to her old tricks. But it can't be her, 'cause she's in an 'ospital bed in Phoenix right now. She don't have access to enough of the right kind of tech."

Kaine glared at the screen. "Are you trying to say the person who interrupted the service station cameras is better than you, Corky?"

The violent way Corky shook his head showed a bubbling anger. For the first time since they'd known him, Corky's cheery smile faded to a deep frown. "Ain't no one better'n Corky. You know that Mr K, right?"

"Sorry, Corky," Lara said, shooting a fierce glare at Kaine.

"Yeah," Corky said, "Corky didn't say he *couldn't* find them. He just said that he hadn't found them *yet*. It's gonna take a little time. They're good, but they ain't Corky."

"So, whoever interrupted the surveillance system will know what car we're driving now?" Rollo asked.

The corners of Corky's mouth dropped. "Possibly. Can't be sure either way."

"Any traffic on the police radio comms?" Kaine asked.

"Nothing," Corky said. "Far as the boys in blue is concerned, they had you bottled up tight. They don't understand how they missed you."

"So," Kaine said, "the interlopers aren't the police."

"Not a chance," Corky answered. "They don't got the skills."

Corky's eyes widened, his hand appeared from the bottom of the screen, and clasped his forehead.

"You've just thought of something, haven't you?" Kaine said.

"Yeah, might have. Leave it with Corky." He lowered his head.

Kaine held up a hand. "Before you go, Corky. Tell me something."

"What's that, Mr K?"

"Are we safe?"

Corky hitched up his bushy black eyebrows. "You ain't never totally safe, Mr K. You know that. Corky's gonna report back as soon as he has something definitive."

"Thanks, Corky," Lara said before the screen reverted to the GPS map.

Rollo stared at Kaine through the rear-view mirror. "What do you reckon, Captain. Abort the mission?"

Kaine scratched at his beard for a momentary consideration before shaking his head. "We've never let a member of The 83 down before, and I don't intend to start now. What do you think, Lara?"

Her eyebrows shot up and disappeared beneath her soft fringe. "You're actually asking my opinion?"

"Don't be like that, this is serious."

"I know. I've never seen Corky so ... I don't know ... so unsure of himself."

"Agreed. That wasn't the only thing different about him, right?"

"You noticed that, too?"

"He's lost a hell of a lot of weight recently," Rollo said. He checked the offside wing mirror, indicated right, and pulled into the outside lane to pass a truck full of car components. "Didn't look like Corky at all."

"You think he's ill?" Kaine asked Lara.

She shrugged. "It's possible. His eyes looked a little bloodshot and dull. He could simply be on a crash diet. Difficult to make a diagnosis without seeing him in person and checking his vitals."

"So," Rollo said, indicating left and pulling back into the inside lane. "Abort or continue?"

"We continue. At least until Corky gets back to us or we have more information. Lara," he said, twisting at the waist to face her. "I still don't know what we're heading into. Mind continuing with the briefing?"

CHAPTER 10

Monday 22nd May – Early Morning

Approaching Brecon Beacons, South Wales, UK

The tree-lined A470 road ran parallel to the River Taff. While Lara continued her briefing, Kaine caught occasional glimpses of silver water through gaps in the vegetation. After Pontypridd, they passed a sign to Aberfan and fell silent at the memory of so many school-children who'd lost their lives in the disaster.

With Merthyr Tydfil behind them, the road veered north-west, the trees slipped further away from the roadside, and they headed deeper into the lush green countryside. Kaine had forgotten how beautiful Wales could be. It had been years since he'd worked in the Brecon Beacons, which matched anything Scotland could throw at the unwary hiker in terms of its ruggedness and wild beauty, but on a much smaller scale.

"Horses," Kaine said after a brief silence. "I should have known it would revolve around horses."

"What's wrong with horses?" Rollo asked. He'd been quiet since the end of Corky's worrying interruption, concentrating on his driving and his mirrors.

"Big beasts I can't reason with or control," Kaine answered.

"Sounds like some of the people we deal with from time to time."

"Ha, ha. Very funny."

Kaine brought back the memory of the first—and so far only—time Lara had convinced him to climb into the saddle and ride a horse—on Mike Procter's farm, some six months earlier. Despite Lara's guidance and encouragement, and her obvious delight in riding alongside him on the powerful black beast that became docile in her hands, Kaine simply couldn't relax or get the hang of it. Nor could he understand the joy. The beast they allocated him, a huge grey and knowing monster, refused to obey Kaine's commands. The animal headed wherever it bloody well chose, irrespective of which way Kaine tugged on the reins or dug in with his heels. In the end, after thirty minutes' bone-crunching, backside-bruising nastiness, he'd climbed stiffly down from the saddle and inwardly vowed never to repeat the process. Although he did lie to Lara and told her he'd loved the experience immensely. In truth, he'd take motorbike saddles over horses' tack any day of the week.

"Horses are wonderful creatures," Lara said, her eyes alive. "You just need to familiarise yourself with them. They can sense fear, you know."

"Me? Show fear?" Kaine dug a thumb into his chest. "The very idea. Totally fearless, me. I faced you down, didn't I?"

"Be serious for a minute, will you?" she said, glaring.

Since the start of their journey, her chill had thawed a little. She'd even relaxed her tense shoulders and smiled when discussing the nags for hire at the *Cadwallader Farm and Trekking Centre, Glyn Coes.* Her eyes always lit up when talking about horses. As a veterinary surgeon, back before he'd unintentionally dragged her into his world of death and destruction, she'd specialised in treating large farm animals. Not for her the cosy veterinary practice which focused on pampering "companion animals" which Kaine still insisted on calling "pets", much to Lara's annoyance.

"The Cadwalladers have had numerous break-ins over the past two months," she said. "The first few were simple vandalism. Stable doors opened and the horses allowed to run free in the paddock. The Cadwalladers wrote them off as local kids playing silly buggers."

"Forgive me for asking, but don't they lock stable doors to stop horses bolting. I mean padlock them?"

Lara shook her head.

"No, the current advice is to avoid putting any type of locks on stable doors. Horse feed and bedding is highly combustible. Padlocked stables would make it impossible to free the horses in case of a fire. Our advice is to use latches on stable doors and lock the gates on the paddocks and driveways instead."

"Okay," Kaine said, nodding. "That makes sense. So, what happened with the other incidents?"

"As Rollo said earlier, sheep have been stolen. Another time, the vandals released all the horses and tried to set some hay bales in the big barn alight. Fortunately, Gwyn Cadwallader's a light sleeper. He managed to douse the fire before it took hold. They were very lucky."

Kaine screwed up his lips.

"So far, this sounds like a job for the police, not The 83 Trust."

"Gwyn called in the police, but the nearest station manned twenty-four-seven is in Merthyr Tydfil, and that's over forty-five minutes from the farm. When he called them after the third break-in, they sent a constable the following morning. According to Gwyn, the officer scratched her head, gave them a crime number for the insurance claim, and left them some leaflets on crime prevention in the countryside. Bloody useless."

Kaine raised an eyebrow. Lara rarely resorted to swearing. It showed her investment in the Cadwalladers' predicament.

"Can't we just stump up the money for some decent surveillance cameras and maybe add a sprinkler system?"

Lara shook her head. "We can't just throw money at this problem."

"Why not?"

"That'll become clear when you meet Gwyn Cadwallader."

Kaine pricked up an ear. "That sounds ominous."

She opened her hands in a shrug, but said nothing more.

"Listen," Kaine said, "I'm not trying to make light of the situation, but I really don't see what we can do other than mount surveillance for a few nights, maybe a couple of weeks, and hope to catch the vandals in the act. If we do that, we can take the little tykes aside and try to intimidate them into submission. As though that's going to work. Soon as we go, they'll be up to the same old tricks again. How large is the farm?"

"Over six hundred acres. You'll see it for yourself soon enough."

"Open land?"

"It's in the middle of a valley formed by the Clantri, a tributary of the River Usk. It's such a beautiful place," Lara said, her eyes shining. "Mostly rolling pasture, but there are about two hundred acres of woodland and scrub. The Cadwalladers run it as a livestock farm all year round and offer pony trekking in the summer."

"Hence the horses?"

"And the ponies."

"And the ponies, right." Kaine nodded, absorbing the information, and wondering what his role in the operation might be, over and above agreeing to sign a large cheque. "By livestock, you mean the sheep, I suppose?"

"Mainly sheep, but there are a few dairy cows. Which takes us onto the most recent incident. It happened last Saturday night."

"The sheep rustling?" Kaine couldn't help smiling.

"It's not funny, Ryan. Theft of livestock is on the rise throughout the countryside, and the police are too stretched to do much about it. Insurance premiums are through the roof."

For almost the first time since entering the car, Lara turned to face him fully, and he felt the full force of her angry glare.

"For your information," she said, moving into full lecturing mode, Corky's ominous news apparently forgotten for the moment, "in the past decade, farming income has declined by close to fifty percent.

And, in the past two years alone, one third of the UK's farmers have sold up and left the industry."

"Bloody hell." Kaine sat up straighter in his seat.

"Exactly. That's about fifty thousand families on the scrap heap."

"I had no idea. How many sheep did the Cadwalladers lose?"

"Fifty."

"And their total value?"

"Around five thousand pounds or so."

"Five grand?" He shook his head. "Is that all?"

Lara gritted her teeth and her frown deepened. "Ryan, that's serious money for the Cadwalladers. And it's not just about the money. You don't understand the commitment involved in raising animals. The Cadwalladers really care for their stock."

Kaine reached out a hand in apology, but she refused to take it.

"No, love, that's not what I meant. I'm just surprised how little a sheep is worth. One hundred quid for a full-grown lamb? That's pitiful."

The tension in Lara's shoulders eased and the lines on her forehead softened. "Pitiful isn't the word. All that work for so little reward."

"And?"

"And what?"

"This isn't only about a few stolen baa lambs, is it?"

Lara shook her head. "No, it isn't."

"What exactly happened last Saturday?"

"The horses were let out again."

"Anything else?"

Rollo slowed to negotiate a roundabout. He took the second exit towards the market town of Brecon and entered the single-carriageway road, still heading north.

Once they'd settled into the lane behind slow-moving traffic, Lara pulled out her mobile phone and accessed her camera app. She scrolled through the gallery until she found the picture she wanted and handed the phone to Kaine. As he took it from her, they brushed fingers—almost their first physical contact since he'd abandoned her in Paris. This time, she didn't snatch her hand away, and Kaine took it as an encouraging sign. He hoped a more extended thaw in the frost would follow.

Kaine studied the picture. It showed an open stable door, to which someone had nailed two items, one above the other. On top, a scrap of paper carrying a handwritten note, below it a photograph. He turned the mobile on its side to view the picture in landscape mode, and spread his fingers over the screen to zoom in. The words on the note remained scrambled and illegible.

"Welsh?" he asked.

"Yes."

"Translation?"

"It says, and I paraphrase, 'This is only the start. Worse is to come! Do as you're told.' Although, I did leave out the expletives."

"Hmm. Interesting. Doesn't sound like kids."

"Slide across to the next picture."

He did as she asked and found himself looking at the close-up of the photo pinned below the note. The image was unmistakable—the rotting carcass of a horse. Flies buzzing all around.

"Ah," he said. "This is serious stuff, and it does make it our business."

"I thought you'd see it that way."

Finally, Lara smiled. It made Kaine's morning and lessened the gnawing worry of Corky's bombshell.

CHAPTER 11

Monday 22nd May – Early Morning

Brecon Beacons, South Wales, UK

A few minutes after they'd negotiated the roundabout, they rolled past an understated road sign—a blue rectangle with a rounded top, bolted to a blue rock with a flat face. At first glance, the logo could have been an acorn in a cup, but closer inspection confirmed it as a fiery brazier—a beacon.

They'd entered the Brecon Beacons National Park.

"What happened when Cadwallader showed this to the police?"

Lara sighed. "He didn't contact the police this time."

"Why not?"

"Said it wasn't worth it. The police couldn't help them."

Kaine tilted his head.

"He said 'couldn't' not 'wouldn't'?"

"Yes, that's exactly what he said. The police *couldn't* help them."

"You think he's holding out on us?"

She shrugged. "I tried to push him, but he wouldn't say. Close-mouthed isn't the word for it. Typical farmer. Stoic, you know? Becky might be more talkative, but I haven't had a chance to chat to her in private yet. She's worried though. Anyone can tell that. In fact, she's the one who called us in, not Gwyn."

"How old are the kids?"

"Dewi's nineteen," Rollo answered, staring straight ahead, but demonstrating his involvement in the briefing. "He's in his second year in agricultural college. Usually spends the weekdays in Cirencester and his weekends at Glyn Coes, helping on the farm."

"What's he like?" Kaine asked.

"No idea. We've not met him yet. He wasn't there this past weekend. Becky said he's away visiting college friends."

"And the other child?"

"Myfanwy's just turned sixteen," Lara answered. "Lovely girl. Bright as a button. Plays rugby for the village. Sings in the chapel choir and attends Brecon Academy School. That's a secondary school about a twenty-mile round trip from the farm."

"Anyone else?"

"What do you mean?"

Again, Lara and Rollo exchanged glances via the rear-view. Once more, the unspoken message passed between them. He tamped down the growing annoyance.

Patience, Kaine. They'll tell you soon enough.

"Anyone else on the farm? Employees? Labourers?"

"No. A few girls from the local village help out as stable hands, but they don't live at the farm. The Cadwalladers employ a full-time guide during the trekking season, but that won't start for another month or so."

She paused. Kaine hoped she'd tell him what was bothering her, but Lara remained silent.

"Okay. Got it. So, who am I?"

"I've told them you are former military. A security expert."

"Staff Sergeant Peter Sidings," he said, nodding. "Okay, we've been through that."

"We thought it would be better than creating a totally new ID for you. Easier for you to remember."

"Right. Does Sidings still work for *Conqueror*?"

"No, he's recently turned freelance," Lara said. "He's currently under contract to The 83 Trust."

"This means we're not married?" Kaine asked, putting on a sad face.

During recent missions, Kaine and Lara had often passed themselves off as the long-time married couple, Mr and Mrs William Griffin.

"Yes."

"Separate beds?"

"Of course," she said, and the twinkle finally returned to her eyes. A huge relief. "The Cadwalladers are Presbyterians. They go to chapel every Sunday, come rain or shine."

"Wonderful."

"They're decent people. Salt of the earth."

"I'm sure they are. So, who's putting the pressure on?"

"No idea. Becky might open up to you, who knows?"

"Meanwhile, we're going in blind?"

"We are."

"Won't be the first time," Rollo said.

A road sign showed a left turn onto the A4215 ahead. Rollo indicated left, braked, and pulled onto the slip road. He braked harder to negotiate a sharp, one-eighty degree turn onto the single-track road. Fortunately, it was free of traffic and Rollo increased speed to a full forty-five miles per hour. Any faster wouldn't have been safe for the road conditions.

"So," Kaine said, "what have you ordered in terms of surveillance equipment, Quartermaster Rollason?"

"Nothing, sir."

"Nothing? Why not?"

Again, Rollo glanced in the rear-view.

"Doc. You want to tell him, or shall I?"

"No, Rollo," Lara answered. "Be my guest."

"What now?" Kaine asked, trying hard to keep his voice even.

"Gwyn Cadwallader's a religious man."

"Yes, a Presbyterian, you've already told me that. What about it?"

"As well as that, he's a pacifist from a long line of pacifists. During the last world war, his grandfather was a conscientious objector, and his family suffered for it. Gwyn won't have anything to do with the military."

"Which means?"

"He won't accept The Trust's money."

"What? Why the hell not?"

"He visited our website," Lara said, "and decided he didn't like where some of our money comes from."

Oh, for pity's sake.

When Kaine considered everything he'd suffered to relieve SAMS of its illicit millions—he'd lost another tooth and gained a few more scars for his troubles—he scowled. And he'd gone through it all with the sole intention of distributing the money to Flight BE1555's nearest and dearest.

"So, Gwyn Cadwallader ripped up the banker's draft we sent him?"

"Don't be daft, sir," Rollo said, slowing and easing tight to the side of the road to allow room for an oncoming tractor. "He might be religious, but he's pragmatic—and Welsh. He wouldn't actually throw away money."

The Audi's nearside front wing scraped the hedge as the vehicles passed each other. Rollo tutted. "There goes our security deposit."

"We can afford it," Kaine said. "What's a few hundred pounds? So, what did Cadwallader do with the money?"

"Put it in a trust fund for his kids. They can decide what to do with it when they turn twenty-five."

"Why twenty-five? Why not eighteen or twenty-one?"

"No idea, sir. Didn't think to ask him."

The narrow road continued generally uphill, and the gentle bends grew into ever tighter curves. Trees crowded in around them, occasionally opening up to reveal rolling fields and hedgerows on either side.

"Okay," Kaine said, after a short pause for thought. "I suppose this means there's no point in trying to throw money at the problem. Not even in terms of surveillance equipment?"

"None whatsoever," Lara said. "Not if it comes from The Trust."

"Is there any way around it? What if we tell him we'll only use sequestered funds that came in from private donations?"

"How would that work? How could we prove the money was 'untainted'?"

"Oh, I don't know," Kaine said, scratching his head in annoyance. "I'm clutching, here. It makes no sense. The bloke takes government subsidies, doesn't he?"

"I imagine so," Lara said. "I've yet to meet a farmer who refused them."

"Well, the government takes taxes from the military sector. What's the difference?"

"You'll have to take that up with Cadwallader," Rollo piped up. "Maybe you can make him change his mind, sir."

"You don't sound too convinced, Colour Sergeant."

"That's because I'm not. You haven't met Gwyn Cadwallader."

"Okay, will he accept our help if it's non-financial?"

"I think so," Lara offered, "but we haven't asked him yet."

"Why'd he call us in, then?"

"He didn't. Becky did."

"Ah, yes. You said."

"I did." Lara's patient smile told Kaine she was almost back on side—not that he'd thought for one minute she'd really desert him.

Well, maybe for a minute or two.

"If he doesn't," Kaine muttered half to himself, "this might turn out to be our shortest mission yet. And given Corky's revelation ... that might not be a bad idea."

He waited for more, but Lara averted her eyes.

"Okay, I've had enough of this. Out with it. What aren't you telling me?"

Lara looked up and met his gaze. Kaine couldn't read her emotions. Still, she refused to answer.

"Lara?"

"Better tell him, Doc," Rollo said. "He'll find out soon enough."

"Yes." Kaine nodded, brows pulled tight together. "You might as well tell me now."

"There's one more member of the Cadwallader family we haven't mentioned."

Okay. Here it comes.

"Go on."

"Rhod, I mean, Rhodri Pierce."

"Who's Rhodri Pierce?"

Lara's expression softened. "Rhodri is Gwyn and Becky's twelve-year-old nephew."

The penny dropped, and Kaine's heart thudded into his belly.

"Sharon Pierce's son?" he asked, his mouth dust dry.

Lara nodded.

Oh dear God.

A twelve-year-old boy whose mother he'd killed. No way he could turn his back on the Cadwalladers. Not now. No matter what Corky's investigations uncovered.

Breathe, Kaine. Breathe.

"Why wasn't he on our list?" Kaine asked, almost choking. He coughed to clear an unresponsive throat. "How could Sabrina have missed him?"

"It's complicated." Lara grimaced and shook her head. "Pierce was Sharon's maiden name, but Rhodri was christened under her married name, Duckworth. When she and her husband divorced eight years ago—acrimoniously, by the way—Sharon reverted to her maiden name and started the process of changing Rhodri's surname. The name change wasn't finalised until a couple of months after she ... passed." She stopped and offered Kaine a sympathetic smile.

"Why did it take so long?" Kaine asked, working hard to process the new information.

"The father, Richard 'Ducky' Duckworth, raised an objection and sued for custody of the lad. The whole process became rather messy."

"But he's Rhodri Peirce now, right? What happened?"

"Money changed hands. In effect, Sharon paid Ducky off."

Kaine stiffened. Where was this going?

"Go on."

Lara shook her head again. "Sharon gave up ownership of the family home and any claims for spousal maintenance. She also applied for full custody of the lad, which Ducky opposed."

Kaine pursed his lips. "Sounds like a lovely fellow. What was the outcome?"

"After Sharon signed over the house, Ducky withdrew his application for custody and sold up. He took all the money and emigrated."

Yep. A really nice chap.

"Where to?"

"Last anyone heard from him, he'd made an offer to buy a bar in Malaga."

"And?"

"The bar owners rejected the offer, and Ducky dropped out of sight again."

"No sign of him since then?"

"None," Rollo said. "Not that anyone's been looking. Useless piece of excrement. When he didn't show up after Sharon's death, the courts agreed to Becky and Gwyn's application for custody. It was either that, or the boy going into care. A no-brainer."

"What's the lad like?" Kaine asked, again pushing out the words through a chalk dry throat.

"Quiet. Shy," Lara answered.

"Skinny little kid," Rollo added. "Keeps to his bedroom most of the time. Never lived on a farm before. I reckon he's scared of the animals. Hates the idea of getting mud on his hands, apparently. And I don't really mean 'mud'." Rollo smiled into the rear-view.

"Right." Kaine couldn't think of anything else to say, but at least his voice sounded closer to normal, less stressed.

He fell silent, trying to prepare for a meeting with a child whose life he'd ruined forever. Would his one mistake ever stop haunting him?

The first child victim he'd actually met, Martin Princeton, had lost his older brother, not his mother. The consequence of Kaine's mistake on Rhodri Pierce's life had to be even more profound. He'd made the boy a virtual orphan, for pity's sake. How would he be able to look the lad in the eye after all the damage he'd caused?

Crap.

"Are you sure I'm the right man for this job?" Kaine asked. "I'm not good with kids."

He tried to swallow but couldn't squeeze it past the rock-hard lump in his throat.

"How do you know that?" Lara asked. "When was the last time you spent any time with a child."

"2008. Mali," Kaine replied, casting his mind back to a different time and place. "Child soldiers. Fearsome kids—"

"Oh for goodness' sake!" she snapped. "Rhodri Pierce isn't a child soldier. He's a sweet little lad who needs our support. As does his family."

Kaine tried another tack. "Won't I just get in the way?"

"You might," Rollo agreed. "If you like, I could drop you off at Brecon. It's not far out of our way. There's bound to be a car hire firm there. You can make your own way back to France."

Rollo's suggestion sounded less like a way out and more like an accusation of cowardice in the face of an enemy. In this case, the enemy happened to be a twelve-year-old boy.

Rollo hadn't been so insolent since they'd first met at SBS boot camp when his role had been to work Kaine and his fellow recruits to near destruction.

"Run away, you mean?"

"Your words, Captain. Not mine."

"It's Staff Sergeant Sidings to you, Mr Bennett. At least while we're at Glyn Coes."

"So, we're not heading to Brecon?"

"No, Adrian. Of course, we aren't."

"I thought not, Sarge."

The tension on Rollo's face eased. His mild rebuke had clearly cost him a great deal.

"So," Kaine said, "how far now?"

"Not far. We'll be reaching Sennybridge before long. After that it's another twenty minutes."

"Twenty minutes. Right."

Not long to prepare himself for the emotional upheaval. Not long enough at all.

"Take all the time you need."

Rollo dipped his head in a curt nod and said nothing.

Again, Kaine reached out for Lara's hand. This time she took it and held it tight, her hand warm in his. She knew exactly how he felt and would do her best to be there for him, but in truth, he'd have to deal with the situation alone.

THEY CRESTED A LOW HILL AND THE ROAD DIPPED INTO ANOTHER WIDE valley. Cows grazed in an upland meadow on their left. Sheep dotted the far-off hills, looking so much like giant puffball mushrooms against the blue-green backdrop. The sun shone bright. Trees cast short and spidery shadows. Stone houses, painted white, appeared in the distance.

Rollo slowed to a crawl behind another tractor, this one pulling an empty trailer, and they entered a small village. On the outskirts, they passed a playing field which proudly sported two sets of rugby posts, confirming their location—deep in the heart of rural Wales. Without indicating first, the tractor braked, turned right, and pulled into an impossibly narrow lane. The road cleared, allowing Rollo to increase speed to a free-flowing twenty-five miles per hour.

The road curved around to the right, they paused at a *GIVE WAY* sign, and ducked into a single-laned street leading to a crossroads.

Movement through the window beyond Lara's shoulder caught Kaine's eye.

Hell!

"Rollo, stop. Stop the car!" he shouted. "Pull over. Now!"

Rollo stomped on the brakes and turned the wheel. The Audi's nose bucked, and the car rode up the nearside kerb. Behind them, a car horn blared.

"Ryan!" Lara shouted.

Before the Audi reached a complete stop, Kaine rammed open his door and dived out.

CHAPTER 12

Monday 22nd May – Mitch Bairstow

Sennybridge, Brecon Beacons, South Wales, UK

Mitchell "Mitch" Bairstow winced. His right ankle and the foot attached to it throbbed. The bloody thing actually throbbed. How could his foot still hurt when they'd buried it in a hole in the dusty ground outside Kabul? His knee, mind, that still remained. The knee had every right to hurt, and by heck did it throb. Ached all the time. Incessant pain. The prosthetic leg didn't fit properly anymore. Rubbed his stump raw every time he tried to walk any distance on it. Truth was the chuffing thing never fit properly. Not since the day they'd presented it to him. Pleased as Punch, they were. Misguided buggers. They didn't have to wear the bloody thing for the rest of their lives.

"It'll be uncomfortable to begin with," the physio told him, a fresh-faced kid straight out of college, "but you'll get used to it."

Lying sod.

"It's too tight," Mitch had said.

"You still have some swelling. Give it time. It'll settle down over the next few weeks."

Damn thing never did.

Back then, booze had helped dull the agony. Back then, before he'd found the peace of the Lord, nothing else helped. Beer. Wine. Whisky. Vodka. God save him, he'd even resorted to cider if there was nothing else on offer.

Alcohol didn't do anything for his balance, though. Kept falling over. But that didn't matter so much. One thing the army did was teach him how to fall and roll without hurting himself. Even with a missing leg, the training still worked.

He'd given up on the booze two years back. The morning after he'd woken in a holding cell, without his backpack, and unable to remember his own name until later that same day. Scary times. Scariest time since the IED blew up in his face.

Since leaving home for good—crappy place with a drunken, abusive father and a dead mother—the only place he'd ever stayed long was the army. But the army didn't want him anymore. He'd outlived his usefulness. Outlived it the day the IED took his leg.

Good old army. Taught him discipline. Let him see the world. Where would he be without it? Who knew, but he'd likely have the same number of legs he'd been born with.

Chuffing IED.

Chuffing insurgents.

Chuffing Taliban.

Mitch dropped his backpack to the concrete beneath the park bench and gently lowered himself onto the slatted seat. His false ankle creaked and clicked as he forced it to bend. Bloody leg needed its annual service, but who had the time to take it in for a proper lube job these days? Mitch certainly didn't. Painful and ill-fitting as it was, he didn't want to do without his prosthesis and suffer crutches for the two days it took them to run it thought the service. Nope, he'd put up with the clicking and the creaking for a few more weeks. Maybe a few more months. He'd survive the upcoming summer easily enough. Maybe next autumn.

Yeah, he'd book it in for the autumn.

Mitch yawned and sighed in one glorious simultaneous movement. Life could be worse for Mitch the Mechanical Man with the missing er ... member.

Ha!

He smiled at the feeble alliteration.

That's it, Mitch. Got to have a sense of humour.

Only thing that kept him going. If he didn't laugh, he'd ... throw himself off the nearest footbridge. But no, he couldn't be doing that. It would be wrong. Suicide was a mortal sin. Or so Father Flannigan had drummed into him at primary school. God would be disappointed in him. Mum would too, may she rest her beautiful soul, wherever she was. The church said she'd be in the Promised Land.

And where was the Promised Land?

Not South Wales, that was for sure. It had its good parts, but beautiful landscapes would only go so far.

Overnight, he'd found a relatively comfortable place to bed down. A place he'd probably use again if he ever passed this way a second time. A good place for an itinerant man. A man on the run from his old life. A man on an unending journey to lose himself in order to find himself again.

Where's the logic in that?

Around the side of a café, it was. Out of sight of security cameras, near an exhaust vent that pumped out warm air. The owner had moved him on when she arrived to open the place that morning. Nice woman, she was. Gave him a sandwich left over from the previous day and pointed him in the direction of the local park. He'd remember such a place. It would keep him alive in the freezing cold nights of deepest winter. Not that it was winter at the moment. More like late spring, early summer. It could still turn chilly overnight, though. Chilly enough to freeze his bones and stiffen his joints.

At least the bright sun had some warmth to it that morning. Later that day, it might even be hot. What a joyous thing that would be.

The rare joy of being truly warm.

Perhaps he should go south. Maybe head towards Portsmouth. He could take a ferry to the continent and find somewhere really warm. Portugal or southern Spain might be a good place to overwinter. Only two things stopped him.

One. He didn't have cash for the ferry ticket. Not without calling home and breaking cover, and that wasn't happening anytime soon.

Two. He didn't have a valid passport. His had expired years back and he'd never bothered to replace it.

Apart from that, he was good to go.

Ha!

Nope. International travel was not for Mitch Bairstow. He'd have to make do with the whole of mainland UK. Not a horrible prospect, but in winter?

A cold breeze picked at the collar of his jacket, fluttering it against his exposed neck. He lifted the collar and folded the lapels up to his throat, but the wind still sliced its way into the sensitive skin around the back of his head. The scar from the IED could be as sensitive as the stump.

Mitch tugged his woollen beanie further down on his head, raised his shoulders, and tucked in his neck—working on his best turtle impression. It helped a bit, but not much. He needed his scarf, or his balaclava, but he'd lost them with his other pack the last time some bastards rolled him over.

Bloody kids.

Mitch had grown to hate kids. The taunts. The disrespect.

The younger ones were bad enough. Dancing around him. Taunting. Calling him names. Where had all the discipline gone? Where were the parents? And him a war hero, too. They'd given him a bravery medal to prove it. Lot of bloody good that did him. Didn't keep him warm at night.

Kids.

Mitch learnt to ignore the younger ones. Turn the other cheek, as the Holy Bible taught him. Them, he could ignore. But the older ones. The teens and the twentysomethings fuelled up on booze and glue, and who knew what.

The bastards saw him as an easy mark since he couldn't run anymore. Couldn't run away. Couldn't give chase neither. Couldn't snatch his stuff back from the thieving bastards. What a comedown.

Enough!

He had to stop feeling sorry for himself. Things could be worse. A lot worse. At least he'd survived. Unlike Chopper, Charlie, and Big Mike. They'd all been blown to tiny, bloody bits. Butchered. Their blood and gore ended up all over the Panther and all over Mitch. During the explosion, he'd swallowed some of Chopper's blood and guts. In that respect, they'd be together forever. Chopper would live on as long as Mitch did. Another reason he couldn't take a swan dive off the nearest bridge. Chopper deserved better.

Looking on the bright side, at least the lower part of his right leg didn't feel the cold any longer. It could only throb, itch, and tingle.

Even though he'd sat and taken the load off, his stump ached worse than ever. No amount of ointment would ever ease the rubbing or cure the rawness. Damned socket needed adjusting.

The chafing had worsened over the previous couple of days. Long days covering big miles. It caused him no end of grief. Made his stump swell up. But he put off going back to the hospital. All the questions they asked that he couldn't answer. If the medics and the headshrinkers really knew how he felt, they might never let him out again.

Nah, he needed to keep his head down. Fly below the radar or they'd send him back to the nuthouse, lock the doors, and melt the key down for buttons.

Better to be outside and freezing his nuts off in freedom than being banged up in a rubber room.

Yep, he'd sit on the park bench until someone moved him on. The park wardens wouldn't let him stay long. They'd shoo him away. Fair enough, they had their jobs to do, but why couldn't they just leave him be? He wasn't doing any harm. Holding out his hand to the occasional passer-by, asking for a donation didn't make him a bad person, did it?

This morning, he'd get three hours tops. That was his bet. Three hours.

One hundred and eighty minutes.

Ten thousand eight hundred seconds.

Mitch did what he always did to pass the time—he started counting. Something about clocking up past the hundreds and into the thousands soothed him. Even though he could read the time off the clock on the church tower, he preferred to count off the seconds for himself. Keeping time—maintaining the correct rhythm—kept him sane.

By the time he'd reached three thousand and forty-five—he liked the fives, too, the halfway points—the sun had crept over the eastern horizon, or at least, the two-storey buildings across the road running parallel to the park.

Eventually, someone would move him along, but for a while they'd leave him alone. After all, he wasn't doing any harm, was he? He didn't smell too bad, either. The washroom in the petrol station last night had hot water. The service staff had filled the soap dispensers, too. Mitch scrubbed and soaped himself red raw. He hadn't been so clean in days. He smelled of roses and changed into his last set of clean clothes. Well, they were cleaner than the ones he'd been wearing for the past week.

Three thousand seven hundred and forty-six.

Difficult to dry clothes when you didn't have money for the launderette and anyway, he hadn't passed one in weeks. Using the same soap dispensers, he'd scrubbed the worst of the filth from his undies and used the hand drier as best he could, but his clothes were still damp. He'd have to air them before too long or the mould would set in. Not good when he only had a few pairs left.

Money.

The root of all evil, but impossible to survive without. Mitch wasn't penniless though. Far from it. Thousands, he had. Maybe tens of thousands by now. It had been a while since he'd checked his account. His back pension and the rest of it, his invalidity benefit. Locked away in a bank. But he couldn't touch it. No way. If he withdrew any of it, *they* would trace him. *They* would track him down and drag him back to the ward, back to the padded cell.

Three thousand eight hundred and eighty-one.

No. No. He couldn't let that happen. Never again. Better be a beggar than a captive. Much better.

Three thousand nine hundred and five.

Mitch closed his eyes and lifted his face to the sun, allowing its heat to infuse deep into his skin. He smiled. Sometimes, life could be tolerable.

Three thousand nine hundred and eight-three.

Something blocked out the light behind his closed lids. A moving shadow.

Mitch held out his hand, palm up.

"Spare a few pennies for an old soldier, buddy?"

"Fuck off, arsehole!"

The shadow moved again. Mitch opened his eyes as the first boot landed. Searing, numbing pain shot through his ribs. He rolled off the bench, fell to the cold ground.

Standing over him, blocking the sun. Four kids. Three laughed, as their mate planted his standing foot and swung the other for a second time.

Four thousand and seven.

Mitch doubled up. He curled into a tight ball. Protecting his head and balls, nothing else to do. He couldn't jump up, couldn't fight, couldn't run.

Pray God they'd get bored and move on after having their fun.

"Want our money, do you?"

The third blow landed, glanced off his shoulder, and grazed the side of his head. The beanie flew off, exposing his scar to the cold breeze. Mitch squeezed his eyes tight shut, lights flashed, searing his retinas. A bell rang in his ears.

Tyres squealed. A car horn blared, and a door slammed.

Running footsteps approached.

"That's enough!" A man's voice. Deep commanding.

Someone close by, one of the attackers, shouted, "Look out, Dai!"

The blows stopped landing, and Mitch's head stopped colliding with the hard-packed earth. Blessed relief, of sorts. The throbbing continued and would do for a while, but at least no more blows landed.

The pounding in his head intensified.

Something thudded against something hard. Air whooshed out of rattling lungs

Someone shouted, "Bastard!" A youthful voice. Trembling.

Mitch tore open his eyes and looked upon a miracle. An honest-to-goodness, Grade A miracle.

CHAPTER 13

Monday 22nd May – Morning

Sennybridge, Brecon Beacons, South Wales, UK

Kaine darted across the road, dodging the slow-moving, oncoming traffic. He vaulted the park wall and raced towards the bench.

"That's enough!" he yelled.

The thug swinging the heavy work boot—long dark hair flapping around his head—had his back to Kaine and didn't see him coming.

One of his partners—short-cropped sandy hair, silver ring through his nose—shouted, "Look out, Dai!" moments before Kaine's shoulder charge slammed the attacker face first into the trunk of an oak tree. Air whooshed out of him, and he slid down the bark onto his knees.

Kaine turned, dropped into a defensive stance, senses on high alert.

"Bastard!" Nose-ring screamed, spittle flying.

The other two gave Nose-ring some space, forming a loose arc. They closed in.

Kaine smiled. Three against one. Not a problem.

The one on the left—squat, blackened front tooth—gripped a rusty metal spike in his right hand. It had a wicked-looking point. The other—taller, rail thin—carried a brick. He raised it and threw in one rapid motion. Kaine ducked. The brick sailed harmlessly over his head and crashed into the bushes behind him.

Nose-ring lunged forwards, raised right arm arcing in a downward strike to Kaine's head and neck.

Metal glinted in the watery sunshine.

Kaine crossed his arms over his head, blocked the knife, and spun on one heel, into the attacker. He slid his hand down the inside of Nose-ring's right forearm, grabbed the wrist, and twisted it out and around. Nose-ring squealed, flipped onto his face, and slammed into the concrete slab surrounding the bench.

Keeping one eye on the still struggling, scrambling Dai, Kaine continued his rotation and wrenched Nose-ring's arm high up behind his back. Under the tortional impetus, the shoulder dislocated. The joint parted, emitting a sloppy wet crunch. Nose-ring screamed, and the black-handled knife with its six-inch blade slipped from lifeless fingers.

"My shoulder!" he wailed. "*Rydych chi'n ffycin* bastard." Tears rolled down his cheeks.

Kaine drove a knee into the small of Nose-ring's back, and pressed a hand into the howling man's head, grinding his face into the gritty slab.

"Mind your language, son," he hissed into Nose-ring's ear, pressing even harder. "And don't attack someone with a knife unless you know how to use it. You're lucky you didn't end up wearing it."

The skinny one, the one who'd chucked the brick, kept his distance. He bent at the waist, and his fingers scrabbled in the dirt, searching for another missile.

In the distance, two of the Audi's doors slammed shut.

Rollo vaulted the low wall and raced down the slope towards them.

Still crouching low, Brick-chucker spun around. His panicked squeal cut short as one hundred and twenty kilograms of hurtling beef and bone crashed into him. He sailed through the air and landed in a crumpled heap on top of the first attacker, Dai. Something snapped. Maybe a tree branch. Another scream suggested a broken bone.

The attacker with the rotten tooth and the metal spike, dropped his weapon, spun around, and legged it. His work boots lost traction on the damp grass, and he plunged headlong into the sloppy mud. Gasping, crying, fists and boots a blur, he clambered to his feet and continued his reckless dash to freedom—heading straight for Lara.

Being the sensible one, Lara stepped aside and let him race pass.

Thug number one, Dai, grunted. He pushed a lifeless Brick-chucker away and tried to stand, but the muddy ground at the bowl of the tree gave his work boots the same lack of traction as the fleeing Rotten-tooth, and his arse squelched into the muddy ground. He flipped onto his front, pushed up with his arms, and made it to his feet, swaying slightly. He thrust out a hand and steadied himself against the tree trunk. A weeping graze on his forehead dripped blood into his eye. He shook his head and blinked hard to clear his vision.

Nose-ring screamed, struggled, trying to buck Kaine off, but he didn't have the purchase or the strength, being only able to use one arm. Kaine allowed his knee to slide down and spear the man's right kidney. Nose-ring whimpered and stopped moving.

Over by the tree, Dai recovered quickly. He stalked forwards, bent at the waist, shoulders rounded, arms outstretched.

Kaine pushed away from Nose-ring, stood, and prepped for action. He and Dai stood five paces apart.

"That's enough," Kaine said, quiet but firm. "Take your mates away before my friend and I turn nasty. This one will need treatment for a dislocated shoulder and a bruised ego. The other one might need traction."

Dai's hand dropped to his side.

Kaine raised a finger in the air. "Don't do it, son."

Dai sneered.

"Don't do what, old-timer?" His hand dipped into his jacket pocket and yanked out a red-bodied modeller's knife. "This?"

Without taking his eyes off Kaine, he thumbed open the blade, held it up, and bared his teeth.

"That looks nasty," Kaine said, edging to his left. "Almost as nasty as this one." He showed Nose-ring's knife, held in an underhand throwing grip.

"You took that from Aled?"

"And I didn't ask nicely."

"You ain't taking mine, old man."

Dai glanced at the long blade. The sneer faltered, his confidence vanishing as quickly as the morning mist. Fear showed in pale blue eyes.

On the ground, Aled's screaming eased.

"Do him, Dai," he snivelled. "Slice the bastard open for me."

Dai waved his knife in the air between them,

"Yeah, right," Dai said, swallowing hard. "I'm gonna cut you, old man."

Kaine shook his head. Time to end this. He snapped out the knife, throwing underhand, deliberately aiming wide.

Dai dodged right, watched the knife fly well past his face, smiled.

"You missed. You pri—"

Kaine dived forwards and slammed the meat of his left hand into the point of Dai's chin. His head snapped back, and the long-haired attacker collapsed to the ground, poleaxed.

Behind him, the scraggy-looking victim stood. The man hopped on his left leg, the right trouser leg flapping free. He held a below-the-knee prosthetic leg high in both hands, paused in the act of dealing a vicious blow to the back of Dai's head. Chuckling in delight, he stopped hopping, lowered the prosthesis, and fell onto his backside.

"Man, you should have let me brain the bugger," he said through the manic giggles. "Had it coming, though. Those steel toecaps of his bloody hurt."

Kaine glanced down at Dai who lay face up, eyes closed, mouth open, but still breathing. Luckily for the vicious thug, he'd missed the concrete and landed in the middle of a patch of weeds. Unluckily, the weeds happened to be nettles.

"Oh dear," Kaine said, "they'll sting like mad when he wakes. You okay?"

No longer giggling, the amputee pushed himself into a sitting position and looked up. He nodded, winced, and touched a hand to his right cheek.

"Apart from this headache, I will be, as soon as I get this thing back on," he said, leant forwards, and started rolling up his trouser leg.

"Need a hand, soldier?"

"Nah, I'm good. How d'you know I was a soldier?"

Kaine nodded towards the backpack on the ground next to the empty bench.

"The Bergen's a dead giveaway."

"Yeah, suppose it must be."

Kaine stepped closer.

"Peter Sidings," he said, holding out a hand.

The man sniffed and wiped his muddy hands on the grass at his sides.

"M-Mitch Bairstow." He reached up, squinting against the light, and they shook. "Pleased to meet you, and thanks for ... this." He glanced towards the three downed men and his face crumpled into another grimace. "Nicely ... done, by the way. Slick."

Kaine waved a dismissive hand.

"I got lucky."

"No, you didn't," Mitch said, pursing his lips and following it with a conspiratorial wink. "That crossed bar block and wrist flip was pure special forces."

Kaine tensed and ran a rapid three-sixty-degree scan of the park. Empty, but for the fast-approaching Lara. Rollo stood guard over the floundering attackers; arms crossed over his massive chest. Kaine forced his shoulders to relax.

"Take it easy, Peter," Mitch whispered, speaking slowly. "Your ... your s-secret's safe with me, mate."

The seated man collected his prosthesis and pulled it alongside the residual leg. As he smoothed out the liner covering his stump, Kaine turned away, giving the man some privacy.

Kaine stepped closer to the groaning Dai, grabbed his foot, and dragged him clear of the nettles. He rolled him into the recovery position and turned his attention to Nose-ring, Aled. The blond attacker had made it to his knees and was still bleating about his dislocated shoulder.

Kaine winced. The misaligned joint looked a mess. Painful. Still, it served him right for attacking a disabled veteran.

Brick-chucker had still to recover from the impact of Rollo's shoulder charge, but, given the difference in their statures, the thug might take a while to recover fully—assuming he ever did.

Lara arrived at the double, carrying her medical bag and breathing deeply.

Aled took a closer look at the size of Rollo and scrambled backwards until stopped by the concrete end on the bench.

"No, please. No!" he squealed.

He held up his good arm, overbalanced, and fell, jarring his damaged shoulder. His pleading turned into another pitiful squeal.

On the far side of Aled, the slim-built Brick-chucker groaned. His left foot twitched and his right hand clenched. At least it showed he'd survived the impact with Rollo, Dai, and the solid oak.

Lara arched a questioning eyebrow in Kaine's direction, pointed at the prone Brick-chucker, but only approached him when she'd received Kaine's nod of approval. Rollo moved in to stand alongside, giving close-order protection.

She placed her bag on the ground at her feet, knelt beside the thin man, and placed her index and middle fingers at the side of his neck. Moments later, she frowned.

"Pulse fast. Breathing ragged."

Starting at the head, she ran her hands over him, testing joints and bones. When palpating the chest, the man groaned, and she paused long enough to say, "Might be a broken rib or two," and continued to the feet. "Nothing else seems broken." She glanced over her shoulder at Rollo. "Adrian," she said, "help me put him in the recovery position. Roll him onto his right side, to keep his ribs clear."

Rollo stooped down and unceremoniously rotated the man onto his right side, lifted his head back, and stuffed his left hand under the chin to hold the head in position.

Once again, she touched her fingers to Brick-chucker's throat. After a few moments, she nodded, apparently happy. Before moving to the other fallen man, she glanced at Kaine once more. Again, he nodded. She scuttled forwards, dropped to one knee, and felt for the carotid artery.

"Pulse strong and slow. Breathing steady."

Her hazel eyes turned towards Kaine. She sighed, shook her head, reached to the inside of her patient's upper arm, and pinched hard.

Dai yelped, tore away his arm, and tried to slither to safety.

"Will you look at that. It's a modern-day miracle!" Rollo announced, gasping in fake awe.

"Playing dead," Lara agreed. "Thought as much."

Rollo reached down, grabbed a fistful of oily hair, and yanked Dai to his feet amid more howls of anguish. Dancing on tiptoes, Dai threw his hands to his head, trying to ease the strain on his scalp. Rollo let go and sent him on his way with a size fourteen boot to the rump.

"Go on, now," Rollo said. "Off you pop."

Dai shouted, "Bastards!" and took off in a good facsimile of a sprinter's race start, his boots scattering the path's gravel. When he reached the park's wall, he tried to vault the locked gate, but caught his foot on the top rail and fell out of sight in another heap.

"Bugger didn't even ... h-hang about to see how his mates were doing," Mitch said, and threw an apologetic glance at Lara. "Excuse my language, Doc."

"That's your one chance," Lara said, showing him a mock scowl. "Don't do it again, soldier."

"No, Doc. S-Sorry, Doc." He held out a hand to Kaine. "Help me up, mate?"

Kaine did as asked, and Mitch grunted on the way to his feet. He swayed a little, his eyes creased in pain, but he remained upright.

"How are you?" Lara asked, staring at the damage below his right eye which had already started swelling.

Mitch shrugged. "I've had worse, Doc. Much worse. I'll ... I'll be okay."

"I'll check you out when I've dealt with this ... fool."

She jerked her head towards the whimpering Aled, who sat cross-legged on the concrete in front of the bench, hugging the bad arm tight to his chest with the good. The deformation of the shoulder joint showed clearly through his tight-fitting T-shirt. He rocked back and forwards in obvious distress.

"Hold still," she ordered, peering closely at the damaged shoulder.

Tears flowing, lower lip trembling, Aled stopped moving and stiffened while Lara palpated the injury. He yelped and whimpered almost before her fingers reached him. She tested his radial pulse and nodded.

"Wh-What you gonna do?"

"How far is the nearest hospital?" she asked.

"B-Brecon," Aled said, gritting his teeth. "'Bout half an hour from here."

Nodding, she pursed her lips. "Okay. We'll call an ambulance. You stay here and keep as still as you can. Watch over your friend there. Make sure he stays on his side."

"C-Can't you do anything? It really hurts."

Rollo stepped forwards. Aled jerked away and let out an involuntary whimper.

"Should have thought of that when you pulled a knife on my mate," Rollo said, edging ominously closer.

"I-I'm sorry," Aled wailed. "Kidding, I was. Honest. Wouldn't have cut him really. Just wanted to s-scare him, like."

Rollo jutted out his jaw. "And when you told your mate—the one who just ran off and left you here at our mercy—to slice him open? Was that a joke, too?"

Kaine left a steadier Mitch and joined Lara and Rollo at the triage area.

"We've got to go," he said. "No telling what'll happen when Dai reaches home. The natives might not be friendly." He winked at Lara. "Can you pop that shoulder back in?"

She jerked up her chin. "Better to do it at the hospital. He needs a muscle relaxant. *Diazepam*'s a favourite, but I don't have any in my bag."

Kaine slapped Aled on his good shoulder and received another squeal for his efforts.

"How old are you, son?"

"Huh?"

Kaine rested a hand on Aled's injury. Sweat bled from the thug's forehead. It mixed with the tears flowing down his face and the snot running from his nose.

"You heard me, son. How old?"

The blond swallowed. "T-Twenty-two."

Kaine and Rollo swapped a glance.

"At your age, I was in Iraq fighting Saddam's Republican Guard. Desert warfare."

"Yeah? So?" Aled's lower lip quivered. He couldn't bring himself to meet Kaine's glare.

"So, I dislocated my shoulder in the middle of a firefight. Had to pop it back in on the move. Want to see how I did it? Adrian, hold him steady."

"With pleasure," Rollo said, the glint in his eye showing how much he anticipated what was about to happen.

The twenty-two-year-old dug his heels into the gravel and tried to push himself away but the bench stopped him.

"No, please. Don't! I-I'll wait for the—"

Rollo tugged Aled away from the bench, took a knee behind his back, and wrapped him in a bear hug. Kaine grabbed the lad's right wrist, jerked it out to the side, and twisted out. The shoulder joint crunched and popped. Aled screamed and fainted. Rollo lowered him gently to the ground and rolled him onto his left side, placing him, too, in the recovery position.

Kaine draped the flaccid right arm across the young man's chest and stood.

"One way of doing it, I suppose," Lara said, adding a shrug.

She cupped her hand over the injured joint, moved the arm a little, and nodded. "A shade warm, but it's moving freely enough. He might get away without permanent incapacity."

"Who cares?" Mitch said, looking at her through his undamaged left eye and showing as much sympathy for the young thug as Kaine felt. "Might ... might stop him pulling another knife and ... beating up on a vagrant." He blinked slowly, as though trying to clear a headache.

"A vagrant?" Kaine asked. "Is that how you see yourself?"

Mitch shrugged. "It's how everyone sees me."

"We don't."

The amputee sniffed. "Thanks."

Kaine marched to the bench. He picked up the muddy and care-worn Bergen, which looked so much like his own.

"We need to be on our way, mate," he said and handed the Bergen to its owner. "Need a lift anywhere?"

"Probably better if you're not here when Dai and his mate return with their mates," Rollo added.

Lara smiled in encouragement. "And when we're safe, I'll check you over. That's a nasty swelling below your eye. Might have a broken cheekbone."

Mitch shot a nervous glance over his shoulder in the direction of the departing attackers.

"Er ... I appreciate the offer, but ... I think I'll have to decline."

"Why?" Lara asked.

His expression changed from nervous to embarrassed.

"I, er ... haven't had a shower for a while. Not sure I'm in a fit state to travel by car. I w-wouldn't want to w-wear out my welcome."

"Nonsense," Lara announced, stooping to collect her bag, "these two are used to roughing it and I'm a medic. We've all lost our sense of smell."

Kaine smiled. "And we can always open the windows if we need to."

"It's what we have to do for Peter all the time!" Lara added and led the way to the Audi, heading in the opposite direction from the recently departed thugs.

Lara shot a quick glance at Kaine. She touched a finger to her eye, indicating Mitch's injury. Worry showed on her face.

CHAPTER 14

Monday 22nd May – Morning

Sennybridge, Brecon Beacons, South Wales, UK

They hurried to the Audi. Despite his panting and his exaggerated shuffle-hop limp, Mitch kept up well enough. He needed no help to scale the stone wall and showed his military training when doing so. How many times in basic training had raw recruits been forced to scale low and high walls on an assault course? During his own boot camp, Kaine had lost count after the first week.

At the car, Kaine lobbed Mitch's Bergen into the boot alongside his own and opened the rear passenger door for their new, if temporary, travelling companion.

"In you pop, alongside the doc. She can check you out while we're on the move. You okay with that, Doc?"

Still carrying her medical bag, Lara nodded. "Yes, that'll work."

Kaine grinned. "We can make the introductions on the way, but I think it would be prudent to leave this village rapid-fast, eh?"

"Makes ... sense to me, sir," Mitch said, touching his temple in a throwaway salute, but his face contorted as a finger brushed his swollen cheek.

"Less of that, Mitch. We're not in the army now, and I'm no officer."

Mitch shot Kaine a look his dad would have called "old-fashioned" and Kaine would class as "sceptical".

"If you ... say so, P-Peter," Mitch said before sliding onto the rear bench seat. His speech was becoming more hesitant, even slurred.

Kaine and Lara exchanged glances. Her almost imperceptible headshake warned him to be on his guard with the amputee. Kaine gave her a grim smile. He didn't need her to warn him, but he understood her caution and was grateful for it. After the better part of a year together, Lara had learnt so much. He only wished she hadn't needed to.

They piled into the Audi, Kaine taking the front passenger seat, slammed all four doors, and Rollo took off, with rear wheels spinning. The village of Sennybridge passed by the Audi's windows in a picturesque blur of grey buildings, slate roofs, low stone walls, and a fast-running river.

Kaine lowered the sun visor and followed Lara's ministrations in the courtesy mirror. After snapping on a pair of surgical gloves, she took a penlight from her bag, shuffled closer to her patient, and shone the light in each eye. Mitch winced both times. Next, she touched the rapidly swelling abrasion beneath his bloodshot right eye. He groaned and jerked his head away.

"Sorry," she said.

"No ... w-worries," Mitch whispered, his left eye tearing. "I've had—"

"I know. You've had worse, right?" she asked.

"Yep." He shrugged and glanced at Kaine. Their eyes met in the courtesy mirror. "I wanted to thank you guys again. Without you, I ... m-might have ... might have been in a spot of bother back there."

"No need," Kaine said, twisting in his seat to face the back. "I'm sure you'd have done the same thing for any of us if the situation had been reversed."

"Nah. Not a chance," Mitch said, his expression deadly serious.

"Sorry?" Lara asked, stiffening her shoulders.

Mitch raised a hand in apology. "No, don't ... g-get me wrong, Doc. I'd have *tried* to help, 'course I would, but I ... I ain't as fast on my feet as I used to be." He punched his right thigh with the side of his fist. "What I ... what I *meant* to say was, I wouldn't have been able to do the same thing. I don't have the skills anymore. Like I said. ... Th-That crossed bar block with the overhead throw." He shook his head slowly. "Man, that was something else. But I would have *tried* to help."

"Okay," Lara said, relaxing and peering at the swollen cheek. "I don't like the look of that."

"Broken?" Kaine asked.

"I think so. The zygomatic bone—the cheekbone—might be fractured, and I'm worried about the orbital surface of the maxilla. That's part of your eye socket."

"B-Bad?" Mitch asked, blinking the water from his eyes.

"Could be serious. You'll definitely need X-rays. Maybe a CT scan."

Mitch winced, scrunching only the left side of his face. "Don't suppose you've got an X-ray machine in that bag of yours, huh?"

She grinned at him.

"Sorry. Don't have one in the boot, either. How are you feeling? Headache?"

"No, thanks. I've ... already got one."

"Funny man," Kaine said. "Let's be serious, shall we?"

Mitch sighed. "Sorry, sir. Defence mechanism. Hate ... Hate hospitals, me. And I can see a visit to the A & E coming up."

"How's your vision?" Lara asked, shining the light into Mitch's right eye once again. "Any blurring?"

"Left eye perfect apart from the tears. Right eye ..." His words tailed off.

"Your right eye," Lara prompted.

"Er ... f-fuzzy."

"How fuzzy?" Lara demanded, clearly sensing evasion.

Mitch gave up another sigh, this one deeper. "Fuzzy as in, I ... can't see ... a thing out of it."

"Okay," Lara said and turned to Kaine. "We need to get him to a hospital right away."

Kaine nodded. "Adrian, program the GPS for the nearest hospital."

"Already on it, sir—er, Sarge," Rollo said, shooting Kaine an apologetic sideways glance. "The toerag with the dislocated shoulder said the nearest one was in Brecon. We're heading that way now." He pointed to a road sign which indicated Brecon at nine miles distance.

Fifty metres later, they reached a T-junction. Rollo gave way to a string of traffic and turned right onto the grandly named A40, which turned out to be a two-lane blacktop running through the centre of Sennybridge village. The first set of traffic lights glowed red. Rollo took the opportunity to reprogram the GPS.

Mitch raised a hand. "Can I ... say something?"

"Fire away," Kaine said.

"No need to ... p-put yourselves out on my account. Really there ain't. You've already done plenty for me. Look,"—he pointed through the window—"there's a bus stop. I'll make my own way to hospital."

"Not a chance," Lara snapped, her tone allowing no argument. "You're my patient. I need to monitor you until we reach A & E. I'll also need to give a full history to the admitting nurse."

Again, Lara locked eyes with Kaine, and he nodded his reluctant consent. The longer they stayed in the open the greater their risk of exposure.

"Look," Mitch said, his voice rising in volume a little. "I ... er, I appreciate what you did back there, I really do. But ... but we ain't in the army, and I ... I don't have to take orders anymore."

At that point, the traffic lights changed to green. Rollo added pressure to the accelerator and the car pulled away.

"Mitch," Lara said, "your head injury could be serious. Life-threatening."

"Really." His right eye drooped into a slow wink.

"Yes," she said. "Really."

"Hate ... hospitals, me," he said, almost whispering. "Spent three months in ... in bed lying flat on my back. Then m-months more in and out of hospital getting this chuffing thing fitted." He side-punched his right thigh again. "And all the ph-physio. You really want me to ... go back?"

"I understand, Mitch," Lara said, her smile encouraging. "I really do, but there's no alternative. Believe me."

Mitch raised a trembling hand to his damaged cheek but lowered it again. He must have thought better of touching the injury. "It's that ... serious. I could die?"

"Yes."

"W-Would that b-be a ... b-bad thing?" He blinked slowly.

Lara dipped her head as though looking over the rim of a pair of glasses to meet his eye. Mitch groaned and raised both hands in surrender.

"Yeah, yeah. Only ... kidding. Me and m-my sick sense of 'umour. A'ways got me into tr'uble."

Mitch frowned in concentration, his speech slowed further, and his words became less distinct. His slurring increased.

Lara and Kaine exchanged a worried look.

"I-I'm sorry," Mitch continued, talking to his knees. "I'll come ... quietly." His eyes lowered and his speech slowed even more. "Head's ... throbbing." His chin dropped to his chest.

"Mitch!" Lara jumped forwards. She reached to the side of her patient's throat and tested for a pulse. "Stay awake, Mitch."

Oh God.

"Adrian," Kaine barked, "put your foot down!"

Rollo punched a button on the dashboard and selected "Dynamic"—Audi's version of sports mode. The engine note deepened, and the car shot forwards. He dropped the indicator and overtook the car in front as though it had been slammed into reverse.

In the back, Lara gently lifted Mitch's chin to keep his airway open.

"Is he still breathing?" Kaine asked above the roar of the racing engine.

Lara nodded. "Breathing's shallow, and the heartrate's slow."

Rollo blared his horn at the next in line—a blue panel van. He jagged out to pass but had to abort the overtake when an oncoming car rounded the corner ahead. Green verges, trees, and hedgerows flashed past on both sides. The faster they travelled, the narrower the two-lane road seemed to become.

The road straightened, a swift twist right to overtake. The panel van disappeared behind them, and the speedo climbed from fifty-eight to seventy-three mph in a few heartbeats.

"How long, Adrian?" Kaine asked, seeing genuine fear in Lara's hazel eyes. Fear for her patient, not the breakneck driving.

"GPS says nine minutes, but I'll do it in six."

"Five would be better," Lara called.

"I'll make the call. Warn the hospital we're coming," Kaine announced.

"Good idea," Lara said. "Tell them we have a serious head injury. Possible cranial bleed. We'll need a CT scan and a surgical suite. If they don't have that, we'll need a medivac to somewhere that does. We'll contact Glyn Coes later."

Kaine stared pointedly at the recumbent Mitch and raised a finger to his lips.

Lara grimaced in apology.

Kaine pulled the mobile from his pocket and dialled 999.

"*Argyfwng. Pa wasanaeth?*" A woman's voice. Musical Welsh accent. She followed up in English with, "Emergency. Which service?"

"Ambulance, please."

A click and a few seconds later, a different woman spoke.

"Welsh Ambulance Service speaking. Is the patient breathing?"

"Yes. Just about."

"What address are you calling from?"

"I'm in a car on the A40, just outside Sennybridge."

"In case we're cut off, what number are you calling from?"

"I don't know, this isn't my phone," Kaine lied. He wasn't about to tell them he was using a burner he'd throw out the window the moment he ended the call.

"What's the nature of the emergency?"

Kaine gave them Lara's diagnosis and added, "I'm heading for Brecon town. Can you warn the hospital I'm on my way?"

"Please hold on, caller."

"My battery's dying," he lied again, allowing desperation to bleed into his voice. "Please hurry."

A clear road and a fast, raking right-hand curve allowed Rollo to increase speed to ninety, pushing Kaine into the door column. They screamed past a tractor, a truck, and three family saloons before Rollo had to ram on the anchors as the serpentine road swept into a sharp left-hander.

Black and white chevrons warned of another bend, but the clear road allowed Rollo to maintain their speed and they hit one hundred and three on the next mini straight—a steep downhill leading to yet another left-hander. They flashed past a farmhouse with a blue-painted gable wall and slowed sharply before overtaking another mid-sized van—this one carrying fresh vegetables and bearing the slogan, "From the fields to your door".

Another long empty straight had them up and over the hundred mark again and the countryside flashed by in a green-blue haze. Oaks, pines, and bushes crowded in around them, darkening the bright sky. A sign for Cwm Camlais and its accompanying stone-built bus stop barely registered. A ninety-degree tight right-hand curve took them past PenPont. The land opened up and the hedgerows fell away, giving Rollo a better view of the road ahead and the oncoming traffic.

The emergency operator returned. "Caller. Are you still there?" she asked, her voice calm and collected.

"Yes, yes. I'm still here."

"I'm transferring you to the hospital admissions block. Please hold."

"Thank you."

The line clicked, fell silent, and clicked again.

"Hello caller, this is Brecon War Memorial Hospital, and I'm Staff Nurse Perry." He had a deep voice, just as calm as the emergency operator, just as strong and musical an accent. "I understand you have a patient with a head injury. Is that right?"

"Yes. He's been unconscious for about three minutes."

"Can you give me an estimated time of arrival?"

The GPS showed an ETA of five minutes. Rollo had already shaved two minutes from the total. Kaine relayed the answer to the nurse.

"We'll be ready for you, caller. Come to the main entrance."

"Thank you. We'll be there as soon as—"

Kaine disconnected the call mid-sentence, powered down the phone and lowered the window. He broke open the case, removed the battery, and lobbed the mobile itself into the verge. The battery, he slipped into the glovebox. The Beacons didn't need the toxic innards of a mobile phone battery polluting its environment. He rolled up the window again.

"Any change?" Kaine asked, holding tight to his seat belt as Rollo negotiated another lightning overtake, this one past a flatbed truck transporting a shipping container. They powered through Llanspyddid—a village of a few dozen houses, a church, and a red telephone box—at fifteen mph above the stated fifty limit and hurtled out the other side where their speed climbed to eighty. More straights, even more curves.

Three minutes.

Another minute shaved off the ETA.

"Doc, how is he?" Kaine asked.

"No change."

"Is that good?"

She turned worried eyes to him, as helpless as he was. On the left, a brown tourist sign announced their approach to Brecon. They whipped past a cyclist, helmeted, riding head down, legs pumping, fluorescent yellow top billowing out behind him.

Without lifting his hands from the steering wheel, Rollo pointed ahead. "There's Brecon. Roundabout coming up. I'll have to slow."

"Be safe but do what you can."

"Will do."

They took the first exit at the roundabout, leaving the tight A40 and joining the tighter B4601. Rollo slowed to an apparently crawling thirty-five mph. Buildings grew up on either side and they crossed the bridge over the River Tarell, heading for the first set of traffic lights. As if knowing the reason for their mad dash, the lights relented and changed to green. Rollo pushed the Audi up to forty, passing another Audi. Its driver blared his horn and shook an angry fist.

A petrol station on the left advertised the inevitable coffee shop. Houses painted in various shades of cream and grey crowded in around them. A pelican crossing, lights also green, allowed them through.

At the next set of lights, on a stone bridge over the River Usk, their luck ran out and they were held up on red. Their progress halted. Nose-to-tail traffic lined up on their side of the crossing. One lane closed for roadworks. Gridlock.

Time marched on.

Thirty seconds.

Forty-five seconds.

One minute.

Oncoming traffic crawled towards them, blocking the bridge. No chance of an overtake.

Kaine leant closer to the driver's side to work a better view of the GPS. Six hundred metres to go. Not far. A ninety-second slog with a heavy load, no longer. He scrutinised the route, committing it to memory.

"Doc, can we move him safely?"

"I don't know. Why?"

"Can I carry him?"

"All that jogging? I don't like it."

"Make the call, Doc."

"I don't—"

"The lights have changed," Rollo said. "We're moving. Hold tight."

Nine cars stood between them, the lights, and the bridge. The first moved off as the oncoming traffic finally cleared the roadworks. The second followed, then the third. Rollo edged the Audi forwards, keeping up with the line. The eighth car, a shiny red Kia, moved forwards slowly. Too slowly. The traffic lights changed to amber.

Damn it.

"Go, man. Floor it!"

Rollo stamped on the throttle and jerked the wheel to the right. The big Audi leapt forwards, beating the Kia to the lights as they turned red again. The Kia's driver braked hard, the bonnet dipping under the kinetic forces. The Audi's nearside wing brushed the Kia's offside paintwork.

They completed the crossing to a ragged chorus of blaring horns flashing lights and open-mouthed pedestrians.

Traffic on the far side of the bridge eased and they increased speed. A left into Market Street. More lights. Green. Straight through. Another set of lights. Red. Rollo crashed through them, narrowly missing a head-on collision with a woman riding a scooter. One hundred metres later, he skidded to a halt at a zebra crossing. A man with a cane hauling a dog who didn't want to walk the right way held them up for an age that was probably less than ten seconds. Down a hill to yet another set of red lights. Rollo drove through them, too, and made a sharp left onto Cerrigcochion Road.

"Not far now," Lara announced, still holding Mitch's head up. Since collapsing, he hadn't moved.

"Get him ready, Doc."

"He is."

They turned right into the hospital campus and followed the signs to the reception. Rollo negotiated a mini-roundabout—bench seating, a large tree, ornamental hedge—and pulled up in front of the main entrance. Blue iron railings protected a ramp off to the left and a set of steps that led up to an atrium sporting a pair of sliding doors.

Kaine jumped out before the wheels had stopped moving. He raced up the steps. Rollo sounded the horn. The entrance doors slid apart. Two blue-clad men pushed a trolley through the opening and down the ramp. A third man wearing a white coat, middle-aged, bald with a rear fringe of greying hair and a chin blurred with designer stubble, faced Kaine.

"Are you the one I spoke to on the phone? The head injury?"

"Staff Nurse Perry?"

"That's me, and you are?"

"The patient is in the Audi," Kaine answered turning and shepherding Perry towards the car.

"What happened? I'll need as comprehensive a case history as possible."

"The doc can give you the details."

"The doc? You have a doctor with you?"

Kaine nodded towards Lara, who had backed out of the car, and started supervising the nurses while they loaded Mitch onto the stretcher.

"Can I leave this with you?" Kaine asked, backing away.

Perry lost interest in Kaine and hurried towards the trolley. Working as a team, with Lara in assistance, the medics wasted no time in fitting a neck brace and securing Mitch in place with webbing straps. Lara talked the whole time, giving details and using medical terms Kaine had heard before but only vaguely understood. The words "CT scan" and "cranial bleed" were obvious, but the rest could have meant anything.

Rollo joined him at the nearside of the Audi, and they watched Lara and her medical entourage wheel their patient up the ramp.

Kaine read the time off his watch. It had just ticked past twelve o'clock. Was that all? The day already seemed to have lasted a week. He rubbed his face with both hands, trying to encourage the circulation to return. His beard itched and the long hair flopped into his eyes.

As the stretcher disappeared into the darkened entrance, Perry stopped and turned. He pointed to the Audi.

"Can you move that? We need to keep the entrance clear for

emergency vehicles. You should find some parking around the back. Follow the signs."

"Right you are, mate," Rollo called. "I'm on it." He leant against the Audi's door and puffed out his cheeks. "Well now, that was a blast."

"Yep," Kaine said, nodding. "Nothing beats a pleasant drive in the countryside."

"Agreed."

They faced the car, leant forwards, and rested their arms on its roof, assuming the role of two mates chewing the fat after a break-neck mercy dash through South Wales. It also served to hide their faces from the inevitable array of surveillance cameras that would be ringing the hospital grounds.

"What do you think of the Audi?" Kaine asked. "Handle well?"

Rollo waggled his head from side to side, non-committal. "Not bad. Dynamic mode stiffened the suspension a little. Improved the handling, but the engine's still massively underpowered. If we'd kept hold of the Beemer, I'd have shaved another thirty seconds off our arrival time."

"Possibly, but the Beemer had to go. As does the Audi."

Rollo nodded and released his breath. "Yes, sir. On the way here from the service station, we'd have tripped dozens of ANPR cameras, and as for our tour though Brecon ..." The ridges on his forehead deepened as he raised his eyebrows.

"Yep. That poor Kia driver's probably in a state of shock right now. You big bully."

"Couldn't be helped. Beat the heck out of having you throw the poor man over your shoulder and bounce him the rest of the way here, though. And you with your poorly back."

"Nothing wrong with my back, Colour Sergeant."

"Not now, there isn't. But after lugging Mitch all that way?" Rollo winked and pushed himself away from the car. "Okay, I'll lose the Audi and pick up another motor."

"Where from?"

Rollo shrugged his huge shoulders. "No idea, sir. It's ages since

I've been to Brecon." He pulled out his secure smartphone and held it up. "My friend, Mr Google, should help."

"Okay, Quartermaster," Kaine said. "I'll leave it with you. Quick as you can though, eh?"

"Right you are, sir. If we take much longer, the Cadwalladers will think we've run out on them."

"That'll never happen." Kaine paused for a moment and frowned at the memory of Lara's slight gaff.

"Something worrying you, Captain?"

"Lara," he said. "She shouldn't have used the name Glyn Coes in front of a stranger."

"Mitch was comatose at the time, sir. He wouldn't have heard anything. We're safe enough."

Kaine patted the Audi's roof and sighed. "Yep, you're right. Too late to worry about it now, anyway. Okay, before you hit the road, let me grab Mitch's Bergen. You can transfer our kit to the next motor. And don't forget Lara's medical bag. It's still on the back seat."

Rollo dipped his head in a curt nod and pulled open the driver's door. Moments later, the big V6 purred into life.

Kaine retrieved what he imagined to be the whole of Mitch's worldly goods and leant further into the boot to pull a baseball cap from his own Bergen. He lowered the boot lid and signalled the "all clear". Rollo and the big Audi rolled away a darn sight more sedately than they'd arrived.

Kaine tugged the cap onto his head, pulled the peak down low, and headed towards the entrance.

Inside the hospital's columned atrium, Kaine found a glass-fronted reception desk and a long queue. He joined the back and resigned himself to an interminable wait. A few moments later, and after Kaine had surreptitiously stuffed a wad of banknotes into one of the Bergen's side-pouches—a wad totalling five hundred pounds—Staff Nurse Perry emerged from a side corridor and approached him.

"Is that the patient's bag?" he asked, nodding to the Bergen.

"I wanted to hand it in to reception before leaving."

Perry nodded. "Your colleague, Dr Silverstein, explained the situation. It seems that you found the patient staggering at the side of the road."

Kaine nodded. "That's right. Just outside a place called Senny-bridge." He managed not to smile in relief. Lara had given Perry a different identity and a sanitised version of the truth.

Good girl.

"Before he passed out," Kaine added, "he mumbled something about being attacked by a gang of thugs. How is he?"

"Too early to tell. Dr Silverstein is briefing our surgical consultant. She'll be out in a few minutes. We're stabilising the patient before giving him a scan. Depending on what we find, we might have to fly him down to Cardiff. They have a top-flight neurological department. Leave it with us. We'll do all we can for him." He smiled and pointed to the Bergen. "Would you like me to take that for you?"

"Yes, please." Kaine passed the backpack across. "Take care of it. I'm guessing this is all the poor man has in the world."

Perry took hold of the carry handle on the top of the backpack and pointed to an unmarked door at the far side of the entrance atrium. "You can wait in there, if you like," he said. "The police won't be long."

Kaine tried not to show any alarm.

"The police?"

"They'll need a statement."

Will they?

Kaine forced a smile onto unwilling lips. "Right, okay. In all the excitement, I'd almost forgotten about notifying the police."

Perry crooked his head to one side in an act of understanding. "As I said. They won't be long. The station's only around the corner."

"Excellent. In here, you say?" He nodded towards the same door.

"That's right, sir." Perry smiled. He shouldered the Bergen and turned away, heading in the opposite direction.

"Oh, Staff Nurse Perry?"

The tall nurse stopped and turned. "Yes, sir?"

Kaine held up his spare mobile. "Am I okay to use this in here?"

Perry pointed at a sign above the reception desk—an outline of a mobile phone inside a red circle struck through with a diagonal bar that Kaine had spotted earlier. "Sorry. You'll have to go outside. You'll find a bench out there if you need it."

"Ah, okay. I'd better pop outside. Thanks for everything. Look after him, won't you."

"'Course we will, sir. Dr Silverstein has my personal number. You can call me for an update anytime."

Kaine raised his phone and headed for the exit, dialling on the move. The main doors slid apart. He stepped into the open and stopped in front of a map of the hospital grounds.

Lara answered on the fifth ring. "Yes?" she whispered.

"We need to decamp right now. The police are on their way."

"Yes, I know. I'll make my excuses. Where are you?"

"I'll make my way to the ambulance bay. It's around the back from the front entrance."

"Wait there. I'll find you as soon as I can."

Kaine ended the call but kept the phone to his ear and sauntered around to his left, following the helpful signage. The moment he'd judged himself out of sight of the entrance foyer, he increased his pace to a brisk military march.

Fifty metres later, he ducked down a narrow side road between two single-storey wards and carried on towards the end. The sun warmed his back, and the white-walled buildings reflected the heat onto his face and neck. The side road terminated at a D-shaped turning arc with markings for five ambulance bays, three of which stood empty. He ducked behind one of the ambulances and waited.

After a few minutes, he pressed the unconnected phone to his ear and started pacing.

CHAPTER 15

Monday 22nd May – Midday

Brecon War Memorial Hospital, Powys, South Wales, UK

Mitch woke fully to a crashing, blinding headache, whining tinnitus in his right ear, and a loose upper right canine. Worse still, some shitting sadist kept shining a bright light in his eyes.

He reached out to slap the light away but missed. Seeing through only one good eye messed with his depth perception.

"Leave it out, will you?" he said, sounding muffled, far away.

"Sorry, sir," a man said. Deep voice, middle-aged, the guttural accent with its harsh sibilance, definitely from North Wales. "I'm a doctor. I need to check your pupillary reflex."

"My what?"

"We need to see how well your pupils react to the light."

Mitch knew that, but he wasn't about to let on to a bloody medic. Best to keep the buggers in the dark.

The light flashed again. Mitch jerked his head away, pressing it further into the pillow. The movement increased the pain, but the pillow softened the blow. The nice, soft pillow.

Could be worse places to stay. It certainly beat a park bench and a heated exhaust vent.

Think this through a bit, Mitch. Work it. Couple of days in a warm bed with free food wouldn't be all that bad. Couple of weeks would be even better.

"Sorry again, sir. Please try to keep still," the medic with the North Wales accent said.

A cool, soft hand pressed against his forehead, and a gentle thumb raised his right eyelid.

The light hit once more.

"Ow! Lord Above. Feels like you're ... stabbing me in the eyeball with a toothpick. Cut that out, will you? Please?"

The hand and thumb withdrew, and the blessed, soothing darkness returned. Darkness interspersed with brilliant orange afterimages. The crashing migraine eased a fraction. On a scale of one to a hundred, it currently registered a ninety-nine-point-three.

There really is a God.

"Can you tell me your name?"

Mitch breathed deep and tried opening his eyes by himself. He squinted against the wash of bright ambient light. Heavy swelling partially closed his right eye and blurred his vision. No wonder his swipe missed the penlight.

"Who wants to know?" he mumbled, deliberately adding an extra slur to his words.

Careful, Mitch. Don't overdo it.

Although he could use a couple of days in a clean hospital bed, he didn't want to push his luck. Play the injured veteran too well and he might end up with probes being stuck where the sun didn't shine.

Sod that for a game of soldiers.

Once again, Mitch pried open his eyes. Wider this time. The swimming vision cleared a little.

A woman, on the left of the bed, beautiful in an understated way, smiled. He recognised her from somewhere.

Where?

Oh yeah, the park. She and her mates kicked some skanky Welsh arse. Yay for the good guys.

What's her name?

Damn. He couldn't remember. The head injury?

Think, man. Think.

Did he even know it?

Mitch blinked hard. The pain below his eye flared.

Idiot. Stop doing that. Stop making it worse.

The good-looking woman. Did she ever tell him her name? What did the other blokes call her? Doc? Yeah, that's right. Doc. A wiry guy and a huge one. Black Ops and Goliath. They called her Doc.

"You're in hospital," the man with the harsh North Wales accent said. "Brecon Memorial. I'm Doctor Rees."

"Hospital?"

"Yes, sir. You've suffered a head traum—er, a head injury. Can you tell me your name?"

"Yep." Mitch smiled and instantly regretted the way it bunched up his cheek and aggravated the stabbing under his right eye.

Damn it.

Could hardly see a thing through the eye, neither. Swelling had all but closed the bloody thing, and it hurt like a bitch.

He finally remembered. The lanky Welsh bastard had kicked him in the head. His boots had steel toecaps, too. Bloody arsehole. Then the wiry one, Black Ops, barged the bugger into a tree and laid out the one with the silver nose ring. A flaming nose ring? What the hell? Stupid thing made him look like a real tit. Yeah. Black Ops went at it like something out of an action movie. He used the crossed bar defence. Followed it up with a swivel, a hip throw, and a torsion twist that damn near wrenched the skanky bugger's arm off. Classic unarmed combat move. Brilliant. Silky smooth. Deadly.

A move carried out with perfect timing.

The big guy, Goliath, only used momentum and his bulk, but looked as though he could handle himself well enough if he had to.

Black Ops with his ninja skills was something though. Something else entirely.

Mitch had struck it lucky. Yes. He'd been lucky all right, but ... Why did Black Ops look so damn familiar? Those moves and those eyes.

Maybe the boot to the head had dislodged some more brain cells. Done some real damage. Screwed with his memory.

Where had he seen Black Ops before? He definitely had. Never forgot a face, didn't Mitch Bairstow.

Leave it, Mitch. Don't try so hard. It'll come if you don't force it.

The good-looking woman, Doc, backed away to answer her phone. She spoke softly. Too quiet for Mitch to hear.

"Well?" Dr Rees asked, sounding confused. Impatience growing.

That's it, Mitch. Keep the medics guessing.

Had to take his fun whenever he could find it.

"Huh?" Mitch asked.

"I asked you for your name."

"No, you didn't."

"Yes, I did."

"No, you didn't. You asked, 'Can you tell me your name?' And I said, 'Yep.' Which is true. I *can* tell you, but you never actually asked me, not directly. Would you like it?"

Ha! That got him.

"My name, I mean."

Dr Rees exhaled and did it noisily. "Yes, please. I really would."

Gotcha!

Mitch hid a smile behind a grimace.

"Me? I'm Mitchell David Bairstow. My friends call me Mitch."

Dr Rees glanced at the nurse on his left, who jotted something onto a form attached to a clipboard—probably Mitch's name. He could tell she was a nurse by her faded purple scrubs, and the name tag pinned to her top. SRN R Hallows. He smiled at her, but the swelling probably made it lopsided.

"What does the 'R' stand for, Nurse Hallows?" he asked, squinting at her through his good eye. "Robyn? Rachel? Rosemary?"

Dr Rees moved across to block his view of the pretty young thing. "Mr Bairstow—"

"Mitch," he insisted. "You can be my friend, if you like."

"Okay, Mitch," Rees said, "please concentrate."

"I am concentrating. I'd like to know the name of the nice nurse."

"That's not important right now."

"Really? Well, now. That's a little dismissive, doctor. SRN Hallows probably thinks her name's rather important. Don't you. Go on. What's your name?"

"Regan. My name's Regan."

"Hi, Regan. What a nice name. It's lovely to meet you. Now, Dr Rees, that wasn't too hard, was it? Didn't take too long, either."

Dr Rees ground his teeth and made his jaw muscles bunch up. "Not at all. We'll need your address next."

Mitch snorted. "You'll be lucky."

"Why?"

"I'm currently between homes. Regan, please add NFA to the form. It stands for No Fixed Address, right?"

"Who's your doctor?"

"Don't have one at the moment."

"But your leg. Who treated you? Who fitted your prosthesis?"

"Is that important? I thought I was here on account of the blow to my noggin. Why d'you need the name of the sawbones who hacked off my leg? Bloody butcher!"

Mitch raised both hands, palms forward, and patted them in the air.

"Sorry. Didn't mean to swear," Mitch said and meant it.

The hot medic, the one Black Ops and Goliath called "Doc", leant forwards.

"Easy, Mitch. No need to upset yourself."

She looked up at Dr Rees and lifted her eyebrows as though asking permission for something. Rees nodded and stepped away from the bed. Regan stayed still, and Doc moved even closer.

"Mitch," she said, "mind if I ask a few questions?"

"Fire away, Doc. I'm all yours."

"Thanks. How's your headache?"

"You've already asked me that. In the car."

Her smile widened, as did Regan's.

"And you said?"

Mitch flushed. Doc made him hot under the collar. "Yeah, I said something like, 'No thanks. I already have one.'"

"Yes, that's right. You did."

"Funny, ain't I?"

"Absolutely hilarious," Doc said, easing up on the pleasant smile and probably extracting the mickey.

She glanced up at Regan and turned towards Rees. "Nothing wrong with his memory." She faced Mitch again.

Lovely eyes she had, too. Hazel with specks of green and yellow near the edges. Regan had clear blue eyes. Just as nice in their own way. Such a pleasant place to find himself. Comfy bed. Wonderful company. Beat lying on a park bench, having the crap kicked out of him. Beat it every way from Sunday.

Make the most of it, son.

"Mitch," Doc said. "Will you do me a favour?"

Uh-oh. Here it comes. Time to be serious.

"If I can."

"Will you behave yourself and let Regan and Dr Rees take care of you?"

Mitch relaxed his shoulders. He'd been holding them tense for a while and they'd started to cramp. "Hell, Doc. Where's the fun in that?"

A gentle frown wrinkled her otherwise smooth forehead. "Mitch. Please?"

Once again, he held up his grubby hands.

"Alright, Doc. You win. I promise to be a good boy. They can ask their questions and do their thing. I'll even let Regan give me a bed bath."

Doc stiffened. "Mitch. That's out of order."

"Yeah, I know. I'm sorry. Regan, I apologise. But the truth is, I stink. Haven't had a proper wash in days."

Weeks, really. But they didn't need to know that much detail.

Doc nodded and backed away. A couple of seconds later, she said her goodbyes, nodded towards Mitch, and slipped out of the room. Such a pity. He'd miss her.

Still, she had her own life to lead—her, Black Ops, and Goliath—and that life didn't include Mitch.

And why would it?

He'd love to know where she was headed. He'd like to thank her and her mates properly for saving his neck. Shame, he didn't know anything about them. Ships passing in the night—or rather, in the morning.

Glenn Close.

Why had the name popped into his head?

Bloody hell.

Doc said something in the car. Something important. Yeah, that's right, when he'd been bouncing around in the back and she'd been holding his head up, she said, "We'll contact Glenn Close later."

Glenn Close? The American actress?

Nah. Unlikely.

No, not Glenn Close. Something else. A different name. He'd seen something like it on his travels. Recently. Glenn Close. Where the hell?

Relax, Mitch. That, too, will come to you.

Dr Rees replaced the attractive Doc, and the prodding, the poking, and the questions restarted.

True to his promise, Mitch behaved himself for the rest of the day, mainly.

The CT scan turned up nothing. No bones broken, but—thanks to Mitch's subtly embellished responses—Dr Rees diagnosed mild concussion and took Mitch's NFA status into account by recommending two days of bed rest and close monitoring. The really nice medic also assigned him a bed in a ward with four-hourly obs.

Result.

CHAPTER 16

Twenty-five minutes later, Lara finally called back. Twenty-five minutes that had Kaine climbing the walls and ready to race back into the hospital and drag her to safety.

Thank God.

"What happened?" he asked, avoiding the pleasantries.

"Where are you?" she asked, doing the same,

When he told her, she poked her head around the side of a building and beckoned him towards her. He hurried across the gap.

"Hi," he said, "you okay?" He reached out a hand and she took it in a firm grip.

"Fine thanks. You?"

"No problem. How's the patient?"

She lifted her chin in an up-nod, her eyes shining. "He regained consciousness as soon as they gave him oxygen. He's coherent. Which is a good sign. He answered all my questions and knew where he was. Complained of a headache, but that's only to be expected."

"Prognosis?"

"Good."

"Excellent." Kaine glanced around them, searching for—and feeling—hidden eyes staring at them. "Great. Let's go."

"Where?"

"Back into town. We need to find a crowd to melt into. Fancy a nice stroll in the sunshine?"

He crooked an elbow. She slipped her arm through his, held tight, and moved in close enough for their shoulders to touch. Her warmth matched the heat of the sun. They ambled along, forcing a slow pace —giving off the vibe of a couple enjoying the scenery—and kept silent until after they'd left the confines of the hospital grounds behind them.

At the traffic lights leading into town, a police patrol car waited, indicating left. In no obvious hurry. No blue lights. Kaine and Lara, still arm in arm, passed right by it. Inside, an overweight constable with a uniform shirt stretched at the seams, yawned. An open packet of salt and vinegar crisps sat on the vacant passenger seat beside him. The hand dropped from the yawn and reached into the bag for another savoury fistful. Kaine relaxed. If the cops weren't in a hurry to interview them, he saw no need to rush. The lights changed from red to green. The patrol car rolled slowly away, turned into Cerrigcochion Road, and kept its speed down.

When they reached the bridge that had held them up for so long, they discovered the little red Kia parked in a slot in front of a bank. The distraught driver—a twenty-something woman with close-cropped hair and a silver nose bar—stood inspecting the damage to her offside front wing. A creased panel and some scratches to the paintwork. Minor. Nothing that would keep the car off the road for long.

"Don't know what the fuss is about," Kaine whispered as they strolled past. "A light buffing with some coloured polish will deal with it."

"You don't feel even the slightest bit guilty?" Lara asked, a gentle rebuke in her tone.

"Not in the least." He shook his head, and they carried on walking. "What's a damaged car? We were on a mercy mission."

"Good point." She sighed and leant in closer. "Still ... I feel for her. That car might be her pride and joy."

"Want me to have a chat? Exchange details for the insurance claim?"

She punched his shoulder gently. "Of course not. I was just ... Oh, never mind."

"Tell you what," he said, squeezing her arm against his side. "If you're really worried about her, take a note of the Kia's registration number. When we have a spare moment, we'll identify the owner through the DVLA database. The Trust's legal department can make a generous ex-gratia payment to compensate her for any distress caused. We'll use the operating budget, of course. Will that work for you?"

"You are a generous man, Ryan Liam Kaine," she said, sotto voce. "And I already have ... Made a note of the licence number, I mean." She tapped her temple and smiled.

"That's alright then. Fancy a coffee while we wait for the quartermaster to work his logistical magic?"

"Yes, please. I'd really love one."

"After all that excitement, I might even stump up for a couple of pastries."

"You old spendthrift, you."

He guided her into *Megan's Tea Rooms*, an establishment with a prime view of the slow-moving River Usk. They sat inside the quaint-but-cramped café, heads bowed towards each other, and ordered coffee and Welsh cakes.

When in Rome ...

Along with the drinks, the Welsh cakes arrived warm and served with, butter, clotted cream, and strawberry jam. Never a fan, Kaine removed the cream and tucked into the rest. Lara ate one half of her serving and left the other for him. The rich roast coffee accompanied the cakes well.

"Sorry," she said, after finishing her half of the cake.

"What for?" Kaine kept his voice low.

"Mentioning Glyn Coes with Mitch in the car. Unforgiveable."

He shook his head and screwed up his mouth. "Not to worry. You had a load on your plate."

"Are we compromised?"

He scratched the fuzz on his chin.

"Mitch was unconscious, right?"

"Yes, I'm certain, but there's no telling what a comatose patient can hear or remember when they wake."

"Really?"

"The brain's a complicated piece of hardware. What do you think? Should we cry off?"

Kaine paused for a moment to consider the question. The café's bustle carried on around them. Waitresses in white starched aprons served. Their patrons enjoyed their midday refreshments, chatting happily. Kaine's deliberations reached a conclusion.

He leant closer and lowered his voice. "From what you told me, the Cadwalladers are in a spot of trouble. I can't turn my back on them. We'll just have to keep our guard up."

"Agreed." Lara said and sipped the last of her coffee.

Kaine drained his cup and wiped his mouth with the cloth napkin provided. Seconds later, his mobile vibrated, and he tugged it from his pocket.

"Rollo," he mouthed. "You pay, I'll take this outside."

"Cheapskate. I thought lunch was on you?" She reached into her jacket pocket for her purse.

Kaine ducked through the low door and headed for the railings guarding the riverbank.

"Hi, Adrian," Kaine said into the mouthpiece. "All sorted?"

"Yep. Not a problem."

Kaine read the time from his watch. "How'd you manage that so quickly?"

"You want me to tell you now?"

Kaine grinned at the grey water flowing southwards, inexorably heading for the sea. "No, not really. You can fill me in later."

"Where are you?"

Kaine told him.

"Megan's Tea Rooms, right," Rollo said, speaking slowly. "Just a sec ... Ah, okay. Got it. I'm five minutes away."

"See you soon. I'll get you a coffee to go."

"And a bun?"

Kaine sighed loud enough for Rollo to hear. "If you insist."

"I do. Haven't had a bite since breakfast at five-thirty. Life on a farm is like being back in the military."

"Suck it up, Marine."

"Up yours, sir." Rollo laughed and broke the connection.

Kaine slid the mobile back into his pocket and turned to face Lara, who'd exited the café, armed with a paper carry-out bag.

"For Adrian," she said, holding up the bag.

"Your big brother will be delighted. He'll be here in a couple of minutes."

"While you were on the phone, I called Staff Nurse Perry," she said, smiling.

"Good news?"

"Very. Mitch is sitting up in bed asking for lunch. The X-rays were clear. The police weren't happy with us for skipping out on them, though."

"They'll survive."

"Staff Nurse Perry said pretty much the same thing."

"Where d'you leave it with him?"

"I said we had an appointment we couldn't break and told him we'd contact the police separately."

"Good. That ought to give us enough wriggle room."

Behind them, a car horn tooted. Rollo arrived in an eighties vintage Vauxhall Astra. Navy blue with buckled panels, its exhaust grumbled and emitted a thin shroud of light blue smoke. The elderly petrol engine rattled and popped but seemed to run steadily enough.

Rollo wound down the driver's window by hand and poked his head through the opening.

"Don't just stand there gawking, jump in."

Kaine yanked on the rear passenger door for Lara. It squealed open and she slid in. Kaine dived in alongside her, and Rollo had them on their way before Kaine could slam the door behind him, and before they'd had a chance to fasten their seat belts.

"Way to keep a low profile, Rollo."

"Beggars and choosers, sir. Besides, look round you." He nodded to a vehicle passing in the opposite direction. It matched their Astra in everything but the licence number. It even had the same rust spots around the nearside headlight cluster.

"Okay, Quartermaster. I take your point. Nice work."

Rollo reached forwards and patted the dashboard. "She'll take us to where we want to go, and ..." He paused for dramatic effect and double hitched his eyebrows. "This vintage predates tracking devices."

"Where d'you find it?"

"Used car showroom behind the bus station. I paid the guy what he wanted, no questions asked."

"No questions?"

"Well, not many. The owner, a real shady type, didn't even ask to see my driver's licence. Couldn't get shot of this heap fast enough."

"Any paperwork?"

"I took a receipt and told him to send the MOT certificate and registration docs to my home address. He was only too happy to oblige."

"What address did you use, big brother?" Lara asked, smiling.

Rollo shrugged. "The Coach House, High Street, Chester. First address that came into my head."

"And he fell for it?"

"Hook, line, and three hundred and thirty quid in cash. It's amazing how a roll of folding money can speed up a business transaction."

"Nice one. We can donate the heap to the Cadwallader's farm

when we've found a better replacement," Lara suggested. "Myfanwy's desperate to turn seventeen and apply for her provisional licence. This will make a half-decent first car. It's better than the first car I ever owned."

"Assuming we can reach the place in this heap," Kaine said, sniffing the dank air inside the cabin. "On the plus side, this beast's unlikely to trigger any ANPR cameras."

"Not many ANPR cameras on the roads we'll be using." Rollo pulled out to overtake a car that was turning into a side road. "Not many traffic lights either."

"Keep withing the speed limits this time, Quartermaster. I'd really like to arrive in one piece."

"Oh ye of little faith." He fed more fuel into the carb. The Astra's 1100cc engine coughed twice, caught, and they pulled away from the centre of Brecon.

"What did you do with the Audi?"

Rollo slid him a sideways grin. "I didn't sell it to Shady if that's what you're thinking. That wouldn't have been particularly covert."

"So, where is it?" Lara asked.

Rollo indicated left and overtook an ice cream van that was turning into a small housing estate, its tinkling audio system blaring out a hideously off-key rendition of *Greensleeves*.

"Dumped it in a car park behind a couple of industrial-sized wheelie bins. I even left a pay and display ticket on the dashboard. I'd put money on it not being discovered for days."

"Good work. Now, changing the subject, what's our ETA?" Kaine asked.

"Doc?" Rollo asked.

Lara worked the GPS app on her mobile. The Astra showed its venerable age by missing a built-in infotainment system. "I assume you'll want to avoid the A40 and take the long way around?"

"Probably a good idea."

"In that case, about forty-five minutes."

"Really?" Kaine said.

She nodded. "'Fraid so."

"Can't be helped. Better call the farm and tell them we'll be even later."

"Will do. Adrian, take the next right and head to a place called *Cradoc*. Then follow the signs for *Battle Fawr*."

"Battle?" Kaine said through a wry grin. "Sounds like my kind of place."

CHAPTER 17

Monday 22nd May – Early Afternoon

Battle Fawr, Powys, South Wales, UK

Battle Fawr turned out to be a tiny Welsh hamlet consisting of a few dozen stone buildings and a pub gathered around a crossroads. They were through it in a matter of seconds.

"How disappointing," Kaine said.

"You expected another Hastings?" Rollo asked, taking his eyes from the road long enough to shoot Kaine an amused look.

"Don't know what I expected. How long now?"

"Twenty minutes, give or take," Rollo answered, after consulting the GPS map on Lara's mobile which he'd perched on the retractable ashtray in the middle of the dashboard. "Can't go too fast in this tin can, not on these roads. She handles like a rowing boat in a heavy swell."

Eight hundred metres beyond *Battle Fawr*, they turned left onto an unnamed road and wound their way downhill to a stone bridge with a single arch that spanned a small river—equally unnamed.

Beyond the bridge, the narrow lane took them uphill on the opposite side of the valley.

On the left and after another sharp bend, the low hedge peeled back to reveal a two-metre-tall chain-link fence topped with shiny barbed wire and broken by a double gate. A sign on one side of the entrance road read:

PROHIBITED PLACE
This is a prohibited place within the meaning of the Official Secrets Act.
NO TRESPASSING NO PHOTOGRAPHY
Unauthorised persons who enter this area may be arrested and prosecuted.

A SECOND SIGN ON THE OTHER SIDE OF THE ENTRANCE REINFORCED THE message with:

MOD PROPERTY
The Ministry of Defence accepts no responsibility for damage howsoever caused to motor vehicles or property in the camp.

BEYOND THE FENCE, A ROW OF PREFABRICATED HUTS STEPPED AWAY INTO the distance. Single-storey, dirty cream walls, grey roofs, and otherwise nondescript. Kaine knew military barracks when he saw them. The gable end of a red brick building crouched close to the unmanned gates. Behind the gates, the entry road fell away into the deep valley and curved to the right, disappearing out of sight behind another building, this one double-storey and more imposing. The camp's administrative building.

"What is that place?" Kaine asked. "Looks deserted."

"Not sure," Rollo answered. "One of the abandoned Cold War listening posts, I imagine. Plenty of them hereabouts. I called Baz Jericho last night. Asked him to check it out for me. On the quiet, of course."

"Of course."

They drove on, passing yet more evidence of MoD activity. A second entrance. More imposing than the first, this showed signs of activity with a few vehicles in the car park, both civilian and military. A guard in full battledress patrolled the gate.

"Doesn't look so abandoned to me," Kaine announced.

"The place was empty when we passed this morning."

Kaine's antennae twitched.

"Chase up Jericho when we reach the farm, eh?"

"Will do."

Lara tapped him on the forearm. "What's wrong?"

Kaine shook his head. "Nothing. I just don't like anomalies, and that's a huge one."

Rollo added a little more fuel to the engine and the Astra chugged up the hill, leaving the anomaly behind.

Three miles or so later, the narrow, tree-lined road crested yet another hill. They scooted through the tiny hamlet of Pentre-felin which consisted of a farm, a few houses, and a bridge over the Cilleni —a stream doing its best to be a river.

Beyond the village, a left turn took them onto another lane and another uphill stretch. They wound through the glorious Welsh countryside for the best part of a mile before Kaine broke the silence.

"Nearly there yet?" Kaine asked, nodding at a pair of horses in a paddock who pushed their heads over the fence and watched them pass.

"Not long now," Rollo answered.

Kaine turned to Lara.

"What are the Cadwalladers like?"

"Becky's lovely. Hardworking, friendly. Always smiling."

"And Cadwallader himself?"

She paused and stared over Kaine's shoulder through the side window as though looking for inspiration. "Stern, but honest. Not an easy man to get to know, I'd say. But we only arrived yesterday afternoon."

"Where did you stay?"

"They have a couple of cottages on the farm. Rollo and I took one of them as paying guests. The other is set aside for the stable hands and the guides."

"They let you share a house?"

"As far as the Cadwalladers are concerned, Rollo and I are brother and sister."

"Of course you are. I almost forgot."

"Thought it would be for the best, all things considered."

"Good idea. The cottage, is it comfortable?"

"Not as comfortable as a Gulfstream, I'd imagine," Rollo said, a wry grin twisting his mouth, "but I've slept in worse places. I took the single room. Doc had the double."

"And I'll have the couch in the front room, I suppose?"

"We'll see," Lara said, smiling.

A moment later, she added a wink, and he finally relaxed in the hopes that she'd forgiven him for dumping her in Paris. He looked forwards to having some alone time so he could apologise properly, but he doubted that would happen until later that night.

A line of tufty grass grew from the centre of the single-track road, which climbed ever higher. A sharp change in altitude caused Kaine's inner ears to compress. He waggled his jaw, and they popped as the pressure equalised. At the top of the next hill, the fifth since leaving Pentre-felin, the land opened up around them and the hedges had been recently trimmed. A wide and undulating river valley spread out below them.

"There you go," Rollo said, pointing through the dirty and wiper-scratched windscreen.

"That's it?"

"Yep, the Cadwalladers own pretty much the whole valley."

"Stop here a moment, will you, Adrian?"

Rollo braked hard and pulled the Astra to a stop in the middle of the lane. Not much chance of traffic so far out in the sticks.

Kaine cracked open the door and slid out. The low hedges restricted his view, and he stepped onto the Astra's sill, hoping the rusted metal wouldn't cave in under his weight.

Rollo wound down his window and handed him up a pair of binoculars.

"Thought these might come in handy."

"Thanks."

Lara scrambled across the seat and climbed up alongside him. She circled one arm around his waist and waved the other arm to encompass the whole sweep of the valley.

"This is Cwm Felyn," she said, making a good stab at the local dialect. "Apparently, it means Yellow Valley."

Kaine acknowledged the comment with a nod, raised the binoculars to his eyes, and turned his attention to studying the lay of the land—his latest theatre of operations.

The wide valley ran from south-east to north-west, its floor mapped out in a patchwork quilt of fields outlined by overgrown hedgerows. Hundreds of sheep and a few dozen cows dotted the meadows. Thick woods covered the upper slopes of both the valley's steep walls, and a stream wound through its centre. Halfway along the valley floor, the little river swelled out into a decent-sized pond. A three-storey, stone-built farmhouse roofed in grey Welsh slate stood back from the pond. It dominated the accompanying outbuildings.

"Picturesque," he said to Lara.

"I already told you that."

"You did indeed. Isolated, though. I'm not sure how a townie like Rhodri will cope being stuck out here without any friends."

"He'll make new friends and grow to love it. The place is idyllic. All that open land and all those animals."

"Hmm."

Kaine took in another sweep.

The road on which they parked dropped down into the valley and joined what seemed to be a much larger road that ran in a great curving arc around the valley.

"Rollo?"

"Yes, sir?"

"That road down there. The one this lane merges into."

"What about it, sir?"

"It seems to hug the valley floor. Would I be right in assuming it's lying in a direct route from that last village we drove through, Pentre-felin?"

"You would be, sir."

"So, why have we been bouncing around on this tank track for the past fifteen minutes?"

Rollo grinned up at him.

"That's easy, sir. Apart from climbing all the way up to yonder crag"—he pointed north-east to a bare outcrop of rock sticking through trees and bushes on the far side of the valley—"this is the best spot to view the farm. You can pretty much see the whole place from here. I thought you'd like to view it first hand before meeting the Cadwalladers."

"Good thinking, Colour Sergeant," Kaine said. "Always knew there had to be a reason for keeping you around."

"Thanks for nothing, sir."

Somewhat reluctantly, Kaine unwrapped Lara's arm from around his waist and helped her back into car, not that she needed any assistance. Such manners had been drilled into him from early childhood.

"Seen enough, sir?"

"I have. Thank you, Adrian. Let's go."

He returned the binoculars and slid back into his seat, but before he'd had a chance to fasten his seat belt, Rollo had them heading down the hill at a much greater speed than earlier.

A kilometre later, they joined the fully tarmacked—if cracked and heavily pitted—road at a T-junction on the valley floor and turned left. After another five hundred metres, a pair of five-bar metal gates blocked their entry to the farmhouse yard. Before Kaine could jump out, Lara beat him to the punch. She jogged to the centre of the road, unlocked the left gate, and picked her way over a cattle grid to push it open and hold it in place.

While Rollo drove the car through, Kaine took his chance to study the farm in close-up.

The basic set-up reminded him of Mike Procter's place in Northamptonshire. To Kaine's left, perched halfway up a small hill overlooking a pair of white-fenced paddocks and the pond, the well-maintained farmhouse stood proud. Its white-painted stone walls and slate roof stood proud and strong against the worst that the Welsh weather could throw at it. A one-metre-tall stone wall surrounded the house, separating it from the working part of the farm and allowing some form of respite from the daily grind.

A muddy courtyard spread out beyond the garden wall, with wooden stables, a paddock, and a riding area he'd heard Lara call a manège beyond. Behind the stables, the huge barn with a rusted, corrugated iron roof stood separate and prominent. Storehouses, garage lock-ups, workshops, and piles of discarded material—rotten wood, rusted parts from abandoned farm machinery, and general rubbish—made up the balance of the farm. A nightmare for a clean freak, but a dream for adventurous children on the hunt for materials ripe for den building. As a kid, Kaine would have loved it. Perhaps the recently arrived Rhodri Pierce would grow to feel the same way.

There's always hope.

Lara danced over the cattle grid, closed the gate, and returned to her seat.

"You've done that a few times, I imagine?" Kaine noted.

"Once or twice."

She smiled and slid a little closer—close enough to hold hands without stretching. Kaine's world gained a little more colour and warmth.

"There's Dancer," she said, pointing to a pocket-sized, light brown horse that danced and pranced in the paddock just inside the gate. "She's really excitable."

The horse whinnied and shook her head as though in disagreement. Then she lifted her tail and released a stream of urine that steamed as it sprayed through the air. Another horse, this one bigger and jet black apart from a white sock on its left front foot, approached Dancer and snickered.

"And that's Black Beauty, I suppose?" Kaine asked.

"Don't be ridiculous," Lara said, grinning. "That's Charcoal. Black Beauty had a star on his forehead."

"Did she? Well, that's told me."

"Black Beauty was a stallion, not a mare."

Rollo rolled the Astra slowly forwards to avoid spooking the animals. The tyres crunched on hard-packed gravel as they progressed along the drive, collecting an entourage of horses on the way. By the time they reached the farmyard, nine horses of varying sizes, shapes, and colours had formed into a small herd.

"Nosey beggars, aren't they?" Kaine said.

"Greedy, more like. They're hoping for some treats. Carrots, apples. Anything healthy."

Kaine glanced at her tight-fitting trousers and form-hugging top.

"I can see you don't have anything like that concealed about your person."

"There's a bag of goodies hanging inside the stable door. With permission, I'll dole them out later. After I've made the introductions. Ready?"

He forced a smile onto a reluctant face.

"Me? I'm always ready."

He couldn't exactly include meeting the relatives of the people he'd killed amongst his list of favourite activities.

Rollo nosed the Astra to a stop in front of the garden wall, and Kaine took a deep and steadying breath. The next part could never be described as easy.

"How do I look?" he whispered.

"Like you've just stepped off a private jet after a relaxing flight over the Atlantic," Rollo answered.

"Don't worry," Lara said, "you look nothing like your mugshot. They'll never recognise you."

"Even with these coloured contacts, are you sure I'll pass inspection?"

Her encouraging smile helped slow his galloping heart rate.

"You'll be fine, Peter," she said.

"Yes, Staff Sergeant," Rollo added. "Even I wouldn't recognise you from your military photo."

He cut the engine and silence fell, save for the whickering, snickering of the horses and the rattling chug of a hard-working and far off diesel engine. Kaine searched and found the source of the noise—a tractor in the fields above the farm, its engine note driven towards them on the gusting breeze.

Get on with it, Kaine.

"Right, here we go."

Kaine pushed open his door and stepped into the warm afternoon air.

Lara and Rollo followed suit, and he trailed them towards the gap in the garden wall, where a wooden gate stood ajar. Rollo stepped back to allow them through first.

The black-painted door stood dark and solid in the granite storm porch. Lara tried the wrought-iron ball handle. It wouldn't budge.

"That's interesting," Lara muttered, a slight frown furrowing her forehead.

"Why?"

"Becky told me they rarely lock the doors. She said there's no need in the country unless they're going away overnight."

A large black bell hung from a bracket attached to the wall. The rope tied to its clapper swung gently in the wind. Lara tugged the rope twice. The bell's deep and resonant chime echoed against the white-painted walls and boomed around the courtyard.

They waited.

Here we go. Look lively, Kaine.

CHAPTER 18

Monday 22nd May – Early Afternoon

Cadwallader Farm, Glyn Coes, Powys, South Wales, UK

After a full minute without a response, Lara repeated the performance with the bell.

Moments later, a lock clunked, the ball handle turned, and the door creaked opened. A woman appeared in the gap between door and jamb. She hugged the door's edge tight to her chest, using it as a shield. Puffy red eyes told a tale. When she clocked her visitors, she forced a smile onto her round and bucolic face.

"Oh, it's you," she said, the disappointment clear in her voice. "I was in the kitchen. Didn't hear your car. Gwyn's Defender is much louder than your fancy German motor." She looked past them to the courtyard and frowned at the Astra. "Oh, what happened to your car?"

"Potholes," Rollo said, grimacing.

"Potholes?"

Kaine took over the explanation they'd devised on the drive from Brecon. "Adrian hit a crater on the A40. Damaged the suspension. We had to wait ages for recovery. That ancient Astra was the only car the garage had available at such short notice." His smile and dismissive shrug ended the tale. "We ended up having to buy it."

Lara pushed her way past Kaine and reached out to take the woman by the hand. "Becky, is everything okay?"

Becky Cadwallader stepped back and fully opened the door. She swiped her eyes with a tissue and used it to blow her nose.

Standing at around one hundred and seventy centimetres tall— sixty-seven inches in old money—she had flyaway, shoulder-length dark hair, deep blue eyes, rosy cheeks, and a gap between her front teeth. She acknowledged Kaine's presence with a nod.

"I ... we had a phone call, from the hospital. Rhodri's had an accident at school."

Lara threw an arm around her shoulders and squeezed.

"Oh no! How is he?"

The woman sniffed, wiped her nose again, and crushed the tissue into a tight ball.

"I don't know. Gwynfor left about an hour ago. Hasn't called me yet."

"Why didn't you go with him?"

"I-I wanted to, but I couldn't. Who'd have let you in?"

"We'd have been happy to wait, Mrs Cadwallader," Kaine said, aiming for quiet reassurance.

"No, no. I called begging for your help. It wouldn't have been right to keep you waiting. And I'm Becky. Everyone calls me—"

A telephone's ring cut her off mid-sentence. She spun away from Lara, rushed inside the house, and snatched up the handset of an old-fashioned telephone standing on a table in the hall. Its tangled, coiled wire pulled the phone's base up with it. She dropped into the adjacent chair and the base clanked back onto the table.

"Gwyn? *Beth gymerodd chi mor hir?* I've been beside myself. *Sut mae e?* Is it serious?" She shot out the questions in a rapid-fire mixture of Welsh and English.

The voice on the other end of the line spoke deep and slow, but Kaine couldn't make out his words. As she listened, Becky Cadwallader slumped against the back of the chair. Her forehead creased in anger, but her shoulders relaxed, and she blinked fresh tears.

"*Dyw e ddim? Ydych chi'n sicr?* ... Thank the Good Lord in His mercy. But why did they call? ... What? ... No! Another one? Who could be doing this to us? ... No, no. I don't understand it, either."

Gwynfor Cadwallader spoke again, this time at length. Becky listened, a catch in her breathing.

Kaine studied Lara's reaction to the part of the telephone conversation they could overhear. She glanced at him and let out a relieved sigh. Her brows lifted, softening her frown of concentration.

"Yes, okay," Becky said, relief clear in the words. "Right. Drive safely."

She untangled the knotted cord, replaced the handset, and sank deeper into the hard-backed chair. She lowered her face into her hands and recited something in Welsh that might have been a prayer.

Lara looked at Kaine, her pained expression showing empathy, but she knew better than to rush the distraught woman for an explanation.

Kaine turned to Rollo.

"Adrian, do you know where Becky keeps the teabags? I'm sure we could all do with a nice cuppa."

"No teabags in this house, Peter," Rollo answered. "Loose leaf only. Nothing but the best here."

"Excellent. Then get to it, man."

"Oh no you don't," Becky said. She clapped her hands to her knees and used them to push herself to her feet. Her joints creaked on the way up, giving away her age, but her breathing had eased, and a grateful smile had found its way to her round face.

"Don't you dare, now. Wouldn't dream of letting my guests make their own tea." She tutted. "The very idea of it!"

From the pocket in her floral apron, she pulled out a fresh tissue and wiped the tears from her eyes and cheeks. Once dry, she turned towards them and bestowed a welcoming smile upon them all.

"Come with me, will you? The kettle's already on the boil. It usually is in my house."

She turned and led the way through the wide entrance hall—off-white walls, dark woodwork, and hung with excellent oil paintings of the surrounding countryside—and into a large kitchen-dining room. The similarity to Mike's farmhouse in Long Buckby struck Kaine. It had a pleasant, homely feel, and the comforting smell of coffee and fresh-baked bread hung in the warm air. Solid and welcoming, made more so by Becky's obvious show of relief at the telephoned news.

"Please, please. *Eisteddwch, nawr.* Take a seat," she said, pointing to a large pine table and the ten dining chairs that surrounded it.

She headed straight for the range oven and busied herself with the steaming kettle. Rollo, familiar with the kitchen layout, opened a wall unit, removed four mugs, and placed them on a tray on the bleached oak kitchen surface. He removed a jug of milk from the huge and ancient fridge and placed it on the tray along with a cup of sugar he'd taken from a different cupboard.

Once she'd filled a large pot of tea with the steaming water, Becky turned to face the room and leant back against the oven's polished steel rail.

"So, you must be Peter. Thank you so much for coming to help. I've been at my wits' end, I really have."

She held out a red and calloused hand. Kaine stepped forwards, took hold. She pumped it twice with the firm grip strengthened by working the land: wrangling sheep, milking cows, and maybe tugging at the reins of wilful horses.

"Peter Sidings," he said. "Pleased to meet you, Becky."

She released her hold and, once again, waved them all towards the dining table.

"We have five minutes for the tea to brew, and I need a sit down. It's been a trying day and it's only mid-afternoon."

Rollo added the huge ceramic teapot to the tray and carried the assemblage for her. She took the chair at the head of the table, her back to a wide window which owned a spectacular view of the rolling wooded hills and the deep blue, cloud-dotted sky, and rested her forearms on the table.

"How much of that phone call did you understand?" she asked.

"Not much," Kaine answered. "But I gather it's good news?"

She nodded and her thankful smile grew a little wider. "Very good indeed, but bad, too. In a way."

"We're all ears, Becky," Lara said.

She'd taken a chair on the opposite side of the table to Kaine, but close enough to Becky to reach out and hold her hand without having to stretch.

"What happened?" Kaine asked.

"It was a practical joke," Becky said. "Made by someone with a wicked sense of humour."

"Go on," Kaine encouraged. "Please, tell us everything."

"Not much to tell really. We received a phone call. Just after midday. It was a man. He claimed to be a nurse at the War Memorial ..." She frowned, and her eyes focused on Kaine. "Oh, that's the local hospital. It's in Brecon. About thirty minutes' drive from here. Anyway, the nurse said Rhodri had taken a fall in school. Cut his head open quite badly. Needed stitches and a scan." She shook her head and released another quick breath. It came out like a short cough. "He made it sound really serious. I'd have gone instead of Gwynfor, but I can't drive on the open roads. Never did pass my driving test, see. Not that I tried at all. Not got the nerves for it, you know." Her chin trembled. "Oh, I can drive tractors and quad bikes on the farm, no trouble. But the public roads?" She shook her head. "All those fast cars. Too busy for this country girl."

"So, Gwyn drove?" Kaine asked.

"Yes, that's right. Normally, Dewi would drive me to town for shopping and the like when he's here. Dewi's our eldest, but he's at college weekdays, so Gwyn had to go. We're Rhodri's guardians, see. Oh, but you know that, of course. Well, apparently, the hospital needed some forms signed for the scan."

"And when Gwyn arrived at the hospital?" Lara asked, no doubt feeling the need to prod her along.

"They looked at him as though he was stupid. They'd never heard of a Rhodri Pierce. Turns out they didn't call us at all. So, Gwyn telephoned Rhodri's school. Took him ages to get through, as per usual. Anyway, they said he was in class, right as rain. And that's when Gwyn telephoned me, just now. On his way home, he is."

Lara clasped Becky's hand in both of hers and squeezed.

"You must have been worried sick."

Chin trembling, she nodded. "It was horrible. Why would anyone do such an awful thing? It's so cruel."

Tears filled her eyes again and spilled down her rounded face. She dabbed them away with the new tissue and blinked hard.

Becky glanced at the clock on the wall and must have decided enough time had passed for the tea to brew. She stood and started pouring. After filling three mugs with the dark brown liquid, she replaced the pot, and rolled her hand over the tray.

"Help yourselves to milk and sugar. I don't fancy one right now. I've drunk enough tea today to float a battleship."

Being closer to the tray, Lara dribbled a spot of milk into Kaine's cup, stirred it in, and passed it across before doing the same for Rollo and herself.

"Thanks, Annie," Kaine said, trying her name on for size and as a reminder.

"Has anything like this happened before?" Rollo asked.

Becky paused for a moment and looked up at the ceiling before answering.

"Yes, all the time."

"What do you mean?" Kaine followed up.

"Well, over the past couple of months we've had more than the usual number of ... what d'you call them ... cold calls? People trying to sell us stuff we don't need. You know the sort of things: double glazing, solar panels, life insurance, a plot at the local cemetery. We even had a man try to sell us a Family Bible, as though we didn't have one of our own already. Then there was the time our vet arrived to treat a cow when we didn't call him first and none of our cows were sick. He swore we called him out, but we didn't. He said the man on the phone sounded just like Gwyn. He tried charging us a call-out fee, but Gwyn wasn't having any of it. Doctor Haviland got really angry. It's a long way from his surgery to the farm. Threatened to strike us off his books."

"No decent vet would ever do that," Lara announced, speaking from personal experience.

"Of course not, but Gwyn wasn't happy about it, and neither was Larry Haviland. They went to school together, see. There's always been a frosty relationship on account of Larry and me once being sweethearts." She flushed and put her hand to her throat. "This was years ago, you understand. When we were all at school."

Becky lowered her hand, reached out reflexively for the teapot, and poured herself a mug apparently without thinking about it. She added milk and two heaped sugars.

"How did it end up?" Kaine asked.

"Oh, well. Gwyn agreed to pay for Larry's diesel, and they set up a password to use in case the same thing ever happened again."

"Good idea," Kaine said, part of him wondering why they'd fallen for the most recent phone call.

"I can see what you're thinking, Peter."

"Really?"

"You're wondering how we could have been taken in by today's hoax call, aren't you?"

"Well ..." Kaine slanted his head to one side and winced.

"Rhodri's our responsibility. Ever since Sharon ... well, you know. Ever since he's been with us, he's been a little, how shall we say, clumsy. Accident prone, you know. Keeps tripping over his own feet or bumping into things. We took him to get his eyes tested. Turns out he's a little short-sighted, but not seriously. We thought that the poor boy might be a little *twp*, you know." She tapped a finger against her temple. "Slow-witted." She finished her tea in three deep mouthfuls, pushed her mug away, and shook her head forcefully. "No, no. That's an uncharitable thing to say. It's just that Rhodri's a quiet boy. Wouldn't say boo to a goose. Scared of the animals, he is. Even the chickens, for goodness' sake." She wiped her eyes again. "Truth is, we never really knew the lad before Sharon passed and we took responsibility for him. Only met him a few times, and then only when he was much younger." She gulped another breath.

"Anyway, the school examined him, you know? Gave him one of those IQ tests. Turns out he's bright. Really, really bright. Genius-level bright. Just doesn't show it. Likes to keep his talents hidden, you know?" Another breath. "Anyway, here's me rattling on."

Automatically, she reached for the pot, refilled her empty mug, and added milk and another two sugars. Then she left it on the table, untouched.

"No, that's okay, Becky," Kaine said. "Please carry on. I'd like to know more about Rhodri and the whole family. It might help us understand what's happening here. He keeps falling over, you say?"

"Yes, that's right. The number of times he's come home from school with bumps and bruises and grazed knees is nobody's business."

Kaine grinned.

"It's not unusual for boys to fall over, Becky. I did it all the time, as a kid. I still have the scars on my knees to prove it."

Becky nodded and lifted the second mug of tea to her full lips. She sipped.

"But looking at you, Peter," she said, giving him an appraising once over, "I imagine you were quite the sportsman, yes? Very active? Adventurous, like?"

"Pretty much. I played football and ran cross-country for the school. Not to any great standard, mind. Couldn't get on with cricket, though, and I never played rugby. Too small and feeble."

"Yes, thought so," she nodded, taking in his frame. "But Rhodri's not like that at all. He's much more into his books. Would rather play on his smartphone or his games console than kick a football or get himself dirty in a scrum or a ruck. Can't tell you the number of times the boy's begged me to write him a note to miss games lessons. I didn't do it, of course. That would be dishonest, and the lad does need his exercise."

Rollo and Kaine exchanged glances. He knew exactly what the big man was thinking, as did Lara, judging by her expression.

"Bullying, you think now?" Becky asked, picking up on their unspoken conversation, and showing herself to be an astute reader of body language.

"It wouldn't be unheard of, Becky," Kaine said. "New boy in school. Slightly different. I'm guessing the school's small and ... he'd stand out from his classmates."

He managed to catch himself from using the word "parochial". Didn't think it would go down too well, and it certainly wouldn't help him build a relationship with his latest "client".

"No, no. That's not it at all. At first, we thought the same thing ourselves, you see. We talked to the headmistress about it at the last parent's evening, but she assured us that bullying was never tolerated at Brecon Academy. We asked her to look out for him, given the upset he's had in his life, and she promised to do so."

"So, Rhodri being accident prone is why Gwyn rushed off this morning without phoning the school to check up first?"

"No, not at all. We *did* try phoning the Academy, but no one answered. They've got one of those fancy automated systems, where you have multiple choice options, and they put you on hold with that mechanical music, you know? Gwyn wouldn't put up with that, and he was worried about the *hogyn bach*—the little lad. I mean, the Good Lord has given him to us, and it's our obligation to take care of him, you see. Rhodri's our family, and we love him dearly. And Gwyn loves Rhodri, of course he does. Loves the boy as much as he loves Dewi."

She spoke forcefully, as though saying it loud enough and power-fully enough would make it true.

Lara caught Kaine's eye and shook her head.

"Any idea who would play such a nasty trick on you?" Kaine asked.

"No, none. None whatsoever. No one we know could ever be so cruel."

"Is Gwyn on his way home?" Kaine asked. "I'd like to meet him. Perhaps he has an inkling of who it might be."

Becky nodded. "He's on his way. Be back soon, I shouldn't wonder. He called from the car when stuck in traffic."

Kaine nodded and sipped at his tea, giving himself time to think.

After a few moments' silence, Becky jumped to her feet and reached for the tray.

"Oh dear. Where are my manners? I haven't offered you any food, and it's close to teatime. What can I get you?"

She lifted the tea tray, the teaspoons rattling as her hands shook.

Kaine stood and prepared to take the load from her.

"Becky, I'm fine, thanks," Kaine said. "I had a decent breakfast on the plane, and we stopped off for a snack on the way here when we had to change cars. We won't be hungry for ages. Tell me about the call from the so-called nurse. Did it come on your landline or your mobile?"

"The landline."

"Did you pick it up or do you have a recording?"

"No, I picked it up right away, thinking it might be Annie." She glanced at Lara before returning her gaze to Kaine. "No telling what trouble you might have had finding the airport. Gwyn and I've only been there the once, and we got hopelessly lost."

"We had our GPS," Lara said.

Becky shivered and shook her head. "Satellite navigation? Seems like magic to me. Don't trust it. What's wrong with reading a map and road signs?"

"Some people can't read maps properly," Kaine said, adding a gentle smile. "They tend to get hopelessly lost."

Their hostess stopped, stared at Kaine for a moment, then she relaxed, and the tray stopped rattling. "Are you having fun at my expense, Peter?"

Once again, Kaine raised his hands.

"Only a little, Becky. Only a little."

"Yes, I see."

"Becky," Kaine said, taking the tray and handing it off to Rollo, "please sit down. We're here to help in any way we can. Annie's given me a briefing, and I know about the note."

"The note?" She frowned in confusion. "Oh, the note. Yes, the note. Strange, it was."

Kaine waited, but she didn't elaborate.

"What were you told, Becky?"

"Sorry?"

"Amongst other things, the note ordered you to do as you were told. Is that right?"

She nodded, her frown deepening. "Yes, that's right. It did."

"So, what were you told to do?"

"That's just it, Peter. Nobody's told us to do anything at all. We've got no idea what's going on. I promise you. No idea whatsoever."

Really?

"That is strange," Kaine said, adding a sympathetic smile. "Maybe we can help you find out why this is happening."

"I don't know how. I really don't." She breathed deeply. "When Gwyn gets back, you can talk to him. He might be keeping something from me ... Oh yes, don't look so surprised. I didn't come down with the last shower of rain, Peter. I know what you're thinking. But if Gwyn is hiding something from me, he'll have a good reason for it. Probably wants to protect me from something. He's always been protective, and he is in charge. As the Good Book says, 'A man's home is his castle', and Gwyn is the king of this particular castle."

Again, Lara shook her head at Kaine, and he bit back his knee-jerk response.

"Yes," Becky said, nodding. "I know some might consider it a little old-fashioned, closed-minded even, but we follow the Way of the Lord in this house, and I'm happy to be led by Gwyn in all things." She breathed in and exhaled long and hard. "Well, now. The kids will be home from school soon. I can't wait for you to meet them."

The throaty roar of an old diesel engine reached them through the thick stone walls and the secondary glazing.

Becky threw a hand to her ample chest.

"Oh, thank goodness," she said. "That'll be Gwyn."

She rushed from the kitchen and along the hall, the hem of her floral house dress flapping around her calves.

CHAPTER 19

Cadwallader Farm, Glyn Coes, Powys, South Wales, UK

Seconds later, with Becky at his side, Gwynfor Cadwallader entered the kitchen, every inch the careworn hill farmer. Of similar height and build to Rollo—six foot three and eighteen stones of beef on the hoof—he matched the vibe of his farmhouse, his castle, and looked as though he could withstand anything the Welsh weather could throw at him. With neatly trimmed grey hair and a face hewn from the red sandstone of the Beacons, he stared at Kaine through piercing dark eyes, assessing his latest unwanted guest.

"So, you'll be the staff sergeant, then," he said, in a shepherd's deep voice designed to carry over the hills and into the ears of his flock.

Kaine, still standing, stepped forwards and offered his hand.

"Peter Sidings, sir."

"Gwyn will do. We don't go in for all that 'sir and madam' nonsense in this house."

Like his wife before him, Cadwallader's grip was firm, but he didn't push it. No unnecessary show of strength. They broke the hold together and Cadwallader nodded.

"You've come to help," Cadwallader said, "and for that, we can only be grateful, but I don't know what you can do for us, Peter. There's a lot of open land out there"—he pointed a stubby index finger at the kitchen window—"and it's not exactly easy to police."

"You're not keen on surveillance cameras, I understand?"

"No point in them out here. I'd have to stay awake through the night watching the screens. When would I sleep?"

Kaine tried a disarming smile. "The Trust could provide some men, Gwyn. Good people. They would act as your eyes and your ears for as long as you needed them."

"Sounds expensive. Who'd pay for all that manpower and equipment?"

"The Trust has the funding."

"*Oes*, yes. And gathered from the pockets of mercenaries and warmongers—"

"And God-fearing Christians who simply want to help the families affected by the—"

"Oh, I daresay some of your donors will offer lip service to the Lord," Cadwallader snapped, "but the bulk of the money is tainted. No, it's out of the question. I—We will not accept your money. Rebecca should not have contacted you in the first place. We will meet these plagues with fortitude. The Good Lord will protect us."

Becky pulled at her husband's forearm. "But these good people want to help us, Gwyn. What if the Lord sent them?"

With a face of thunder, Cadwallader turned to her. "I've discussed this with the minister, and he said I must abide by what the Lord tells me. And He tells me it would be wrong to accept money from these people."

"But they're here now, Gwyn. Surely, we can let them help?"

Cadwallader's dark brown eyes alighted on Kaine, and the appraisal continued.

"Do you believe, Peter?"

"In a God?"

"Yes, mun. In God. Are you a believer?"

Bloody hell.

How could he answer such a question without giving offence? Did he believe in a god? Did he heck. Any faith he might have held after the two decades he'd spent in the military, witnessing the worst acts that humans could commit upon each other, had been seared from his soul by the fireball that engulfed Flight BE1555. The fireball *he* released upon it. How could he answer?

Kaine returned Cadwallader's gaze. He could see no other way but the truth.

"No, Gwyn, I am not a believer, but I will defend to the death your right to believe in anything you wish, so long as it doesn't offend or upset others."

Cadwallader narrowed his eyes and turned to his wife. "*Onest, onid ydyw. Rwy'n ei hoffi.*"

"Excuse me?" Kaine asked, half expecting the huge and sinewy farmer to sling them all out on their ears.

"No, no," Cadwallader said. "I'm the one who should be excused. I slipped into Welsh for a minute. Rude of me, with guests. Actually, what I said was, I like your honesty, Peter. You could have thrown all sorts of lies and deceits at me, trying to appease, but you didn't. I like that in a man."

"Thank you," Kaine said, relaxing a little.

"So, what's the next step? Can we do anything to help?"

Cadwallader turned his head and took in Kaine's apparently insubstantial frame.

"After tea," he said, "I'll be heading up to Ten Acre Field. There's a gap in the wall that needs rebuilding. It needs mending to stop the sheep wandering into the woods and getting lost. Dopey, they are. Get lost easy enough in the open. If you and Adrian fancy a bit of manual labour, I'd appreciate the help."

"Happy to," Kaine said. "Aren't we, Adrian?"

"Delighted," Rollo answered, but with all the enthusiasm of a condemned man ordering his final meal.

Cadwallader laughed. "That's wonderful. Either of you ever done any drystone walling?"

Kaine shook his head. Rollo did the same.

"Nope," Kaine said, "but we're fast learners. Tell us what to do and we'll do it."

"Right you are, boys." He wrung his hands. "It's tough going, but toiling in the fresh air, under the watchful eyes of the Lord, is rewarding. You'll work off tea and build a healthy appetite for supper. And on the way out, I'll be able to show you a bit of the farm."

Cadwallader paused, and once again, his brown eyes ran an appraisal of Kaine from head to foot and back again. He didn't seem too impressed with what they told him. "Peter, you look like you could do with a good meal, if you don't my saying."

"No, Gwyn. I don't mind at all," Kaine said. He recognised a challenge when he heard one.

At his side, Rollo smiled knowingly. The first time they'd met—on the SBS assessment trails—Rollo had said pretty much the same thing. A raw lieutenant, Kaine had taken up the unspoken challenge and proved himself up to anything Rollo and his fellow training staff could throw at him.

"And," Lara said, shaking her head at the men as they virtually flexed their muscles at each other, "if you don't mind, I'll spend some time with the horses."

"Bless you, dear," Becky said, "we don't mind at all. We could use a helping hand in the stables. Always plenty of work to do coming up to trekking season. But first, you can help me with tea."

She spread her arms wide and swept Lara along with her to the kitchen.

Gwyn wrung his hands again and faced his newly volunteered workers.

"Right then, boys. It'll be windy and wet this evening, and you can't work on the hills in those togs. Adrian, I'll borrow you one of my boiler suits, but they won't do you, Peter. Dewi's work gear will be more suitable. I'll ask Becky to fetch one out for you."

"Dewi's about my size?" Kaine asked.

"Not really," Cadwallader shot back, smiling, "you'll have to roll up the legs and arms a bit. I just thought you'd be upset if I said you could wear Fan's gear."

He pronounced it "Van's gear".

"By 'Fan', I take it you mean Myfanwy, your sixteen-year-old daughter?" Kaine asked, one eyebrow raised, the other lowered into a mock scowl.

Cadwallader laughed and clapped Kaine on the shoulder.

"No offence, Peter. But Fan's from farming stock. Already taller than her mother and just as solid."

Kaine refused to rub his smarting shoulder, nor did he check it for dislocation.

"None taken, Gwyn. But I wouldn't let Myfanwy hear you call her 'solid'. I doubt many teenage girls would appreciate that description, especially from her father."

Cadwallader kept laughing.

"Wouldn't dare, Peter. That girl of mine can already match me in an arm wrestle. Now, I need to freshen up for tea. Do you know where you're staying?"

"I assume I'm bunking with Adrian?"

"Oh no, mun. Adrian's with his sister in the Lodge. We can't have you in with them. Unmarried singles under the same roof and unchaperoned? What would the minister say? No, you're in the attic room next to the boy. Er, Rhodri, I mean."

Wonderful.

Kaine shot Rollo a glance, but the former marine refused to meet his eye.

Cadwallader pointed to the staircase.

"Keep on climbing 'til you reach the top and see three doors. Yours is the one on the right. Knowing Becky, she'll have made up your bed already. The door in the middle is *yr ystafell ymolchi* ... I mean, the bathroom." He read the time from his scratched analogue watch. "Afternoon tea will be ready at three o'clock sharp. Don't be late or we'll start without you, and you wouldn't want you to begin work hungry, now. Would you?"

He winked, opened the nearest door, and entered what seemed to be a downstairs cloakroom.

Rollo pointed towards the staircase and moved away from the cloakroom door. Kaine followed.

"Interesting man," Rollo whispered.

"Interesting's one word for it. Eccentric's another," Kaine answered, just as quietly.

"Agreed."

"So, tell me. What's your gut saying?"

Rollo puffed out his cheeks.

"To be honest," he said, still keeping his voice down, "you'd need a fully armed infantry platoon to defend this farmhouse from a frontal assault, and a battalion to protect the land. You've seen it, sir. Open fields, woodland, scrub."

"Are we expecting a frontal attack?" Kaine asked, pulling in his neck.

"Well, no. Of course not. I'm just making a point. The farm's indefensible."

"Have you had the chance to quiz him about the thefts? Dates, times, locations?"

"I tried, but Cadwallader's been a bit offhand about it. Reluctant to talk, you know."

Kaine nodded. "Maybe spending time working the land together will help him warm to us. He might open up."

"Yes, sir. I'm so looking forwards to lugging blocks of stone around a Welsh field all afternoon and evening."

Kaine slapped Rollo's rock-hard stomach with the back of his hand. "You need a bit of graft, Colour Sergeant. Work off some of that middle-aged spread you've developed since getting spliced. I wouldn't want my second-in-command going all soft on me."

"Yes, sir. Very good, sir. We'll see how soft I've become on that wall this afternoon. You could probably do with a bit of a workout your-self, what with all that lounging around in private jets."

"Challenge accepted, Colour," Kaine said. "The first to take a break loses."

"What's the wager? A tenner?"

"Nothing. I doubt Cadwallader would appreciate gambling on his farm. We're playing for pride only. Agreed?"

"You're on, sir."

After shaking hands on the non-wager, Kaine headed out to the car to collect his Bergen.

CHAPTER 20

Monday 22nd May – Evening

Cadwallader Farm, Glyn Coes, Powys, South Wales, UK

"I'm telling you, lass," Cadwallader said, jabbing a fork in the air towards his wife. "Never seen anything like it in my life. Almost put me to shame they did."

The Cadwallader clan and Kaine's party were sitting around the kitchen table, tucking into a huge "supper" that might well have been sufficient to feed the whole of Kaine's old troop.

Myfanwy sat next to her mother, matching her for height and power, and confirming that Cadwallader hadn't exaggerated his daughter's physicality. By her own admission, she played rugby for the village women's team, and lamented the fact that the rules didn't allow her to take on the boys at their own game. She hoped one day to play for Wales. Like her mother, she wore her wavy dark hair cut to shoulder length. She had the health, vigour, and clear complexion of a person brought up in the open air. Unlike her mother, the girl's eyes were hazel, with long dark lashes that didn't need mascara to help them stand out on a pretty, round face.

Beside her and opposite Kaine sat the diminutive and near-silent Rhodri Pierce. With long, sandy hair, pale skin that looked as though it had never seen the sun, his prime distinguishing features were his eyes. Large, deep blue, and partially obscured behind a pair of wire-framed glasses, they rarely looked up from his supper plate. The first time those eyes locked on Kaine's, they carried so much hurt—the same sort of hurt Kaine saw looking back at him in the mirror on his darkest days. In Rhodri Pierce's underdeveloped shoulders, twig-like arms, and the skinny legs dangling from his baggy shorts, Kaine also recognised his twelve-year-old self. He felt an instant empathy and a deep sympathy for the boy.

Unless prompted directly, Rhodri sat in silence, picking at his food, head down. He added nothing to the conversation, apparently lost in his own private world of pain.

"Stuff and nonsense," Becky said after swallowing a mouthful of creamed potatoes, cabbage, and roast lamb.

"It's true, I tell you," Cadwallader continued, still brandishing the empty fork. "Of course, Peter couldn't lift the same sized rocks as Adrian and me, but he wasn't far off, and he kept going forever. Worked faster than we did to make up for it. They hardly even took a break for water. Wouldn't think of it to look at him, but Peter's a powerhouse, he is. Both of them are, really. Finished the work in half the time I expected."

Kaine flushed at Cadwallader's effusive report, but the man wasn't prone to exaggeration. With neither wishing to lose their ridiculous wager, Kaine and Rollo had worked themselves to a near standstill.

During his uncle's report, Rhodri threw a number of cautious and wondrous glances at Kaine as though unable to believe so slightly built a man as Peter Sidings could hold his own with two oversized specimens such as Rollo and Cadwallader. Kaine hoped it would allow him to the lad's world. If Rhodri was being bullied at school, as they suspected, maybe he'd open up to someone closer to him in size and bulk than his huge uncle.

Time would tell. Assuming Cadwallader didn't send them all packing the next day.

Apart from Rhodri, who left most of his food, they cleaned their plates in record time. Despite Lara's silent but frowned reprimand, Kaine copied Cadwallader's actions and mopped the last of his meaty gravy with a hunk of the delicious home-made bread. He placed his knife and fork together on the plate, leant back, and patted his slightly distended stomach.

"Becky, that was wonderful," he said through a sigh. "Thank you."

"Yes," Rollo added. "I needed that. Thanks indeed."

The farmer's wife threw them both a dismissive wave.

"Wasn't just me. Annie helped, too. Insisted on it, she did. Even after all her work in the stables. And you can thank Fan for the gravy. It's your speciality, isn't it, Fan?"

"I do my best, Mam." Myfanwy beamed, casting a furtive peep across the table at Kaine.

The teenager's smile held none of Rhodri's shyness but radiated the confidence of a person happy with their lot in life, and comfortable in their own skin. Kaine wished Rhodri could learn the same things from his cousin.

"We're not finished yet," Becky said, standing and waving for the empty plates. "We've still got pudding to come."

Kaine patted his stomach once more and shook his head.

"Sorry, Becky. I'm podged. Couldn't eat another morsel."

"Me too," Lara said.

She stood and helped Becky pile the dishes into two neat stacks.

"Lightweights," Rollo said, dabbing his lips with a cloth napkin. "I could manage a spot of dessert."

"Excellent, there's a choice of apple pie and cream, or rhubarb crumble and custard," Becky announced.

Rollo chose the pie. Cadwallader and Myfanwy opted for the crumble. The sweet aroma issuing from the oven smelled great, but Kaine really couldn't force in another crumb.

"Rhodri," Cadwallader said, "no pudding for you until you've finished your mains."

The boy looked up at his uncle through cowed eyes.

"I-I'm not hungry, Uncle Gwynfor. M-May I leave the table, please?"

"You've hardly touched your food, boy. We do not allow waste in this house."

"But Uncle—"

"The Good Lord has provided this bounty," Cadwallader announced, pointing at the boy's plate, "and you should be grateful for it."

He clenched a giant fist, making the knuckles crack. Rhodri shuddered, and his lower lip trembled.

"Gwynfor," Becky said, her voice calm and low, "he's done his best, poor lamb. It's all my fault for piling too much on his plate."

Cadwallader shot Kaine a sidelong glance, relaxed the clenched fist, and stretched out his fingers.

"Perhaps you're right, dear," he said, and turned to face the boy again. "But you should try a little more, Rhodri. You need to put some meat on your bones. From tomorrow, we'll reduce your portion size, but we'll also give you a few more chores around the farm other than collecting the post of a morning. Feeding the chickens and collecting the eggs will prob'ly help build your appetite. What d'you say, lad?"

Rhodri's blue eyes widened, and his startled gaze darted around the table. He wore the expression of a prisoner searching for an ally, or a means of escape. Kaine yearned to help the boy, but it wasn't his place to intervene.

"I-I … don't know how," Rhodri whined, fighting to hold back his tears.

"There's nothing to it, lad," Cadwallader said. "Fan will be happy to show you. Won't you, Fan."

Myfanwy focused her bright smile on her father.

"'Course I will, *Tad*. If Rhod takes over in the hen house, it'll give me more time in the morning with the horses."

"And it'll help get you used to working with the animals, lad. It's settled then." Cadwallader's expression showed a degree of finality that allowed no argument.

Rhodri's hands trembled and he lost his fight with the tears, which drizzled down his deathly pale cheeks.

"What time do you check the chickens, Myfanwy?" Kaine asked.

The girl met Kaine's gaze. Her eyes shone with excitement.

"Six o'clock," she said, slightly breathless. "We need to do it early so we don't miss the school bus."

"I've never handled chickens," Kaine said. "Would you mind if I join you? I'd like to see how it's done."

The excited smile stretched out even further.

"No, I don't mind at all. So long as you don't mind getting up at that time in the morning."

Kaine returned her smile. "I'm a former 2 PARA. Early mornings don't hold any fears for me. You okay with me tagging along one day, Rhodri?"

The boy sniffled and swiped away his tears with the heels of his hands.

"N-No, I don't mind," he said, seemingly surprised to be asked.

"Okay, I'll knock on your door at oh-five-fifty hours tomorrow. Okay?"

Rhodri's brows knitted together.

"That's ten to six, Rhodri," Kaine said.

"I know," he said, blinking rapidly to clear his eyes, "I learnt all about military time from *Call of Duty*. H-Have you ever played?"

The lad's excitement showed in his rapid speech, and in the fact that he hadn't strung so many words together in one go since he'd returned from school. He had a strong Midlands accent, which stood out clear against all the Welsh voices around the table. No wonder he found it difficult to settle in at a school full of home-grown locals.

Kaine shook his head.

"Afraid not, Rhodri. Maybe you can take me through it sometime?"

"Yes, it's great. You can set up battles and patrols and skirmishes and choose your weapons. My favourite is the Armalite AR-15—"

Cadwallader slammed the flat of his hand down on the table.

Rhodri jumped and folded in on himself.

"War games!" Cadwallader roared. "Is that what you do on that *cyfrifiadur* of yours all day long? War games?"

Rhodri cowered under his uncle's furious onslaught. Kaine's heart went out to the lad. Rollo's bunching chin muscles told Kaine he felt the same way. Lara tried to keep her expression blank, but colour rose to her cheeks—whether in anger or embarrassment, Kaine couldn't tell.

"We thought you were using it to do your homework, boy!"

"But I-I do, Uncle Gwynfor. I do."

"Is that true, boy?"

"Y-Yes, sir. Honestly."

Cadwallader turned to his daughter. "Fan?"

"*Ie, Tad?*"

"You know how to remove all the games from his computer? Delete them, I mean."

Myfanwy hesitated. She glanced at the weeping boy before saying, "Yes, *Tad*."

"Soon as you've finished loading the dishwasher, do that for me and make sure he can't reload it. Right?"

Myfanwy nodded slowly. "*Ie, Tad*. I can set up the parental controls," she said.

Again, her reluctance was evident and appeared genuine. Kaine saw no evidence of the triumph of one sibling lording it over another.

"Please don't," Rhodri begged his cousin.

"Rhodri," Cadwallader said, "you can use your computer for schoolwork only and that's my final word on the subject. We'll review these parental control things when you've proven yourself reliable and hard-working. But there will be no 'war games' under this roof. Do I make myself clear, boy?"

A teary-eyed Rhodri sniffled and lowered his head.

"Yes, Uncle Gwynfor. M-May I leave the table now, please?"

"Yes, you may. Help your cousin clear the dishes. And don't make a noise while you're doing it."

Silence fell, apart from the lad's sniffling and the muffled rattling of dishes, and it dragged on until the youngsters had finished loading the dishwasher, Rhodri had left the kitchen, and Myfanwy had reclaimed her chair.

Once outside, Rhodri's shouted words, "I hate this place! Everyone's horrible," made their way through the closed door, as did his footfalls as he tramped up the stairs.

"*Annwyl, Duw,*" Cadwallader muttered, eyes closed, head bowed, hands clasped tightly together. "*Rho nerth imi.*" He continued in a similar vein but lowered his voice to a mumble.

Kaine slid a glance at Lara who shrugged and shook her head. They both turned to Becky. Rollo studied his hands.

Becky sighed. "He's asking the Divine Lord for strength and guidance."

Cadwallader stopped praying and looked up.

"My apologies for that outburst," he said, "but the boy does try my patience. I hate raising my voice to him after all he's suffered, but ..." He scrubbed his careworn face with his hands and then lowered them to the table. "I cannot have *war games* played in this house. Do you understand, Peter?"

"Your house, your rules, Gwynfor," Kaine said, refusing to answer the question directly.

"I try to treat the boy the same way I treated Dewi and Fan at that age, but all I do is end up sounding like an angry bully. He's in pain. I can see that. ... Am I being too hard on him, d'you think?"

"Not for me to say," Kaine answered. "You can only do what you feel is best."

Cadwallader shook his head slowly, sadness deepening the creases on his angular face.

"The way he talked to you, Peter. Excited, you know. He never speaks to me that way. Annie, Adrian," Cadwallader said, looking up, "do you think I'm being too hard on the boy?"

Rollo pursed his lips and shook his head. Lara took a breath and looked as though she wanted to say something but must have decided against it. Eventually, she shook her head, too.

Becky broke the short silence.

"He's not the same as the others, Gwynfor. He's much more sensitive. Sharon tried her best, but she was too soft on him. Didn't have a husband to help her. The nasty wastrel left them when Rhodri was little more than a toddler ..." She made the sign of the cross and shook her head. "Give him time, *cariad*. He'll toughen up."

He'll have to in this house.

Becky placed her hands on the table and used them to push herself to her feet. "Now," she said, "it's way past time for pudding. Peter, Annie, are you sure you don't want any?"

All appetite gone, Kaine raised both eyebrows.

"Not for me but thank you for the offer."

"Nor me," Lara said.

Rollo took his lead from the others and also refused, going against his grain.

"Oh dear," Cadwallader said, "that's done it. I've gone and ruined everyone's appetite. I'll go upstairs later, after the boy's calmed down. I'll try to make my peace with him."

"Good idea, *Tad*," Myfanwy said, accepting her bowl of crumble and pouring on a generous serving of thick, deep yellow custard. "He's a good lad, really. Just needs to learn to fit in a little better. If he played rugby it would help."

"I thought he *did* play," Cadwallader said. Another frown deepened the ridges on his forehead.

"No, *Tad*. He gets changed into his kit, but then hangs around on the fringes, avoiding the ball at all costs. Shame really, because he's lightning fast. Would make a really good winger."

"A winger?" Cadwallader scoffed. "What on earth makes you say that?"

"I saw him run once ..." She blushed and stopped talking.

She scooped up another spoonful of pudding, but let the spoon hover over her bowl, undecided.

"When was this?" Kaine asked.

The girl lowered the spoon and her eyes, but she didn't respond.

"Fan," Cadwallader said, his tone insistent. "When did you see him running? I've never seen him do anything but shuffle about this place, dragging his feet."

Becky spoke next.

"Myfanwy," she said, "answer your father, child."

A pained expression crossed the girl's face.

"It was at dinner break last Wednesday. A couple of the older boys were chasing him. Taunting him about his accent, you know? He left them in the dust. A mean sidestep he has on him, too. He'd have gotten clean away from them if he hadn't run straight into Frankie Hughes. Bounced off him, he did. Fell into a puddle of mud."

"Is that why his *trowsus* were so filthy after school that day?" Becky asked. "He told me he'd fallen over."

"Some big boys were chasing your little cousin and you let them?" Cadwallader growled.

"It happened over on the far side of the playing fields. I couldn't do anything about it at the time. I did cheer him on, mind," she added, nodding.

"What happened when the 'big boys' caught him?" Rollo asked, his growl matching that of their host.

He hated bullies almost as much as Kaine.

"Nothing," she answered, through an embarrassed smile.

"Nothing?" Lara asked, tilting her head towards the girl, and making it clear she wasn't impressed by the way Myfanwy looked after a family member either.

"That's right, nothing," she said, on the defensive. "Ronnie Jones and Huw Parry just stood there, pointing at him and laughing their stupid heads off."

"And Rhodri?" Kane asked. "What did he do?"

"He tried to pick himself up but slipped again. By the time I reached him, he was crying his little eyes out. I felt so sorry for him. The whole school was laughing."

"Is that it?" Cadwallader demanded, still glowering at his daughter. "Didn't you help?"

The girl straightened in her chair, offended.

"'Course I did, *Tad*. I helped him up and took him to the changing rooms so he could dry himself off. He still had a towel in his PE kit, see? I also stood guard to make sure no one went in to have a go at him, and then I ..." She lowered her head to hide an embarrassed glow.

"And then you what?" Cadwallader demanded, rolling his hand forwards, insisting she kept going.

Myfanwy winced. "I'm not proud of it, *Tad*. But no one messes with my cousin and gets away with it."

"Myfanwy Cadwallader," Becky said, placing both hands flat on the table in front of her, "what are you not proud of?"

"After Rhodri had sorted himself out, I um ... well, I gave Ronnie Jones and Huw Parry a taste of their own medicine."

"In what way?" Cadwallader asked, glancing at his wife, who hadn't taken her eyes from Myfanwy.

"I pushed them into the same puddle and held their faces under the muddy water for a bit. Not so long as they'd drown, mind. Just long enough so they'd remember. I also made them apologise to Rhodri in front of the whole school and promise never to make fun of his accent ever again. Sorry, *Tad*."

"What are you sorry for, girl?"

"You taught us to turn the other cheek, but I couldn't stand by and let them pick on Rhodri just 'cause he's different, could I?"

"No, Fan, you couldn't," Cadwallader said, both his voice and his face softening. "And I'm proud of you, *merch*. You're a good girl."

Myfanwy sat up straighter, and her smiled returned. "Thanks, *Tad*." She picked up her spoon and returned her attention to her pudding.

"Those two lads, Ronnie and Huw," Kaine said, "how old are they?"

The girl chewed rapidly and swallowed her food before answering.

"They aren't younger than me if that's what you're worried about. That would make me as bad as they are. No, they're in my year. We're about the same age. Smaller than me, of course, but there were two of them and only one of me. So, it *was* fair, right?"

Kaine nodded. "Yes, it was fair. You did well."

"Thank you ... Mr Sidings."

"Please, call me Peter."

She paused a moment before saying a hushed, "Thank you, Peter."

Myfanwy fluttered her long eyelashes at him, blushed, and returned her concentration to the dwindling remains of her rhubarb crumble.

Lara covered her face with a hand, trying not to make it look like a facepalm. Rollo winked at Kaine but made sure to hide it from the teenager. He wouldn't have wanted to embarrass the lass.

Yeah, yeah. Very funny.

They settled down to watch three large bowls of pudding disappear in record time.

"If you like," Cadwallader said, speaking between mouthfuls, "after dinner I'll show you the fastest way up to Great Scar. It's the highest point for miles. You'll be able to see most of the farm from there. I'll also point out where the stock disappeared from."

"Thanks, Gwyn," Kaine said. "That'll be a great help."

"Not sure what you can do about it, mun. They were taken from different fields and on different days of the week. No pattern that I can see."

"Random dates and sites of entry? Doesn't make it any easier to predict or prevent future attacks," Kaine commented, staring hard at the big farmer.

"Attacks? I wouldn't call them *attacks*, mun."

"What would you call them?"

"Robberies is what they are. That's all. *Attacks* makes it sound personal."

"These thieves are targeting your farm, stealing from you, damaging your livelihood. I'd call that personal, wouldn't you?"

Cadwallader hiked up his shoulders in a shrug and met Kaine's stare straight on. "Looking at it that way, I suppose you're right. It *is* personal."

"Do you have the dates of the robberies? We might be able to see a pattern you've missed."

"Fan, you've got all the *incidents* on one of those spreadsheet things of yours, haven't you?"

Myfanwy scraped her bowl clean and pushed it forwards.

"Yes, *Tad*. It's on my laptop in my bedroom. I'll go get it. Can I leave the table?"

Without waiting for an answer, the teenager shot to her feet and hurried from the kitchen, not taking her eyes from Kaine until she'd passed his chair. As with Rhodri, her scampering footfalls on the bare wooden treads echoed through the hall and into the kitchen.

"She's a good girl," Lara said to Becky, her smile sweet and innocent. "You should be proud of her."

"We are, *annwyl*. We are indeed."

Seconds later, the scurrying footsteps fired up again, growing louder as they descended the stairs. A breathless Myfanwy burst back into the kitchen, carrying a solid-looking laptop, covered in faded stickers. She retook her seat, flipped open the lid, and started tapping. All ten fingers flew over the keyboard. Kaine smiled. Today's youth had grown up with tech. To them, typing had become second nature. It made his two-fingered pecking even more of an embarrassment.

"Here it is," she announced, a proud smile replacing the frown of concentration. She spun the laptop around enough for the screen to face Kaine. "See?"

He glanced at the screen but couldn't make out the tiny numbers and text in the cells.

"Fan," Cadwallader said, "print it off, please. It'll be dark soon and I promised to take Peter and Adrian up to Great Scar."

"Can I come?" she asked, practically bouncing on her chair.

"No, *annwyl*," Becky said. "You have homework and chores to do before bedtime. Those horses won't feed themselves. You know that."

"Oh, *Mam*!"

With those two words and the way she delivered them—eyes lowered, shoulders dropping—Myfanwy's age fell from sixteen going on twenty, to sixteen going on twelve.

In deference to the girl's feelings, Kaine tried not to show any amusement.

Lara raised her hand.

"Fan, I'll help you feed the ponies, if you like. I'd love to look in on Bright Star. She's not far off, now."

"Are you sure, *annwyl*?" Becky asked. "You've already done so much."

"No, it's fine. I love horses. Before coming here, I hadn't had the chance to be around any for months and months." She flashed a glance at Kaine and added a cute grin.

"Right, now," Cadwallader said. He pressed his hands together and lowered his head in prayer. Becky and Myfanwy assumed the same posture.

Cadwallader, who had said grace in Welsh before the meal, spoke in English for the benefit of his guests.

"Dear Lord, we humbly thank you for the great bounties you have bestowed upon this humble family. Amen."

Becky, Myfanwy, Lara, and Rollo all repeated the "Amen".

Kaine couldn't force himself to speak.

After a moment's quiet reflection, Cadwallader stood.

"Now then, gentlemen," he said. "Are you ready?"

Can't wait.

CHAPTER 21

Monday 22nd May – Evening

Cadwallader Farm, Glyn Coes, Powys, South Wales, UK

The grandly named "Lodge" turned out to be the largest of four detached buildings partially hidden from the main farmhouse by the barn and the stables. Built over a century earlier for labourers and their families, it stood two storeys tall and commanded almost as good a view of the valley as its grander companion, the farmhouse. Two bedrooms and a basic bathroom upstairs, and a large kitchen-diner downstairs, it hardly met the requirements of its imposing name, but Kaine had endured far less comfortable billets. Not that it mattered since he would have to decamp to his cramped bedroom in the loft to hit the sack—and he'd have to do it before Cadwallader's midnight curfew. Still, they wouldn't be in Wales for long.

Hopefully.

Kaine, Lara, and Rollo, huddled around the dining table, making ready to review the printed spreadsheets Myfanwy had hand-delivered before reluctantly heading back to the farmhouse. She left them with a "See you in the morning, Peter," but nothing for the others.

"Don't know what you've got, sir," Rollo said, unable to stop himself chuckling, "but the poor lass is smitten. Must be your after-shave. What d'you reckon, Doc—I mean, Annie?"

"Possibly," Lara answered, also grinning. "Can't be his boyish charm since he doesn't have any."

Kaine sliced a hand through the air, trying to cut off the frivolity. "Don't be so ridiculous. I'm the same age as her father!"

"It's not all that ridiculous," Lara said, her tone considered and her expression slightly more serious even though her eyes still sparkled. "When I was her age, I had a crush on my father's best friend."

"You did?" Rollo asked, eyes wide, playing along.

"Leyland Morris," she said, nodding. "Sleepy blue eyes and a deep, rasping voice that made my insides tremble."

"Leyland Morris?" Rollo scoffed. "You sure he was a bloke and not a vintage car?"

"Oh no," she said, "Leyland was a man, alright. All man."

"A bit like our Staff Sergeant, then," Rollo said, refusing to let it lie.

Kaine leant against the straight back of his less-than-comfortable dining chair. "Pack it in, you two. We've got work to do."

"Yes, Peter," Rollo said, and straightened his face.

"Will you promise me one thing, Ryan?" Lara asked.

Kaine sighed. "Go on."

"Please let the poor girl down gently. Teenage crushes can be every bit as serious as the real thing."

Kaine chewed the inside of his cheek, searching for patience and struggling to find it.

"Okay, I promise. You finished now? Can we get started?"

"Yes, sir," she said, tipping a finger to her temple in perhaps the least respectful salute he'd ever seen.

"Oh," Rollo said, "before I forget, I finally heard from Baz Jericho."

"What did the old soak have to say?" Kaine asked, more than a little happy to be changing the subject.

"Baz thinks most highly of you too, sir."

Nearly two years on from the event, Kaine still had trouble remembering all the details of Jericho's retirement bash. He wondered whether the refurbishments to the venue, *The Harbour Arms*, Poole, had been wholly successful. They'd certainly charged enough in damages. Over the years, the SBS base, Hamworthy Barracks, had built a fierce reputation for celebrating whenever one of the team lived long enough to reach retirement age. Baz Jericho's retirement celebrations had done nothing but add to the legend.

Jericho's new life, as part-time reporter for *Soldier Magazine*, the official publication of the British Army, made him the go-to guy for in-house news and gossip, and Rollo kept in touch on a regular basis.

"What did he have to say about the activity outside Battle Fawr?"

Rollo scrunched up his face. "The boffins are testing a new range finder. The artillery field trials have been on the calendar for months. Like I said, nothing to do with us, sir. We won't even hear them firing unless the wind's in the right direction."

"Excellent. One less thing to worry about." Kaine read the time on his watch. Less than two hours until his host's curfew. "Let's get down to business, shall we?"

He picked up the neat stack of paper Myfanwy had left and distributed a copy to each, and they settled down to read.

"So, what's the first thing you notice?" Kaine asked, waving a hand at the printed spreadsheets.

Rollo cast an eye over his copy.

"There are far more than the four incidents Becky told us about. Myfanwy's done a bang-up job with collating the data. Apart from the nuisance phone calls, which are nothing more than annoyances, I count ten incidents that match the 'serious' criteria. All occurred overnight. The police were called for five. They only attended the ones related to the theft of sheep and the attempt to burn down the stables. And did nothing useful."

"Why not?" Kaine asked, wanting Rollo to confirm his interpretation of the data. A second opinion was always valuable.

"On each occasion, the police didn't arrive until the day after the Cadwalladers called them in."

"Even for the attempted arson?" Lara asked.

"Yep. For that one, they turned up first thing—which for them meant eleven hundred hours."

"What's the police force in these parts?" Kaine asked.

"Just a minute."

Lara grabbed her mobile from the table, thumbed a search string into the browser, and squinted to read the results.

"Around here it's the Dyfed-Powys Police," she said, frowning. "Wow. They cover a huge geographical area. Their patch runs all the way from the southwest coast to the English border. Nearly nine thousand square kilometres." She enlarged the map on her screen, held up the phone for a moment to show Rollo and Kaine, and continued reading. "It says here, they have less than twelve hundred officers to police the whole area."

"It's no wonder they're so stretched," Kaine muttered. "What's the population on their patch?"

"Er ... around half a million permanent residents, but that swells with holidaymakers in the summer months."

"The nearest police station's in Brecon, I suppose?" Kaine asked.

"Yes," Lara said, nodding, "but it closes overnight. The nearest full-time station is in Cardiff, which is operated by the South Wales Police."

"During the day, Cardiff is a ninety-minute drive from here," Rollo said.

Kaine twisted his lips in a grimace and tilted his head. "At night and on blue lights, they'd be faster, but there's bound to be a mobilisation delay." He leant forwards and took a short breath. "Unless there happens to be a patrol in the area, I'd say the crims can count on at least a ninety-minute window to escape from the moment the alarm's raised. Basically, we're on our own here."

"Which gives us the advantage," Rollo said. He rubbed his hands together and allowed a wolf-like grin to form, showing his readiness for the operation. "I hate it when bad people take advantage of good ones."

Me too.

"Okay, moving back to the spreadsheets, do you see anything else?" Kaine asked, looking at Lara.

She lowered her phone to the table and picked up her sheet of paper. "The incidents are becoming more frequent and more costly. Looks like a concerted attempt to drive the Cadwalladers out of business."

"Someone wants to take over the farm, you think?"

"Possibly," she said. "If so, neither Becky nor Gwyn has mentioned anyone making an offer."

"Do you think Gwyn's holding out on Becky?"

"Could be," Rollo answered. "He definitely rules the roost here. Wouldn't surprise me if he keeps business matters to himself."

"Maybe you should ask him?" Lara said, looking at Kaine.

"Will do, when the time's right." Kaine nodded. "If someone wants them out of the farm, it will give us a suspect and someone to lean on. And I agree with you, there's no way these are random acts. It's a concerted attack, alright." He fell silent and pored over his copy. "She's good, though, isn't she," he said after a few moments.

"Who, sir? Your young girlfriend?"

"Don't go there, Rollo," Kaine snapped. "Not even in jest. But, to answer your question, yes, Myfanwy. She's given us the dates, times, and locations of every incident, which should prove useful." Like Rollo had done moments earlier, Kaine rubbed his hands together, although he refused to resort to a wolfish snarl.

"You've had an idea?" Lara asked.

"I have."

Lara and Rollo hunched closer to the table.

"Care to enlighten us, sir?"

Kaine grabbed a pen from the table and marked a cross on each cell where the livestock were taken.

"Here," he said. "On the 29th of April, and the 3rd and 11th of May, the thieves made off with twenty, thirty, and thirty-five sheep, respectively. Agreed?"

Rollo and Lara nodded.

"And?" she asked.

"They must have had transport. I can't see our boys driving a flock of stolen sheep over the fields on horseback or using quad bikes, can you?"

"Sir, I know you've just returned from the Wild West where they made an industry out of stealing cattle," Rollo announced, "but no, I can't see them herding the sheep away on horseback. Or on quad bikes."

"Okay, I get you," Lara said. "But there aren't any traffic cameras for miles. And we can't exactly expect the police to trace all the trucks in the area large enough to hold thirty-odd sheep. They don't have the manpower."

"Or the inclination," Rollo added. "A few dozen missing sheep isn't a high enough priority for them."

"I know," Kaine said, adding a smile.

"Where are you going with this, Ryan?"

"There's a top-secret MoD camp just up the road. The one we passed this morning."

"What about it?"

"And ..." Kaine added, ignoring the question, "Special Forces have been running selection test assessments and training courses on the Beacons for decades. We've yomped these hills ourselves often enough, remember."

"How could I ever forget?" Rollo asked, adding a theatrical head-shake and shudder.

"Ryan, where are you going with this?" Lara repeated, this time with exaggerated patience.

Kaine raised a hand and pointed at the ceiling.

"What's the betting there's at least one military satellite up there, taking pictures of the area the whole time?"

Rollo clicked his fingers and excitement shone in his eyes.

"Of course!" he said. "Why didn't I think of that?"

"We have a couple of very gifted friends. I imagine at least one of them might be able to give us access to satellite photos of the farm for the nights in question, don't you?"

Lara shook her head. "Sabrina won't be in a fit state to hack into military satellites for a while. Her grandfather won't allow it for a start. Which leaves us with Corky."

"Okay," Kaine said. "Corky it is then. Let's give him a shout. I take it you have a comms unit handy? I left mine in my room."

"I'm on it, sir." Rollo stood. "Won't be long."

He left the room and climbed the stairs, his tread much lighter than would be expected of a man his size.

"Alone at last," Kaine said, after a door upstairs closed as Rollo entered his room. "Are we okay, love?"

"Not really. Don't ever abandon me in a foreign country again without discussing it first. Okay?"

"I'll try."

"You'll try? You'll try!" She clenched her jaw but kept her voice down. "That's not good enough! What you did in Paris was unforgivable."

He raised both hands in an attempt to placate.

"Lara, I don't want to lie to you. I can't promise something that's out of my control. What if I'm called away at a moment's notice? The police call it 'exigent circumstances', by the way." By way of an apology, he shot her a lopsided smile. "Look, I will promise not to do anything underhanded like I did in Paris. Okay?"

He reached out to take her hand, but she snatched hers away.

"We'll talk about this later," she said. "When we have more time."

"Good idea," he said, lowering his head in an act of deep contrition.

"I still haven't forgiven you."

"I know, and I'm sorry. But in my defence, I only did it to protect you."

"So you keep saying, but you make me sound like a liability, Ryan. How many times do I have to prove myself? We're in this together, you and me. At least, I thought we were."

"I dragged you into this life, and it's my job to keep you safe."

"We've been through this before. We need to work together. Safety in numbers, right?"

"Right."

No arguing with that logic.

"You can't act alone," she continued. "There are plenty of people who want to help you."

And plenty more who'd like to see my head on a silver platter.

"Yes, love. I know."

Lara reached out and squeezed his hand. He enjoyed the warmth of her grip.

"We're a team, Ryan. A partnership. I feel safer with you than with anyone else." Her gaze slid up to the ceiling. "Even Rollo."

He nodded. "I get that, love. I really do. Are we good now?"

"No, we're not. But ... I will let you earn my forgiveness. Probably."

Her gentle smile lifted his spirits.

"Might take a while, though," she added.

Above their heads the floorboards creaked rhythmically. Rollo had started pacing his room.

Kaine cleared his throat.

"So," he said, "where were we?"

"The satellites. Okay, let's assume Corky can access the pictures. How's that going to help?"

"Have you seen the quality of satellite imagery these days?"

She arched an eyebrow.

"Not recently. Why?"

"Assuming there was no cloud cover on the nights in question, and the azimuth is low enough—"

"The azimuth?"

"Sorry. I mean the horizontal angle of the satellite in relation to the object it's photographing. Assuming the azimuth is good enough, we should be able to read the registration number of any vehicle used in the robberies."

"The picture resolution is that good?"

"Given the air is so clear in the Beacons, yes, it is."

"Wow. And we can use the DVLA's database to trace the owners of the truck?"

"Exactly."

"And if this azimuth thing is wrong?"

"With luck," Kaine answered, "we should be able to follow the truck all the way home, which I'm guessing, will either be a nearby farm or a slaughterhouse."

Lara winced.

"Sorry, love," he said, "but I'd put money on a butcher being involved in this somewhere along the line. It's much easier to hide cuts of meat than whole, live sheep. Worst case scenario, they could transport the sheep across the border into England and maybe onto the Continent. In which case ..." He shrugged and let the thought trail off.

"Sheep are tagged, you know."

"They are?"

She nodded. "Of course. Farmers are required to add an EID tag set when the lambs reach nine months old. The EID includes a unique flock number, year of birth, the names of the sire, dam, and so on. They're used for quality control and to prevent theft."

"Ah, I see. But there must be ways to bypass these tags," Kaine said.

"I imagine so. No security system is foolproof."

"How true."

Upstairs, a door closed and floorboards creaked, as did the staircase. Rollo re-entered the room, his expression thoughtful.

"Did Corky give you a hard time?" Kaine asked.

"Nope. He didn't even answer."

"Really? That's a first."

"Hmm. Believe it or not, he left a recorded message."

"What did it say?"

"'Corky can't answer the comms right now, he's on a break. Don't know when he'll be back, neither.' Or words to that effect."

Kaine rubbed his chin.

"That's a shame. He's been even more stroppy than usual recently. Maybe we've pushed his generosity too far."

"He's only ever done what he wanted to, Ryan," Lara said.

"I know, but we've been relying on him rather a lot lately. He's pulled my plums out of the fire more than once. If you'll excuse the expression."

"Expression excused. So now what are we going to do?" she asked, glancing from Kaine to Rollo.

Kaine arched his back and stretched his arms over his head. "We'll have to do things the old school way."

"Yep," Rollo said, nodding slowly and stretching out a yawn. "I was afraid of that."

"Old school?" Lara asked.

"We're gonna be staying up late and missing some sleep. Well, at least Rollo and I are going to be missing sleep. Lara, you're excused boots."

"What does that mean?"

Kaine shot Rollo a look, giving him permission to answer.

"You get a pass."

"Why?"

"Sorry about this but, put simply," Kaine said, wincing in apology, "you're not skilled enough. We'll be up through the night on a watching brief."

"All night, every night?" she asked, disbelief in her voice.

"Until the next attack at least," Kaine admitted.

"That could be days or weeks."

"Yep, I know. And we can't tell anyone about it, or the news might get out. Not even the Cadwalladers."

"Night watch behind enemy lines," Rollo announced.

"That's right," Kaine agreed. "We're mounting a clandestine operation in the middle of Wales. At least there won't be any insurgents hell-bent on putting a bullet through our foreheads—"

"Or an IED up our tailpipe."

"Yes indeedie."

Lara jumped to her feet. "Will you two be serious for one moment? There's nothing funny about any of this. You can't stay up all night and sleep all day without someone noticing."

"Who said anything about sleeping during the day?" Kaine asked, glancing at Rollo, and nodding for him to take over.

"For the time being, we'll be catching our zeds as and when we can. What do you say, sir? Four-hour shifts through the night until the support arrives?"

"Support?" Lara asked.

Rollo nodded. "When I couldn't get through to Corky, I took the liberty of calling in reinforcements. Didn't think you'd mind, sir," he said looking at Kaine.

"Good idea. We'll need warm bodies to mount a twenty-four-hour, fully supported operation."

"If they're spotted, they can pass themselves off as a military unit on manoeuvres," Rollo said.

"So," Lara interjected, "some of the guys are going to camp up on the hill and watch for the enemy?"

Kaine and Rollo nodded.

"Yep, that's about the size of it," Kaine said.

"And what will they do when they spot them?"

Kaine scratched an itch at the side of his left eye. "That, Annie, will depend on who the enemy are, if and how they are armed, and how they react to being snatched up by a team of men in face masks and full battledress."

Lara's face paled by a few shades.

"Are you expecting the rustlers to be armed?"

Kaine shrugged. "Not necessarily, but we certainly will be. I can't ask my people to go into battle unprepared. Who knows what the enemy's capable of doing."

"I don't like it. I really don't."

"Neither do I, love. But we have to prepare for the worst—"

"And hope for the best?"

"No, love. I'll leave hope to you and the Cadwalladers. Okay, Adrian. Ideally we're looking for up to four people. Who's available at short notice?"

Rollo grimaced. "I'm afraid we'll be pretty thin on the ground for the next few days."

"Cough and Stefan?"

"They're currently in the Shetlands. Can't reach here until Thursday at the earliest. Travel issues. Who knew?" Rollo shrugged.

"What are they doing all the way up there?" Lara asked.

"Would you believe they're working security for a heavy metal rock group?"

"I'd believe anything of those two."

"What's the band called?" Kaine asked, eyebrows raised. "Anyone I'd know?"

"Ever heard of *The Wild Axemen*?" Rollo asked.

Kaine screwed up his face. "Nope. A guitar band, I take it."

Lara held up and waggled her mobile. "Want me to find them on YouTube?"

"Oh Lord, spare me," Kaine answered, cutting his hand through the air. "I'll take a pass on heavy metal. If it were *Oasis* or *Blur* ... that'd be different."

"Some of the younger guys would call that 'Dad Rock'," she said, grinning.

"And those same guys would end up cleaning latrines for a week." Kaine turned to Rollo again. "What about Fat Larry and Slim?"

Rollo's face crumpled into another wince. "On close protection duty in Dubai. Can't free themselves up until the end of next week. I have them on standby in case this drags on longer than we'd like."

Rollo continued the roll call, rattling off the details from memory. As standard practice, they left no paper trail.

"Paddy's in Ireland visiting family. He's on his way. Should be here by Friday afternoon. Saturday morning at the latest."

"PeeWee?" Kaine asked.

"Out of commission. Fell and broke his collarbone on a training run. Won't be fit for active duty for at least a month, maybe two."

"Chances are we'll be finished here well before then. What about Nate and Jeff?"

"Unavailable. On an op in Slovakia. Can't get here for a couple of weeks. There is some good news, though. Connor Blake's between jobs. Should be here by Thursday morning. He'll be bringing us a motor. We can't rely on that crappy little Astra for too long. And I've given him a shopping list."

"Such as?" Kaine asked.

"He'll bring some basic camping equipment. We'll set up a bivouac on the far side of the valley"—he pointed through the kitchen window—"behind Great Scar. I'll start shipping in the more specialist equipment from Wednesday. Military equipment."

Kaine nodded. "Good."

"But," Rollo continued, "until Connor and Paddy arrive, we'll be on our own."

"Not a problem."

HALF AN HOUR LATER, AFTER KAINE HAD OUTLINED THE RULES OF engagement, he called the briefing to a close.

"I can't be seen to stay after curfew," he quipped. "Wouldn't want to upset our hosts."

"No, we wouldn't," Lara agreed.

She glanced expectantly at Rollo. Quick on the uptake, he took the hint.

"I'll give you two a moment," he said, standing. "I'll go prep for tonight."

Once again, he left them alone, climbing the staircase in near silence.

Kaine wandered across to the nearest window, confirmed there were no gaps in the curtains, and held out his hand to Lara. This time, she took it with little hesitation. He helped her to her feet and pulled her into a hug. Their bodies moulded into one and they kissed, long and gentle. Lara broke the embrace first.

"I love you, Mrs Hallam," he whispered into her ear.

She smiled. "I know."

"And?" he asked, hoping for a different response.

She pecked him on the cheek and backed away.

"Nothing more to say?"

"Nope," she answered, her smile a little warmer. "You can keep apologising, though."

"Don't make it easy on a bloke, do you?"

"Nope," she repeated. "Now, off you go, Peter Sidings. You need to show your face in the house, before heading out into the night."

He allowed his shoulders to slump.

"Yes, ma'am. Anything you say, ma'am."

He straightened, snapped out a smart salute, and leant in for another kiss. She returned it, and he headed for the door, a spring in his step and feeling much lighter.

CHAPTER 22

Monday 22nd May – Night

Cadwallader Farm, Glyn Coes, Powys, South Wales, UK

Helped by the single, low wattage outside light, Kaine made his way from the guest house to the rear of the farmhouse and tried the handle on the back door. It turned and the lock clunked open. Becky had left an internal light on for him, but otherwise, the kitchen stood warm, dark, and deserted. He headed towards the staircase.

A small canvas bag on the kitchen table drew his attention, as did the folded sheet of paper sticking out beneath it. He freed the paper and read the handwritten note.

PETER,

Since you'll be out and about tonight, I thought you and Adrian might need something to keep you going. I hope you like cheese and pickle sand-

wiches. You'll also find a couple of flasks of coffee to keep you warm, and some sweets for energy.

May the Good Lord bless and protect you for helping us.
Becky.

KAINE SMILED IN APPRECIATION, FOLDED THE NOTE, AND SLIPPED IT INTO his pocket. He left the canvas bag on the table for later and headed through to the back stairs. At the first-floor landing, he paused to listen. Four closed doors. Silence. All asleep. Early risers couldn't stay up late and still function properly in the long term.

He planned to keep Gwyn Cadwallader in the dark as to their ongoing plans. No telling how the giant Welshman would react to armed men camped on his land, even if their sole aim was to protect his family, his property, and his livelihood.

As he grabbed the banister to start the climb to the top floor, a lever handle lowered, and one of the doors creaked open. Myfanwy's face appeared in the gap between door and jamb, her big hazel eyes wide.

Uh-oh.

"Oh," she gasped, "it's you, Peter."

Kaine smiled.

"Sorry to wake you," he said, keeping his voice low, little more than a whisper. "I'm just collecting some things from my room."

She stepped into the corridor, wearing a baggy T-shirt and nothing else. The hem of the T-shirt barely covered her modesty, revealing a pair of long, muscular legs, bare feet, and toenails painted bright red.

Kaine wondered whether her deeply religious parents knew their daughter coloured her toenails.

She took another pace towards him.

"Can I help with anything?" she asked, rushing her words.

Dear God.

Her hazel eyes shone, and a flush darkened her cheeks. Not a brazen temptress, but a nervous teenager stretching her wings, risking everything.

"No thanks, lass. I'm fine," he said, smiling to let her down gently. "Sleep tight, Myfanwy."

"Oh. Okay." She lowered her head and looked up at him through long, dark eyelashes. "I-If you need anything ... anything at all, just let me know."

"I will. Thanks again. Goodnight."

"*Nos da,*" she said. Sadness tinged her voice.

Kaine waited while she backed into her bedroom and softly closed the door. He sighed in relief and climbed the remaining stairs to the top floor two at a time.

He reached his tiny attic room and crouched to avoid hitting his head on the sloping ceiling. Out of pure habit, he ran the check. As expected, the place hadn't been disturbed, and his Bergen remained on the single, metal-framed bed where he'd left it. To reduce the weight, he removed all the rolled-up clothing, and packed it into the cheap pine drawer unit under the small dormer window. In the daytime, the age-misted glass allowed a modest rectangle of natural light into the bedroom, but this long after sunset, the window remained black, foreboding, and curtain free. He stood, hefted the lightened Bergen onto his shoulder, and turned to leave.

Outside, in a darkened corridor lit only by the night light on the first-floor hallway, he paused. A muffled sobbing disturbed the silence. Kaine moved along the hallway, past the adjoining bathroom, and pressed an ear to Rhodri's bedroom door. The boy's sniffling sobs tore at Kaine's heart. He raised a hand to tap on the door but cast his mind back to his twelve-year-old self and lowered it again. At that age, the last thing in the world he'd have wanted was for a total stranger to know he cried himself to sleep.

Quietly, Kaine backed away, leaving the lad to his despair.

Back in the kitchen, he paused long enough to stuff the provisions into his Bergen before heading into the chilly evening air, delighted to be out of the house and away from the kids.

Realisation hit home. He'd rather face an angry mob of Taliban insurgents than a couple of needy kids.

Pitiful coward.

He met Rollo in the courtyard.

"Ready?" Rollo asked, glancing at his wristwatch.

"As always. Let's go."

USING THE ROUTE GWYNFOR CADWALLADER HAD SHOWN THEM THAT evening, Kaine and Rollo climbed a well-worn trail up to Great Scar —an outcropping of old red sandstone that dominated the surrounding area. The steep climb on a gravel-and-rock-strewn track had Kaine panting and straining under the load of his Bergen. The afternoon spent wrangling heavy rocks had taken its toll, and he'd yet to fully recover.

Shape up, old man.

Since becoming a fugitive, he'd been unable to maintain his high-intensity training programme, and his fitness levels had taken a slight hit as a result. Maybe spending a few weeks on a farm would have some side benefits.

Once at the ridge of Great Scar, they set up temporary camp with a perfect view of the valley below. The starlight and gibbous moon provided enough light to pick out plenty of detail.

"I'll take the first shift," Kaine announced.

"Pulling rank again, sir?"

"Only out of necessity. I've got an appointment tomorrow morning, early doors."

"You have?"

He snorted. "I'm going on an egg hunt."

"Ah yes. I remember now." A worried expression crossed Rollo's usually unreadable face.

"What's up?"

"Okay, the kid needs a friend, I understand that, but don't get too close. We can't hang around here for long."

"I know. It's just that ..." Kaine puffed out his cheeks. "Oh, I don't know. The kid's hurting and it's my fault."

"That's what I mean, sir. Rhodri has family. I'm less worried about him than I am about you." Rollo fixed his dark eyes on Kaine. "All I'm saying is don't get too close."

"Yeah, I know. Thank you."

They stopped talking and silence grew around them.

After a few moments, Rollo leant against the flat stone rising near-vertically at their backs. He stretched out his legs allowing his feet to hang over the edge. "This is just like old times."

"Only here, no one's looking to blow our heads off."

"Not that we know of," Rollo said, showing what was for him, an unusual level of pessimism.

"Okay, Colour Sergeant. Snap to it," Kaine said, handing him a pair of Zeiss binoculars he'd taken from his Bergen. "Let's make sure we're on the same page. Read off the clock face to me. Start with the farm at twelve o'clock, which means we're sitting at six."

Rollo groaned and pushed himself away from the rock face. He tucked his boot heels into his rump and braced his elbows on his raised knees to steady the glasses.

"Right," Rollo said. "Listen up. Twelve o'clock sets the farm buildings directly ahead of us. It puts the rise of the eastern valley as afternoon, and the western valley forenoon. All set so far?"

"All set," Kaine said.

"The pond in front of the farmhouse stands at one o'clock. The stable block and paddocks lie between two and three o'clock. Check?"

"Check," Kaine acknowledged, following Rollo's description with his naked eye.

"The road leading to the farm entrance runs in from five o'clock and terminates at the farm, noon."

"Check," Kaine repeated. "We're sitting at six o'clock here. Go back to the farm and head west."

"Okay, right then. We have fields and woods between noon and eight o'clock. Nothing stands out but that burnt oak at ten o'clock.

Then, at eight o'clock, we have a break in the woods and bushes made by a farm lane. Beyond the lane, from seven o'clock to us at six o'clock we have nothing. Nothing that is, but wooded hills, fields, and hedges cut through with farm tracks."

"Agreed," Kaine said.

"Excellent. Are we done now, sir? You're eating into my sleep time." He handed the binoculars across.

"Ten Acre Field," Kaine said, waving a hand towards three o'clock.

"What about it?"

"The terrain dips away. Makes the fields beyond the road something of a blind spot. We'll need to position someone on the other side of the entrance road."

"You or me?" Rollo asked, straightening his legs and preparing to move out.

"Rest easy. It's too late to change positions now. The night will be over before you get down there. We'll address it tomorrow."

"So, who's going to be up here in the cold, and who'll be the other side of Ten Acre Field, in the nice warm Astra? Toss you for it?"

"Wouldn't dream of it," Kaine said. "You can have the crappy Astra. I'd rather be up here in the fresh air."

"Works for me," Rollo said. He stretched out his arms and yawned. "Wake me in four hours."

No, "Thank you, sir"? Typical.

Kaine smiled.

"That rock's likely to act as a sounding board," Kaine said. "Keep the snoring down to a dull roar, will you?"

"Bugger off, sir. I've never snored in my life, and you know it."

"No, Colour Sergeant. Of course you don't."

"Marie-Odile doesn't complain," he grumbled, leaning back.

"Either the poor woman's stone deaf, or she wears earplugs. And talking about your new wife, how's she taking you being away for so long?"

"As far as she's concerned, I'm a defence consultant for the UK government. She understands that I'll have to disappear at the drop of a hat from time to time."

"Nevertheless, if we don't find out who's targeting the Cadwalladers by the time the rest of the team arrives, I'll send you home. Can't have Marie-Odile upset with me for keeping you away for so long."

"Not a chance, sir. I'm staying as long as I'm needed."

"That's just what I'm saying. When Connor and Paddy get here, you'll be superfluous to requirements."

"Ouch. Now you've hurt my feelings."

Kaine snorted. "Feelings? You? Never."

"Ha, ha."

"Get some sleep. That's an order."

"Yes, sir." Rollo crossed his arms, tucked his hands into his armpits, and squirmed lower against the rock face. After a moment, he let out a long sigh.

Kaine reached into his Bergen and dragged out a rolled sheet. He spread it on the lichen-covered ground, dropped to his front, and scrambled closer to his edge of the ridge. The damp rocks smelled of mud and mildew, and the wind ruffled the long hair sticking out below his knitted cap.

Gradually, Rollo's breathing settled into the long slow rhythm of sleep. Kaine smiled. Like so many experienced soldiers, he'd developed the knack of snatching sleep as and when he could.

By the pale light of a billion stars, Kaine spent his watch scanning the valley, identifying each potential point of weakness, of which there were many. The road running along the valley floor gave easy access to most areas of the farm, and the dirt tracks leading off the road granted simple entry to the rest.

Not for the first time in their relationship, he agreed with Rollo. As a military target, the Cadwallader farm was completely indefensible.

CHAPTER 23

Tuesday 23rd May – Early Morning

Cadwallader Farm, Glyn Coes, Powys, South Wales, UK

Sweating and breathing hard after their fast downhill jog from the ridge followed by a three-lap, eyeballs out sprint around the pond— which Kaine won at a canter—he and Rollo slowed to a warm-down trot. As they approached the farmhouse they dropped into a fast walk.

The sun peeked its head over the eastern valley and promised a bright, warm day. A cockerel's raucous crow reinforced the new day's imminent arrival and reminded Kaine of his promise.

"Adrian," Kaine said once he'd recovered enough to talk without struggling for breath.

"Yes, Peter?" Rollo answered, also fully recovered.

"You're slowing down, mate. Too much easy living in France."

Rollo coughed out a short laugh. "Haven't you worked it out yet?"

"Worked what out?"

"A subordinate can't beat a superior officer in a foot race. It wouldn't be seemly. I let you win, sir. Always do."

"Don't give me that nonsense," Kaine said, not missing a beat. "You've never backed down from a challenge in your life."

Rollo cut his stride length to match Kaine for pace.

"Yes, well. I'm heavier than you ... Carrying more muscle bulk. You'll probably always beat me over a short distance. And anyway, I'm a marathoner not a sprinter."

Kaine allowed himself a sideways grin. "Fair enough. Next time, we'll increase the distance a little. How does a twenty-five-kilometre race in full battledress suit you?"

They stopped at the fork in the path where Rollo needed to turn left for the Lodge, and Kaine would bear right to the main house.

"Sorry, sir," Rollo said, straight-faced, looking him directly in the eye. "No can do."

"Why not?"

"We can't leave the farm unprotected for so long, and there's always the doc to consider. Wouldn't be safe."

Kaine snorted. "Excuse accepted, Colour Sergeant. And I'll take it as your acknowledgement of my inevitable victory." He clapped Rollo on the shoulder and had to reach up to do it. "Okay, mate. Go have your shower. I'll see you at brekkie."

He headed towards the farmhouse and left Rollo calling foul.

KAINE RANG THE BELL ON THE FARMHOUSE PORCH AND WAITED. HE huddled in the shelter of the high stone walls, trying to maintain his core temperature. While he stood still, the chill morning wind freeze-dried the sweat on his face. He shivered under its slicing power.

Overnight, a heavy breeze had driven in half a dozen squally showers into the face of Great Scar, and the wind chill factor on the hill had pushed the temperature towards freezing. Exposed as he and Rollo had been on the valley side, their vigil had been unpleasant but otherwise uneventful.

In answer to Kaine's ring, Becky opened the door wide and stepped back into the boot room, giving him room to enter.

"Come in, come in," she gushed. "Friends don't need to ring to enter this house."

Kaine stepped over the threshold and stood, dripping rainwater onto the welcome mat. He swiped moisture from his hair with his hands.

"Oh my goodness, you must be frozen."

"I've had worse nights," he said, smiling.

Much worse.

"Come into the kitchen where it's warm."

"Thanks. I'll remove my boots first."

"Where's Adrian?"

"He's gone straight to the Lodge for a tidy up. Don't worry. As soon has he smells a whiff of breakfast, he'll be battering the door down."

She laughed and disappeared into her domain, the kitchen.

Kaine wiped his muddy boots on the mat, untied his laces, heeled off the footwear, and peeled himself out of his sodden jacket. When he pushed into the superheated kitchen, the sweat poured out of him once again. By way of compensation, the enticing aroma of bacon and sausages frying gently in onions and butter made Kaine's mouth water and his stomach gurgle.

"Sit, sit," Becky said, ushering him towards the kitchen table. "You must be starving."

Kaine shook his head.

"Sorry, Becky. I'm in a rush. I promised to wake Rhodri and see to the chickens with him and Myfanwy. I'll need to shower and change clothes first."

Becky waved him into a dining chair.

"Sit down there, Peter. There's no rush. Indeed, I've just sent the boy back to bed. The poor thing's absolutely exhausted."

"Really?"

She nodded effusively. "Everyone's been up for hours on account of Bright Star delivering us a beautiful jet-black foal in the middle of the night. A colt, it is. One of the Lord's most wondrous creations."

"Up on the ridge we saw the stable lights come on. Thought it must be the foaling. So, Adrian and I missed all the excitement?"

"You have indeed. Horses," she said through a sigh, "I don't know. Contrary creatures never seem to deliver during the day."

"Annie loves horses. I imagine she enjoyed watching the delivery."

"Not just watching," Becky said, beaming. "She helped, so she did. Without her, I don't know what we'd have done. The colt presented breach, you see. That's rear first. Oh my goodness, Annie was amazing. Took over completely. It meant we didn't have to call out Larry Haviland. She saved us a small fortune in vet's bills."

"Shame I missed it. Never seen a foal delivered—except on TV."

"You'd have loved it, Peter. Witnessing the miracle of new life is one of the Divine Lord's most wonderful gifts to humanity. If you like, after breakfast, I'll get someone to take you to see the new foal. The very best thing was that Rhodri took to the little creature right off. Wonderful to see, it was. As a special treat, we're letting him name the foal."

"That's a lovely idea. Is everything okay between Rhodri and Gwynfor this morning?"

"Oh yes. That nasty business last night is all forgotten. My Gwyn always forgives and forgets."

A moment later, she placed a huge pot of tea in the centre of the table. "Help yourself. Breakfast won't be long. I told the others to be here at half past six. You've plenty of time to get ready."

Kaine poured himself a brew and added a splash of milk. He took a sip. The boiling tea scalded his lips, and he blew across the top of the mug. "Mind if I take this upstairs? I'm starting to catch a chill after my jog."

"What? You jogged down from Great Scar?"

"It's not that far."

"No, but it's so steep. Dangerous. All those loose rocks. You could have fallen. Hurt yourselves."

Kaine shrugged. "We took it easy on the crag, and we're used to running over rough terrain. Thanks, but there's need to worry about us, Becky." He showed her his mug. "Do you mind?"

"No, of course not. I've left you out a fresh towel. One of the nice new fluffy ones. And there's plenty of hot water on the go."

"Thanks. Won't be long."

He took another sip to lower the level of liquid, stood, and headed off.

"Take your time. I'll keep everything warm for you."

"Thanks again. Be right back."

Kaine walked his tea from the room and climbed the stairs as quickly as he could without spilling any.

At the top landing, Kaine listened at the door to Rhodri's room, happy to hear nothing but silence. He headed straight for the bathroom, stripped, and folded his sodden clothes into a neat, military wash pile.

Becky hadn't exaggerated. He luxuriated under a powerful waterfall of piping hot water and took longer than his usual sixty seconds to absorb as much heat as possible. The towel, as soft and fluffy as promised, did its job. He wrapped it tight around his waist and picked up the wash pile. He opened the door and walked straight into a red-face Myfanwy Cadwallader. She stood, hand raised, frozen in the process of knocking on the bathroom door.

Her eyes swept over him from head to toe, lingering on the horizontal scar running across his abdomen—a legacy from the first day of his life as a disgraced and wanted man. Whereas he expected to see revulsion on her face, the teenager didn't seem at all fazed by any of his battle scars.

"Oh, I-I'm sorry, P-Peter. *Mam* asked me to tell you breakfast is ready."

"Thanks, Myfanwy. I'll be right down."

He waited for her to move, but she stood still, blocking the way to his bedroom and staring at his chest. He lowered a hand to where he'd tied the towel and grasped the fold tightly. God alone knew what would have happened if the towel had loosened. The girl might have had a screaming fit. Or worse.

"Is there anything else, Myfanwy?"

She jerked herself aware and turned sideways, and seemingly by intent, left him barely enough room to squeeze between her and the wall.

He stood still, growing colder by the second but refusing to shiver.

"Myfanwy, please," he said, meeting her eye and holding her enthralled gaze. "Excuse me."

"Oh, sorry," she said, a shy smile forming. "Not much room up here, is there."

She turned and skipped down the stairs, calling out, "Don't be long, now."

Kaine waited until she reached the first-floor landing before releasing his breath.

Kids.

"Weird," Rhodri said.

Kaine snapped around. He hadn't heard the boy open his door or step into the landing.

Pity's sake, Kaine. Wake up.

"What is?" Kaine asked.

"She's been acting funny ever since you arrived."

"Has she?"

"Yeah." The lad nodded. "All nervous and ... well, funny. Funny strange, you know. Not funny ha-ha." He lifted a hand and pointed. "You've got loads of scars. Is that on account of you being a soldier?"

"Yes, Rhodri. But it's rude to point."

The lad dropped his arm and mumbled an apologetic, "Sorry, Mr Sidings." His hand dropped to his side and gripped the leg of his pyjamas. "I'm always getting things wrong." His lower lip started to tremble. The lad was close to losing it again.

"Have you chosen a name for the colt yet?"

In an instant, Rhodri brightened. His thin lips stretched into a smile, and his eyes gleamed with excitement rather than tears.

"Not yet. I was thinking of Anthracite in honour of all the mines around here. Did you know that anthracite's a coal? The economy of South Wales was built on coal mining."

The boy rattled on, his excitement clear, eyes shining ever brighter. Although a chill breeze whipped up the staircase and leached away all the warmth he'd absorbed from the shower, Kaine didn't have the heart to interrupt the lad. He tensed his muscles and listened patiently.

"Miss Lazenby, she's our history teacher," Rhodri continued, "was telling us all about it. Trouble is, there aren't many active coal mines left in Wales on account of coal being a fossil fuel and burning fossil fuels is bad for the environment. You know that, right? And, anyway, I want to name him something else. Something special."

"Is he pure black?"

Rhodri nodded. "Completely. Even his feet ... I mean his hooves."

"How about Nightwatch? After all, he arrived in the middle of the night, and you'll have to watch out for him."

A thoughtful frown buckled his pale forehead.

"Nightwatch?" he said slowly as though trying the name on for size. "Nightwatch. Yes. Brilliant. I love it. Sounds like something out of *Call of Duty*. Better still, Uncle Gwynfor won't work out the link."

Somewhere in the house an outside door opened, sending another icy blast of chilly air up the centrally positioned staircase. Again, Kaine tensed his abs and suppressed a shiver.

"Sorry, Rhodri. It's perishing up here. Are you going down for brekkie or heading back to bed?"

"Breakfast. I'm starving."

Judging by the way the lad had picked at his supper, he wondered whether the kid had it in him to wolf down a hearty breakfast.

"Me too," Kaine said, grinning, "but we'd better get dressed first, eh?"

The lad looked down at his pyjamas and smiled, too.

"We wouldn't want to shock the ladies," Kaine added. He tousled the lad's unruly mop of blond hair and headed for his room.

"So," Cadwallader said, "how long do you plan to keep up your vigil on Great Scar?"

The table, groaning under the weight of six enormous breakfasts and a normal-sized plate for Rhodri, fell silent. All eyes turned on Kaine, the recognised leader.

"Until the next attack," Kaine said, slicing into the last of his three sausages.

"That could be ages."

"I doubt that. In fact, I'm expecting another visit from your tormentors very soon."

"What makes you think that?" Becky asked.

"Myfanwy's excellent records," Kaine said. He nodded to the teenager, who flushed bright red at the compliment and beamed. "Whoever's targeting the farm has been stepping up their attacks recently. If they follow the pattern, their next visit will likely take place within the next few days."

"Are you sure?" Cadwallader asked.

"As sure as we can be," Rollo answered for Kaine.

As Kaine had predicted, Rollo had blundered into the kitchen the moment Becky began serving breakfast. The Colour Sergeant's ability to sniff out a meal bordered on precognition. Lara arrived shortly afterwards, dressed in preparation for a day in the stables—white T-shirt under a plaid shirt, tight jeans, walking boots, and a cheerful smile.

"And when you do stumble upon some unwanted 'guests', you'll capture them in the act and hand them straight over to the police," Gwynfor said, making it a statement not a question.

"Not necessarily," Kaine said.

Again, all eyes around the table turned towards him. In fact, the only time Myfanwy looked away from Kaine was to scoop another forkful of food into her mouth. Lara's amused patience showed on her beautiful face.

"Peter Sidings," Cadwallader snapped, "I will not have you dispensing summary punishment! Judgement must be left to the Lord and the Welsh courts. If you cannot agree to that, you must leave this house right away. I will have nothing to do with vigilantism."

Kaine lowered his cutlery to the plate and held up both hands as a sign of appeasement.

"That's not what I meant, Gwyn. We have no intention of meting out range justice. If and when the rustlers return, I plan to follow them back to whoever's in charge. The paymaster."

"You think they're being paid to do these horrible things?" Becky asked.

"Don't you?" Kaine asked.

"I never thought—"

"Given the note they left on the stable door," Lara said, "this is personal."

"A note? What note?" Rhodri asked, speaking up for the first time since sitting at the table.

"Never you mind, Rhodri Pierce," Cadwallader said, dropping his voice. "Adults are talking."

Rhodri lowered his head and mumbled an apology. He dug a fork into his last rasher of streaky bacon, sliced off a piece and stuffed it into his mouth.

"As Annie suggested," Kaine said, "these attacks are personal and they're going to carry on until we stop them. And I can't see the person in charge getting his or her hands dirty, can you? Which is why we have to follow the lackeys back to their leader. Back to the source."

Cadwallader frowned and stared into the fire Becky had lit before breakfast as though searching for inspiration. "Put like that, I suppose you're right."

"So, when we find out who's orchestrating these ... incidents, we'll provide you with all the proof you need to take to the police. Is that acceptable?"

Cadwallader slid a surreptitious glance at his nephew, who sat with his head still bowed and still chewing on the same piece of bacon. The boy was definitely earwigging the "adult conversation" but trying hard not to show it.

Eventually, Cadwallader's head dipped in a nod.

"*Ydy, mae'n dderbyniol.* Sorry, I meant to say, yes. That would be acceptable."

The conversation slowed as they tucked into their food. Cadwallader, a man with an appetite to match his enormous frame, finished first. He lowered his knife and fork to his plate, wiped his mouth with a napkin, and folded it into a triangle before placing it on his side plate. Satisfied with its position, he pushed the plates away and turned his bearded face towards the boy, who had made a good fist of clearing his plate. Only one rasher and half a fried egg remained.

"Now then, Rhod," Cadwallader said, his voice warm and low, "it would appear that staying up late and helping in the stables has improved your appetite. *Hogyn da.* Good lad."

The boy's knife scraped on his plate as he cut the last rasher in half, scooped both halves and the egg onto his fork and popped the whole lot into his mouth.

Rhodri nodded and started chewing. He chewed fast, blushing under his uncle's scrutiny. The rest of them looked on in a slightly awkward silence.

Cadwallader waited for the lad to finish before speaking again.

"Now tell me, Rhod. Have you decided on a name for the colt, yet?"

The lad helped his food down with a gulp of milk and nodded.

"Yes, sir," he said. "I have."

"Well," Becky piped up, teacup held close to her lips, "don't keep us in suspenders"—she grinned at her deliberate mistake—"what's his name?"

"Nightwatch," Rhodri announced, pride evident in his smile.

Myfanwy's eyes popped wide. She looked at her father, without doubt understanding the relevance of the name.

"On account of him being born overnight, and I need to watch over him," Rhodri added, looking down at his cleared plate. He seemed to be holding his breath, awaiting his uncle's response.

"Nightwatch? Hmm, Nightwatch," Cadwallader said, as though deep in thought. "Yes, I like it. It's a great name, lad. It's a keeper."

"It is?" Rhodri asked, looking from Cadwallader to Kaine and back. "I can?" The pitch of his voice rose with his excitement.

"Yes, lad," Cadwallader said, breaking out a huge grin. "I'll contact Larry Haviland, the vet"—he glanced at Becky and returned his scrutiny to the boy—"and set the registration in motion. We'll need to have him tagged and inoculated."

"Inoculated?" Rhodri asked.

"Against equine flu and tetanus," Lara said. "Which can be fatal in horses."

"It's nothing to worry about, Rhod," Myfanwy added. "It won't hurt him. If you like, I'll talk you through it. *Tad*, can you arrange the vet's visit for after school?"

Cadwallader nodded. "Yes, okay. Assuming Haviland doesn't mind."

"He won't," Becky piped up, grinning wide. "I'll call him this afternoon. After that nasty business last month, he'll be keen to make amends."

"So," Cadwallader said, rounding on the boy again, "what do you say, Rhodri? Do you want to learn how to look after your horse?"

"My horse?" Rhodri's jaw dropped. "You really mean it?"

"You know me, Rhodri," Cadwallader said, his expression stern. "I never say anything I don't mean. So, are you up for it, lad?"

"Yes, please," he said, the response instant.

"You want to learn to ride, too?"

This time, the lad took a little longer to reply. "Er ... yes. I would."

"That, Rhod," Becky said, "is the correct answer."

"We'll make a cowboy of you yet," Myfanwy added, chuckling.

The chatter around the table grew in volume. Rhodri, sitting next to his cousin, fired question after question at her.

"How many injections will he have? Will they hurt him? What does he eat? Can I brush him? When will he be big enough to ride? Can we go see him?"

Myfanwy answered each query with clarity and patience. On hearing the final question, delivered like an entreaty, Myfanwy turned to her mother.

"*Mam*, may we leave the table, please?"

Becky frowned. "What about school?"

"The bus won't be here for half an hour, Aunty Becky. Please? We're already ready for school, look." Rhodri jumped up and showed everyone his uniform.

"Okay, okay," Becky said, shooing them away. "Off you go."

Rhodri grabbed hold of Myfanwy's hand and almost dragged her from her chair. The girl, every bit as enthused as her cousin, raced him through to the boot room, laughing all the way. Closest friends.

Becky clasped her hands to her ample chest. "God bless him. Never seen the boy so lively." She looked at her husband, beaming with obvious delight.

"You did a good thing there, Gwyn," Kaine said when the kids' excited chattering had faded into the distance.

The big farmer screwed up his mouth. "It was a clear sign from the Lord. The boy fell in love with that foal the moment he saw the blessed thing. Wouldn't surprise me if he's found his calling. We'll soon find out. Looking after a foal takes much more work than you'd think."

"Talking about looking after horses," Lara said, "if you don't mind, I'll pop over to the stables and check on the new mother."

"I looked in on her before *brecwast*," Cadwallader announced. "Bright Star's doing fine. A little tired after her ordeal, but nothing a bit of rest and a good diet won't cure. What's more, Nightwatch is feeding well. Latched onto the teats easy as you like. And Peter Sidings," he said, fixing Kaine with a fierce stare, "don't think I'm unaware of the undertone here."

"The undertone, Gwyn?" Kaine asked, playing the innocent.

"*Nightwatch*," Cadwallader said, coughing out the name. "You think I'm unaware of the name's military association? I'm a Presbyterian, not a monk. I know more than you think."

"But you're okay with the name?"

"Not really, but the lad showed *yspryd*, spirit, when he told me the name of the foal. And no matter what I think, I admire spirit in a man. So, okay. Nightwatch it is."

Before Kaine could respond, a mobile phone buzzed.

"It's mine," Rollo announced. He dug into his pocket and showed Kaine the caller ID. Connor Blake.

Rollo stood. "Excuse me, but I need to take this in private." He accepted the call, said, "One moment," into it, and headed out in the same direction as the kids.

Lara stood. "That's my cue to help clear the dishes before heading out to the stables."

"I wouldn't hear of it." Becky flapped her hands, shooing Lara away from the table. "You pop in on Bright Star. I'll do these. It's only a question of loading them into the dishwasher, anyway. Won't take but a minute."

Lara didn't need a second invitation. She waved goodbye, smiled at Kaine, and left almost as fast as the kids had.

After she'd closed the door behind her, Becky stood and reached for Kaine's plate. "Are you finished, Peter?"

"Yes, thanks," he said, adding his plate to the pile the kids had started. "I'd help you with these, but I think Gwyn and I need a quiet chat. Don't you, Gwyn?"

"We do?" the big man asked, frowning in concern.

Kaine nodded and stared him down.

"Yes, Gwyn. We do."

The big farmer used his hands on the arms of his chair to push himself to his feet. "Better come into the office with me, then."

CHAPTER 24

Tuesday 23rd May – Guy Gordon

GG Cleaning Systems Ltd, Cheltenham, Gloucestershire, UK

Guy Gordon yawned deep and long. Ever since the phone call, life had been manic. He and his team of techies had worked through the night, using every weapon in their technological arsenal. The result? A big, fat zero. Nothing. Nada. Zilch.

Well, almost.

Wales. Goddamn it. What a miserable sodding backwater.

Outside of the three main cities of Cardiff, Swansea, and Newport, South Wales might as well have been on the bloody moon, at least in relation to national surveillance systems.

Fair enough, the ANPR network operated on the main trunk roads—the M4, the A40, and the A470—in pretty much the same density as the rest of the UK, but the minor roads turned out to be a disaster. A virtual blind spot. In surveillance terms, years of underinvestment had left Wales a technological desert.

As for the tinpot market town of Brecon, bloody place might as well have been the centre of a black hole. His team had managed to pull up barely-in-focus pictures of the Audi arriving in town and sideswiping a little red Kia. After that, they'd followed its rapid progress to the hospital entrance and three people had exited. Again, the pictures had been useless in terms of providing a definitive identification of the suspects. Within minutes, the Audi had sped off, heading along the main road back into Brecon town centre. Hacking a dozen shopfront surveillance cameras had proved child's play for his team, but it eventually turned out fruitless. None of them had collected a clear shot of the driver. Then, after the car had dived down a side street on the outskirts of town, nothing. Absolutely sod all. The Audi might as well have been swallowed up by the same black hole.

Then again, the bloody car had to be somewhere. There'd been no sign of it leaving town, at least not on the main road, but that left dozens of minor roads it could have used to slip out of the area.

Damn it, he'd have to admit defeat, but not to Enderby and definitely not to Hartington. Oh no. His report to the professional spooks could wait until he'd exhausted every single line of enquiry. No way would Gordon risk souring what had become a highly lucrative and self-serving relationship. If his firm failed, it wouldn't look good moving forwards. He'd invested heavily in GG Cleaning Systems Ltd, and the unofficial tie-up with Enderby could be the making of his fledgeling operation.

So, what to do?

The search needed feet on the ground. Not something Gordon would ever contemplate doing personally. Not for him the schlepping around streets, wearing out shoe leather, knocking doors. GG Cleaning Systems Ltd—a private entity on the periphery of government—employed people to carry out the grunt work. Operatives with access to false identity papers the envy of even the country's biggest organised crime groups. Yep, their papers were as good as those produced for the UK government itself.

He pulled in a deep breath, scrubbed his face with his hands to wake himself up, and picked up the phone. He dialled the ops unit and didn't have to wait long for an answer.

"Ops. Stacy speaking."

Gordon smiled. At least he could deploy the company's top operative. Poached four months earlier from the intelligence services and skilled in the dark arts, William Stacy had been an expensive recent acquisition who had, as yet, been given little opportunity to earn his expensive corn. This task would give the man his chance to shine. And not before time, too.

"Good morning, William," Gordon said, keeping his tone soft and his delivery even. "How do you fancy a trip to South Wales?"

"Wales? Anything interesting?"

"Ryan Kaine's been spotted near Cardiff."

"Kaine? He's finally surfaced?" If excitement infected Stacy's mind, his taciturn response certainly didn't show it.

Gordon allowed his smile to grow.

A cold fish, William Stacy.

"My private office, five minutes. Bring McKenna with you."

"Can't do that, sir. He's on sick leave. Broke his wrist rather badly."

Bugger.

"How and when did that happen?"

"Last night, sir. After work. We were sparring in the gym."

"For God's sake! You broke his wrist?"

"Not intentionally. I'm afraid he got a little carried away, sir. Tried something he shouldn't have. An unfortunate accident. As you know, accidents can happen."

Stacy's lack of emotion chilled Gordon to his core. He swallowed back an angry response for fear of upsetting his latest acquisition. If Stacy could best Paul McKenna, a man with a black belt in *tae kwon do*, a man fifty kilos heavier and eight centimetres taller, there was no telling what the man would do if he took offence.

"Who else do we have available? It'll have to be someone with current and legitimate firearms accreditation—in case you do locate Kaine."

"Of course it will," Stacy said, maintaining his monotone speech pattern, almost sounding bored. "In that case, I'll bring Maureen Reilly."

"Reilly? Is she up to the task?"

"You employed her, sir. You tell me."

Insolent bugger.

"Reilly's a little ... volatile."

"Keen, sir. I'd call her keen rather than volatile. No need to worry though. I'll keep her in line."

I bet you will.

"Five minutes," Gordon repeated and ended the call.

EXACTLY FIVE MINUTES LATER, A DOUBLE RAP ON GORDON'S OFFICE door announced the strike team's arrival.

Gordon hit mute on the base unit of his desk phone and called out, "Enter."

The handle turned, the door cracked open, and Stacy slipped into the room. Maureen Reilly followed close behind.

Gordon beckoned them in, raised a finger to his lips, and pointed to the phone in its cradle on his desk. Silently, Stacy and Reilly took their seats across from him and waited.

Gordon released the mute. "You were saying, sir?"

The man on the other end of the line, Permanent Secretary Ernest Hartington, Head of the NCTA, and Gregory Enderby's immediate boss, grunted. "I'm not used to having to repeat myself, Gordon."

"No, sir. Sorry again, sir."

What else could he say?

"As you know," Hartington continued, "I've made no secret of my opposition to allowing any private sector involvement in the nation's security network, but austerity budgets have forced my hand. Reluctantly, I might add."

"No, sir. You haven't, and I do understand."

"Nonetheless, if you can take down Ryan Kaine without causing any waves, you can be assured of my wholehearted support moving forwards."

"Yes, sir. Thank you, Mr Hartington."

"And Gordon ..."

"Yes, sir?"

"When I say, take Ryan Kaine *down* you do understand my intention, don't you?"

"You mean take him out, sir. Permanently."

"Exactly so, Gordon. Exactly so. But there must be no blowback on Her Majesty's Government. Absolutely none. When you remove Ryan Kaine from the equation, no one is to know about it. Not the local police, the media, no one. Do you understand me, Gordon?"

"Yes, sir. I understand perfectly."

Gordon looked at Stacy and Reilly. She slid Stacy a sidelong glance, trying to make eye contact, but Stacy didn't accept it. He just sat still, eyes front, staring unblinkingly at Gordon. Silent and intense.

Jesus wept.

The man just sat there, taking everything in, nothing more than a weapon. A loaded gun without a conscience. A killer for hire. Gordon had contracted Stacy for high profile cases such as this. Didn't stop him giving Gordon the willies, though.

"Good," Hartington said. "Keep me informed as to your progress."

The line clicked into silence. Gordon picked up the phone, listened for the dial tone to confirm the call had fully disconnected, and returned the handset its cradle. In this game, there was no such thing as being too careful.

"What did he mean by that?" Reilly asked, a frown furrowing the forehead beneath a severe and unflattering fringe.

God, the woman could use a makeover. She had decent foundations, and it wouldn't take much to improve the package. With a little help, she could move up the scale from plain to half-decent. Although, it would take a miracle—and cosmetic surgery—to make her look anything close to beautiful. On the other hand, half-decent would be a vast improvement on the look she currently adopted.

Naughty, Guy. How cruel.

"He meant," Stacy answered for Gordon, "we have carte blanche to do whatever we want. We could take Kaine apart, drop him down a Welsh mineshaft, or bury him at sea, and the UK government will not only turn a blind eye, they will reward us handsomely."

"Are you serious?" Reilly stared at Stacy before turning her unremarkable, pale blue eyes on Gordon. "Sir?"

"Yes, Reilly?" he answered, almost amused by her response.

"The government has put a Grey Notice on Ryan Kaine?"

"Reilly," Gordon said, trying not to groan, "wake up. Of course it has. Not that anyone outside of a very few will ever know. I doubt even the PM is truly aware of it." He smiled and looked at Stacy. "I believe the Americans have coined a term for it."

"Plausible deniability," Stacy said, his response dry and totally free of emotion. "It means we can kill Kaine with total impunity. Occasionally, our colonial cousins can produce a colourful turn of phrase."

He might have been discussing the cost of a non-fat cappuccino in the local coffee bar when they were actually talking about killing a human being.

Yes. Someone very high up had decided that it would be too embarrassing for the UK government if the case against Ryan Kaine ever reached trial. Hence the private sector contract. Compact, well-managed firms like GG Cleaning Systems Ltd could hide their operations much more easily than vast departments like the poorly resourced public sector.

Plausible deniability—what a wonderful expression.

A world in which Guy Gordon was about to make a great deal of money.

And long may it last.

Reilly shot Stacy another glance. "Are you okay with this, Will?"

William Stacy stared her down for a moment before nodding.

"Yes. Are you?"

She smiled. "Hell, yes."

"So, what was the mock horror all about," Stacy asked, as dry as ever.

Reilly's expression transitioned from a deep frown to a wide smirk.

"Just checking. I wanted to avoid any point of confusion." She turned to face Gordon. "Will we have the Grey Notice in writing, sir?"

Stacy turned away from her and closed his eyes for a moment longer than a blink. It could have been his version of rolling his eyes or a facepalm. If so, it was the only emotional response Gordon had ever seen from the man.

"Don't be ridiculous, Reilly," Gordon snapped. "You think we're about to receive a death warrant signed by the attorney general in our inbox?"

"Get real, Maureen," Stacy muttered under his breath.

"Just trying to cover our arses, Will."

"You know the score. We're covered," Stacy said. "End of."

Once again, Gordon studied the man sitting across his desk.

No James Bond wannabe, Stacy couldn't have looked less like the Hollywood version of a spy if he tried. Nondescript didn't even cover it. Average height, medium build, greying hair, thinning on top. Inside a rounded face sat a pair of dark brown eyes that seemed to absorb the daylight rather than reflect it. When he turned those dead eyes on Gordon, they could sometimes make him shudder—and the two of them happened to be on the same side. Although Gordon suspected it wouldn't take much for Stacy to switch teams. An offer of increased pay. A perceived slight. The merest whim. Who knew?

As part of the recruitment process and in the interests of full disclosure, Enderby had given Gordon access to Stacy's unredacted service record. Poached by MI6, after twelve years in the British Army which included two tours of Iraq and three tours of Afghanistan. Apart from the casualties of war, he'd killed for the state already. Three times, in fact. Yes, Stacy knew the score much better than Reilly ever could.

"So, South Wales?" Stacy asked, his voice quiet, the accent as unremarkable as his face.

Reilly relaxed back into her chair and the smirk disappeared. She'd made her point and seemed happy to carry on with the briefing. Reilly would do anything Gordon told her to. After leaving the Metropolitan Police under a disciplinary black cloud, a cloud that might well have ended in a long prison term, she couldn't afford not to. She had limited options and came extra cheap as a consequence. Beggars couldn't choose which party to gatecrash, and her cut-price salary offset Stacy's exorbitant one.

Such was the price of being so hot-tempered.

"We aren't the only private team in the hunt, but we do have a hot lead."

Gordon hit return on his keyboard and the screen on the wall off to the side lit up with the passport photo of a Major William Griffin, taken straight from the border control station at Cardiff International Airport. "Cheeky beggar disembarked from a private jet at around five o'clock yesterday morning."

"Yesterday *morning*?" Stacy pulled back the cuff of his shirt to expose a cheap wristwatch. "And we're only being told this now?"

"Commander Enderby informed me of Kaine's arrival late yesterday evening. Hours late."

"Typical," Reilly huffed.

"Permanent Secretary Hartington's call just then was by way of a chivvy-up. The arrogant prick was trying to shove a red-hot poker up our arses."

"Sounded to me like he's running scared," Reilly said. "I wonder what Kaine's got on Hartington."

"Not just Hartington," Gordon said. "If someone's placed a Grey Notice on Kaine it means he knows something that might well take down the government."

Stacy crossed his right leg over his left and folded his arms. Gordon took it as a signal for him to move the conversation along.

"Yes, Will?"

"Since Enderby's call, I imagine you've had our techies on the trail?"

Yes. That's it, Stacy. Cut to the chase.

"I have indeed."

"Can I assume the trail's gone cold?"

Gordon smiled. "Not quite."

Stacy uncrossed his arms and sat up a little straighter. "Do tell."

"Kaine and two unidentified associates were last seen entering Brecon hospital, and they"—he paused for dramatic emphasis—"left a man behind."

Reilly frowned. "That doesn't sound like the Ryan Kaine I've read about."

"He murdered eighty-three people on that plane," Gordon said, trying to match Stacy's calm tone. "There's no telling what he's capable of doing."

"I've heard rumours that Kaine was set up," Reilly announced, glancing at Stacy, no doubt trying to gauge his thoughts from his body language.

Yeah. Good luck with that.

Stacy remained immobile.

"There are always rumours, Reilly," Gordon said. "Conspiracy theories. I read one that involved Sir Malcolm Sampson of SAMS."

"He lost the knighthood when they banged him up for embezzlement, sir," Reilly countered. "He's plain old *Mr* Sampson now."

Gordon snorted. "I stand corrected, Reilly. *Mr* Sampson it is. Nonetheless, our job is to track down Ryan Kaine and take him out."

"Sir?" Reilly said, raising a finger, but keeping it low, being unusually timid.

"Yes, Reilly?"

"There's a black market reward on Kaine's head."

"Last I heard, it stood at half a million," Stacy said. "How much is it now?"

"It's been rounded up to a full million euros," Reilly answered.

Gordon slammed the flat of his hand down on his desk. The crack made Reilly start. Stacy didn't react.

"Let me make this perfectly clear. If you *do* manage to fulfil the contract on Ryan Kaine, neither of you will try to claim that reward. Am I making myself perfectly clear?" He paused again, this time, to drive the message home. "We are being paid handsomely for our work and Kaine's upcoming death must be kept quiet." He held up a hand to forestall Reilly's attempted interruption.

"And please remember this. Apart from the contract fee, which will be reflected in your end-of-year bonuses, think of the cachet involved if we're the firm to end the Kaine debacle. You heard what Hartington said. The company will be right up there at the very top table. We'll be able to write our own cheques."

Gordon's heart pounded as the excitement coursed through his system.

"Mr Gordon," Stacy said. "This man Kaine left behind ..." He paused and rolled his hand forwards.

"Ah, yes. Well, leaving him behind is maybe a little fanciful a description. According to the police reports, Kaine and his friends rescued an old soldier who'd been injured in a fracas."

"A fracas?" Reilly asked, arching one of her pencil-darkened eyebrows.

"Yes. Apparently, they found a vagrant wandering in the middle of the road and raced him to hospital. And do you know what's better?"

"What?" Reilly asked.

Gordon allowed a smile to form. "The vagrant's still in his hospital bed."

"Which hospital?" Stacy asked, not a man to waste words.

"Brecon Memorial."

Stacy nodded. "I suppose you'd like us to go ask the man a few questions?"

Gordon let his grin spread wider. "That's what I like about you, Will. You're so very quick on the uptake. Draw the requisite firepower from the armoury on your way out."

"Thank you, sir," Stacy said, failing to return the smile. He eased to his feet and signalled Reilly to follow him towards the door. "We'll keep in touch, sir."

They left the office, the door swung closed on its pneumatic soft closer, and Gordon breathed again. The bloody man with the unreadable eyes gave him the creeps.

Gordon permitted himself a brief shudder.

With William Stacy hot on his trail, Gordon almost felt sorry for Ryan Kaine. He definitely felt sorry for the vagrant should he be reluctant to answer the away team's questions. If the poor man didn't need a hospital bed already, he'd certainly require one after Stacy had completed his particular form of interrogation.

CHAPTER 25

Tuesday 23rd May – Early Morning

Cadwallader Farm, Glyn Coes, Powys, South Wales, UK

Kaine followed Cadwallader through the hallway and into a small and cluttered back room. A dark oak desk dominated the centre of the office. Three grey metal filing cabinets lined the left-hand wall, their tops laden with papers, folders, and farming trophies. A large built-in bookcase filled the opposite wall, each shelf stacked with books, periodicals, photographs, and more trophies—one of which, a silver cup, proclaimed something as being "Best in Show". A deep and wide window cut into the wall opposite the door, and the bright daylight framed Cadwallader in a golden corona of sunlight.

"Well now, Peter," the big Welshman said, after dropping into his threadbare seat behind the desk and waving Kaine into the only other chair in the office. "You asked for this 'quiet chat'. Carry on."

Before he could sit, Kaine had to remove a stack of folders from the seat and balance them on the edge of the desk.

"One second," he said and pulled his mobile from his pocket. He opened the photo app and searched through the library until he found the picture he wanted—the threatening note pinned to the stable door. He enlarged the image until it filled the screen and turned the phone towards Cadwallader.

As he studied the image, the big farmer breathed deep and slow. He ground his teeth and his nostrils flared. Anger clear in every movement.

"Becky gave you this?"

"She gave it to Annie."

"Which is pretty much the same thing, I imagine?"

Kaine nodded. "We work closely together, Gwyn. Do you mind translating the note for me?"

Cadwallader lifted his broad shoulders in a shrug. "Rambling nonsense, it is. Nothing but threats wrapped up in cursing. Bad grammar, too. Some of the words are misspelt."

"'This is only the start. Worse is to come! Do as you're told,'" Kaine recited from memory. "We have a translation app, but I left out the more colourful phrases."

"This is all you wanted to talk to me about?"

"It is. What were you told to do?"

Cadwallader leant back in his chair and swivelled it to one side, showing Kaine his profile. "That's just it," he said. "I have no idea. I haven't received any messages apart from that one." He waved a giant hand at Kaine's mobile. "No letters. No threatening telephone calls. Nothing. It's a complete mystery."

"What about Becky? Has she been threatened in any way?"

"No, definitely not. She would have told me. There are no secrets between us."

"Really?"

He squirmed in his chair. "None related to this matter."

"You showed this to the police?"

"Of course we did. And they asked the same questions you did. Only, I don't think they believed us. The way they acted ... it was as though we'd brought this upon ourselves."

"So," Kaine said. "No one's threatened you?"

"No. Well, Howell Powell said I should go to the Devil," Cadwallader said. "But he didn't use those exact words, you understand. Actually, he cast doubt on my legitimacy ... my parentage, you know. But I didn't take it that seriously. The beer was flowing."

Kaine leant forwards. His chair creaked so much he feared it might disintegrate beneath him. "Howell Powell? Seriously?"

Cadwallader nodded. "Yes, seriously. Howell's father didn't have much of an imagination."

No kidding.

"You can guess how the kids teased him at school."

"I can. Who is he and why was he so angry?"

Cadwallader's lips curled into a sad smile. "Don't know why I mentioned it, really. This"—again he indicated the picture on the screen—"has nothing to do with Howell. He's our nearest neighbour. Been jealous of my success in the county shows for years." He pointed to the silver cup taking pride of place in the bookcase. "We won that that last year for Magnolia, our prize ewe. Howell cried foul. Accused me of bribing the judges. Me! As though I'd ever do such a thing. Bribery's a black sin. Howell's always been a tad ... volatile. Especially when he'd been sitting in the sun all day, drinking beer. He'd convinced himself that his Petunia would beat our Magnolia. Not a chance."

All this over an animal beauty pageant?

Kaine tried to keep the surprise off his face.

"Howell's an angry drunk?"

"You could say that. We nearly came to blows over it, but I'm way bigger than him, and Howell's a coward at heart. In the end, the stewards ejected him from the show."

"Have you seen Howell since?"

"No, mun. Me and Howell's never been what you'd call buddies. Unless we happen to bump into each other at market, we don't see each other for months on end."

"You think all this might be over a silver cup?"

"No. Like I said, it wouldn't have anything to do with Howell. But you did ask if anyone's ever threatened me, and the incident with Howell's the only one I can think of."

"What about the farm. How's it doing financially? Are you in debt to anyone?"

Cadwallader hesitated, no doubt uncomfortable discussing finances with a stranger.

"We're trying to help, Gwyn. I promise you this information will stay between us."

"Between you and me? What about Annie and Adrian?"

"They don't need to know the details, unless you say I can share them."

"Do I have your word?"

"Yes."

"Right then. Apart from the usual credit arrangements with our feed and fertiliser suppliers, we owe nobody but the bank. We have a hefty mortgage on the farm and took out a development loan for the pony trekking business."

"And you're managing to service the debts?"

Cadwallader wavered for a moment as though debating how forthright he should be before answering. "Just about. The winters are a struggle with the closed tourist and trekking seasons, but we are managing to make the mortgage and loan payments. I won't say it's easy, but the Good Lord has provided us with his bounty, and we are grateful for it."

"What about the business in general? Has anyone tried to buy the farm recently?"

Cadwallader surprised Kaine by smiling and barking out a laugh. "Yes, how did you know?"

"I didn't. Was the offer serious?"

Cadwallader swayed in his chair, wavering. "At first, I thought it was a joke, but we had an offer for the farm only the other month. It came out of the blue from an English company called Ridgemont Capital Holdings Limited. Ridiculous, it was."

"Too low? Insulting?"

"No, too high. Way above the market value. Thirty percent above, in fact. The fools wanted to turn the place into a health and beauty spa, or something equally ludicrous. How *twp* is that?"

"*Twp?*"

The big farmer tapped his temple with the tips of his index and forefingers.

"Foolish," he translated.

"In what way?"

"For a start, Ridgemont Capital would never get planning permission to change the use of the land. Farming land is protected, you know."

"I thought it must be, considering we're in the Beacons."

"Actually," the big farmer said, "we fall just outside the National Park." Cadwallader shook his large head. "Makes no difference, though. Farming land is still protected."

It may be protected for now, but money talks.

Kaine changed direction. "Were they serious? Did they have enough capital behind them?"

"I have to admit, I was intrigued. Out of curiosity, I visited their website and downloaded their latest annual report from Companies House. They *seemed* legitimate. Reported a couple of billion pounds of liquidity and a pre-tax profit of eleven million for the last financial year."

A pained expression crossed Cadwallader's face.

"I'll be honest with you here, Peter. For a few moments, the Devil himself tempted me, but the Good Lord cast Satan from my mind. I could never sell the farm. This is my family home. Has been for generations."

"How did they contact you?" Kaine asked, leaning forwards slightly.

"By post, initially. They sent a letter of introduction, a prospectus, and a company brochure—full colour, it was. Most impressive."

"Initially, you say?"

Cadwallader's stare drifted off into the middle distance above Kaine's head. He might have been dreaming of a life without the incessant heavy farm work. A life of ease, lying on a beach in the sun.

After a moment, the Welshman snapped to a seated attention and focused his gaze back on Kaine.

"They followed up with a telephone call." He glanced at the phone on his desk, black and as old as the one in the hallway. "Well, they called twice, actually. I hung up on them the first time. The nerves got to me, see."

"And the second time?"

"I answered," Cadwallader said, through a barely audible sigh, "and I rejected their offer."

"You've heard nothing since?"

"A couple of emails. One reconfirming their offer, and the other asking to visit the farm for what they called a 'face-to-face'. I imagine they were going to try and tempt me by waving fifty-pound notes under my nose."

"No contact since the emails?"

"No. They seem to have given up."

Kaine scratched at his beard.

"You don't agree, Peter?"

"When there's so much money involved, people don't tend to give up so easily. Mind if I look a little more deeply into Ridgemont Capital?"

"Not at all."

"Thanks. I'll need everything you have from them. The prospectus, letter of intent, brochure, everything. Then I need your permission to tell Annie about the offer and—"

"Do you have to?"

"Yes. She's not just good with horses. She also one of The Trust's best techies. Annie will be able to dig much deeper into these people than I can. And she doesn't have to know about the ... er, Devil's temptation."

Cadwallader breathed deep. "In that case, you can tell her, and Adrian too, if it will help. But please keep the information from Becky and the kids."

"I will, and thanks. You never know, Ridgemont Capital might just be what they claim to be—honest and above board, and keen to buy your beautiful farm. Conversely, they might be aggressive and greedy enough to be organising the campaign against you. They might see it as a way to change your mind about the sale."

Cadwallader folded his arms over his massive chest. "That's never going to happen. Any more questions?"

"One or two. Apart from its obvious natural beauty, does the farm have any other assets you are aware of? No untapped mineral resources?"

"No. Definitely not."

"Any right of way issues that would make the farm more intrinsically valuable?"

"Not at all."

"Are there any large-scale infrastructure works in the pipeline?"

Cadwallader placed his hands flat of the desk in front of him. "This close to the Beacons? Not a chance. There are all sorts of covenants and planning restrictions in place. For goodness' sake, I have to apply for permission to fart!" He smiled at his own joke. "No, there are no plans for any large-scale building works. That, I can assure you of."

Kaine scratched at the stubble on his cheek. He'd run out of questions. "That's all I can think of. If you have the paperwork from Ridgemont Capital, I'll leave you in peace."

Cadwallader leant to one side, straightened his leg, and pulled a set of keys from his trouser pocket. He selected the smallest key on the ring and used it to unlock the bottom drawer of his desk. After walking his fingers through to the back of the suspension files, he found the one he wanted, and tugged out a large manilla envelope.

"That's everything I have from Ridgemont Capital, including printed copies of the emails."

"Thanks, Gwyn." Kaine stood and relieved Cadwallader of the hefty envelope. "What are your plans for the day?"

"Right now, I'm heading to the shed. Cows can't milk themselves. After that, I'll be in the barn most of the day, servicing the Massey Ferguson."

"Need a hand?"

Cadwallader lifted an eyebrow.

"I'll never refuse an offer of help, Peter. You know farm machinery?"

Kaine shook his head. "I don't, but I know a man who does."

"Adrian?"

"Yep. He's one of the best mechanics I know. I'm sure he'd be happy to smother his hands with engine oil. After the way he tucked into his breakfast, he needs to earn his keep."

A few moments later, Kaine exited the office armed with the envelope and two possible lines of investigation. Later that day, he'd pay a clandestine visit to the neighbour, Howell Powell. As for Ridgemont Capital, if Corky remained incommunicado, Lara would have her work cut out for her—assuming she could tear herself away from the stables. If she couldn't, he'd ask Rollo. Maybe even try searching the internet for himself.

After all, how hard could it be?

CHAPTER 26

Tuesday 23rd May – Maureen Reilly

A40 Westbound, South Wales, UK

Maureen cast a sly glance towards the man in the driving seat, Will Stacy. Such a cold fish, but somehow exciting in a dark and mysterious way. Cool.

Since he'd joined GG Cleaning Systems Ltd—what a great name, it sounded more like a horse grooming service than a bespoke security firm—they'd worked together twice. She still knew next to nothing about him on a personal level.

Despite his unexceptional appearance—he was no oil painting— Will could handle himself physically. No doubt about that whatsoever. The way he dealt with Paul demonstrated his physical prowess to perfection. Geordie Boy Paul had been begging for it, though. He'd been goading Will for weeks, banging on about his lack of stature, his age, his thinning hair. Kept calling him vanilla too. All couched as light-hearted banter. Will had absorbed it all with apparent good humour, even smiling occasionally. Then Paul "accidentally" spilled the dregs of his coffee over Will's favourite pair of shoes.

Maureen could see the event, clear as the road ahead through the Range Rover's dusty windscreen. Will seemed oblivious to the dirt. Should have cleaned the screen miles back, but she wasn't about to suggest it. No way of telling how he'd react to her instruction.

A hush had fallen over the office. Five techies and Maureen waited for Stacy's outburst. She could almost feel the group intake of breath.

"Sorry, man. My bad," Paul said, showing a cheesy grin and clearly not meaning a word of the apology. "Someone must have jogged my arm."

Will simply stared at Geordie Boy who didn't have the brains to recognise calm calculation when faced with it. Where Maureen saw cold confidence and steely determination, Geordie Boy saw cowardice.

Silly boy.

"Accidents happen," Will said, politeness itself. He strolled across to his desk, took a tissue from its box, sat, and wiped the shoe.

Paul laughed, a scornful bray that set Maureen's teeth on edge.

"Why aye, man," Paul said. "Accidents happen. Really sorry. See you laters."

He waved, turned his back on Will—he actually turned his back in an act of pure defiance—and swaggered away. Will finished drying his shoe and the office breathed again. She could almost describe it as a collective sigh of relief. All seemed forgiven and forgotten.

Things finally came to a head a week after the coffee spillage incident, when Will engaged Paul in a pleasant, if apparently aimless, conversation. The chat started with a review of the unseasonably warm weather and graduated onto the topic of Paul's secondary passion, Newcastle United FC, his primary passion being Paul himself.

Will must have read up, since he knew the team's current form and their debate became quite animated, but friendly.

"I haven't seen you in the gym, recently," Will said after a natural lull in the conversation. "You're not injured, are you?"

Paul leant back in his chair and puffed out his chest, showing off an impressive pair of Arnie-sized pecs and washboard abs.

"Nah, man," he said, making sure the whole office could hear him. "I've been working with a new *sensei*. He's recently arrived from Seoul. Invited me to join his *dojo*." He made it sound like a real feather in his cap.

"Sounds like a serious honour," Will said, nodding with keen interest.

"Sun-Yung Choi," Paul announced to anyone who cared to listen, chest puffed out with pride. "You've heard of him, surely?"

"'Fraid not," Will answered. "An important man in the field, I take it?"

"A world leader. He doesn't accept just any student."

"I don't doubt it. As I said, a real honour. You must be delighted."

"Why aye, man. Hundreds applied to join his *dojo*, but he only took on twelve students."

"I guess that must make you one of the Dirty Dozen?" Will asked, smiling.

Paul laughed. "Dirty dozen? Yeah, I like that, man."

Will paused for a moment as though lost in thought. "I've never practised *tae kwon do*. A little too energetic for me, I'm afraid. *T'ai chi*'s more my style. Much more gentle."

Paul fell right into Will's trap and didn't even know it. "Why don't we spar sometime? Your *t'ai chi* against my *tae kwon do*. It'll be a hoot."

Hook, line, and sinker.

"Sounds like a plan. I'm free tomorrow evening. How about you?"

"It's a date," Will said. "But it needs to be closed session. I don't want an audience."

Paul laughed and fired off a quip suggesting Will wouldn't want the whole world seeing what was about to happen to him.

Later that evening, she'd sat in her car parked outside the gym, watching them spar on her mobile phone via a feed she'd instructed one of the techies to set up from the gym's video system.

It ended so fast, Maureen had to replay the throw in slow motion a number of times before she could work out exactly how he'd done it.

After an extensive warm up, Paul attacked. He danced around Will, moving clockwise and anticlockwise, throwing controlled and precise punches and kicks. Will avoided each blow with deceptive ease, barely breaking into a sweat. After five minutes' furious action, Paul lunged, closing the gap. Will struck in a blur of arms and hands, with a bend at the waist. Paul flew over Will's back. As Paul's feet left the ground, Will stepped into the throw, and pulled back hard, taking Paul's arm with him.

Paul's scream rattled the gym's windows. The silent video didn't capture the howl, but it did capture the anguish driven into Paul's face clearly enough. The slow-motion playback made it clear. Will's actions had been intentional. The iron certainty he displayed couldn't have been more obvious. If he'd released the wristlock when Paul's feet left the canvas, Geordie Boy would have landed in a heap on the mat and suffered no more than bruises, defeat, and embarrassment. As it was, he might never regain full use of his right hand. The hideous mess that remained, looked more like a loose bag of nuts and bolts than a functioning wrist. After finally releasing his wristlock, to another shriek from the beaten man, Will lifted his face to the camera and did something extraordinary.

He winked!

He winked as though he knew she'd been watching. Then he strolled away—without turning his back—leaving Paul writhing in agony and hugging his useless hand. Maureen had watched the recording dozens of times since, scrutinising the technique, hoping to learn the move herself. Who knew when such a throw might come in handy.

Now, sitting in the Range Rover's passenger seat, recalling the previous night's action, she blushed and turned her head towards the passenger window.

To say watching Will Stacy in action turned her on would have been an understatement. At the time, if he'd asked, Maureen would have offered to carry his children. But Will Stacy had never responded to any of her advances, more's the pity. Perhaps he didn't roll that way.

Okay, even on her best days, not even her best friends would call her beautiful, but no one would call her ugly. At least not to her face. She would never let anyone do that again. Not after the way she'd let Reed beat her into docile subservience over so many years. But that was then, and this was now. The worm had turned. By God, had it turned.

Reed would never bully anyone again. Never cheat on anyone again, either. Not after Maureen the Worm had transformed into Maureen the Monster and buried a paring knife into the back of his neck. Severed his spine. The bastard had dropped like a brick to the garage floor. At the time, she'd wondered whether the knife in through the neck had answered the last question he'd ever asked.

"What's this tarp doing on my garage floor?"

Typical of him, that. *His* garage floor. *His* house. The bloody nerve of the man. *Her* name was on the mortgage deeds. *She* paid all the bills. *She* did all the housework, but it was still *his* house, *his* garage. *His* bloody worm.

Well, he was long gone. Worm food. And good riddance, too.

She never expected to get away with it. Never in a million years. But she had. No one even suspected. As far as the world was concerned, Reed Reilly had just disappeared. He'd left her for another woman. A prettier woman, no doubt. How could it be otherwise?

Reed had no family and few friends. At least no one who cared enough to chase him up. No one asked about him. No one called. She stored his corpse in the chest freezer in the garage. Over the following few weeks, she carefully removed pieces of the carcase with a hacksaw—*his* hacksaw—and distributed them in wheelie bins all over London. Not one piece had been found. At least, nothing untoward had made it into the media.

She'd gotten away with it.

A miracle. One that left Maureen Reilly free to live her life the way she wanted to. It left her free to grow. Free to develop. Free to be her own woman. Free to take her revenge on anyone who stood in her way.

A pure joy.

She'd found her calling. After all, if she could get away with murder once, why not twice? Why not a third time? Why not turn it into a career? The rest became a matter of historical record. Two years as a beat officer in the Met. Firearms training. An armed siege or two. Three shootings. Two dead drug dealers. Both deemed justified. Then the worst mistake of all. An innocent bystander. The inquiry. Out on her ear as a failure. Humiliation. Then Guy Gordon knocked on her door. A pay cut, but a chance to continue. And the icing on the cake, a return of her firearms certification.

She was back in the saddle.

Maureen pressed her upper arm against her side to feel the reassuring bulk of the SIG P226 in its shoulder harness under her armpit. Positively orgasmic. To top it all, they were on their way to kill a wanted man. A fugitive. A killing sanctioned by those in the highest offices in the land. Couldn't improve on that. Not a chance.

And she didn't forget the Remington locked in the luggage compartment. What if she actually got to fire it in anger instead of popping away at cardboard targets on the shooting range? Man, what a buzz.

Will had barely said word one since they'd climbed into the Range Rover and left Cheltenham. He insisted on driving, and she let him. He was a good, steady driver, if a little uninspiring. Although she'd have preferred to drive, she'd never argue the toss with Will Stacy. Especially not after seeing the way he'd dealt with Geordie Boy.

"I need a pit stop," he said, pointing through the windscreen to a sign that read "Services 2 miles".

The statement came so far out of the blue, Maureen nearly jumped out of her seat.

"Good idea. I could use a coffee, Will."

What else could she say? As team leader, he called the shots. If he needed a break, he took a break. At least he'd given her warning.

They pulled off the main drag of the A40 and into a service station with an unpronounceable name. While he filled the tank, she paid for the fuel and bought the provisions, two coffees to go. Black for him. White with two sugars for her. As a treat, she also picked up a couple of energy bars. She'd seen him munching on the dust-dry things during their most recent operation together, a stakeout of a cabinet minister who was becoming far too chummy with an attractive member of the Russian delegation to the G8 Summit. Shortly after Guy Gordon presented their report to Commander Enderby, the same cabinet minister gave up his government post and his parliamentary seat to "spend more time with his family". The real reason for his decision to quit remained a mystery to all but the most close-mouthed members of the establishment.

She returned to the car armed with her refreshments and the receipts and slid into the passenger's seat. He pulled away from the pumps and parked in the shade of some trees.

"We're stopping here?" she asked, handing him his cardboard cup and the bar.

"Thanks," he said, pressing his cup into the handy holder in the centre console and opening the energy bar. "And yes, we are."

"Why? I thought we were in a hurry to interroga—I mean, interview the vagrant?"

"We are, but I need a rest break. And, anyway, Mitchell Bairstow's staying put for the time being."

"We're sure of that?"

"Think about it. He has the chance to put his feet up in bed and eat three squares a day. Even hospital food must taste good to a travelling man."

"I could drive if you like."

He shook his head emphatically. "I don't make a good passenger."

"Why not drink on the move?"

"Mo," he said, turning those deep brown eyes on her, "I'm surprised at you, being an ex-police officer. It's illegal to eat or drink while driving. We wouldn't want to be pulled over by the traffic police. We're supposed to be undercover."

"But our cover stories—"

"Are just that, stories. You may be able to pass yourself off as an officer of the law, but I'll struggle. If a cop talks shop to me, I'm toast. Your background is the main reason I wanted you on this op."

"That and the fact Geordie Boy's out of commission?" She smiled through the question.

"Exactly."

"You know that's a myth, right?" she said, staring through the windscreen and watching the trees bend in the wind.

"What is?"

"That it's illegal to eat and drink while driving."

"It is?"

"Yep. Drivers are only *advised* to avoid eating or drinking while driving, since it could be a distraction. Police may decide that a driver might not be in proper control of their vehicle."

"Then we could still be stopped, right?"

"Well, yes."

"Which is why we're parking here while I fuel up. Okay?"

"Okay," she nodded.

He bit into the bar, chomped it quickly, and helped it down with a swallow of coffee. Unable to face it, she dropped her unopened bar into the centre console and took another drink.

"What do you know about the target?" Will asked, coffee cup held up to his face, covering his mouth although they'd parked in a spot that had no surveillance cameras. At least none they could spot.

"I've read the file."

Will nodded almost to himself. "You've read the file? Hmm."

She dared to ask. "Why?"

Evidently immune to the heat, Will took another sip and kept the cup high while answering. "I need to know whether you understand the kind of target we're facing."

He's testing you, girl.

She pursed her lips before launching into an abridged history of Captain Ryan Liam Kaine.

"...then, last September, he went rogue and shot down Flight BE1555, a civilian plane carrying eighty—"

"If we find the target, do you understand what Hartington and Enderby want us to do?" Will interrupted, cutting her off, mid-flow.

Taking a leaf from his book, she hid her mouth with the cup before answering.

"I thought we'd covered this in Gordon's office."

"We did, but I wanted to make sure you were happy with it. Are you?"

"Aren't you?"

"Answer the question."

"'Course I'm happy with it."

"You don't mind that Kaine won't have his day in court? You don't have trouble with the moral issues?"

He is *testing you.*

Will wanted to know he could rely on her when push came to shove. Well, hell yes.

"You want the truth?" she asked.

"The whole truth, and nothing but."

He smiled while saying it. He actually smiled. Practically a first for Will Stacy.

"To be honest," she said, returning his smile, "I don't give a flying fuck for the morality of it. Someone high up has placed a Grey Notice on the arsehole, and we're being paid well to carry it out. We get to kill the prick with total impunity. And if we get a kick out of it, where's the harm? I can't wait to have the bugger in my crosshairs."

"You'll enjoy it?"

"Too right I will. Does that make me a bad person?"

He snorted. Another first.

"You know what?" he said, softly. "It probably does."

"What about you?"

"Me? Oh I'm bad to the bone."

"So, we're two bad people on the way to have a little fun."

"We certainly are. Sorry for the inquisition, but I needed to know where you and I stood. And now I do." He drained his coffee and replaced the top. "You finished?" he asked holding out his hand.

"Sure am, Will."

She passed the empty cup across, and he climbed from the car. She watched him stroll, no, stalk towards the restrooms. Being ever so environmentally sound, he deposited the cups in the recycling bin and disappeared into the gents.

Maureen took the opportunity to lower the sun visor and scope herself out in the vanity mirror. Like Will Stacy, no one would ever mistake her for a fashion model. For a moment, she contemplated applying some lippie but decided against.

"Maybe later, girl," she said to her reflection. "You never know but killing Ryan Kaine might not be the only bit of fun you have on this little trip to Wales."

She chuckled and settled back in her seat to wait for the man who just might be the one she'd been waiting for all her life.

CHAPTER 27

Tuesday 23rd May – Mitch Bairstow

Brecon War Memorial Hospital, Powys, South Wales, UK

Mitch Bairstow relaxed into his pillows and pondered his good fortune. He had a full stomach, a warm bed, and time to think. After a night's interrupted sleep, he'd finally decided to make the most of the situation.

The first evening, he did receive a bed bath, from a hefty male nurse called Dafydd, who had three-day stubble and reeked of cigarettes. A real passion killer, it was. At least the wash freshened him up. The second-hand baggy T-shirt and shorts they gave him helped too. Well worn, but clean and comfortable. The whole thing was transformational. Mitch rejected Dafydd's offer of a shave on cosmetic grounds. Although the beard helped to keep him warm on the coldest nights, he'd also grown to consider the facial fluff a close friend.

After the bath, a volunteer helper arrived with a smile, a bowl of warm soup, and a slice of buttered bread. He'd torn the bread into tiny pieces and soaked it in the soup. Made it easier to chew. Tasted okay, too, and who was he to complain?

That night, he had the best sleep in forever. Not even the coughing, spluttering, and groaning from patients in the surrounding beds could keep him awake for long.

At one stage strange dreams disturbed his rest. A boot to the ribs followed another to the face. A man with a nose ring screamed in agony, his arm ripped from his body and lying detached and limp at his side. His face morphed into another—the serious, bearded face of Black Ops. So strangely familiar.

In his nightmare, Black Ops' beard melted away and the long, wavy hair changed into a military crop. Who the hell was the guy?

Don't worry about it, Mitch. It doesn't matter.

He didn't expect to see Black Ops or his mates ever again.

At oh-four-hundred hours, a nurse had woken him for the second of three overnight obs. Heart rate, blood pressure. Both close to normal. A whispered, "How's the headache?" netted his response, "Fifty-five," on the same scale he always used. Since falling asleep, the rating had lowered from a solid "eighty-eight".

At oh-six-hundred hours, the bell rang for reveille, or in this case, breakfast. He vacuumed up a bowl of crispy cereal with milk and sugar, a slice of cold toast, butter, and marmalade. Rounded off with a mug of warm, sweet tea. Delicious. Even better than his usual morning dive though rubbish bins.

At ten-hundred hours, they let a cop in. Apparently, he'd returned from the previous day and had already been waiting over an hour. Such a shame.

Big bloater, he was. Sweated heavily into his stab vest. It certainly said something about life when a cop felt the need to wear a stab vest inside a hospital. The world was turning to crap in a big way. Mitch was well out of the mainstream.

Without asking permission, the cop tugged the modesty screen around the bed, dragged a visitor's chair closer, and flopped into it.

Bloody cheek.

"Mr Bairstow," the cop said, "I'm PC Newton. May I ask you some questions?"

"Dunno," Mitch said, meek as a kitten and dragging out his secondary persona. The persona of the ignorant, invalid former squaddie who didn't speak the Queen's English so good. For added effect, he winced. "Got an 'eadache, I have. Can't this wait?"

Newton's washed-out grey eyes narrowed, and his thin lips stretched out into an even thinner smile. If he imagined it made him look sympathetic, he'd have been wrong.

"Dr Rees tells me you're fit to be interviewed."

"Oh, he did, did he?"

Damn his North Wales heart.

It meant they'd probably be turfing him out of his comfy hospital bed sooner than he'd hoped.

"Yes, sir. He did." Newton pulled an old-fashioned police note-book from a pocket inside his stab vest.

And there was Mitch, thinking all cops used computer tablets these days. Newton was old school.

"Can you tell me what happened?"

Mitch paused to gather his thoughts. He lifted a hand to the side of his face and felt the lump. They'd given him a mirror earlier in the day. Bruising made the swelling look even worse. It had to earn him some extra points for sympathy, surely?

"Give me a sec," he said. "Everything's a bit fuzzy. I've got an 'ead injury, you know."

"In your own time, Mr Bairstow," Newton prompted.

Mitch nodded slowly, adding another grimace for good measure. "Okay, yeah. It's coming back to me. I were in a park, minding me own business ..."

He told his story, egging up the attack, but said nothing about the way Black Ops and Goliath dealt with the fuckers who'd attacked him. None of Newton's concern.

"Where was this, sir?" Newton asked, writing in his notebook.

"Dunno the name o' the place, Officer. Sorry. Don't take much notice o' where I lay me head these days. One place is the same as any other."

"And these people, the Good Samaritans," Newton said, "they just appeared out of nowhere?"

"Nah, they appeared out of a car, far as I know." Mitch chuckled softly, but Newton didn't join in.

"What sort of car?"

"The one they drove me here in, I guess."

Newton added another note.

"Make and model?" Newton asked, his grey eyes staring hard, as though he didn't believe a word that came out of Mitch's mouth.

A two-year-old, silver-grey Audi A5. Sleek and shiny. Lovely motor. Handled like a sports car, and driven by a pro.

"No idea, officer. Cars ain't me thing, y'know? Anyway, I were pretty well out of it by then. Don't remember nothing much. They half-carried, half-dragged me into it. Alls I know is the seat were soft and leather. Dark leather, grey or black."

"Can you describe them?"

"What? The seats?"

"No, Mr Bairstow, the Good Samaritans."

Mitch shook his head and, again, wished he hadn't. The headache flared up a little. He worked through them all in his mind.

Doc. Hazel eyes, longish dark hair, smooth skin. Tall and slim but nicely curved. Beautiful, in fact. A mature version of Regan. She smelled nice, too.

Black Ops. Blue eyes. Long, untrimmed beard. Longish hair, brown but turning grey. Wavy. Lean, fit. Forearms bunched like coiled ropes.

Goliath. Shortish dark hair. Craggy face. Ripped. Massive shoulders. Trim at the waist. Not a gram of spare fat on him. Eyes ... no idea.

"Not really. Everything's a bit of a blur, y'know? Two blokes and a bird—a woman. 'Fraid I can't tell you no more."

Newton stared at him for a bit, then started scribbling.

"Thank you, sir. We have two of them on the hospital's surveillance system."

"Why'd you ask me, then?"

"We like to get as much detail as possible."

"Why's you looking for 'em? They didn't do nothing but save an old soldier who were on the receiving end of a good kicking."

Although, come to think of it. Is there any such thing as a "good" kicking?

"A complaint has been made, sir."

"What sort of a complaint?"

"The complaint came from a member of the public. A driver. During your Good Samaritans' reckless drive to the hospital—"

"Reckless drive! Their mercy dash, you mean?"

Newton's lips stretched, again forming the thinnest of smiles. The forced, patient smile of a disinterested man. "As you say, sir. Their 'mercy dash'. They sideswiped the complainant's car. We actually have the incident on film."

"Did you tell the driver what were happenin'?"

"Yes, sir. We did, but ..." Newton's words trailed off and he took his turn to wince.

"Go on."

"Well, sir. Your saviours left the scene of a road collision, and that's an offence under the Road Traffic Act 1988."

Mitch reached up to his throbbing eye. For the first time since he'd regained consciousness, his missing foot itched. Finally, things were returning to normal.

More's the pity.

They'd be kicking him out soon. Maybe, if he played it right, he could squeeze out one more night of comfort.

"Ain't there summat called ... Oh, I dunno, 'extension' something or other?"

"You mean 'extenuating circumstances'?"

'Course I did, doughnut breath. I'm playing you.

"Yeah, yeah. That's right, officer. Don't saving my life count as these here 'extenerting' circumstances?"

"Ordinarily, they would, sir," Newton said. "Ordinarily, we'd take a statement from both parties and let the insurance companies deal with the matter."

"So, why isn't you doing that now?"

"The three individuals who rescued you and brought you here have disappeared. They failed to make a statement, and by doing so, they broke the law."

"Oh. I see."

Good on 'em.

"That's why I'm asking these questions, sir."

"Oh, I got you." Mitch raised one shoulder in a short shrug. "Sorry, Officer. Can't help you none, I'm afraid. I ain't never seen none of them before."

"And you've no idea where they are now, I suppose?"

"No, Officer. None whatsoever."

Newton grunted. "In that case, sir. I have no more questions at this time." He wrote some more notes, drew a line under his writing, and stabbed a full stop into the paper with the point of the pen. "If we find the men who attacked you, we'll be back in touch to arrange an identification—"

"Yeah, do me a favour, Constable Newton. They's hardly gonna walk into the local cop shop and hold up their hands to attacking me, is they?"

"You never know, sir. A witness might come forward with information."

And pigs could start applying for landing permission at Heathrow.

"Yes, they might."

"Now then, sir. Thank you for your time, and ... get well soon." He climbed to his size twelve feet and reached for the privacy screen.

"Thanks, Constable Newton. Have yourself a really wonderful day."

Newton stopped tugging on the screen mid pull. He turned, arched an eyebrow at Mitch, and nodded. "Mind how you go, sir," he said and ducked through the curtain.

"I will, Constable."

Good bloody riddance.

CHAPTER 28

Tuesday 23rd May – Mitch Bairstow

Brecon War Memorial Hospital, Powys, South Wales, UK

A few minutes after Constable Plod left, the double doors opened, and a couple of suits marched into the ward as if they owned the place. They ignored the other beds and headed straight for his bunk in the corner. The middle-aged bloke of average height, pushed slightly ahead of the tall, square-shouldered, and wide-hipped woman at his side. Both wore surgical face masks.

Face masks?

None of the medical staff wore face masks. Anyone would think Mitch carried something contagious, or they did.

The bloke stopped near the foot of his bed, and the woman moved a little closer.

"Mr Bairstow?" she asked.

"Yep, that's me."

Her cheeks bunched out into a smile—at least he imagined it was a smile. Not easy to tell if someone was smiling with their mouth hidden behind a face mask. Could have been a sneer or a grimace.

"Mr Bairstow," the bloke at the foot of the bed said, keeping things formal. "I'm Detective Sergeant William Sykes, this is Detective Constable Folly."

"Sykes, you say? Bill Sykes. Where's Oliver?"

"Very drole, sir," Sykes said, unamused. Eyes dead.

"Sorry, my bad sense o' humour. Cops make me nervous, and I crack jokes when I'm nervous. Can we start over?"

"No need to be nervous around the police, sir," DC Folly said. "Unless you've broken the law."

"Nope. I've been sinned against, I ain't the sinner."

Not this time.

"We're here to ask you about what happened yesterday," Sykes announced, speaking quietly.

"What, again? Don't you people talk to each other?"

A frown appeared on Sykes' high and shiny forehead, and the skin around his dark brown eyes creased. "Excuse me?"

"Constable Newton's just finished interviewin' me. You must've passed him in the corridor."

Sykes slid a quick glance at his partner and nodded. "We did. But he's a local. We're not."

"Not local?"

Folly stepped even closer. She had blue eyes and thick eyebrows. Didn't bother plucking them, neither. She'd tucked her shoulder-length dark hair behind her ears, which made them stick out big time, but she didn't seem to care. Her loose-fitting trouser suit hid any curves she might have had, not that it mattered. The woman had all the sex appeal of a cold, part-eaten burger.

Something about the two masked cops gave him the willies. Mitch took an instant dislike to them. Enough of a dislike to give them a hard time, but he'd keep it within reason. Couldn't take it too far or he'd wind them up too much. No telling what might happened if he went overboard.

"You didn't show me your warrant cards. Your proof of ID."

"Didn't we?" the bloke said.

"No, you didn't."

"How remiss of us," Folly added.

"Well?" Mitch said. "Let's see 'em."

Sykes speared Mitch with a pair of eyes so brown and opaque they could have been pools of muddy water.

Folly dipped a hand into the inside pocket of her grey jacket and tugged out a small, black leather wallet. She flipped it open—a metal badge flashed under the harsh strip lights—and closed it half a second later. Before she could return it to the pocket, Mitch held out his hand and beckoned with his fingers.

"Uh-uh, Constable. Gimme 'nother butcher's at that, will ya?"

Sykes bunched his hands into fists and clenched them so hard, his knuckles cracked. In anyone else, it would have appeared like a form of grandstanding, designed for effect. Somehow, on Sykes, it didn't.

"Come on," Mitch said. "If you don't give us another gander, I ain't tellin' you nothing. Hand it over. I need to see it up close on account of me 'aving this bad eye."

With more reluctance than he'd expected, Folly passed the ID wallet across.

Mitch flipped it open and took his time to study it carefully. On the left inside flap, an embossed metal badge glinted above a braille insert. The right flap held a photo, the name and rank, and a holo-gram. The name read Maureen Folly, the rank showed Detective Constable, and the top line attributed her as a member of the Metropolitan Police. It certainly *looked* genuine. He'd seen a few police warrant cards in his time.

"Let me see your face," he demanded.

She glanced at Sykes again. He dipped his head in a nod and she tugged down the mask to reveal a pair of thin, almost cruel lips. No lippie. No make-up of any kind. Her face matched the photo on the card. Not pretty. Not ugly, either. Average.

"Now you," Mitch said, looking at Sykes.

Even more reluctantly than Folly, the DS held up his ID wallet, which matched hers apart from the photo and name. Sykes didn't lower his mask and didn't offer the ID across. Mitch let it slide. No need to take things too far.

"Thanks," Mitch said.

Behind the detectives, a nurse entered the ward, pushing the locked meds trolley. She parked it just inside the doors and consulted a clipboard before she started doling them out.

"You from the Met?" he asked Folly, stating the bleeding obvious for want of anything more inciteful to say.

"Didn't we tell you?" she asked, offhand.

"No. You didn't, love. Long way off your beat, ain't you?"

"We're part of a Special Task Force—"

"Wow. A 'Special Task Force', eh," Mitch interrupted, trying not to be too sarcastic. "I am impressed. Honoured, too."

"Cut the sarcasm, son," Sykes growled. "We've had a long drive. Don't need a scrote like you pissing us about."

"Whoa there, Sarge." Mitch held up his hand once again. "Ain't no need for the hostility nor the language. This is an 'ospital, y'know."

Folly shot Sykes a glance and arched an eyebrow, silently asking him to leave her to it. After a moment of almost palpable tension, Sykes nodded and backed further away. He glared at Mitch, grabbed the bed's foot rail with both hands, and stood there, glowering at him.

"Forgive my sergeant, Mitch." Folly smiled, or sneered, again and softened her voice. She'd started playing it all nice and chummy. "We've been on the road all morning and he had to go without his breakfast. Makes him a tad irritable."

"Apology accepted from you, DC Folly. But I ain't inclined to forgive your sergeant. Nasty piece o' work, he is. Upsets me, he does."

"No, Mitch. He's a pussycat once you get to know him."

"Yeah, right. I believe you. Thousands would call you a bare-faced liar. Only you ain't bare faced, 'cause you's wearing a mask." Mitch watered down the insult with a smile that aggravated his throbbing cheek.

Bloody hell, man. Stop doing that!

The meds nurse reached the end of her round and looked at him from across the end of the bed opposite from his.

"How's the head today, Mr Bairstow?" she asked and held up the clipboard. "Need anything?"

Mitch placed the palm of his hand over the swelling. "No thanks, Nurse Hopkins. I'm okay. I'll struggle through as I am."

"Don't forget to take on plenty of fluids. You need to keep hydrated."

"I won't, but I will need a ... uh, bottle when my 'friends' have gone."

He waved a hand in the air between Sykes and Folly. Then, to placate her and show willing, he reached across to his bedside cabinet and picked up the water bottle with its disposable straw and sucked in a noisy mouthful.

The nurse smiled at the three of them and reversed her meds trolley back out through the doors. His fellow patients carried on doing what they'd been doing all morning. One sat up, eyes closed, listening to something through his earphones. Another lay on his side, facing away from Mitch, unmoving. The rest hadn't moved much all morning. None seemed to be taking any notice of Mitch and his visitors. Each had his own concerns.

"Wonderful staff here," he said to Folly, ignoring Sykes' deepening scowl—impatient bugger. "They look after me real good."

He almost winced at the bad grammar, but he loved playing the semi-literate vagrant.

Folly took a breath and looked ready to ask a question but stopped when Mitch held up a finger and took another pull on the straw.

I'm in charge here, Missy. Not you.

Once finished, he groaned for effect while returning the bottle to its place on the bedside table.

"So," he said, nodding, "what brings you two all the way to Wales from the Big Smoke?"

"Tell us what happened to you yesterday, and we'll tell you why we're here." Folly reverted to her earlier, more formal approach.

Seemed as though she couldn't maintain the warm and cuddly act for long.

"Well, sorry Officers, but you've had a wasted trip. I don't remember nothin' much. Everything's a bit of a blur, you know. I woke up on a park bench with a bunch of Welsh morons usin' me head as a rugby ball ..."

He repeated the story he'd laid out for Newton, going just as easy on the role Black Ops and his mates played in the event.

Mitch ended his tale with, "Next thing I knew, I woke up on a trolley in A & E with a bloke shinin' a bright light in me eyes. That's all. 'Fraid I don't got nothin' else to tell ya."

Really, I haven't.

"And you've never seen them before?" Folly asked.

"Nope. They was just a bunch o' thugs pickin' on a cripple. If it helps, one of 'em wore black boots with steel toecaps."

"Don't be dense, son," Sykes snarled from the foot of the bed. "You know who we're talking about."

Something about the way Sykes looked at Mitch with his dead, brown eyes worried him. Much worse than the arrogance and aggression, he came across as malicious. Spiteful.

"No, I don't," Mitch said. "I'm a bit thick, me. You'd better explain it and use little words to avoid confusion."

Sykes tightened his grip on the footboard. He opened his mouth to speak, but Folly interrupted him.

"We'd actually like to know about the people who brought you here," Folly said. "The ones who helped you."

"The ones what 'elped me? Oh, I see. Trouble is, I can't remember nothin' on account of me head injury. Why's you after them? Gonna give 'em a medal?"

"Just answer the question, son," Sykes said, seemingly having a hard time keeping control.

Son? Fuck you, arsehole.

Mitch turned to Folly, a slightly less offensive sight.

"No idea who they was, and I don't give a damn 'bout them fleeing the scene of no road accident, neither. That's what Constable Newton were bangin' on about. Those three picked me up off the street and drove me here. That's all as 'appened. Good people, they was." He paused long enough to swallow before carrying on. "They don't deserve being persecuted by a 'Special Task Force' down here from the Met. ... Is that it? Really?" Mitch scoffed and shook his head gently to avoid causing pain. "That's your job, is it? Chasin' people what skip out on traffic accidents?"

Folly shot Sykes another look. This time, Mitch couldn't read the message passing between them.

Again, Folly dipped her hand into her inside jacket pocket. This time, it came out clutching a mobile phone. She tapped the screen a couple of times, found what she was looking for, and turned the phone towards him, tilted sideways. The image flipped to landscape and displayed the identity page of a passport, showing a man with longish hair and a full beard. His name appeared at the side of the image, black on pale green and clear enough to read.

Black Ops!

For definite. No mistaking his face. Mitch had seen it before, too. Damned if he knew where from though.

"Do you recognise this man?" Folly asked.

"Nope." He reached out to the screen, but Folly pulled the mobile away.

"Are you sure?"

"Yeah."

"This is one of the people who drove you here," Folly said.

"It is?"

"Yes."

"How d'you know?"

"We've seen the hospital's surveillance footage."

"Right. That's his name, huh? William Griffin?"

"No, Mitch. It isn't," she said.

"That's his passport, right? Is you tryin' to tell me it ain't kosher?"

Sykes peeled his fingers from the footboard, leant forwards, and rested his forearms where his hands used to be. Not trying to be tough. The man didn't need to try. He had the dead eyes of a killer.

Mitch had seen plenty of blokes like him in the army. Blokes who couldn't wait for battle. Blokes who loved killing for killing's sake. Every army had its share of them. Sick fucks, the lot of them. A shiver rolled down Mitch's spine.

Dial it back, Mitch. This shit's getting serious.

"This man's a terrorist, Mitch," Folly said. "He's top of the UK's most wanted list."

"That," Sykes added, pointing to the mobile, "is Ryan Kaine."

Ryan Kaine! Shit!

Of course. Mitch knew he'd recognised Black Ops from somewhere. The story had been all over the news a few months back. The bombed plane. All those dead people. The papers banged on about it for weeks. Been quiet ever since, though.

Ryan Kaine. No wonder the Welsh mutt with the nose ring hadn't stood a chance. The kid was lucky Kaine let him live.

This time, Mitch managed to swallow.

"Don't be daft. That"—he jabbed a finger towards the image on the screen—"don't look nothin' like Ryan Kaine. His photo's been in the papers. Nah. Can't be him."

Folly withdrew the mobile from out of his face, tapped the screen again, and showed Mitch a new image. This one paired the first photo from the passport alongside Kaine's mugshot. Superficially different —one with long hair and a beard, the other with military crew cut and clean shaven—but the similarities were so obvious there could be little doubt.

Holy crap.

He'd been in the same car as a man wanted for murdering eighty-three innocent civilians. And he'd survived! In fact, he hadn't even felt threatened. On top of that, Ryan Kaine had probably saved his life. Why would a terrorist do that? It made no sense.

"You can't be serious."

"See for yourself, Bairstow," Sykes said. "Griffin and Kaine are the same person."

"Yeah." Mitch sniffed and raised his chin. "Looks like him, I grant you that. But ..."

"But what?" Folly asked.

"Why would a murdering *bastard*"—he mouthed the word to avoid disturbing the other patients—"like Ryan Kaine go out of 'is way to drive me to 'ospital? Don't make no sense, do it?"

"Who knows, Mitch," Folly answered. "No telling what drives a madman like Kaine."

"We'll ask him when we find him," Sykes added.

Yeah. As though a man like Kaine would sit still long enough to answer police questions.

"So, Mitch," Folly said, reverting to her friendly cop persona. "Can you help us? Can you help us find Ryan Kaine?"

Mitch stared at the paired photos again. Doing it allowed something in the back of Mitch's head to work free.

Glenn Close. Glenn ...

Bloody hell.

Not Glenn Close ... Glyn Coes!

The words hit him like another boot to the head. He'd seen the name on a road sign. Glyn Coes. Not a person, a farm on the edge of the Brecon Beacons. Mitch had trudged past the place a few weeks back.

Black Ops and his mates were heading for Glyn Coes.

Well, well, well.

He, Mitch Bairstow, had the answer. He knew the whereabouts of the UK's most wanted man. At least, where he was heading yesterday. Mitch allowed a smile to stretch across his battered face—didn't even mind the discomfort it caused. He turned to face Sykes.

"Dunno," Mitch said, playing it cagey. "Might do."

"You know where Kaine is?" Folly said, edging forwards, almost thrumming with excitement.

Slowly, carefully, Mitch tilted his head to one side. "Like I said. I might do. Might have overheard them talkin' in the car when they thought I were out of it."

Folly's free hand shot out. She grabbed Mitch's right forearm and squeezed with a grip so hard, she had to have developed it from slinging weights around in a gym.

"Where is he, Mitch?" she demanded, voice low, teeth clenched.

"Oi, leave it out, will ya?" Mitch tore his arm free from her grasp. "I's an injured man."

The intensity of Sykes' stare increased, and Folly drew even closer to the edge of the bed. She stood over him, a leaning tower of menace.

"Don't bugger us about, Bairstow. We could arrest you right now for ..." Sykes hesitated and turned to Folly.

Hello? Who's the boss here?

Bloody hell. Sykes wasn't a cop. He couldn't be. It meant Folly probably wasn't one either. That knowledge changed things. Changed them big time.

Folly took over from the man claiming to be her boss. "Aiding and abetting a criminal, obstructing the police in the execution of their duty, and perverting the course of justice. All of which are punishable by long terms of imprisonment. For perverting the course of justice, you could get life."

Mitch looked each so-called police officer in the eye and focused on Sykes.

"Bollocks," he said simply.

"What?" Sykes demanded.

"I said, bollocks. I didn't just fall out the nearest tree, you plonker. Cut the crap ... whoever you are."

"What do you mean by that?" Sykes asked, his voice deep, but his expression remaining blank behind the face mask.

"If I keep schtum, you don't got nothin'. Look around you. I'm in 'ospital with a serious head injury. If I clammed up and claimed to have lost me memory, no jury in the world would convict. Bloody case wouldn't even get to trial. So, don't you go threatenin' me with the law. It won't wash here, boyo."

"What about your civic duty?" Folly said.

"Civic duty? Fuck that." He pointed at his missing leg. "I've done me civic duty and look what it got me!"

"There's a reward," Sykes said, quietly.

Money? Now, there's a thought.

Mitch sniffed. "Now, that's a different story entirely. Who couldn't use a bit o' extra dosh."

Folly's cheeks expanded and her eyes narrowed into something that could have been a smile, but again the face mask made it difficult to tell. As he'd come to expect, Sykes' expression remained the same —unreadable.

"How much?"

"Five hundred pounds," Folly said.

"It ain't enough."

"Five hundred isn't enough?" Folly said. "Are you taking the mick?"

"Nah," Mitch said, adding a sneer for emphasis. "Last I heard, the reward on Ryan Kaine stood at half a million smackers. Wouldn't surprise me to learn that it had gone up a bit since then. I want a bigger cut."

"How much?" Sykes asked, leaning even closer.

That was too easy. Something really is up.

"One third."

"Fuck off," Folly snapped, anger bubbling in her low voice. "We're doing all the work and you want a third share? That isn't happening. No way."

Bingo.

He had them. How stupid did they think he was?

"Without me," Mitch said, still smiling, "you don't got nothin'. I know where Kaine is, and you don't got a clue. If you want your cut, I need a better share. And I want some up front. No way is I gonna trust a couple o' bozos claiming to be cops."

Folly tensed and shot another glance at her partner.

"What are you talking about?" she asked, lowering her voice to a stage whisper. She and Sykes turned to scan the rest of the ward, making certain no one was taking an undue interest in their conversation.

Mitch folded his arms across his chest. He had their attention and the upper hand, and he'd damn well keep it.

"If you two really was cops, you wouldn't be in line for a share of nothin'. Serving cops ain't entitled to claim no reward for doin' their jobs. Summat called a conflict of interest. So, let's get real, shall we? Who is you? And who is you really workin' for?"

Sykes and Folly shared another non-verbal exchange, after which, Sykes dipped his head.

"Okay, Maureen," he said. "He's made us. Tell him the truth."

The truth? This'll be interesting.

"We work for a ... private contractor," Folly began. "No point in telling you its name. You won't have heard of us. Suffice it to say, Her Majesty's Government have tasked us with finding and ... detaining Ryan Kaine."

"How you gonna do that when the whole police force has been searchin' for months and come up empty?"

"The police have plenty of other things to deal with," she said. "We, on the other hand, can dedicate all our considerable resources to any specific challenge we choose."

"What's more," Sykes interrupted, "the police are tied up in red tape. We aren't."

"You mean the cops have to abide by the law?" Mitch asked, masterfully stating the blindingly obvious.

"You have it in one, Mitch," Sykes said, taking on the charm offensive. A task he couldn't have been less suited for. "Furthermore, the police can't offer the same inducements we can."

"Bribes, you mean?"

Sykes stared at him through the dead, brown eyes. He lifted a thin eyebrow.

"Exactly," the so-called detective sergeant said. "Right, now we understand each other a little better, let's move this along. Time's passing and we want Kaine put away before he can hurt anyone else."

"Okay, fair enough," Mitch said. "What's your revised offer?"

Sykes paused for a second before answering. "The best we can do is ten grand. One now, the rest when we have Kaine in custody. Deal?"

"You've got one thousand quid in readies on you?"

"Yes, Mitch. We have."

"Bloody hell."

"We always come prepared," Sykes said and nodded to Folly.

Folly opened her jacket, removed a leather wallet, and counted out twenty crisp fifties.

"Nice. You'd better hand it over." Mitch smiled and held out his hand.

"Not until you tell us where Kaine is," Folly said. She folded the notes in half and held them close to her chest.

Mitch gave her what he considered his most winning smile.

"You got an internet connection on that fancy phone o' yours?"

She drew in her chin and frowned. "Of course."

Mitch held out his hand again. "Give me the money and I'll give you his location. Not before."

"You don't trust us?" Sykes asked.

"Nope. Not one bit. Give me the cash and don't give me no bollocks about payin' me the rest after Kaine's in jail neither. I know that ain't gonna happen. Bloke like Ryan Kaine won't give himself up. He'll go down fightin'. If I'm right, you is part of a bloody hit squad, ain't ya? *You're here to kill Ryan Kaine.*"

Mitch whispered the final part. No one in the ward could hear him but the fake cops.

"Does it matter?" Sykes asked.

Mitch twisted his lips into a sneer and snorted.

"Not to me, mate. The murderin' bugger killed eighty-three people on that plane. Deserves everythin' he got comin' to him. So, I'm happy with the one grand. That okay with you, *Detective Sergeant* Sykes?"

After a fleeting moment, Sykes nodded to Folly. She handed over the cash and he stuffed it down the front of his pyjama bottoms.

Let her try taking it back from there.

"Okay, Bairstow," Sykes said. "You've got your money. Where's Ryan Kaine?"

Mitch scratched his chin. Now he had their money safely hidden, he could play with them for a while.

"Ryan Kaine. Where is Ryan Kaine? Now, let me think ..."

Folly bent at the waist, leant over the bed, and rested her hand lightly on Mitch's stump through the bedding. Her eyes glistened with pleasure.

Evil. Pure evil.

"Don't mess us about, Bairstow," Sykes whispered. "You have your money. Where's Ryan Kaine?"

Folly leant down harder, increasing her weight on the stump. Pain exploded through Mitch's leg. Hot, throbbing pain. He gritted his teeth. Sweat poured out of him.

"Okay, okay," Mitch said, gasping. "You've made your bleedin' point. Pack it in. I'll give you Kaine."

"Good," Sykes said.

Folly pushed herself away from the bed, but not before patting the stump hard.

"Bitch!" Mitch muttered.

Folly snapped up her head, her pale blue eyes on fire. "What did you call me?"

Mitch kept smiling. "Nothin'. I didn't say nothin'. *Arsehole.*"

"You really are a nutter, aren't you," Folly said, staring at Mitch as though he'd fallen out of the nearest tall tree. "You know what we can do—with complete immunity—and you're still lying there winding us up."

"A nutter? Yep, that's me," Mitch answered through the same smile. "At least, that's what the psychiatrists say." Mitch double hitched his eyebrows. "Only they used fancier language. PTSD's one o' the nicest ways they described what I've got. Can't take the stress of ... well, life really. At least the quacks don't think I'm dangerous no more. Only to meself."

"What does that mean?" Folly asked.

"Self-destructive, I am. Wouldn't hurt a fly otherwise."

Sykes stood taller and pulled in a breath. "Are you going to tell us where Ryan Kaine is, or do we have to drag you out of here and find the nearest place suitable for some waterboarding? And don't think screaming's going to save you. You're a nutter. Screaming's what people expect of you."

"Yeah, yeah. Okay. A deal's a deal." Mitch turned to face Folly. "Pull up a satellite map of the Beacons, and I'll show ya where they is. I might let people call me a nutcase, but ain't no one gonna call Mitch Bairstow a liar or a thief. Always help 'the police' when I can. Just 'cause Ryan Kaine rushed me to 'ospital, don't mean he should get away with killin' all them poor innocent souls."

Folly's shoulders relaxed. Sykes' didn't, but an almost imperceptible sheen of excitement brightened the formerly dead eyes.

CHAPTER 29

Tuesday 23rd May – Late Evening

Cadwallader Farm, Glyn Coes, Powys, South Wales, UK

Ryan Kaine tugged on the rope he'd belayed the previous night, slid past the gnarled roots of a bush with tiny purple flowers, and pulled himself higher.

Nearly there.

Five metres later, he threw a leg over the edge of the ridge and rolled onto just about the only piece of flat land on his side of the valley. He scrambled the last few metres on hands and knees until he found a secure spot where he'd be hidden from the farm by more of the same purple-flowered bushes.

After a moment's pause to collect his breath and his bearings, he unclipped the waistband, slipped the backpack straps off his shoulders, and lowered the heavy Bergen to the exposed rock. He lay it flat on its back, and tested its stability, making sure it wouldn't topple. He'd lost count of the number of times he'd seen rookies lose all their equipment thanks to a carelessly positioned Bergen.

On his knees, he unzipped the Bergen's top flap, removed the field glasses, and took in his view for the upcoming few hours.

Perched on the edge of Great Scar, a high and rocky outcrop cut into the side of a steep valley by erosion and a quirk of nature, Kaine stared out over one of the most beautiful sights his eyes had taken in. A pure joy to behold. No wonder Gwyn Cadwallader called this part of Wales, "God's Country".

He reached up and tapped his earpiece.

"Alpha One to Alpha Two, are you receiving me? Over."

"*Alpha Two here.*"

Rollo's instant response made Kaine smile.

"*Receiving you, strength five. Been here ages. What's taken you so long? Over.*"

"The scenic route's a 'mare, Alpha Two. You had the nursery slopes. Over." Rollo also had the use of a car.

"*Sounds like you're panting hard, Alpha One. Perhaps you need to step up the training. Over.*"

Cheeky beggar.

"Keep your eyes and ears open, Alpha Two. No falling asleep like last time. Alpha One, out."

That'll get him.

Kaine double tapped the earpiece into silence, and sat cross-legged, his back pressed against the hard rock. He settled down to watch as the sun dropped closer to the rugged western hills.

KAINE FLEXED AND EXTENDED HIS FEET TO WARD OFF THE CRAMP threatening to tighten his calf muscles. Next, he tensed and relaxed all the major muscle groups in his body, working from feet to head: thighs and quads, hamstrings, glutes, abdominals, back, shoulders and arms, and finished with tiny head moments to keep his neck loose and largely pain free. Finally, he pulled in a deep, slow breath through his nose, held it for a fifteen count, and released it through his mouth, just as slowly. Following such a routine helped him to remain a mobile, relatively warm, and effective fighting machine.

Not that he expected to fight anyone in the immediate future.

Without fail, he'd repeat the same process every fifteen minutes throughout his vigil. The routine had saved his life many times in the past and would, no doubt, do so again.

Without specific countermeasures, lying still and prone on cold rock for hours on end would result in stiffness and cramp—an inevitable and invariable human weakness. If the enemy did arrive that night, he'd need to be swift and silent, and that couldn't happen if his body failed to react instantly to his mental commands.

He'd once spent five days lying in wait for his shot. His personal record in the field. Not long in the overall scheme of life, but long enough while enduring it. Back then, deep behind enemy lines with no one to rely on but himself it had been a nightmare of watching and waiting and wondering whether his target would arrive before the enemy found him or he died of exposure. He'd run out of water halfway through day four and lay in the searing, blinding desert heat for another whole day before the man—the insurgents' regional leader—finally fell under his cross hairs. Kaine's dehydrated condition nearly caused him to miss. His focus almost failed him, but not quite.

The shot, eleven hundred and fifty-five metres—not a record, not even close—had its own challenges. Downhill, with a gently gusting left-to-right crosswind, and without a spotter, the bullet missed the target—the centre of the insurgent's forehead—by a full fifteen centimetres. He'd missed it low, but the terrorist still died.

The .338 Lapua Magnum's FMJ bullet had smashed through the man's bearded chin, blowing it apart and carrying on through to shatter the spinal cord at the base of the neck. The man collapsed to the sand-and-dust-covered earth, dead before his fanatical buddies had even heard the report from Kaine's rifle—his preferred and trusty Accuracy AXMC.

The percussive crack from the shot bounced off the surrounding hills, the echo repeating as it decayed to silence, replaced by the angry whooping, hollering screams of the tribesmen who let loose a fusillade of unaimed small arms fire—hitting nothing but rock and plant life. The nearest shot didn't strike within one hundred metres of Kaine's nest. He remained still, fighting the desire to scramble away, waiting for the uproar to diminish and the insurgents to swarm the area. They didn't have a clue where he hid.

Sniping.

Some might call it a cowardly way to kill, but when the target's prime method of operation was to send suicide bombers—some of them children—to murder and maim innocent civilians, including other children, Kaine lost no sleep over his kills. No sleep at all.

This current operation, though, involved no weapons other than stealth. For this task, he wouldn't need his rifle with its specially commissioned targeting 'scope. In fact, for this operation, the only weapons he carried were a comms unit, a ceramic dagger, and his wits.

"Come on," he muttered to the surrounding rock, "where are you? Don't be shy, now."

He sat, leaning against the old red sandstone, eyes clamped to his Zeiss 20x60 binoculars, sweeping the same bucolic scene—the farmhouse, outbuildings, stables, paddocks, fields, and their immediate surroundings—in the valley below.

Nothing moved except the wildlife. Nightjars on the wing churred their unnerving calls, owls hooted in the trees, and bats bounced and weaved through the air. A lone fox barked into the night. Horses whinnied in their stables. Cows and sheep slept and passed wind, destroying a fraction more of the ozone layer. The brook winding through the valley babbled over rocks. The sounds carried on a stiffening south-westerly breeze.

The mist-shrouded sun would slip beneath the western crags in an hour or so and would leave enough residual light to see the farm and the valley floor for at least another ninety minutes. After that, he'd have to resort to the imperfect view through his FLIR Scout thermal camera. At nine hundred metres, the main targets remained within the FLIR's maximum operating distance, a factor that had determined the location of Kaine's observation point—a point more suited to a mountain goat, or a nesting nightjar than a human watcher. A point where he could take in the majority of the farm in a single, slow, and sweeping pan of the binoculars.

A light rain started falling. Slowly, it increased in intensity, adding to Kaine's discomfort.

The things he did for members of The 83. But he'd never complain.

Not ever.

They deserved everything he could give them. Everything he had. It wasn't much. It didn't compensate for the pain he'd caused them. But it was all he had to give apart from the money.

Rustling.

Movement!

Behind and to his right.

At last!

Stone tumbled over rock, falling away into the valley.

Whoever made the noise, knew precious little about a covert approach.

Amateurs.

Kaine eased away from his slightly exposed position and ducked deep into the patch of bushes, moving slowly to minimise his effect on the undergrowth. With the vegetation in front and the sandstone stretching up behind him, he'd be hidden from view.

He pulled the dagger from its sheath at his calf, listened, and waited.

Come on, come on.

CHAPTER 30

Cadwallader Farm, Glyn Coes, Powys, South Wales, UK

Kaine held his breath.

More scuffling, quiet panting, as the intruder drew ever closer.

The rain stopped.

Moments later, a small, dark shape appeared over the broken edge of the ridge. Small and lithe. Too small to be a danger. Blond hair reflected the ambient light. Kaine jumped to his feet.

"Rhodri! What the hell—"

The boy squeaked, jerked backwards. His feet slipped on loose gravel. Arms flailing, he toppled sideways, teetering on the edge of nothingness. His high-pitched scream split the night.

Kaine threw out a hand, caught the lad by the front of his jacket, gripped hard, and tugged him close.

"Help!"

"It's okay, son. I've got you."

Thin arms encircled Kaine's waist, squeezing tight. Rhodri panted. His fluttering heartbeat thumped against Kaine's midriff. The boy sniffled, and the breath caught in his throat.

"I've got you," Kaine repeated, this time more softly. He released his grip on the lad's jacket, wrapped an arm around his skinny shoulders, and backed them away from the edge. "You're safe now," he said, as much for his own benefit as the boy's.

Rhodri eased his grip, pulled his head back, and looked up. Tears glistened on his pale cheeks and his chin trembled.

"Y-You scared me," he said, his voice thin and reedy.

You terrified me!

Kaine caught hold of the boy's upper arm, dragged him closer to the bivouac, and dumped him down on his skinny backside.

"Bloody fool," he snapped in anger fuelled by fear. "Sneaking up on me like that. What the hell do you think you were doing? You could have been killed."

"I-I wasn't sneaking up on you," Rhodri wailed.

He tried scrambling to his feet, but Kaine dropped firm hands on his shoulder and pressed him back into the dirt.

"I-I didn't even know you were up here. How could I? You didn't tell me."

Kaine opened his fists and flexed his fingers. The boy had a point, unless he'd been earwigging them discussing their plans in the Lodge. If he'd tried following Kaine up the trail, he would have given himself away. During his approach, the lad had made enough noise to wake Rollo, on the other side of the valley.

"Wait right there," Kaine ordered, jabbing an index finger at his charge. "Don't you dare move one inch. Understand?"

Tear-filled eyes wide, chin-trembling, Rhodri nodded.

"Say it," Kaine insisted.

"Y-Yes. I understand. I-I'll stay here." His breathing still faltered, but it had calmed since his brief flirtation with the precipice.

Kaine turned away to hide a shudder from the lad. He pulled in a deep breath and released it slowly. The combination of fear and anger had flooded adrenaline through his system, and he fought the familiar after-effects—the shakes, fatigue, and nausea. He couldn't let Rhodri see his reaction. The lad could only see a man in full control.

Kaine bent low, searching with his eyes, not with his fingers. He'd made that mistake once before, years ago, and wouldn't make it again. Sliced fingertips weren't exactly fun.

Where the hell was it?

Ah. There you go.

Despite its matt-black finish, he found the discarded dagger easily enough. It had fallen, point first. The blade had buried itself three centimetres into the dirt, and its handle offered itself up for safe retrieval. Kaine wiped the blade on his trouser leg, re-sheathed it, and returned to his nest. True to his word, Rhodri hadn't moved.

Kaine squatted in front of the boy, who stared at the dagger in wonder.

"Explain yourself," Kaine ordered.

Rhodri swallowed hard. He pulled his eyes from the knife handle and found focus on Kaine's chest.

"Look at me, son. I won't bite."

The shimmering blue eyes met Kaine's. He blinked and they spilled more tears.

"I-I come here all the time. To get away. I-It's my favourite spot."

"You come here at night?"

Rhodri dipped his chin and lowered his eyes.

"Yes. Sometimes. I-It helps."

"In what way?"

"Quiet up here. Helps me ... think. Helps me remember."

Oh hell.

In an instant, Kaine understood.

"Remember your mother?"

Rhodri sniffled. He pulled a tissue from his coat pocket and blew his nose. After another sniffle, he blew his nose again and wiped it dry.

"Sometimes, during the night," he said, his tiny voice little more than a whisper carried on the gentle breeze, "I forget what she looks like. Being up here helps me ... see her again. Up here, I can ... talk to her. Tell her what's happening. Share my life."

The lad made perfect sense. When Kaine lost his dad at about the same age as Rhodri, he used to disappear into the fields around their home to talk with him. It helped ease the pain a little.

"What was she like?" Kaine asked, although the last thing in the world he wanted to learn about was one of his victims. "Tell me about her."

The youngster shook his head, but he carried on in his soft Midlands accent. "Always smiling, she was. Trying to pretend she was happy and things were good. Always tried to protect me from ... the bad stuff. When Dad left us, it was better, but we ... struggled, but she did her best. Me and Mum against the world. We didn't have much money, but"—he looked up at Kaine, defiant—"we had each other. Then she left, too."

"She didn't want to go, son," Kaine said, the words tore from his throat as though wrapped in barbed wire. He held out a hand, but the boy flinched, and Kaine lowered it to his knee.

"You're not my dad," Rhodri said. He almost sounded wistful. "My dad went and didn't come back, and I'm glad."

"Why?"

"Huh?"

"Why are you glad?"

Rhodri clamped his lips together and shook his dishevelled blond head.

"Did he hurt you?"

Again, the lad's chin trembled. "No ... not ... not me, Mum."

"He hit your mother?"

He sniffled and lowered his head.

"Have you heard from him?"

Another shake of the head, this one violent. Rhodri swallowed and lowered his gaze, trying to hide his emotions.

"Social Services tried to contact him, but he's disappeared. No one knows where he is. That's why I'm here. In this ... place." He spoke quietly, keeping his head low, studying the dark ground.

Kaine cast his eyes over the valley as it spread out below them. Even in the gathering dusk, its beauty stood out clear and strong. Something in his expression must have reached through to the lad.

"I-I know. It's really beautiful. It is, and Aunty Becky's lovely. Dewi and Myfanwy are really kind too, but ... Uncle Gwynfor ... he's horrible. He hates me, and I hate him back. I do!"

Kaine reached forwards and rested a hand on the lad's shoulder. "He doesn't hate you, son—lad. He has his own beliefs and they're sometimes difficult for anyone else to understand. But he loves you. I can tell that. Remember, he's hurting, too."

"He is?"

"Of course he is. You lost your mother in the ... crash, but he lost his sister. He's having to come to terms with that, and ... I've seen photos of you and your mother together. You look so much alike. You must remind him of her. Think how that must make him feel."

The boy's chin trembled. "I don't look anything like Mum, do I?"

"You do. Same hair colour, same eyes, and that cleft on your chin. You're the spitting image of her."

"No, no." The boy's hand shot up to his chin and rubbed it hard as though trying to iron out the small crease. "Dad had the cleft, not mum. I hate it. Hate it. Mum was beautiful. Dad was ... horrible."

"Sorry, Rhodri. I never met your mother."

And he'd only glanced at the picture. Whenever possible, he avoided looking at photos of his victims. The words "gut" and "wrenching" didn't do the sensation justice.

Rhodri sniffled and wiped his nose with the tissue again. "That's okay. You weren't to know."

"Either way, give your uncle a break, eh? He might be finding life a little difficult, too. And remember, he did give you Nightwatch."

Rhodri frowned in thought, and his lips rolled in on themselves.

"Nightwatch. Yes, I suppose you're right. He's why I came up here tonight. I wanted to tell Mum all about him. I would have gone to see Nightwatch tonight, but Fan said he needs his sleep, and I didn't want to disturb him." The words tumbled from the boy's mouth. Excitement overtaking the other emotions.

Kaine patted his hands in the air for the boy to lower his voice. Sounds travelled so far at night the lad's excited words might even carry into the valley.

"Did you see him? Did you see Nightwatch yet?" Rhodri asked, using only slightly less volume. "Only a day old and he's already eating from my hand. Beautiful, isn't he?"

"He certainly is, Rhodri. Best looking calf I've ever seen."

"He's not a calf, he's a foal!"

"Is he?" Kaine grinned.

"Oh, ha-ha. Very funny."

"I try my best, Rhodri. Bet you're looking forwards to riding him, eh?"

"Can't do that for ages. Fan said he won't be big enough to ride for at least two years. And I've got to learn how to take care of him first. Got to learn to ride, too."

"The time will fly, lad. You'll be putting a saddle on him before you know it."

"But two years!"

The comms unit in Kaine's ear clicked.

"Alpha Two to Alpha One, are you receiving me? Over."

Kaine pressed the earpiece harder into his ear, stared at Rhodri, and raised a finger to his lips. Quick on the uptake, the lad took the message and nodded. His eyes shone, but this time with excitement rather than tears.

"Alpha One to Alpha Two," Kaine said, voice low. "Receiving you strength five. Over."

"Alpha One, do you see it? Over."

"See what? Over."

"Check your eastern perimeter. Three o'clock. Over."

"Alpha Two, hold tight. Over."

Kaine dived into the nest and grabbed the binoculars. He turned towards the valley, took a knee, and raised the glasses to his eyes. Two miles to the south. A large truck showing only sidelights crawled along the road leading to the western edge of Ten Acre Field.

Contact.

Kaine gripped the glasses tighter, steadying them by resting an elbow on his raised knee.

Damn! Why does it have to be tonight?

He lowered the glasses and tapped his earpiece.

"I see them, Alpha Two. Contact, Ten Acre Field. West gate. Give them time to do their thing. See you in twenty. Alpha One, out."

Kaine tucked the binoculars into their pocket in the Bergen and turned to face the boy.

"What's happening?" Rhodri whispered.

"Rustlers," Kaine said, pointing down towards the valley. "Looks like they're after more sheep."

"What are you going to do?"

"Follow them."

Rhodri shot to his feet and peered into the gathering gloom. "Can I come?"

"Not a chance. Things could get dangerous."

"Oh, please?"

"No," Kaine said, adamant. Where he and Rollo were going was no place for kids. "But ..."

"Yes?" Rhodri asked, almost bouncing on his heels.

"How are you for heights?"

"Okay. I climb up here all the time. Sometimes in the dark, too. And in the rain."

"Ever done any abseiling?"

The frown creasing the youngster's brow and the accompanying shrug gave Kaine his answer.

"Okay. I need to get down to Adrian ... and fast."

He pointed to the rope he'd anchored to the rock face in preparation. It dangled over the edge of the rocky outcrop and disappeared into the darkness. The drop was almost vertical. "If I take you with me, will you promise to head straight back to the farm?"

"I-I can't go down there."

"Yes, you can. It's easy."

"Wh-What do I do?"

"Remember piggyback rides? Hold on tight, and I'll lower us both down."

"Oh God." The boy swallowed hard.

"Quickly, Rhodri. We don't have much time. They'll be getting away."

Kaine turned his back to the lad and squatted. A pair of thin arms wrapped around his neck and squeezed. Kaine stood. The boy weighed less than a fully loaded Bergen. He tapped the lad's skinny forearm.

"Not too tight, Rhodri. I need to breathe."

The grip loosened enough for Kaine to draw breath.

"That's better. Don't forget your legs."

He grabbed the backs of Rhodri's thighs, placed them in position around his waist, and crossed the ankles at the front. The lad pressed his chin into the crook of Kaine's neck and shoulder, his breathing rapid, and his breath warm.

"Ready?"

The boy nodded.

"Don't drop me."

"Hold tight. This won't take long."

Kaine shifted the minimal load to a slightly more comfortable position and bent at the knees to pick up the rope. He tugged hard. The anchor held firm.

Good enough.

He removed the belay plate from its pouch on his safety harness, attached it to the central strap, and did the same with the prusik cord. He fed a small loop of rope through the anchor point in the belay plate and fastened it to the carabiner. Ordinarily, he wouldn't have bothered with a prusik loop for so short a drop, but with Rhodri's added weight he needed it for safety. He wrapped it around the leading run of the rope and used it as a dead man's handle.

He patted Rhodri's knotted hands.

"Ready?"

The lad's chin dug into Kaine's neck twice. He took it as a nod.

"Okay, here we go."

Moving more cautiously than normally, Kaine released the rope through his lower hand and backed out over the edge. Rhodri's breathing rate increased as they hovered out into space and his arms and legs gripped tighter. Kaine release his upper hand and hooked it under the lad's rump, adding to the security.

Feet wide apart and planted flat to the rocky outcrop, Kaine descended, gaining speed as he grew more confident.

Rhodri's head pulled away from Kaine's neck, leaving a cold space where his hot breath used to be.

"Okay?"

"Yes," Rhodri squealed. "This is brilliant!"

"Pipe down, lad," Kaine snapped, smiling with relief. "We're supposed to be running silent."

"Sorry," the boy whispered directly into Kaine's ear.

Kaine loosened the prusik cord, kicked away from the rock face, and bounced down to the foot of the Scar. The wind whistled in his ears and Rhodri's barely subdued squealing added to the excitement.

Kaine increased the grip on his brake hand and pulled it away from his body, slowing their descent. He touched down gently and bent into another a squat.

"Down you get, lad."

Rhodri peeled himself off Kaine and stepped back onto firm, flat ground.

"That was fantastic!" Rhodri said, barely able to contain his excitement. "It felt like we were flying. Can you teach me how to do it on my own?"

"Maybe one day. Stay there. Don't move."

Kaine unclipped himself from the rope, removed the harness, and turned to face the boy. He dropped to one knee and signalled for the lad to do the same.

"Listen carefully," he whispered.

Rhodri nodded, the movement a faint blur in the growing darkness of the valley.

"Are you wearing a watch?"

"Yes."

"Wait here a full five minutes, then head back to the farm and get to bed. Okay?"

"Yes."

"Promise?"

Another nod barely visible in the darkness. "I promise."

"You can't tell anyone what we just did. We must keep it as our secret."

"Oh, but—"

"Listen, Rhodri ... Rhod. If anyone finds out about what we just did, I'd be in real trouble."

"Why?"

"Abseiling at night is dangerous."

"But it was brilliant. You were—"

"If you promise not to tell anyone, I promise to teach you how to abseil safely. Deal?"

The lad hesitated.

"Deal?" Kaine repeated.

"Okay. It'll be our secret."

He reached out and tousled the boy's hair.

"Good lad. Five minutes, okay?"

Rhodri tugged back the sleeve of his jacket to expose his wristwatch. "Five minutes," he said. "I promise."

Kaine stood and turned to leave.

"Mr Sidings?"

"Yes, Rhod?"

"Go kick some slimy butt!"

Kaine shook his head. "Your uncle's right, lad. You play too much *Call of Duty*."

The blond head shook. "There's no such thing as too much *Call of Duty*."

"See you in the morning."

"Will you tell me what happened?"

Kaine pretended not to hear the question, turned, and melted into the night.

CHAPTER 31

Tuesday 23rd May – Late Evening

Cadwallader Farm, Glyn Coes, Powys, South Wales, UK

Blanket clouds scudded across the night sky, driven by a stiffening south-westerly breeze. No moon, no stars, but the sunset's afterglow bathed the western horizon a pale grey, offering plenty enough light to see by. When he reached the woods, some eight hundred metres from his destination, Ten Acre Field, Kaine's earpiece clicked again.

"Alpha Two to Alpha One. Can you hear me? Over."

"Alpha One to Alpha Two. I hear you. Over."

"You know I heard all that, Alpha One? Over." Rollo couldn't hide the amusement in his voice. He didn't appear to be trying too hard, either.

"Heard all what? Over."

"Abseiling down the face of a vertical cliff with a twelve-year-old on your back? Naughty, naughty. Over."

"Don't exaggerate, Alpha Two. It's nowhere near vertical, and the drop couldn't have been much more than seventy metres. Seventy-five, tops. Over."

"*How many health and safety rules did you break? Over.*"

"Alpha Two, the lad was perfectly safe. Over."

"*Wouldn't let the doc hear about it, Alpha One. You'd be in even more trouble than you were for the France thing. Over.*"

Kaine winced and intentionally changed the subject.

"Where are you and what are the targets up to? Over."

"*I'm at the eastern end of the field. Four o'clock. Pick up the lane from the farm, head east, and you can't miss me. The targets—three of them on quad bikes—have collected about thirty sheep. They're herding them towards the truck now. They'll be on their toes soon. Over.*"

"On my way. Alpha One, out."

Hands held up in front to protect his face from low hanging branches and twigs, Kaine hurried downhill through the patchy woods and scrub. He broke through the treeline, reached a level pasture, and high-stepped over the long grass, heading north-east. The effort made him breathe more heavily. Up on the rock, the stiff breeze had carried the quad bike's angry buzzing away from him and from the farm, but as he drew closer to Ten Acre Field, the noise became clear. A hornet's drone left and right.

Kaine reached the hedgerow marking the pasture's border, turned right, and followed it east until he found the rusted five-bar iron gate. He vaulted over it, landed softly on the grassy verge, and stepped out onto the gravelled lane. Still heading downhill, he picked up the pace, keeping to the side of lane and dodging the deep, rain-filled potholes, keeping the quad bikes' drone to his left.

The lane curved around to the north-west and ended abruptly at a T-junction, where it joined a metalled road that ran east to west. Kaine scurried close to the hedge and took a knee.

Straight ahead stood another hedgerow, two metres tall and densely packed with brush, hazel, cherry, and hawthorn, forming a great natural barrier to the field beyond. Fifty metres to his left, a break in the hedge showed another iron gate, this one open but blocked by a large DAF truck, closed side panels, enclosed roof, hydraulic tilting trailer. Dark green, lights out, it blended into the surroundings as well as any non-camouflaged vehicle had a right to do. The driver had partially reversed the DAF into the field, ready for a fast getaway.

Dipped headlights from the quad bikes filtered through the hedgerow, gathered close to the rear of the truck. Sheep bleated. Hooves clattered on wooden boards as the rustlers loaded their bounty.

Kaine tapped his earpiece.

"Alpha One to Alpha Two. Show a light. Over."

For a moment, a dim red glow flashed to Kaine's right. He locked its position into his memory and took off at a sprint. Twenty seconds later, he dived into the Astra's front passenger seat and closed the door quietly, breathing hard.

"Evening, sir," Rollo said, without turning his head. "What took you so long?"

Kaine ignored the question and slowed his breathing.

"How many?" he asked.

"A driver and the three on the quad bikes," Rollo answered, keeping his eyes straight ahead, trained on the view through the windscreen. Like the truck's driver, Rollo had reversed the Astra into another break in the hedge, ready to head out in either direction. "Won't be long now," he added.

Kaine checked the time on his watch. 22:37. The targets had been on site for less than twenty-five minutes. Efficient. No wonder rustlers were getting away with so much livestock.

The quad bikes' lights stopped moving and the dull triple-drone softened to a burbling idle. Hinges squealed, and a tailgate slammed into place. Another door banged and the truck's diesel engine roared into life.

"Here they come," Rollo said, but made no move to fire up the Astra's motor.

Lights out, the truck edged through the gap in the hedge and turned right, heading away from Rollo and Kaine. The three quad bikes followed, in a red, firefly tail, weaving in and out, bumping fists. Kids having fun. Playing high jinks.

Still, Rollo didn't move a muscle. His arms remained crossed over his powerful chest.

Kaine leant back into his seat. "I take it you planted a bug?"

Rollo smiled knowingly. He freed a hand and keyed the ignition. The Astra purred into quiet life, sounding a million times healthier following Rollo's hours of attention that afternoon. As it turned out, the workshop in Gwyn's barn contained all the equipment Rollo needed to turn the Astra from a coughing, grumbling disaster into a reliable car fit for their purposes. He'd also attached a phone mount to the windscreen which held his mobile in its secure grip.

"I uploaded the app this afternoon. It's so neat. Watch this."

He touched a finger to the phone's screen. A night-time map of the valley appeared, and a flashing red light crawled along the road, heading west.

"What's the range?"

"Under optimal conditions, five or six miles. But all these hills will reduce that quite a bit."

The flashing red dot reached the turning on to the A4067 and headed north, towards the A470.

"Time to go?" Kaine asked.

Rollo answered by selecting first gear and adding a little pressure to the throttle. The Astra took off, the front wheels throwing gravel into the floor pan. A quick twitch on the steering wheel centred the car into the middle of the lane and they rolled through the gathering night.

"Myfanwy won't appreciate you treating her new car like that."

"This isn't her car yet. If I break it, I'll buy her another one out of my wages," Rollo said through a happy smile. "Since this is an official 83 operation, I'm on expenses for the duration. Right?"

"Right. In that case, floor it. I don't want these buggers getting away."

"They won't."

Rollo pushed the aging Vauxhall faster. They reached the junction with the A4067 and turned right, closing quickly on the GPS screen's blinking red dot. The road straightened and the DAF's lights glowed red some five hundred metres distant. The quad bikes had disappeared. Rollo slowed enough to match the truck's speed and they settled in for what they expected to be a long haul.

"WHAT DO YOU RECKON?" KAINE ASKED. THEY'D BEEN TAILING THE DAF for thirty minutes. "Local abattoir or smuggled to the Continent?"

"My money's on the local abattoir. It's easier to shift cuts of meat in a refrigerated truck than live sheep in an animal transporter."

"Yep. That's my guess too."

"Hang on, what's this?"

The road dipped into another valley, the DAF slowed sharply, and its indicator signalled for a left turn.

Rollo eased his foot off the throttle. He pulled the Astra onto the side of the road and cut the lights. The engine ticked over on fast idle. On the screen, the GPS showed a minor road leading deep into the heart of nowhere.

The DAF turned left and stopped.

"That's interesting," Kaine said.

"What's he doing?"

In the gathering darkness they had no idea what was happening on the road below them.

Rollo reached up and pressed the "zoom out" button on the GPS screen. The map expanded in size, revealing more and more of the surrounding area. To the left, it showed nothing but a narrow, winding lane, empty space, and the wriggling blue line of a small watercourse. The lane ran parallel to the blue line. Kaine traced its route north to a string of four small bodies of water, the largest and furthest north marked as *Ceri Reservoir*.

A full minute later, the DAF pulled forwards a little way and stopped again.

"That's a private road," Kaine announced. "The driver's opened a gate and now he's locking it again."

"Private land? Out here in the Beacons? Must be a farm."

"Some of these tracks lead to quarries and abandoned coal mines."

"Really?"

Kaine nodded. "I saw a few signs when I scoped out the Powell farm this afternoon. I've also been running some research on the area."

"Research? Hmm." Rollo arched a quizzical eyebrow.

"Didn't get much sleep today. Still jet-lagged."

"You slept long enough on the Gulfstream, though." He couched the statement as an accusation and said it po-faced.

Cheeky beggar.

"Will you ever let that lie?"

"Doubt it." Rollo grinned.

Below them, the DAF started moving again. Rollo released the handbrake and the Astra rolled slowly down the hill. He kept the speed to a sedate thirty mph and switched on the sidelights.

"Apart from disused coal mines," Kaine continued, "there are a couple of gold mines hereabouts, too."

"Really?"

"Yep. Welsh gold is incredibly rare and incredibly valuable. Didn't you know?"

"Welsh gold? Oh yes, that's right. The Royal Family ... wedding rings and such?"

"Exactly."

They reached the turning and pulled tight to the side of the road. A pair of steel mesh gates blocked their way, and a big brass padlock shone bright under the Astra's yellowing sidelights. A faded sign attached to the left-hand gate read:

Lloyds & Sons Ltd.
Quarry Works.

Danger. No swimming. No entry.
Trespassers will be Prosecuted.

A SIMILAR SIGN ON THE OTHER GATE REPEATED THE MESSAGE IN WELSH.

Beyond the gate the deeply rutted and potholed track wound up the hill, hemmed in either side by rusty wire fences.

"Don't suppose you've got your picks with you?"

"You know me, Colour Sergeant." Kaine winked. "Never leave home without them. Keep your eye on the screen. We've no idea how far they're going or how long they'll take."

He unfastened his seat belt, cracked open the door, and slid out.

The DAF's engine thundered into the distance, straining to climb the steep hill towards the rocky outcrop at the summit. Its headlights bobbed and weaved, bouncing around in the darkness, showing the woeful state of the track. Kaine pitied the animals being thrown around in the back of the truck. The poor things would be terrified. Maybe injured, too. This had to stop.

Kaine pulled a set of house keys from his pocket. He removed the false metal sheath covering two of the brass Yale keys and revealed a tensioner and a rake pick. The Chubb padlock, new and well oiled, took just a few seconds to open. Kaine unclasped the padlock, released the bolt, and swung open the gate. He held it open until Rollo passed through with the Astra and closed it again, refitting the padlock but leaving it unclasped.

Once back in the car, Kaine nodded, and Rollo took off.

"Can you turn off the sidelights?" Kaine asked.

"Good idea." Rollo threw him a sideways glance and smiled. He reached forwards and rotated a switch on dashboard. The lights cut out and darkness grew all around them.

"Couldn't do that in an Audi," Rollo said. "More brownie points for the Astra."

"Take it easy," Kaine said.

Rollo slowed the car even further.

"No telling what we'll find up there," Kaine said. "For all we know we could be heading towards a pop-up abattoir and a gang of heavily armed butchers."

"This road's little more than a farm track. No way I'm going to speed. I'd hate to throw a tyre or crack a suspension arm. It's a long walk back to the farm."

They climbed the hill slowly and crested a rise. Ahead of them and to the west, stretched out the Ceri Reservoir, showing as a silver disk in the darkening twilight.

Higher up and to their right, the DAF's headlights had stopped moving. They showed bright behind a dense stand of bushes, turning the plants into transparent-leaved, black-limbed skeletons.

Rollo stopped the Astra in the middle of the lane. The deep ruts, high verges, and rusted fences on either side gave him no other option.

The DAF's headlights pulled forwards, the twin funnels of light raked the night sky, and then reversed. Fortunately, the Astra's position, three hundred metres back down the hill, kept them out of the headlights' glowing arc.

"What the hell's he doing? That's the quarry. He's getting damn close to the edge."

"I don't like it," Kaine said, noting the urgency in Rollo's voice. "Kill the motor for a minute."

Rollo cut the ignition and an eerie silence flowered around them. Seconds later, the Astra's crinkling-hot engine clicked and spat as it cooled.

In the distance, the DAF's heavy diesel engine roared, the noise reverberating through the valley, increasing in pitch as the truck reversed up a steep incline, heading towards the quarry's vertical drop. The DAF stopped again, air brakes hissed, and the driver's door opened. The cab's courtesy light flared and remained lit as the driver left the door open.

Illuminated by the backwash from the headlights, the driver—a tall, trim man, wearing faded torn jeans and a dark sweatshirt—climbed down from the cab and sidestepped towards the rear. He moved slowly, pressing his back against the side of the truck to avoid taking a headlong tumble into the darkness. A howling gale driving into the driver's face whipped his wavy blond hair around his head. Terrified sheep screamed and bleated behind the truck's metal sides —the pitiful, gut-wrenching sounds driven by the same storm force gale.

"Oh God. He's unloading them!"

"Get me up there, Rollo. Hit the lights!"

Rollo keyed the ignition, the Astra's ancient engine fired up, coughed, and died. He tried the ignition again. Nothing happened.

"Damn it, Rollo," Kaine roared. "I thought you'd sorted the bloody thing."

Kaine threw open the passenger door and slid through the gap. The courtesy light threw out a pitiful yellow glow. It dimmed and faded with each turn of the starter motor.

"Give me some lights and sound your horn. Scare the bugger off!"

The headlights flared for a moment, then died. Nothing. The screaming from the sheep and the howling gale the only sounds.

"Main fuse must have blown!" Rollo called, but Kaine barely heard him.

Roaring at the top of his voice, a screaming banshee, Kaine took off up the hill, keeping to the deep ruts and treading carefully, he ran as fast as he dared.

"Stop, you bastard!" he yelled. "Stop!"

The wind whipped away his words, carrying them down into the valley, away from the DAF and its driver.

Two hundred and fifty metres separated Kaine from the truck.

It might have been a mile.

Two hundred metres.

Legs driving, pounding, stomping. Fists pumping, grasping at the empty air, trying to pull him forwards. Lungs pulled in cold air, sucked oxygen into starved blood. He raced on.

A full lung-bursting minute later, blowing hard, Kaine reached the tiny spur where the DAF had turned off the lane and reversed towards the quarry's edge.

One fifty.

At the opening, a sign attached to the fence read:

Danger:
Risk of Rockfall

HE BARELY HAD TIME TO READ IT.

One hundred.

The closer he drew to the truck, the louder the sheep's hideous crying became. The track grew steeper, the underfoot conditions worsened, became more treacherous. Kaine slowed his pace. Safety first.

"Stop!" Kaine screamed, the words lost to the squally wind.

At the tailgate, the blond driver pulled a lever at the rear of the truck. Slowly, the top of the tailgate peeled away from the trailer. It teetered for a moment and fell. After clattering into the cliff's craggy edge, it bounced, and settled. A large rock broke away, plummeting into the darkness. Sensing freedom, the sheep's bleating increased in volume and stridency. Blondie stepped back against the rear wheel.

Nothing happened.

Fifty metres.

Blondie lowered his head, studying something in his hand, a rectangular box attached to a cable. He pressed a button on the box. An electric motor whirred. The front of the trailer started to rise, pulling away from the cab.

Hooves scraped metalwork. Squeals turned to tortured shrieks. Fluffy white clouds with wide eyes and open mouths, erupted from the rear of the truck and tumbled into the night, screaming as they fell.

CHAPTER 32

Tuesday 23rd May – Night

The Quarry, Powys, South Wales, UK

"No!" Kaine yelled.

Blondie's head jerked up and snapped around to face Kaine. Fear and shock flashed onto a handsome and vaguely familiar face.

"What the fu—"

"You total bastard!"

Kaine reached out to snatch the control box. Blondie jerked upright, yanked his arm away, stepped backwards. The edge crumbled beneath his feet. Terror filled his dark blue eyes, and his mouth jerked open. He dropped like a rock, following the tumbling white clouds.

Kaine shot out an arm, grabbed a fistful of disappearing dark sweater, held tight.

The man's hips slammed into the rock face, threatening to break

Kaine's grip, but he held on. Rocks crumbled around them. Blondie's belly scraped the edge, air burst from his lungs.

"Help me! For God's sake, help me!"

Eyes wide, legs kicked, boots scraped rocks, searching for a foothold. He reached up, fingers scrabbling for Kaine's forearm. They missed. The arm flailed, snatching at empty air.

The man's weight pulled Kaine out and forwards. He dropped to his front, moving with the forces, using friction to slow their impetus. He hit the hard ground and started sliding, out, out towards the new, still-crumbling edge. The raging wind in his face and at Blondie's back drove hard into them, helping to press Blondie into the rock wall, but not enough to prevent their inevitable sliding plummet.

Kaine struck out with his feet, searching for something to hook onto. He found nothing.

Blondie, larger and much heavier than Kaine, tugged them both down and over the precipice.

Let go. Damn it. Leave him.

Kaine tightened his grip. Unable to let the man fall to his death.

He stretched out his other hand, grasped Blondie's collar and held tight.

Blond hair flayed around a terrified face.

Gravity's pull worked against them. The man's weight pulled them inexorably downwards. The gravel-strewn rock offered precious little traction. Kaine couldn't hold him. The edge slid closer, reaching Kaine's outstretched forearm, his elbow, his upper arm. He peered into the blackness, the abyss. Below them, nothing but a void.

Blondie stared up, eyes wide, terrified, his face inches from Kaine's. His legs dangled, kicked out, found nothing but empty air. He reached up again, this time with his left arm, the hand grasping, grabbing. It found the shoulder of Kaine's jacket. Fingers latched on.

"Help me," he wailed. "Don't let go."

"Can you find a foothold?" Kaine said, teeth gritted against the strain.

"I-I ..."

Kaine's chest ground against the stones, the rocky edge moved, crumbled beneath him. They slid closer to the tipping point. Much further and he'd have to let go.

Electric motors still whirred. The trailer tilted higher. Another fluffy, screaming cloud slipped from the back. Kicking, bleating as it plummeted to its death. It sideswiped Blondie, snapping his flailing right arm—the noise of breaking bone loud, obvious. Blondie shrieked. His right arm flopped, hanging loose and useless. But his left hand still held tight to Kaine's jacket, knuckles blanching under the grip.

At Kaine's back, skittering stones and heavy breathing brought a flash of worry. His current position—lying flat on his front, trying to avoid being pulled over the side of a quarry—left him totally vulnerable.

A heavy hand slammed into his back between his shoulder blades, pressing him hard into the gravel pathway. His chin ground against the scraping rocks. They stopped sliding.

"Why didn't you let the bugger drop?"

Rollo's shouted words made Kaine smile. Relief made him light-headed.

"In a couple of seconds, I would have done," he said. "Come on, man. What are you waiting for? Pull the bugger up."

Keeping his hand pressing hard into Kaine's back, Rollo leant forwards, grabbed Blondie's mop of flying, flapping hair, and yanked. Blondie seemed to levitate. The weight eased from Kaine's arm and back. Rollo lifted and tossed the injured man over Kaine's head and dumped him on the ground in a crumpled, yelping, crying mess.

Kaine rolled over onto his back and levered himself into a seated position. He sat hunched, gasping, pulling the delicious clean air into his oxygen-starved lungs. Moments later, he lifted his head. The rectangular control box dangled in front of his face, tethered to the side of the trailer by a thick power cord. He reached up and grabbed it with his left hand. His right arm throbbed, ached, and refused to work properly—muscles and tendons stretched almost beyond their limits. The control box held three buttons, each illuminated by an LED light. Taking a risk, he hit the red one.

The electric motors stopped whirring and the trailer juddered to a halt.

It worked. Lucky.

Two more buttons, one green, the other black. He pressed the black circle and the trailer bed started lowering.

Thank God for that.

Were any sheep left? He wasn't going risk a fall by leaning out and beyond the truck to find out, but the ominous silence from within the trailer told its grim story.

Kaine sat still for a moment, trying to calm his rapid breathing, paying back the oxygen debt to his muscles, and lowering his heart rate. After a few more deep breaths the pain flared. Pain everywhere. His knees, hip bones, chest, and chin stung where they'd scraped over the rocky track. His right shoulder, arm, wrist, and hand locked tight with cramp. But the fire raging in the tips of his index and middle fingers trumped everything else.

After a judicious stretch of each major muscle group in his hand and arm, the cramp eased, and he could breathe again. Taking care to keep well away from the newly-formed rim of the precipice, he leant out from the trailer and held his hand up to the light. Blood oozed from the tips of his index and middle fingers, stinging where the nails had torn from the nail bed. Fortunately, they both remained attached at the root.

Kaine winced.

He gritted his teeth, carefully folded each nail back in place, and made a loose fist to hold them in position until he could find a first aid kit or some gaffer tape. The fingers thudded in time with his pounding heartbeat.

Suck it up, Kaine. You've had worse.

To take his mind off the pain, Kaine turned away from the drop and edged towards the brightness. In the halo of light bouncing off the hedgerow, Rollo stood over the whimpering Blondie. A menacing figure to most, but to a man with a smashed arm and clumps of hair torn out, he must have appeared monstrous, terrifying.

"You okay, Peter?" Rollo called.

Kaine scrambled to his feet, tugging on the control box for help, and using his left hand. "What the heck took you so long?"

Rollo flashed him a pained smile. "The view's too good to rush." He gazed over Kaine's shoulder, towards the edge of the track where the world opened into blackness. "Stunning, isn't it?"

Kaine turned. The blustery gale whipped back his hair and dried the sweat on his face and throat. A chasm stretched out below him, inky black, seemingly bottomless. In the distance, some one hundred metres away, the opposite edge of the quarry loomed high over them, its jagged, crumbling face picked out in silvery moonlight. On its lip, squat trees and gorse bushes quivered and trembled, the wind threatening to uproot them and drive them into the chasm to cover the dead or dying sheep.

The ridge opposite stretched around on either side in a ragged, wide oval, to meet up with the edge where they stood, the track being the only obvious break in the rim. The GPS map had showed this as the first puddle in the small string of watery pearls. The sheep would have drowned in the rain-filled quarry pond, or they would have been smashed to pieces on rocky outcrops and quarry spoil. Only daylight would show them.

With his little finger, Kaine tugged back the cuff of his jacket and read the time on his watch. 23:13. They had at least four and a half hours before enough daylight would reveal the carnage. Too long to wait.

Kaine covered his watch and dug his throbbing right fist into his trouser pocket. His fingers burned as though he'd been holding them in the glowing flame of a blowtorch.

"Injured your hand?" Rollo asked.

"Tore back a couple of fingernails."

Rollo winced. "Ouch."

"Yep. Nothing the doc can't sort out."

He marched away from the quarry's edge and stopped at Blondie's feet. The broken man cowered in a tight heap, hugging his shattered arm tight to his chest, in much the same way as Nose-ring had done in the Sennybridge village park a couple of days earlier.

Kaine held no sympathy for either. Both men deserved worse. Much worse.

Kaine gritted his teeth against another flare of pain from his fist.

"Hurting?" Rollo asked, again wincing in sympathy.

"A tad."

"Should have let the bugger fall," he said, loud enough for Blondie to hear.

The stricken man, much younger than he first appeared—early twenties at most—stopped his snivelling and jerked up his head. He stared at them through frightened and tear-filled blue eyes. A pitiful sight.

"I was going to," Kaine said, "but then we wouldn't have had the chance to ask him any questions."

"Good point," Rollo said, "but still, you shouldn't have bothered."

As they talked about him, Blondie followed their conversation, his eyes swivelling in his head like a spectator following an extended rally at Wimbledon.

"Recognise him?" Kaine asked.

Rollo shook his head. "Nope. Do you?"

"He looks familiar somehow. Maybe we should ask him his name?" Kaine asked, hiding a wink from the blond sheep murderer.

"He might not want to tell us," Rollo said, picking up Kaine's inference.

"In which case," Kaine said, turning his eyes on Blondie, "you can have him."

"Thanks, but what would I do with the scrawny bugger?"

"Oh, I don't know. Why not lob him over the cliff? See how far out you can chuck him."

Rollo scratched at the day's growth of stubble on his square chin. "Sounds like a plan. He isn't that big. If I take a bit of a run up, I could probably toss him quite a distance."

"Further out than those poor sheep?"

Rollo fell silent for a moment, considering his reply. Then he nodded. "Reckon so."

"Fifty quid says you can't chuck him over the edge from here without a run up."

Rollo flicked his gaze from the terrified Blondie to the quarry's lip and back again. He pursed his lips as if estimating the distance. "Can I spin like I'm throwing a discus?"

Rollo's response broke Blondie. The man lowered his head and cowered into a tight, whimpering ball. Kaine kicked his foot—kicked it hard.

"What's your name, son?"

Still snivelling, Blondie lifted his head. Long blond hair flapped in the wind and tears rolled down his face. He tried to blink them away, but more fell in a stream.

"M-My arm," Blondie whimpered, his chin trembling, "it's broken. Help me."

"Your name."

"R-Robbie," he said, "Robert Powell."

The kid's surname struck a chord. He knew why the kid seemed familiar.

"What's your father's name?"

"Huh?" Blondie's face wrinkled in confusion.

"Your father," Kaine said, "is his name Howell?"

The creases in the lad's forehead and around his eyes deepened. "H-How'd you know that?"

"You look like him. Your father and I had a pleasant little chat this afternoon. He seems like a reasonable fellow. Maybe I misjudged him."

"Y-You talked to my dad?"

Kaine kicked the lad's rump. He used the side of his boot to soften the blow. The sheep killer didn't need any more tenderising.

"I'm asking the questions, Robbie." Kaine spoke loud enough to be heard over the howling wind, but no louder. He saw no need to shout at a terrified and compliant captive. "So, your dad put you up to this?"

"No, mun. No." Robert shook his head. His hair flopped into his eyes and made him look even younger. Little more than a teenager.

"Dad would never hurt sheep. Loves the bloody things. He'd kill me if he knew what I'd done. Don't say anything to him. Please. I'll tell you everything I know, but please don't say anything to my dad."

Kaine straightened.

Are you serious?

They'd just watched the kid destroy a truckload of sheep and all he cared about was keeping it from his father. Even if the penalty for sheep rustling in Wales didn't include a custodial sentence, the police would be involved. Keeping the crime from his father was never an option.

"Keep talking and we'll think about it."

Powell collapsed in on himself again. "Oh God. What have I done?"

"Don't be so pitiful. Tell me a story. Start from the beginning. Don't leave anything out."

The kid lowered his head, stared at his feet, his chin quivering. "My arm. I-It's killing me. C-Can't think straight."

"The bugger's stalling," Rollo said. He leant in and grabbed Powell's good arm. "Over he goes."

The boy squealed. He tried to scramble away, his boot heels digging into the gravel, doing nothing but kick up dirt and dust.

"N-No, please. I'll tell you everything. A bloke, a stranger walked up to me in the pub, waving a bunch of tenners under my nose. Asked me if I wanted to earn a few hundred quid. Easy money, he said. No questions asked."

Kaine scoffed. "A total stranger sidles up to you in a bar and offers you money. You expect me to believe that bull?" He turned to Rollo. "Adrian. I've had enough of this nonsense. Lob him over the cliff and be done with it."

"No! No. Please. It's true. Every word." Powell bleated more pitifully than the sheep had as they tumbled through the air. "I swear it. On my mother's life. He paid me to steal the sheep."

"He told you to dump them here?"

"No, no. He told me to get rid of them. I found this place. It's been abandoned for years. No one ever comes up here. It's t-too dangerous."

"You have a key to the padlock?"

"Yeah. My dad grazes his sheep here over winter. Pays rent for the land. I-I borrowed the key."

"You dumped all those sheep here? Over a hundred animals?"

Powell lowered his head. "What else was I gonna do with them?"

"Sell them to a dodgy butcher?" Rollo suggested.

"Don't know one I could trust. Safer dumping them here. They disappear quick. You can't hardly see nothing. Even in the daylight. The water down there's dark green. Summat to do with the minerals in the rocks. I dunno."

Powell shrugged and bleated out another whimper. The movement must have jerked his broken arm.

"The man. The one who paid you. Who was he?" Kaine asked.

"I-I dunno, mun. I-I mean, I'd seen him around town a few times recently, but never to speak to, like."

"Describe him."

Powell shifted his position, careful not to jog his arm again.

"I dunno how to. Can't think straight."

"How old?"

"My d-dad's age. 'Bout forty ... maybe forty-five. Really old."

Cheeky sod.

"Height?"

Powell closed his eyes as though trying to visualise the man in the bar. "Taller than you, but shorter than me. Tubby, like. Round face, beer belly. Liked his booze, I reckon."

"Hair colour? Length? Did he have a beard?"

Powell opened his eyes and gawped at Rollo. "Dark. Like his, but longer. Scruffy. No beard, but"—he gulped—"he had a-a double chin. And a hole—a dimple—in the middle, like that old actor. Y-You know ... the one as played Spartacus in that movie?"

"A cleft chin?"

Kaine and Rollo exchanged a glance. Rollo's expression showed that he'd picked up on the snippet, too.

"Y-Yeah, that's right. A cleft chin. Really stood out on him. Looked funny, like. Like he'd drilled it with a pencil."

Powell's hearty nod couldn't have been much more enthusiastic, but it must have jerked his broken arm again. He blanched, gagged. He tried to lean towards his good side but mistimed his lurch and puked orange and yellow vomit down the front of his sweater.

Lovely.

Kaine waited for him to recover before throwing the next question.

"Where was he from?"

"I-I dunno, mun. English, though."

"What accent did he have?"

"I-I dunno. *Saeson*, English people ... you all sound the same to me. Not from London, though. Didn't sound like no one on *EastEnders*."

"How much does he pay you?"

"Three hundred quid a job."

"Cash?"

The kid frowned. "Yes, of course. I don't work on credit."

"How astute of you," Rollo said.

"Huh?"

"Never mind. Where does he make the exchange?"

"In the same pub. He phones me. Tells me what to do and when to do it. Then we meet in the same pub, and he hands over the readies. As proof, I take photos of ... you know." He gulped, stared towards the quarry, then lowered his eyes. "And he hands over the money. Simple."

"And your mates on the quad bikes?" Rollo asked. "Who pays them?"

"I do." Powell snorted. "Well, they don't get paid, really. I give them enough to fill their petrol tanks and buy them a few ciders. They do it for *yr hwyl ohono*. The fun of it, you know."

"Why?"

"Sorry?"

"Why rustle the sheep only to kill them?"

"I dunno, mun. I just do as he tells me. No idea why he's taking all them sheep or what he has against Mr Cadwallader. I just do like he says and don't ask no questions."

"You just obey orders?" Rollo growled.

Powell's keen nod showed he didn't understand the reference.

"When are you collecting the money for tonight's little outing?"

"Later this morning. After the pub opens. Eleven o'clock, or there abouts."

"What do you do? Call him to confirm the meeting?"

"No, no. I just turn up and wait. Don't normally have to wait too long. He's never later than midday."

"How extraordinarily efficient of him. What's the name of the pub?"

Powell swallowed hard and gagged. He definitely didn't like the taste.

"The Red Lion in Brecon," he said. "It's on the river. Serves a decent pint, and doesn't ask for IDs, if you know what I mean."

"Underage watering hole. I understand."

"Is that all? Can you take me to hospital now? My arm ... it's killing me."

"Let me take a quick look-see."

Kaine dropped to his haunches and leant closer. Powell held his right arm cradled in his left, his hand showing clear under the DAF's bright headlights. The fingers were red and puffy, but not heavily swollen. Kaine reached out with his left hand. Powell whimpered and tried to scramble away but stopped moving when Rollo raised a finger and shook his head. Kaine pressed his index finger to the radial artery at Powell's wrist. Pulse strong if a little fast, but it did indicate good blood flow throughout the limb.

"Can you move your fingers?"

"I-I don't know."

"Try."

Powell's chin trembled. "But my arm ... it hurts."

"Move your fingers, damn it."

Slowly, the kid straightened and flexed his thumb and fingers. Sweat bathed his face, and he whimpered the whole time.

The movement suggested no nerve damage, and with good blood flow to the extremities, the kid's treatment could wait.

"No, son," Kaine said. "You're staying with my large friend, Adrian, until I've met your paymaster. Wouldn't want you calling him from the hospital and warning him off now, would we."

"No. Please. I-I won't call. I p-promise. I need a doctor, please."

"You'll get your doctor, boy. But the hospital can wait. Adrian, would you mind taking him back to the farm, please? The doc might be prepared to treat him even when she learns what he's done to all those poor sheep."

"But ... you promised."

"Promised what?"

"Not to tell anyone what I done."

"No. I said we'd think about it. And, by the way, I wouldn't expect too many painkillers if the doc needs to reset the break if I were you. She loves animals. I doubt she'll be inclined to waste sedatives on a sheep murderer."

Rollo reached down and dragged the shrieking lad to his feet by the collar. Powell looked ready to puke again, and Rollo held him at arm's length.

"Will the Astra fire up?"

"Should do. I stuck a set of fuses in the glove compartment yesterday while you were visiting Powell Farm. There's a first aid kit in the boot, too. We'll take care of your fingers before you leave."

"Thanks," Kaine said. "In that case, I'll take the car. You can have the truck."

"Wh-What about my arm?" Powell squealed. "I-I can feel the bones grating against each other."

Kaine nodded to Rollo. "Use his belt as a sling. I'd do it myself, but my hand hurts." He shrugged, but only used his left shoulder.

"Good idea," Rollo said, turning towards Powell. "Don't move, now. This'll probably hurt."

Rollo unfastened the kid's belt and slid it through the loops. The saggy, low-slung jeans threatened to slip down a set of slim hips and Powell spread his legs to keep them up.

How modest.

It took Rollo little more than a minute to fasten the belt into a loop, slide it over Powell's head, and slip the hand through to hold it at chest height. It made a half-decent, makeshift sling. Powell squealed and whined the whole way through the field operation. The kid would never make a soldier.

When finished, Rollo clapped the lad on the back.

"There you go," he said. "Good as new."

The kid carried on crying. A piteous sight.

"I'll run the truck down the hill a little way," Kaine said, addressing Rollo. "When its well clear of the edge, you can lob Mr Powell in the trailer. He'll have a first-hand experience of what the sheep suffered before they died."

"B-But you can't. My arm—"

Rollo silenced him with another raised finger.

Kaine almost pitied the lad. He could well imagine the state of the trailer after two dozen terrified ewes had been bouncing around in the back for the better part of an hour. At fifteen metres away, the stench wafting from the back did its best to make him gag. God alone knew what it would smell like from inside.

CHAPTER 33

Wednesday 24th May – Morning

The B4520, Powys, South Wales, UK

Kaine drove slowly through the night. No need to rush. He had plenty
of time to kill before meeting the paymaster. On a quiet road outside
town, he pulled to a stop and called Lara. He outlined the events on
the lip of the quarry, skirting over his part in the process and his and
Blondie's dice with death.

"Oh my word," Lara said, the emotion heavy in her voice. "All
those poor sheep."

"We couldn't save them, love. Tried our best."

"I know, I know. But ... how they must have suffered."

"We should have intercepted the DAF before he took the track up
to the quarry. If we'd known what he planned—"

"I understand. Who are we dealing with here, Peter? Who could
be so cruel?"

"I'll find out in a couple of hours." He hadn't mentioned Powell's description of his paymaster or voiced his suspicions. No point in speculating ahead of the event. He had that joy to come.

"Adrian's on his way to you now. He's bringing the head rustler to you for treatment."

"He's injured?"

"Broken arm. You'll never guess the kid's name."

"Go on."

"Robbie Powell."

"Powell? Howell Powell's son?"

"Got it in one. But the lad swears his dad had nothing to do with the attacks on the farm."

"And you believe him?"

"I do. He wasn't in any condition to lie about it. And after meeting Howell yesterday, it rings true."

"A fractured arm, you say?"

"At least one break, and a possible dislocated shoulder. It'll need setting."

"Serves him right."

"Yep, but you will treat him?"

"He'll need an X-ray and hospitalisation. There could be complications."

"His radial pulse is strong. The blood flow isn't compromised, and he can move his fingers. Can you at least keep him stable until I've spoken to his paymaster?"

She faltered before responding. "I'll try, but if there's any chance of his recovery being compromised, I'll have to rush him straight to hospital. There's no question about that. Not sure I'll give him much in the way of sedation, though."

"Ha! I told him to expect that very thing. I also told him you loved animals. Mind you, after being bounced around in the back of the truck for an hour, you can bet your life he'll be compliant."

"It won't do much for his injury."

"I don't doubt it. Oh, before I forget, did you have a chance to dig into Ridgemont Capital?"

"Yes, I did."

"And?"

"From what I can tell, they're legitimate. Not particularly sound in environmental terms, though. They have a reputation for building high-value executive housing estates on green belt land. Had the Countryside Alliance up in arms more than once, but they act within the law. Or so it seems. To be honest, I can't see them trying to pressure the Cadwalladers by stealing a few sheep and setting fire to their stables."

"Me neither."

"They're more likely to up their offer or try another location. So, you're on your way to the meet?"

"Heading there now."

"Be careful. There's no telling what you'll be up against, and you'll be on your own."

"I'm always careful, love."

He ended the call, powered down the mobile, and slid it into his jacket pocket.

THE RED LION PUB ON THE RIVER USK WOULDN'T HAVE MADE MANY tourist brochures. A go-to destination it wasn't. To call it a dive would have insulted dives around the world.

After a brief recce of the surrounding area, Kaine pushed through the part-glazed entrance door—two of the panes were cracked, all six were filthy—and squelched the ten metres to the bar. The beer-soaked carpet sucked hard to his walking boots the whole way.

Lovely.

At ten minutes past the hour, the place already held a smattering of patrons keen to immerse themselves in the alcohol and the vibe, such as it was. An old man wearing work boots, faded dungarees over a plaid shirt, and a weather-beaten cloth cap, hogged one corner of the bar. He nursed a pint of golden liquid and studied a red-topped newspaper. Three stools separated him from his nearest neighbour, another man of similar vintage who wore the same uniform, only his plaid shirt was blue, not red, and he didn't sport a cap. Two others, both men, sat opposite each other at a table in front of the unmade fire. Neither spoke and each seemed happy to sit in silence, staring at their drinks.

Kaine ordered himself a pint of the local beer from a disinterested barman, who asked him nothing but what he wanted to drink. He found an empty seat in the darkest corner—a table with a commanding view of the place—and settled down to wait.

Fifteen minutes and two sips of insipid, badly kept beer later, the front door opened, and a man entered—a rotund man with a belly-button-shaped hole drilled into his chin. The paymaster. He stood in the doorway and searched the bar with a pair of dark brown eyes. On finding no sign of Powell, he frowned and made his way to the counter, where he ordered a double whisky, neat. He knocked it back in one, ordered another, and found an empty chair at an equally empty table in the corner adjacent to Kaine.

Seconds later, the main door opened again, and a large bruiser barged into the room. Tall, heavily muscled, and wearing a dark blue suit one size too small for his muscular frame. The overly tight suit performed two prime functions. It prevented him walking about in his undies, and it showed he wasn't carrying a weapon. Bruiser studiously avoided looking at Paymaster and crowded the counter. The big man ordered half a pint of lemonade with a splash of lime and took a seat at the bar next to the elderly gent with the flat cap. He sat and studied the room through the mirror behind the bar, trying not to be obvious about it but failing miserably.

Bruiser's whole performance screamed cut-price minder. His appearance reinforced it, all the way down to the close-cropped hair, the heavy scarring over both eyes, and the flattened, oft-broken nose.

Kaine had seen enough. He took another sip of the disappointing beer and stood. He left the glass on the table and headed to the only other door in the place, one carrying a sign that read "Toilets" in two languages. The door led to a small corridor with three others, a ladies, a gents, and a third marked "Private"—this time only in English. He tried the handle on the third door, locked.

He took a breath, held it, and pushed through to the gents toilets. The place met his expectations. A stainless-steel trough lined one wall; the single drain partially blocked with cigarette butts. Urine, presumably left over from the previous night's excesses, remained in the bottom of the catch tray. Yellow tablets sat in the liquid and failed to mask the stench of stale pee. The wall opposite the urinal housed two cubicles. Both doors stood partially ajar. Kaine didn't need to see inside them to know what he'd find. The place hadn't been cleaned in forever.

With no exit through the gents, he assumed the same would be true for the ladies. Again, he'd seen enough. More than enough.

Kaine performed a rapid about-turn, pulled on the least obvious place on the handle, and rushed back out through the door into the small corridor. He released his pent-up breath and pushed out into the slightly less fuggy air of the bar.

On his way to the exit, he nodded goodbye to the barman, who failed to return the farewell, and stepped out into the fresh, crystal-clear South Wales air. Why anyone would choose to spend time in the stinking atmosphere of The Red Lion when they had the wonders of the Beacons on their doorsteps defeated him. It wasn't as though the beer tasted much better than the liquid contents of the stainless-steel trough in the toilets.

Outside, he made a left turn and headed for the car park where the Astra waited. After Rollo had changed the main fuse, she'd behaved perfectly on the drive from the quarry to Brecon, and he'd arrived in plenty of time for a leisurely breakfast—a bacon roll and two large coffees—in the same place he and Lara had taken after-noon tea. After the meal, the GPS took him to The Red Lion, but he'd arrived an hour too early and spent the time driving though the small town, taking in the scenery and familiarising himself with the quickest exit routes.

KAINE WAITED BEHIND THE WHEEL OF THE ASTRA FOR FORTY-FIVE minutes before Paymaster stormed out of the pub, thunder on his face. Bruiser, close behind, slammed a meaty paw into the middle of Paymaster's back.

Paymaster staggered, stumbled forwards, and caught a toe on an uneven paving slab. He only managed to stop himself falling headlong onto the path by catching hold of a lamp post on his way down.

"No, please. Don't," Paymaster wailed.

What's this?

Kaine tensed, his senses on high alert.

"We've waited long enough," Bruiser growled, his accent more refined than expected in a man so large and so ugly. "Mr Baker's patience only goes so far. Time to pay your debts."

Paymaster spun to face the man who wasn't his minder.

"No, wait. Please, give me a moment."

Bruiser threw out an arm. He grabbed a fistful of Paymaster's leather jacket, yanked the fat man towards him, and lifted him up so high he had to stand on tiptoes. Paymaster squeaked. He pawed at Bruiser's fingers, trying to loosen the man's iron grip. His efforts proved ineffective.

"You've had two months. Long enough with nothing to show for it. The interest on your loan keeps rising."

"But ... Let me find out what happened. He's only a few minutes late."

Bruiser sneered and shook his head. He pulled Paymaster closer, until their noses nearly touched.

"You are a miserable arsehole," Bruiser growled. "I've had more than enough of your bellyaching. Don't know why Mr Baker's cut you so much slack. You've had all the time you're getting. Time to pay up or shut up."

Kaine had heard enough. He opened the door, climbed out of the Astra, and sauntered towards the grappling men.

"But I'm so close to the pay-off," Paymaster whimpered. "I only need a few more days. Please."

Bruiser straightened his arm and released his grip. The unexpected move took Paymaster by surprise, and he collapsed to the path in a bedraggled mess of flailing arms and legs.

"Oh dear," Kaine said, standing over the downed man. "Had too much of the falling over water, did he?" He held out a hand in an offer to help Paymaster to his feet.

Bruiser took a couple of paces closer. Crowding in on Kaine. Standing tall. Imposing.

"Fuck off, arsehole," he said, voice rumbling deep inside his throat. "This is none of your concern."

"Arsehole you say?" Kaine asked, forcing confusion into his tone. "And me just showing concern for a person in distress. That's a little harsh, I must say."

His scowl deepening, Bruiser took another step closer, leaving himself wide open. He balled his right hand into a massive fist.

"Listen, buddy—"

Kaine swayed back, took the balance on his left leg, and shot out his right. The heel of his boot connected with Bruiser's standing leg, shattering the kneecap. The big man howled and collapsed to the path beside Paymaster.

"My knee," he screamed, tears flowing. "You broke my fucking knee." His hands clawed at his damaged joint, trying to hold the splintered bones together. "You bastard!"

Kaine stepped back and swept the surrounding area. Seeing no one else about, he relaxed and shook his head. "That'll teach you not to swear at complete strangers, boyo. It'll also teach you not to stand too close when you make your move. Yours is no job for amateurs."

The giant squirmed around in the dirt. He tried to roll onto his back.

"My knee—"

"Keep holding it tight, son," Kaine said, taking pity on his inept victim. "And keep still. Stop rolling about like that or you'll make it worse."

Paymaster sat up and leant against the lamp post he'd used to prevent his first fall. He stared at Bruiser and then at Kaine, wonder in his eyes. He opened his mouth, but Kaine held up a hand to forestall any questions.

Kaine stood over Bruiser and held out a hand.

"Mobile."

"What?" Bruiser asked, teeth gritted.

"Give me your mobile phone."

"Why?"

"Do you want an ambulance or not? I'm not using my own phone. It can be traced."

Bruiser gulped and nodded. "Jacket. Inner pocket."

Kaine found the device, dialled the emergency number, and asked for the ambulance. He had to wait another few seconds.

"Hello caller," the jaunty operator said. "This is the Welsh Ambulance service. Is the patient breathing?" She sounded very much like the operator he spoke to in the Audi.

"A man's taken a nasty fall outside The Red Lion in Brecon," Kaine said, disguising his voice, just in case. "Might have hurt his knee." He cancelled the call before the operator could ask any more questions. He wiped the mobile on his sleeve and dropped it in the dirt beside Bruiser.

"The hospital isn't far away," he said, offering Bruiser an encouraging smile. "They shouldn't be too long."

"Bastard."

Kaine sighed. "The thanks I get for such a kind gesture. Won't bother next time."

He turned and indicated for Paymaster to stand. The tubby man made it to his feet with all the poise of an inverted turtle trying to right itself.

"I-I don't know who you are," Paymaster said, "but thank you. Thank you so much."

Don't thank me too soon, buddy. I'm not your saviour.

"That's okay. I hate bullies, me. What was that about?"

"You were brilliant," Paymaster said, ignoring the question. "So fast, I hardly saw you move."

Kaine threw a one-shouldered shrug. "He wasn't expecting it. I got lucky. Shall we get out of here in case his mates come running?"

Paymaster's effusive nod risked whiplash. "Good idea. We came in his car, and I don't have the keys."

"Wait a minute," Kaine said, feigning surprise. "You know that bloke? He's a friend of yours?"

"It's a long story. Can we go now?"

"I dunno, man. I should really hang around to make a statement when the police get here. No telling what that big bloke's going to tell them."

Paymaster rounded on Kaine.

"You just said we can't hang around in case his mates—"

Kaine held up his hands to keep Paymaster at bay. "Yes, but I changed my mind. The cops are going to be here soon."

"Listen, I promise you, Blackstone"—he shot a look at the crippled Bruiser—"won't tell the cops nothing. Baker wouldn't let him."

"Blackstone? Baker? Who are these people?"

"Look, I'll tell you all about it when we're well away. Give me ten minutes to explain and it'll all be clear. I'll make it worth your while, too. I could use a man like you. A man with your skills. I mean, the way you took care of Blackstone. You did good."

"I told you, man. I got lucky."

"Don't give me that bull. I know a man who can handle himself when I see one in action."

Distant sirens announced the imminent arrival of the emergency services.

Paymaster turned his head towards the sound, his expression changing from pleading to frantic.

"You'll make it worth my while?" Kaine asked.

"Look," he said, patting his back pocket. "I've got three hundred quid in my wallet. It's yours if you get me away from here before the cops arrive."

"Three hundred notes?"

"Cash money."

Kaine smiled. "Why didn't you say that before? Let's get out of here." He turned and led the way to the Astra.

"Is this yours?" Paymaster asked, no doubt unimpressed with their getaway car.

"What's wrong with it?"

"Is it a runner?"

"Hey, don't talk about Betsy like that. You'll upset her."

"Sorry, mate. No offence."

"Offence taken. Now hop in," Kaine said, pointing to the front passenger seat. "Door's open on account of the central locking system being busted."

On the way around the front of the car, Paymaster shot him a look that said, "You need the money as much as I do."

Kaine slid behind the wheel and fastened his seat belt. In his haste to leave the car, he'd left the keys in the ignition.

"Where are we heading?" Kaine asked, firing up the motor. This time, she started on the first turn.

"Anywhere but here."

"Right you are."

He slipped the Astra into first gear and rolled slowly out of the car park, passing within a few metres of a red-faced, sweating, and highly distressed Bruiser who mouthed all sorts of obscenities at their bumper.

CHAPTER 34

Wednesday 24th May – Midday

Near Brecon Town, Powys, South Wales, UK

They reached the outskirts of Brecon Town in minutes, and Kaine headed north-west on the B4520, picking up speed on a two-lane minor road in much better condition than some of the main roads he'd driven in England. Probably had something to do with the reduced traffic in the area. Hedgerows crowded on each side, and they wound uphill into the Beacons.

Once the last house had disappeared from the rear-view mirror, Kaine took the next right turn onto a single-track farm lane which led them deep into a wooded hillside. With no other vehicles in sight, not even a tractor, Kaine pulled into a passing spot which lay deep in the shadow of the trees, and turned off the engine. Neither had spoken since leaving The Red Lion's car park.

He twisted in his seat to face the bloated Paymaster.

"Okay," Kaine said. "This is as far as I take you. I want my money. Pass it over."

Paymaster released his seat belt, stretched out his legs, and struggled to remove a leather wallet from the back pocket of his jeans.

He pulled out a wad of crisp twenties and placed them, uncounted, in Kaine's outstretched right hand.

"Three hundred quid. It's all there."

Paymaster took in the light dressing Rollo had applied to Kaine's fingers, which still throbbed but the pain had lessened as the bandages offered plenty of protection.

"You hurt yourself?" Paymaster asked.

Kaine twisted his mouth in denial. "Bite my fingernails. Nervous habit. Can't break it no matter how hard I try."

He transferred the money into his left hand and, for show, took time to count it. Once certain he had the correct amount, he nodded, and slid it into his pocket.

"Right then," he said. "Start talking. What's your name?"

Paymaster hesitated. He broke eye contact and shifted in his seat. "Alfie," he said. "Alfie Smith."

Kaine managed not to laugh. If "Alfie Smith" wanted to play the game, he needed to learn how to tell a better lie. For the moment, Kaine let it pass.

"What's yours?" Paymaster asked.

"You don't need to know that."

"The way you handled yourself back at the pub, you're trained, though. Military. Right?"

"You don't need to know that, either."

"Yeah, military. What should I call you?"

"We'll get on to that if I like your story. Who are Blackstock and Baker, and what do they have on you?"

"Blackstone," Paymaster said. "The one you crippled is Jerry Blackstone. Former heavyweight boxer, but probably not a very good one."

The truth.

Maybe the first true words Paymaster had spoken since they'd met.

"And Baker?"

"The moneyman. I mean, the investor."

Evasion. A half-truth.

"By 'moneyman' you mean 'loan shark'?"

Paymaster smiled. An unpleasant thing that made his round cheeks bulge, and his chins wobble—including the chin with the bellybutton crevice. "Don't let Baker hear you call him that. He has delusions. Fancies himself as an 'entrepreneur'." Paymaster waggled his head when saying it. "And he has better, more skilled employees than Jerry Blackstone."

"How much are you into him for?"

The wince mutated into a petulant frown. "You don't need to know that."

"I want the whole story, Mr 'Smith'. All of it, or I'm dropping you here and buggering off home."

Paymaster sagged deeper into his seat, and his shoulders rounded in on themselves.

"Okay, okay. The whole truth. Three months ago, I borrowed … twenty-five grand off him, just to tide me over while I worked my side hustle, you know?"

Still not the whole truth, but we're getting there.

"What's the debt stand at now?"

"With interest? Fifty and it's still growing."

Kaine whistled. "That's one hell of an interest rate. You'd have been better off taking out a payday loan."

"Tell me about it."

"No," Kaine said, shaking his head, "I'm telling you nothing. This is your story. If you owe Baker all that money, how can you make it worth my while to help you, like you said back at the pub? This so-called side hustle of yours?"

Paymaster's eyes gleamed—the glimmer of pure greed. "Exactly. It's a sure-fire winner. One hundred percent guaranteed."

"Oh please. Don't tell me. You're a maths teacher and you've developed a system for the ponies that can't possibly fail?"

Paymaster's smile returned, this one oozed smugness and greed.

"No," he said. "I'm a father, and my son's worth a whole bundle of money. Help me out and I'll cut you in for ... ten percent."

Bastard.

"Hang on a minute," he said, "you're gonna kidnap your own son and then what? Hold him for ransom?"

"No way. That's illegal. I don't need to break the law ... well, not really. This deal's totally kosher. I'm simply gonna take back custody of my own kid and ... then I'm going to be rolling in it. Hundreds of thousand, maybe more."

"You're making no sense, man." Kaine held out his left hand and beckoned with his fingers. "The whole story. Spill it. And the truth this time. No more bullshit. What's your real name?"

More hesitation, but it didn't last long before the truth came.

"Duckworth." He sighed and the smile stretched wider. "Although my friends call me Ducky."

Rhodri's father.

What a surprise. Now tell me something I didn't know.

Kaine wanted to slap the smug grin from Duckworth's face, but that could wait. First, he needed to know the greedy pig's story.

"Go on. Keep going."

"Remember that plane crash last year, the one up near Hull? Flight BE—something or other?"

Kaine dipped his head.

"The one shot out of the sky where eighty-odd people died?" Duckworth added.

"I remember it. Terrorism, they say."

"Yeah, that's right. Ryan Kaine, ex-army."

"Royal Marine," Kaine corrected. "Not army."

Duckworth jerked up his chins in a nod. "Same difference."

No, it isn't.

"So, what's the plane got to with your kid?"

Duckworth sat up straighter. He twisted, trying to look straight at

Kaine, but the restricted size of the Astra's cabin made it awkward for such a fat man.

"Ah," he said, "that's where it gets interesting. My wife was on that plane. She was one of the victims." He didn't even try to sound sad. In fact, he smiled and the glee in his voice made Kaine want to slap the emotion from his face.

Such a lovely chap.

"And you're going to claim the insurance?"

"Nah, she didn't have much cover. A few grand. Nothing but a pittance, but ... here's the interesting part. Ever heard of The 83 Trust?"

Kaine blanked him and Duckworth carried on almost without pause.

"It's a charity set up to support the families of the victims. I checked them out. Rolling in it, they are. Millions of quid in the bank and they're dishing it out to the families of the victims. By rights, some of that money's mine."

"So, what's to stop you collecting?"

"That's just it, me and the wife were separated, part-way through a divorce and she had custody of the kid on account of ... legal issues."

"What legal issues?"

"The bitch made up all sorts of lies about me, and the stupid fat cow of a magistrate fell for it."

"What sort of lies?"

"Doesn't matter," Duckworth said, shaking his fat head so hard, he dislodged the bead of sweat that had gathered on the tip of his nose. It landed on the front of his sweatshirt, and the material absorbed it in an instant.

As soon as they'd stopped, Kaine had wound down the driver's window by hand—no electric windows in so venerable a car. It did little to help diminish the heat rising inside the Astra's cab or the increased stench emanating from his passenger, who seemed disinclined to lower his own window.

"The whole truth, remember," Kaine said.

Duckworth hitched a fat shoulder. "The bloody woman told the court I used to hit her and the boy."

"Did you?" Kaine asked. He formed fists and ignored the pain spiking in his right hand.

"Nah. It was total bollocks. I slapped her a couple of times, but she was into it. Heavy foreplay, you know." He double hitched his bushy eyebrows. "As for the boy ... never. A little smack now and again, to keep him in his place. Nothing serious. Used to be called 'gentle chastisement' back when I was a kid. Parental discipline. Nothing wrong with that, is there."

"Where's your son now?" Kaine asked, keen to move the story along. If he had to suffer much more of Duckworth's self-justification, he might snap.

"On a farm in the middle of nowhere. His aunt and uncle took him in. Took some money from The Trust, too. Thieving bastards. By rights, that was *my* money." Duckworth ground his teeth and prodded his chest with his thumb. "I wrote to them, asking to see my boy, just to see him, mind, but they totally blanked me. Wouldn't reply to my letters or answer my calls. Nothing. I would have set my solicitor onto them, but that would have taken forever and cost a bloody fortune. That's when I decided to take direct action. Put the squeeze on the money-grubbing arseholes. See how they liked it." He chuckled, an ugly noise that reminded Kaine of water gurgling down a partially blocked toilet.

"In what way?"

Duckworth explained how he'd found a local lad to organise a series of attacks on the farm. He hoped to drive the Cadwalladers into what? Bankruptcy? Selling their farm? Intimidate them into giving up the boy? Complete nonsense. A hare-brained scheme that made no sense to anyone but Ducky Duckworth. How had he managed to sell the plan to Baker the Shylock? Madness. Neither Duckworth nor Baker could have understood the make-up of a man like Gwynfor Cadwallader. He'd have suffered the Ten Plagues of Egypt before buckling under Duckworth's loopy plan.

"What was Baker's money for?"

"I already told you. It helped tide me over, and I needed to pay the little scrote to steal the sheep and torch the stables. Useless fucker couldn't even get that right. In fact, that money in your pocket was supposed to pay the bugger, but he didn't turn up for his payment."

"What was Blackstone doing there?"

"Baker was getting impatient for his money. I convinced him to give me a little more time, and he sent Blackstone along to put the pressure on."

"So, what's my role in your grand scheme going to be?"

Duckworth's eyes turned away. He scanned the scene beyond the windscreen which showed nothing but bushes, trees, and leaves rippling in a stiff breeze. Shadows danced around them.

"Well?" Kaine said, prompting a response.

"Dunno, really," Duckworth said at length. "The way you dealt with Blackstone showed me your capabilities. It made me think you might be prepared to do something more ... radical. To be honest, I panicked, too. I mean, fuck knows what Baker's gonna think. Christ, he might even reckon I put you up to it. My guess is, we're both in the crapper now, you and me. Baker's likely to go apeshit. Wouldn't surprise me if he's already put a contract out on the two of us ..."

Another contract on my head?

Kaine almost laughed out loud at the idea of a cut-price Shylock putting a contract on his head when the might of the UK establishment had failed in all its efforts to take him in—or take him down.

"...and you know what that means?" Duckworth continued.

"No, do tell."

"We're both in this together, you and me. The only way out is to pay off Baker and to do that, you need to help me claim my fair share of the money. Deal?" He held out a sweaty hand.

Kaine smiled to himself. There was another way. A way Ducky Duckworth would find unacceptable.

"Let me think about it."

Duckworth's hand dropped into his lap. "Don't take too long. Like I said, we're both in trouble now."

"Before I make my decision, I have some questions you can't answer. Do you have Baker's phone number?"

Duckworth jerked into a seated attention. His head swivelled on his flabby, grease-stained neck.

"What?"

"Listen, Ducky," he said, "in the military, one of the first things they teach you is to get to know your enemy."

"So, you *are* a soldier. I was right?"

"Royal Marine."

"What, like Ryan Kaine?"

Kaine stared back, his face stone. "You could say. So, Baker's number. You. have it?"

"Um, yeah. Just a minute." He reprised the stretch-legged performance he used to retrieve his wallet but pulled a mobile from a different pocket. "Here." He held it out. His hand glistened with sweat, and the mobile, a cheap black burner, seemed just as damp.

"Call him and put it on speaker."

A confused frown crinkled Duckworth's forehead.

"Really?"

"Do it. As you said, we don't have a whole lot of time here."

Duckworth touched the mobile's screen, which opened to the phone's keypad. He scrolled through to "recents" and selected the first number on the list. Evidently, Ducky Duckworth didn't have many friends.

Kaine smiled. The next part should prove interesting.

CHAPTER 35

Off the B4520, Powys, South Wales, UK

The mobile shook in Duckworth's trembling palm, threatening to slip off.

The call barely had time to connect before a deep male voice answered—a voice with a strong Welsh accent

"What the fucking hell are you up to, Duckworth?"

"No need for the language, Mr Baker," Kaine said, modifying his accent to make it more cultured. "I assume this *is* Mr Baker?"

"You're not Duckworth," the voice answered.

"Well spotted. Am I speaking with Baker the Shylock?"

"I'm Baker, but I'm an entrepreneur not a fucking loan shark."

"Please don't swear, Mr Baker. I find that swearing is the last resort of the feeble minded. Any more swearing from you, and I'll hang up the phone. I'm not prepared to listen to foul language on such a lovely sunny day."

A strangled growl leeched through the phone's speaker.

"Okay, smartarse, speak to me. What d'you want?"

"That's a little better," Kaine said. "Now we can have a proper, adult conversation."

Kaine smiled at Duckworth and winked before snatching the mobile from Duckworth's hand.

"Who are you?" Baker asked, barely under control. His rage bubbling close to the surface of his Welsh baritone. "What's your name?"

"You can call me Ryan." Kaine threw another wink at Duckworth who failed to stifle a derisive snort.

"Okay, 'Ryan'," Baker said. "Are you the one who attacked Blackstone?"

"I'm afraid so. How is the poor fellow?"

"In the hospital waiting for a scan. You fu—broke his knee."

"Thought I might have. And I apologise wholeheartedly for it. Please send him my best regards. Still, he shouldn't go around attacking innocent bystanders. He never knows who he's tangling with. Most unprofessional of him."

"Yeah, you're right. He's always been useless. I only keep him on out of sympathy. Used to manage him back when he was in the ring, see. Never made me a penny piece. I tend to give him the easy jobs. But listen to this, 'Ryan'. Don't be fooled into thinking he's the best I've got."

"I'm no fool, Mr Baker."

"Yeah, right."

"And I do hope your employees have a good healthcare plan. Pension scheme. Invalidity benefits?"

"Stop taking the pi—mick. What's your game?"

"There is no game, Mr Baker. I just wanted to ask you a couple of questions."

A brief pause before, "Go on then, ask away."

"Why did you lend money to a no-hoper like Richard Duckworth here?"

Duckworth frowned in confusion.

"You surely didn't take his scheme seriously, did you?" Kaine added.

"Scheme?" Baker snapped. "What pigging scheme?"

"No!" Duckworth tried to snatch back his phone. Kaine pulled it away and slammed the side of his fist into Duckworth's ribs, twice. The fat man grunted and folded in on himself, gasping for breath. Kaine wasn't too worried. The rolls of blubber had absorbed some of the punches, and he hadn't hit the man hard enough to cause any significant damage. The shock would have had as much effect as the force of the blows.

Duckworth whimpered, still struggling to breathe.

Kaine held up a finger for silence.

"What the hell was that?" Baker demanded.

"Not much," Kaine said. "Ducky made the mistake of trying to interrupt our conversation. Very rude. I hate rudeness almost as much as I hate bad language and bullying."

"What's that noise. Sounds horrible. Is he dying?"

"No, but he's not a particularly happy bunny at the moment. In fact, he's turned a rather peculiar colour. I'd call it a sort of puce. Now, where was I?"

"Something about a scheme."

Duckworth's breath rattled in his lungs. He still whimpered, but his colour had improved. Less maroon, more red.

"Yes, I thought that must have been a crock. No serious 'entrepreneur' such as yourself would even consider it as viable. Let's go back a little. Why did you lend Ducky twenty-five thousand pounds?"

"Twenty-five grand? Don't be daft, mun. He ain't worth that sort of risk. I loaned him five grand three months ago, which he still hasn't paid back. He now owes ten. That's why I sent Blackstone around. To lean on him a little. He was only supposed to break a couple of fingers. Nothing too damaging. But you got in the way."

"Yes, I really am sorry about that. If I'd known the sort of creature I was saving, I wouldn't have bothered. So, cutting to the chase,

Ducky here tells me you're likely to put out a hit on me. Is he correct?"

"Too bloody right I am. Can't have any toerag thinking I'm an easy mark, can I? Bad for business. Trouble is ..."

"What?"

"I don't have any idea who you are."

"But I've already told you who I am. I'm Ryan. Actually, my full name's Ryan Kaine."

Duckworth gagged again, but this time it wasn't the result of a double punch to the ribs. His eyes nearly popped out of their sockets.

Baker huffed out a disbelieving sigh. "You're who now?"

"You heard. Ask Ducky. He's finally recognised me from my mugshots. Furthermore, I think he's just wet himself all over the passenger seat. I'm going to have to dump this car now. Such a shame. I've grown to like this Maybach." He smiled at Duckworth and gave him a thumbs up. "Why not ask him yourself? We're on speaker. Go on, ask him."

"Well, Ducky?" Baker demanded. "What you got to say for yourself?"

"It's him," Duckworth gasped. "It's Ryan Kaine. He's ... He's ..."

"Annoyed," Kaine said, speaking for the fat man. He raised a silencing finger. "Annoyed is what I am, old chap. Do you believe me now, Baker?"

"Dunno, mun," the Shylock said, "but after the way you dealt with Blackstone, I'm inclined to."

"Good. Think of it this way. Blackstone's only breathing now because I didn't finish him off. Agreed?"

Baker hesitated again before saying a reluctant, "Agreed."

"Good. Putting our personal situation to one side for the moment, one of the things we have left to discuss is what happens to Ducky. Yes?"

Another hesitation, this one shorter. "Suppose so."

"Okay, cards on the table, Baker. From the looks of him, I don't think dear old Ducky has the money to pay you back. And I imagine you don't offer easy payment terms?"

"No, I don't. I'm a businessman not a bank."

"My thoughts exactly. So, if I hand Ducky over to you, what's likely to happen?"

"He'll disappear," Baker said, the response instant. "And it'll be permanent, like," he added, leaving no room for doubt.

"And you'll write off his loan as a bad debt?"

"Yeah, I'd have to wear the loss. It ain't much, though. It's not as though it ain't happened before—not that I'd ever admit to it in court, like." Baker barked out a low, cruel laugh.

Kaine smiled at Duckworth and added another wink, this one sly. Confusion compounded the overweight man's clear discomfort.

"Thought so," Kaine said. "And I suppose you believe I owe you something for what I did to Blackstone?"

"Yes. You do."

"Why don't we rationalise the situation? Cut out one layer of the cake, as it were."

A pause.

"How we gonna do that?"

"It's simple, really." Kaine smiled at Duckworth and stretched it into a leer. "Why don't I 'disappear' Ducky for you?"

Duckworth let out a strangled cry. He twisted away and scrambled for the handle on the passenger's door. Kaine flicked out his left hand and backslapped the man's ear. Duckworth squealed and flopped back into his seat. He covered his stinging lug with a cupped hand.

"What was that?"

"Ducky tried to get away. He isn't overly impressed with my plan, but he doesn't have any say in the negotiations. Well, Mr Baker? Do we have a deal?"

Another pause before the response.

"Yeah, yeah. I reckon so."

"Good, but let's make this perfectly clear. I dispose of Ducky for you, and you forget about what happened this morning with Blackstone. Deal?"

"Yeah. Deal. I guess it'll make us even. But if Ducky ever reappears, all bets are off, and you'll be back on my radar."

"Trust me, Mr Baker. When I disappear someone, they don't reappear. Not ever."

"Okay. Are we done now?"

"We are."

Kaine pressed the red symbol to disconnect the call.

"Well," he said, turning to his passenger, "that went rather well, don't you think?"

Duckworth held his ear with one hand and clutched his ribs with the other, apparently unable to decide which injury to concentrate on.

"Y-You just agreed to k-kill me."

"Did I? Did I really?"

"Yes ..." Again, confusion showed on his mobile face, and the creases on his forehead deepened. "Didn't you?"

"Nope. I agreed to make you go away. The way I see it, I've just saved your life. Not only that, but Baker's written off your debt. In my book, that's a win-win."

"You're not going to kill me?"

"Kill you? Of course not. Why would I do that? I'm no killer."

"But you're Ryan Kaine ... aren't you?"

Duckworth lowered the hand from his ear but kept the other in place. Maybe the blubber hadn't protected the ribs as much as Kaine imagined.

"No," Kaine said, "my name's Peter. Peter Sidings."

"You lied?" Duckworth gasped.

Kaine nodded. "It doesn't make me a bad person."

"Who are you?"

"Me?" Kaine said, smiling again. "I'm Chief Security Officer to The 83 Trust, Mr Duckworth. My prime directive it to prevent people like you from gaining fraudulent access to our funds. You would not believe the number of hoax calls we receive each week. In short, you've been sussed, Ducky, my man."

Duckworth closed his eyes and his shoulders slumped even

further. A few moments later, he opened his eyes again and turned them on Kaine. "Is that why that Welsh plonker, Powell, didn't turn up to collect his money this morning?"

"Correct. Last night, my colleague and I followed Robbie Powell to where he disposed of those sheep. A nasty business. Another of my colleagues loves animals, if I let her anywhere near you, she'd volunteer to carry out Baker's plans for you. I promise you this. In terms of pain delivery, she can be rather imaginative."

"Oh God." Duckworth's eyes closed again as understanding dawned. "That's how you knew my Christian name."

"Yep, I rather messed up there," Kaine said, easing out a tight wince. "Shouldn't have used it. No way I could have known your first name at the time. Don't sweat it though. Your eyes were glued to the mobile. No wonder you didn't notice. In any case, what could you have done differently?"

Duckworth raised his shoulders and grimaced as the movement jarred his injured ribs.

"S-So, what happens next?" Duckworth asked, eyes and voice lowered. He evidently expected the worst.

"We clear the air."

Duckworth's head lifted and the eyes showed hope.

"Yes?"

"First," Kaine said, raising his bandaged index finger, "and I'll make this perfectly clear. The 83 Trust will never, ever give you any money. Understood?"

The fat man's head lowered again.

"Understood," he whispered.

"Second." Kaine's bandaged middle finger joined its injured partner. "And this follows on nicely from the first point. All the attacks on the Cadwalladers and their farm cease as of now. Right?"

"Right." Another mumble.

"Third." The ring finger joined the other two. "You'll give up all claims of custody over Rhodri, forever. Agreed?"

"Agreed," Duckworth said, his response louder and faster than for the previous two. "Why would I want anything to do with that stupid little ru—"

Kaine backhanded him so hard across the face, his head snapped around and smacked into the side window.

"Will you never learn?"

Duckworth clamped his jaws together. Tears spilled down his face.

"Fourth and final point." The pinkie finger extended to join the other three. "And this one's only common sense. Leave Wales and don't come back. Are we clear on all four points?"

The piteous creature nodded.

"Say it."

Duckworth pulled in a snivelling breath. "All clear. I understand. You wouldn't catch me in this shithole—"

Kaine's clenched fist cut off Duckworth's rant mid-sentence.

"If I were you, I wouldn't say another word. Now get out."

Duckworth's eyes popped.

"What?"

"Get out of the car. Now!"

"But we're in the middle of nowhere."

"Go."

"B-But I'm totally skint."

Kaine stared long and hard at the wretch. Eventually, he took pity on him. He pulled out the wad of notes he'd stuffed into his pocket and handed it over. Duckworth ripped the money from Kaine's fingers as though it was a lifeline thrown to a drowning man. The passenger door screeched open when he worked the catch, and he stumbled out of the car. A damp patch on the seat and on his jeans confirming he'd emptied his bladder as Kaine had suspected.

The moment Duckworth slammed the door, Kaine fired up the Astra's engine and engaged first gear. He pulled out of the passing space and executed a tight right turn to head back the way they'd come.

"Wait!" Duckworth shouted. "My phone! You've still got my phone."

"Have I?" Kaine looked down. The rectangular object nestled in the passenger footwell. "Well now, so I have."

Kaine slipped into second, added some pressure to the throttle, and picked up speed. In the rear-view mirror, the sight of an overweight man jumping up and down, waving a fist in the air, and screaming at the top of his voice made Kaine laugh out loud. Duckworth had plainly been milking the rib injury.

"Count yourself lucky, Ducky. I could have let Lara loose on you," he muttered.

Four hundred metres later and still smiling, he slowed at the T-junction with the B4520 and turned right, heading north-west towards Glyn Coes.

A mile further along, he stopped at another T-junction and threw Duckworth's mobile out of the window after removing the battery.

CHAPTER 36

Wednesday 24th May – Early Afternoon

Near Glyn Coes, Powys, South Wales, UK

Behind the wheel, Kaine felt relaxed enough to whistle. Apart from the evil business with the sheep, it had been a decent day. A successful day. They'd uncovered the cause of, and ended, the attacks on Cadwallader Farm, and they'd removed all prospect of Rhodri being reunited with his abusive father. The kid might not appreciate the fact that they'd saved him from his dad, but he didn't need to know the truth. At least not until he was old enough to understand the situation fully.

Yes, it had been a good day. With the mystery over the attacks solved and the culprit banished on pain of death, there was nothing holding them in Wales. The prospect of a few weeks' rest and recuperation in Aquitaine loomed large in Kaine's mind. The coastal towns and villages facing the Bay of Biscay would be glorious in late May. The sea warm and the weather acceptable. It would give him the chance to make up with Lara, who still hadn't forgiven him for ditching her in Paris.

He'd left the B4520 far behind and picked up the even more minor roads leading towards the farm. The mobile's GPS easing him south and west. Forty minutes after dumping Rhodri's father, he turned onto a familiar stretch of winding, single-lane road that ran uphill and parallel to a river valley. After a slow left-hand turn, the road stretched out two hundred metres before a right turn would lead him into Glyn Coes.

In the distance, on the left-hand side, a small figure faced him, arm held out, thumb on full show.

As the distance between them closed, the figure grew and became familiar. Mitch Bairstow.

Oh hell. What now?

Kaine trod on the brake pedal, and the Astra lurched to a stop alongside the smiling former soldier.

"Well, blow me down," Mitch said, "fancy seeing you here." He removed a stained and tattered baseball cap and scratched the top of his head.

"What are you doing here?" Kaine asked, trying not to snap.

"On my way to a place called Glyn Coes. Fancy giving me a lift?"

"You'd better get in the back. My last passenger had a bit of an accident." He pointed to the damp patch on the seat and then to the rear door. "It's open."

Mitch cranked open the door, threw in his backpack, and slid in beside it. He leant forwards and sniffed the air over the front passenger seat.

"Your last passenger took one look at your mug and released a stream of ... invective, did he?"

Kaine stared at him through the rear-view. "Mitchell Bairstow, you have a wonderful turn of phrase."

Bairstow shot him a cheeky grin. "I know. Famous for it the world over, I am." He dropped the grin and became serious. "Did he wet himself when he learnt who you were, Captain Kaine?"

Kaine twisted at the waist and stared straight into his latest passenger's deep brown eyes, where he found nothing but honesty and openness.

Bairstow raised both hands in calm submission.

"Please don't be worried, Captain. I'm not here to shake you down or nothing."

Bluff it out. He knows nothing. He's guessing.

"I don't know who you think I am, Mitch, but my name's Peter Sidings, and I never made Captain. I was a Staff Sergeant."

Bairstow glanced over his shoulder checking the view through the rear window. The road remained empty. He turned and locked eyes with Kaine.

"Don't treat me like an idiot, Captain Kaine. I've trudged twenty-five miles today to warn you, and that's not easy for a bloke with one leg. Give me a break, will you?"

"Warn me?"

"Yeah, too right." He nodded for emphasis. "I wanted to warn you."

"What about?"

"There are people looking for you."

Really? That's a shock.

"What people?"

"We're too exposed here. Take us somewhere safe, and I'll tell you all about them."

"We're safe enough here. Start talking."

"At least take us off the main road. We're too visible."

Bairstow crossed his arms in a sign of defiance. He had the upper hand. Kaine wasn't about to manhandle a disabled veteran and eject him from the car. Nor would he take a relative stranger to the home of a member of The 83. Not without a thorough vetting first.

"Seat belt on," Kaine ordered and turned to face the wheel.

"Now we're getting somewhere," Bairstow said, grabbing the seat belt and clicking it into place.

They drove past the turning to the farm, and Kaine studiously ignored the sign that read *Cadwallader Farm and Trekking Centre, Glyn Coes*. He took the third turn on the right, where a sign pointed to

Howell Farm, and headed uphill on a farm track that needed remedial work. Half a mile later, Kaine pulled into a small gap in the hedge blocked by a moss-covered, five-bar gate and yanked on the handbrake. He twisted in his seat again.

"Okay, Mitch. Take it away."

CHAPTER 37

Wednesday 24th May – Maureen Reilly

East of Glyn Coes, Powys, South Wales, UK

"Where is he now?" Maureen Reilly asked.

She couldn't see the tracker screen clearly from the passenger seat and Stacy still refused to let her drive, the misogynist pig. Not that they were driving, of course. Oh no. That would be too damn easy. No, they were parked near the limit of the tracker's range, fifteen miles from the target, who was making snail's progress, hitching a lift in a place with no traffic. The wait couldn't have been much more excruciating.

Stacy just sat there, drumming his fingers on the rim of the steering wheel. Couldn't even keep to a recognisable beat or a consistent rhythm.

So flaming irritating.

She'd been primed to take down Ryan Kaine for a couple of days now. Could there be anything more frustrating than an extended wait for action?

If she'd had her way, they'd have picked up Bairstow the second he signed himself out of the hospital. She'd have happily beaten the truth out of the cripple. How she would have enjoyed taking the weasel apart. The way the little prick had whimpered and squirmed when she squeezed his ugly stub of a leg through the bedding had been a hoot. It not only gave her utter joy to feel him tremble under her grip, but it also demonstrated how he reacted to pain, how easy it would be to break the little fruitcake.

Still, Stacy was the lead. At least for now. Nothing else for it but to obey his instructions and bide her time. Yes, she'd follow his lead, and see where the cripple took them. And then, she'd do her thing. She almost wet herself at the thought of taking down the UK's most wanted criminal.

Ryan Kaine.

It had to be Bairstow's destination. He'd tried to throw them off by spending the night in a filthy dive in Merthyr Tydfil of all places. She'd pleaded to move on him then, but Stacy overruled her yet again.

"Patience, Mo," he'd said. "Patience. Given time, he'll take us right to the target. I can feel it."

Arrogant prick.

Maureen took her time to review her new partner.

After spending so many full days with the man, she'd lost all romantic interest. To imagine she'd actually fancied him once.

God alive.

The very idea.

Despite his cool manner and his obvious physical skills, Will Stacy had about as much charisma and sex appeal as a four-day-old pizza. No matter how hard she tried, she could not engage the man in any sort of conversation that didn't involve the immediate operation or their work in general. In short, she'd learnt nothing of his personality. She had no idea what drove him or how he ticked.

The previous night, she'd practically thrown herself at him, but he turned her down flat, and he hadn't been too subtle about it. So embarrassing. She could have killed him, but no. Not yet. Killing Stacy would have to wait until after they found Ryan Kaine and fulfilled the Grey Notice.

She could do far better than the likes of Will Stacy. By God, she could. And she would. If she looked hard enough, she'd find a partner who met her wants and needs. Someone who wouldn't turn up his nose at a little wanton violence.

"He's a couple of miles away from a place called Glyn Coes," Stacy finally answered. He kept drumming his fingers on the rim of the steering wheel.

Annoying bugger. Why doesn't he stop?

"The place barely registers on the map," he continued. "Nothing more than a crossroads and a couple of farms, by the looks of things."

"You really think Kaine's hiding out on a farm?"

"No idea, but Bairstow's heading somewhere, and he's the only lead we have."

They lapsed into silence again. Silence apart from the incessant, infuriating finger tapping.

"Will," she said, "I need to ask a question."

She'd been waiting to broach the subject for ages, and this seemed as good a time as any. At least it might stop him tapping his bloody fingers against the pigging steering wheel.

"Go ahead," he said, not taking his eyes from the tracking screen.

"When we find the target ..." She hesitated, and her heart rate increased as her inner tension mounted.

Go on, girl. Out with it.

"Yes?" He gripped the wheel and had the decency to tear his eyes from the screen and look at her. Progress of sorts. And he'd stopped the bloody tapping.

"When we locate the target," she repeated, "can I take the kill shot?"

There, she'd asked the question that had been worrying away inside her head since Gordon had tasked them with the Grey Notice job. How would Stacy react?

The bugger did what he always did when asked a question. He took his sweet time to consider the answer. What she once found reassuring, she now found exasperating. Why couldn't he just answer the bloody question?

By the time she'd made it all the way up to an eleven count, Stacy opened his mouth and took a breath in preparation to speak when something on the screen drew his attention.

"The tracker's picked up speed," he said, pressing the ignition button on the dashboard. "Bairstow must have found a lift."

He selected drive and stamped on the accelerator. The Range Rover took off like a startled hare, stirring up gravel and raising dust.

Once their speed had increased to sixty, Stacy eased back on the throttle, and they cruised at just below the national limit. Even though they were sanctioned to work for the government, Stacy would keep below the radar. The man never took a risk.

So damned boring.

Ten minutes later, Stacy feathered the brakes and they slowed to make a tight left turn onto an even narrower road. Overgrown hedges crowded in on either side of them, narrowing the lane even further. They had to pull in tight to the side to allow an oncoming tractor to pass. How the mud-spattered monster didn't remove a layer of paint from the Rover was anybody's guess. The farmer waved a thank you at them, and Stacy responded with a raised hand before pulling out into the middle of the road and building speed again.

One left turn later, Stacy pulled into a passing place and activated the parking brake. He left the engine running.

"What's up?" Maureen asked, leaning over, trying to see the screen.

"Signal stopped moving again. Looks like they've parked up. Two miles west of us."

"That Glyn Coes place?"

"No." Stacy shook his head. "They drove past the turning and stopped on a lane leading to a place called Howell Farm. My bet is Bairstow is waiting to see if he's being followed before making contact. It's why he overnighted in Merthyr. Don't let the false leg fool you, Mo. The man's a trained soldier. He knows how to cover his tracks."

Trained soldier, my arse.

Bairstow may have been a squaddie back in the day, but she couldn't think of him as anything but a useless cripple who'd lead her straight to her share of a one-million-pound reward. Her share being all of it. No way was she going to let Stacy have a penny of it. She'd made the decision the second Gordon had sent them on the job. The old skinflint had been underpaying her since she'd joined the firm. Peanuts. At the job interview, Gordon told her he'd only considered taking her on as a favour to an old friend, Maureen's former superintendent. At her first annual review, Gordon also claimed she hadn't done enough to prove herself worthy of a pay hike. Well fuck him. Fuck the lot of them.

No one shat on Maureen Reilly and got away with it. No one. Reed was the first to find out and others had learnt since.

"You never did tell me where you planted the tracker," she said after they'd been silent for a full five minutes. Anything to break the tension.

Stacy's thin lips stretched out into a lopsided grin. "Tucked it into the shoe of his false leg. I figured he wouldn't feel it and he wasn't going anywhere without his leg."

"Neat."

Maureen gave him points for smarts and another for finally answering one of her questions. Maybe she'd make it quick. Originally, she'd planned to gut shoot Stacy after he'd helped her to the pay-off. Have him die slowly. But maybe she'd take pity on him after all. Kill him quick. A bullet to the back of the head when he wasn't looking. Quick and painless.

"I thought so," Stacy said, smugness itself.

Smugness didn't suit him. Nothing suited Will Stacy. How could she ever have considered him attractive?

The Rover's automatic start-stop system killed the engine and they waited.

CHAPTER 38

Mitch couldn't really blame Kaine for being overly cautious and a little defensive. With every law enforcement agency in Europe hunting him down, it was a wonder the man hadn't gone stark staring bonkers. Although he should have been a nervous wreck, bouncing up and down in his seat, spitting nails, he simply sat and listened, taking it all in. He barely asked any questions. He also kept scanning the area outside the car, forever on the lookout.

"So," Mitch said, reaching the end of his tale, "there I was in my hospital bed, with a cool one thousand pounds in my crotch. Such a hoot, man. I can tell you that for nothing. I nearly wet myself trying not to laugh. I mean, I couldn't believe they folded so easily."

"Okay," Ryan Kaine said, nodding but still maintaining his steady watch. "What happened next?" he asked—one of his rare interruptions.

"I told them I overheard you in the car on the way to the hospital. Said I recognised the name of the place on account of schlepping through it a couple of weeks back. All of which is true, by the way." Mitch forced out a smile that wasn't reciprocated. "What isn't true is the name I gave them. Trefecca. Pretty little place about ten miles due east of Brecon Town. Well away from here."

Ryan Kaine narrowed his eyes and stared hard at Mitch. Unnerving, it was, too. Mitch could imagine people wilting under such a withering stare. Blue eyes, he had, but the news articles described his eyes as brown. Had to be wearing coloured contacts. Couldn't blame him for changing his appearance, though. The long hair and the beard helped, too. They softened his tough-guy image.

"And they believed you?" Ryan Kaine asked, turning his gaze to their surroundings, forever guarding his back.

"Yeah, I think so. Of course, they gave me a load of guff about taking back the money and making sure the police came after me for wasting their time if I was lying." Mitch sighed and shook his head. "The woman, evil bloody creature built like a middleweight boxer, also threatened to come back and inflict serious physical pain on me. Ha!" Mitch slapped his right thigh. "As if I'm a stranger to pain. Live with pain every day of my life. Anyway, after that, they skedaddled out of the ward like flames were coming out their backsides and they were in dire need of a fire hydrant."

Mitch laughed. Ryan Kaine nodded slowly, as though having trouble taking it all in.

"Okay," he said, "keep going."

"Well, the moment they left," Mitch said, allowing a hint of triumph to enter his voice, "I asked for my clothes and my backpack, and discharged myself. Used a borrowed phone to call a taxi and had the driver take me south, to Merthyr Tydfil. All the while, I kept checking my rear to make sure Sykes and Folly weren't on my tail. Spent the night in a nice little B & B. Oh, thanks for the five hundred quid, by the way. I assume that was down to you?"

Ryan Kaine nodded. "A thank you for your service." He flicked a glance at Mitch's right leg and made eye contact again.

"Yeah, well ... it's appreciated but not necessary. I've got plenty of money coming in, but ... what I do with it is my business. Right?"

"Right."

"I'm a travelling man by choice," Mitch said, urgency in his voice. "Can't stand to settle down anywhere. I need to be on the move. Get me?" On recognising the growing stridency in his voice, Mitch took a breath and reined himself in. "Sorry, Captain. Sore subject. People just assume I'll do anything for a handout. Sykes and Folly tried to buy me with thirty pieces of silver, like I was a Judas."

"So, you spent the night in Merthyr Tydfil?" Ryan Kaine asked, glossing over Mitch's semi-rant, no doubt trying to move the story along.

"Yeah, didn't get much sleep, though." He raised a hand to the side of his face. "Still had a bit of a headache, and I kept an eye open for any signs of a tail. Didn't see anything. Then, in the morning, this morning, I had a very nice breakfast and started hitching a lift here."

Mitch threw up his hands.

"And there you are, bang up to date," he said.

"Okay, thanks for the warning."

"You're welcome."

"However, it does leave one final question," Ryan Kaine said, his expression stony.

"It does?"

"Yes."

"Go ahead."

"What do you want now?"

Mitch smiled. "Aha, I see. Don't worry, like I said, this isn't a shakedown. Your money's safe. I already told you I'm not after a handout."

"What *are* you after?"

Mitch sighed. This part wasn't exactly easy to explain. "You and your mates saved me from a right kicking, and then you drove me to hospital. Didn't have to. Put yourself out for me. Could have called an ambulance and left me in the street, but you didn't. It put me in your debt. Hate being in anyone's debt, me." He smiled.

"Then, last night I got to thinking. What sort of a man risks everything to save a total stranger, and a filthy vagrant at that? Would a terrorist killer really do that?"

"And what answer did you arrive at?"

"That was the simple part. Of course he wouldn't. So, I reckoned the papers got it wrong. You can't be the cold-blooded killer they paint you to be."

Mitch paused a moment to rest his voice. He hadn't spoken so much in ages. No surprise it hurt his throat so much.

"Anyway, I decided you were a good man, and I wanted to warn you about Sykes and Folly. Don't worry, I didn't come here direct from Merthyr. I took a roundabout route. Went by bus from Merthyr to Brecon and hitchhiked the rest of the way. You'd be amazed how easy it is to spot a tail when you're walking. And I didn't. Spot a tail, I mean."

"That's it? You wanted to warn me?"

"About Sykes and Folly. Yes. If they know you're in the area, other people will, too. You're not safe here, Captain Kaine. You need to scram. Get out of Wales. Go."

For the first time since he'd picked Mitch up at the side of the road, Ryan Kaine's tense shoulders relaxed. He even showed Mitch a smile. Not much of a smile, mind. More an easing of the scowl. Still, it softened the fugitive's tough-as-nails appearance to something a tad less harsh. Might even have made him look friendly.

"Thanks again for the warning," Ryan Kaine said, twisting in his seat and turning his back to Mitch—a sure sign of a thaw in the defences. "As it happens, our business here is done. We're getting ready to move on."

Thank the Good Lord for that.

Mitch couldn't have been more relieved. Although desperate to ask what business a hunted man would have in the Brecon Beacons, he wouldn't dream of interrogating the notorious Ryan Kaine. No way.

Just be happy you've paid off your debt, man.

"Hungry?" Kaine asked.

"Famished," he said, telling the whole truth.

"Me too. I'm sure a farmer's wife I know will be happy to sort us out with a spot of grub."

Mitch rubbed his hands together.

"Home cooking?"

"Yep. Becky's a great cook."

"Excellent. Can't wait."

Ryan Kaine fired up the Astra and slipped it into first gear. He executed a rapid five-point turn on the narrow track and had them facing back the way they'd come in an instant.

"Oh," Ryan Kaine said, "before I forget. The people we're about to meet, the Cadwalladers, know me as Peter Sidings. *Staff Sergeant* Peter Sidings."

"Ex-military?"

"That's right. 2 PARA." Ryan Kaine's blue eyes fixed on Mitch through the rear-view mirror. "The Cadwalladers can't know who I really am. They mustn't."

"Understood."

Mitch didn't really understand, but he didn't care, either. He'd delivered his message, paid his debt of honour, and that would be an end to the matter.

"I'll introduce you as a hitchhiker I took pity on—"

"On account of the limp?"

"If you like. And ..." Ryan Kaine refocused his attention on the twisting road ahead. "They don't know anything about the business at Sennybridge the other day. As far as they're concerned, we've just met."

"Got it," Mitch repeated. "What about your buddies, Doc and Goliath?"

"Goliath?"

"Yeah, the big man who drove like a nutcase."

"Oh, I see. Goliath, nice one." This time, Ryan Kaine smiled properly. Took the harshness from his face. "What about my buddies?"

"How are they going to react to seeing me?"

"Don't worry about them. They won't say anything."

"They know who you really are?"

Ryan Kaine nodded. "Of course."

"And they don't mind helping you? Despite ... you know ... despite what you're supposed to have done?"

"They're old friends. They know me."

Mitch settled back in his seat. He'd been dead right about Ryan Kaine. Dead right. A man who generated such fierce loyalty in his friends had to be a good man. He couldn't have done what they accused him of.

No way.

CHAPTER 39

Wednesday 24th May – Early Afternoon

Cadwallader Farm, Glyn Coes, Powys, South Wales, UK

Kaine took a left at the end of Powell Farm Lane and joined the road leading to Glyn Coes and Cadwallader Farm. He kept glancing in the rear-view mirror, but his latest passenger did nothing other than stare through the window, taking in the scenery.

He'd taken a bit of a gamble, but something about Mitch Bairstow made Kaine want to trust him. If he couldn't rely on his instincts, life would prove impossible. Bairstow would keep Kaine's secret and the Cadwalladers would be none the wiser. And if he didn't, would it matter? They'd completed the mission, protected the farm, and kept the boy safe from his money-grubbing father. If they learnt the truth about him, would they see the real him in what he'd done for the boy? Could they learn to forgive him for his God-awful mistake?

Grow up, Kaine. That's not going to happen.

He indicated right and took the turn. The Astra chugged up the hill on the scratchy farm lane. It took ten minutes to crest the brow and for the sunlit valley to stretch out below them.

Bairstow leant forwards and wrapped his arms around the front seat. He pursed his lips and emitted a low whistle.

"Man," he breathed. "What a pretty place."

Kaine smiled. "Certainly is."

To give Bairstow time to take in the glory, Kaine reduced speed, and they cruised downhill at a sedate twenty-five mph.

"Horses!" An excited and agitated Bairstow pointed to the paddock, where a dozen of the wilful beasts poked their heads over the fence, whinnying and begging for food. "Love horses, me. Used to ride all the time when I was a kid. We lived next to some stables. I used to help out during the holidays. Pay for my rides that way. Happy days."

"Doc's just the same," Kaine said. "Potty over the beasts. If you ask nicely, Myfanwy will put a saddle on one of them for you. It'll have to wait until she's back from school, but I'm sure it'll be okay."

Bairstow faltered and leant back in his seat again. "Not sure I'm up to riding these days. Haven't been on a horse since way before losing the leg."

"They run a trekking school here. I'm sure they'll be able to find a docile nag for you to wander about on. If you're up for it."

Bairstow lowered his chin to his chest, the initial excitement seeping away until a horse whickered, and his head jerked up again. He stared out the window, eyes smiling.

At the gate with the cattle grid, Kaine stopped. Bairstow opened the door and bounced out. He hobbled away, unlatched the gate, and tugged it open. Kaine drove through and waited, but after closing the gate, Bairstow waved him away.

"I'll stay here until you've made the introductions. To be certain it's okay for me to scrounge some food."

"And give you a chance to say hello to the gee-gees?" Kaine grinned as he asked the question.

Bairstow returned the grin and limped closer to the paddock fence.

"Hello, boy," he said to a large black beast. "Aren't you the fine-looking fellow." Tears gleamed as he rubbed the animal's nose, unmistakably lost in the moment.

Kaine eased the Astra away and turned into the yard. Before he'd pulled up the handbrake, the front door flew open and Lara raced out, concern written all over her face. A worried-looking Becky followed her out but stayed in the doorway, clutching the big, wrought iron handle.

Hell. What now?

"Peter," Lara called. "Where were you? We've been calling you all morning."

Kaine jumped out of the Astra and met her halfway along the garden path. "I powered my phone down. What's wrong?"

"It's Rhodri," Becky cried from the porch. "He's gone. The boy's run away."

"What?" Kaine shook the cotton wool from his ears. "When?"

Lara leant close and spoke quietly. "Rollo arrived and brought Robbie Powell to the Lodge. While I set his arm—a clean break, by the way, should heal well enough—he started rambling. Pain meds will do that to some patients. He ended up talking about the dead sheep and saying how sorry he was."

"What else did he say?"

Lara shook her head. "He confessed to being paid by a fat man with a cleft chin."

Hell.

"Where was Rhodri during this confession?"

"I don't know. Why?"

"The paymaster, Mr Cleft-chin is Rhodri's dad, Richard Duck-worth." Kaine gritted his teeth. "Rhodri must have overheard you. He's sneaky that way. Quiet as a ghost when he wants to be. Inquisitive, too. He might have heard Powell's confession."

"Oh Lord. There's no telling how he'd react to hearing something like that."

"No wonder he's taken off. Where is everyone?"

"Rollo, Gwyn, and Fan are out searching for him. Gwyn's taken the Land Rover and the others are on quad bikes. My God," Lara said, pointing towards the paddock. "What's Mitch Bairstow doing here?"

"He's come to warn me off."

"Sorry?"

"Long story. He knows who I am, but he's on our side. At least, I think he is. I'll explain later. Meanwhile, I'm off to find Rhodri."

"You know where he is?"

"Think so. Back soon, I hope."

He touched her arm and turned away.

"Wait, where are you going?"

Over his shoulder, he called out, "Great Scar!" and took off at a fast jog.

CHAPTER 40

Wednesday 24th May – Maureen Reilly

East of Glyn Coes, Powys, South Wales, UK

Ten interminable minutes dragged by with Stacy staring at the screen attached to the holder, and Maureen craning her neck to view it, before he sat up straighter.

"They're off again," he announced.

"Is Bairstow on foot?"

"Can't be. The signal's moving too quickly. He must still be in the car."

Stacy added a little pressure to the accelerator to wake the Rover's dormant engine, checked his mirrors, and pulled out of the passing space. He kept the speed below twenty.

"Why so slow?" she asked at the risk of annoying the great man.

"He's reversed direction and coming towards us. Be prepared to duck down in your seat." He paused at a T-junction, apparently unable to decide which direction to take. "Rest easy, Mo. He's taken the turn into Glen Coes. It's marked as a pony trekking centre."

"What are you waiting for?"

He shot her one of his withering sideways glances. At least it *used* to be withering, but that was back when Will Stacy wasn't a dead man walking—or in this case, dead man driving.

"It's a dead end, I'm making sure they don't double back on us."

"Oh."

"They've stopped at the farm."

Stacy pulled out at the junction, turned left, and picked up speed. A sign pointing right read *Cadwallader Farm and Trekking Centre, Glyn Coes.* Stacy ignored it and carried on going.

"What's wrong? Why aren't you—"

"There's another turn further up the hill. A lane. Looks like it'll give us a good view of the farm."

The right turn immediately after the farm entrance found them bouncing along a dirt track, lined on either side with neatly trimmed hedges, heading uphill. At the top of the rise, the road levelled out and the hedges merged into woods. Stacy pulled into a lay-by and stopped the car. He hit a button on his side of the dash. The tailgate popped and powered open. Then he cracked open his door and jumped out. Maureen followed suit.

They gathered at the tailgate. Stacy unhooked the flap of his backpack, pulled out a pair of binoculars, and hung them around his neck from their leather strap. Working in silent tandem, Maureen broke open the lock box bolted to the floor pan and slid out the rifle case, feeling the reassuring weight of her beautiful new toy, a Remington CSR. Her latest sniper rifle of choice. It broke down into three pieces, each less than forty centimetres long, and could be reassembled and fired within sixty seconds. Maureen left the lethal beauty in its case and pulled her SIG P226 from its shoulder holster. Not a fan of the Glock 17 issued to her as a police firearms officer, she preferred the SIG for its lightness and accuracy at shorter range. She released the magazine from the handle, confirmed the load, and snapped it back into position. She was ready to go.

Stacy did the same to his Glock 17, which he kept in a holster clipped to the belt at his hip, the better for a rapid draw, which Maureen had never mastered. Hadn't even tried to master.

"Oh," Stacy said, looking directly at her for the first time since leaving the driving seat. "If Kaine *is* down there, you *can* have the honours. But wait for my signal."

Her heart rate leapt.

"Thank you."

She didn't really want or need his permission, but it felt good to have the go-ahead. Her only intention in asking was to ease his suspicions. He'd have expected her to ask, and she'd met the brief.

"Follow me," he said and headed into the woods.

Maureen hefted the Remington's case onto her shoulder and let Stacy take point to her Tail End Charlie. They'd covered less than fifty metres before she'd reaffirmed Stacy's skill set. He floated over the terrain and skirted the trees like a ghost, barely making a sound, while she clomped and scratched and rattled in his wake. No matter how much care she took, Maureen couldn't keep her noise down.

He turned his head to scowl at her but said nothing. If he'd said anything derogatory, she might well have shot him in the back, to hell with the consequences. Instead, she slowed and allowed Stacy to stretch the distance between them.

The rifle case dug into her shoulder, its weight dragging her down, making her a liability, but she couldn't let Stacy see how it affected her. He'd probably offer to carry it for her and that wouldn't do. She needed it for the kill shot.

Up ahead, Stacy had reached the treeline. He dropped to his right knee, lifted the binoculars—a powerful pair of Zeiss Rangefinders. He rested his elbow on his raised left thigh to steady the glasses.

Maureen closed the gap, took a knee beside him, and waited, breathing slightly more heavily that she wanted or expected.

An open valley stretched out below them. Fields, hedges, farm buildings, animals, a stream, yadda, yadda. Some would have called it picturesque. Maureen called it a battlefield with a single target, then glanced to her left at the silent Will Stacy.

Check that. Two targets.

She smiled at her own joke but made sure he couldn't see it. Wouldn't want him thinking she was enjoying herself too much. To Will Stacy this was business. Deadly business maybe, but business, nonetheless. To Maureen Reilly, this was pure, unadulterated joy. Positively orgasmic.

Okay, woman. Get serious. Scope it out.

The main buildings stood about half a mile distant. Without the binoculars, she could just about make out a figure standing by the fence close to a bunch of horses, a small blue car parked in front of the farmhouse, and another two people standing close together. She couldn't make out any of the details.

"What do you see?" she whispered, fed up with waiting.

Stacy lowered the binoculars, removed the strap from around his neck, and passed them across.

"Check it out for yourself."

Maureen lowered the Remington case to the ground at her side, raised the glasses to her eyes, and rotated the nut to sharpen the image to its maximum. She found focus on the dark-clad figure by the horses. He patted the head of a big black monster and stepped to one side to pet a smaller, brown one. No, not stepped, limped.

"Bairstow," she said. "The one petting the horses is Bairstow. I'd recognised him anywhere."

"Agreed. And the other man?" Stacy said, voice low and steady, "The one near the old Astra standing close to the woman?"

She panned around to the left, past the rust-pitted car, and towards the farmhouse. A man and woman stood close, talking. The woman animated. The man stood with his back towards Maureen. He seemed to be listening intently. He half-turned, showing his profile. Longish brown hair, beard.

"Kaine!" she yelped. "It's Ryan Kaine. We've got him!" Excitement made her speak way louder that she'd intended.

"Calm down, Mo," Stacy whispered, keeping his infuriating voice down and unemotional. Did nothing faze the man?

Such a cold fish.

Maureen practically threw the binoculars back to Stacy and reached for the rifle case, tugging it towards her. She unfastened the buckle from the rear flap and released the strap. Next, she removed the chassis stock and the barrel, slid one into the other, and finger-tightened the locking nut. Finally, she removed the handguard and slid it into place.

"What are you doing?" Stacy asked, speaking a little louder.

"I can take him out from here. Easy shot. Let's get this over with."

"No," he said firmly. "This must be covert. No witnesses, remember."

Maureen ground her teeth together. What was wrong with the man?

"We're government sanctioned, and Kaine's a multiple killer. I'm taking the shot."

"No, you aren't." Stacy snaked out a hand and unclipped the magazine from the Remington. "Covert, Gordon said. And I agree. No witnesses. We bide our time."

"But Kaine's right there!" she hissed, trying her best to lower her voice, but anger took over.

"Maureen," Stacy said, "Mo. Kaine's going nowhere. We'll do this my way. There are at least two non-combatants in the field of fire. We don't risk collaterals. Understood?"

"Fuck's sake, Will," she said, forcibly relaxing her jaw. "I understand. We wait 'til Kaine's alone. But I still get to take him down, yes?"

Stacy nodded and raised the glasses again.

"Hang on," he said. "You might just get your chance sooner than you think."

"What?"

"Kaine's on the move."

Maureen changed her attention from glowering at Stacy to following the target.

"He's heading west," Stacy said. "Where's he going? ... Looks like he's making for the cliff over to the west, there."

"My God, he's going to pass right by us. More or less."

Maureen glanced at the Remington.

Pity.

She wouldn't be "blooding" it. Not today. On the positive side, she'd be taking Kaine out up close and personal. She'd be able to look him in the face while the light died in his eyes. A much better option.

"See that track?" Stacy asked, pointing at a pale line slicing through the woods and the bushes to their left. It headed towards the woods and emerged at the top of the ridge to the left of the cliff.

"Yeah, I see it."

"It's the fastest route. Move quickly and you'll be able to head Kaine off."

"While I'm doing that, what are you going to do?"

He waved a hand over the Remington. "We can't leave this lying around here for anyone to stumble over, and it's too heavy. Neither of us will beat Kaine to the ridge carrying that great lump."

He had a point.

"You head Kaine off," he continued. "I'll take the rifle back to the car and catch you up. Hurry up, he's moving faster than you'd think. And remember, make sure he's alone before you take him out."

Yeah, right.

Maureen checked the security of the SIG in its holster and raced off, dodging tall trees and low bushes. It didn't take long for her to pick up the track. It ran gently downhill, but the underfoot conditions—jutting roots and deep potholes—made a flat-out sprint way too dangerous. She measured her tread and risked a quick glance over her right shoulder.

Jesus wept.

Kaine, moving impossibly fast, had already made it to the upper boundary of the first large field. Unless the uphill climb slowed him down, she wouldn't reach the ridge ahead of him. She was already blowing and any faster risked a headlong plummet into the footpath or, worse still, face first into the gorse bushes running alongside it.

Steady, Maureen. You've got this.

Three hundred metres after she'd joined the twisting path, it dipped away more steeply, and the bushes to her right thinned and disappeared. She skidded to a stop and ducked behind a tree.

Her jacket!

Bright blue, it would stand out a mile in all the greenery. Beneath it, she wore an off-white blouse. Even worse. Kaine only had to look up to his left and he'd spot her in an instant.

Damn it, she should have worn something dark, more camouflaged. Basic errors on a covert field trip. What the hell was wrong with her? Before the trip, she'd packed her bags full of clothes to impress Will Stacy. As though she could ever do that.

Stupid, stupid, stupid.

Breathe deep. Slow down.

She had to slow down. Go dark.

Panting heavily, she hugged the trunk of the tree, the bark grooved and rough under her palms, and poked her head around the side. No sign of Kaine. Damn ... where was he? Ah yes, there.

Kaine's dark-clad figure jogged over the lush, knee-high grass of another field, still making good time. He hardly seemed to have slowed. Less than a quarter mile separated them, and the distance closed with Kaine's every stride.

She cast her eyes around the bushes on the other side of the track, searching for something.

There.

A couple of metres away she found it. A puddle. Perfect. She stripped off her jacket and dunked it into the muddy water.

CHAPTER 41

Cadwallader Farm, Glyn Coes, Powys, South Wales, UK

Kaine made good time from the farm and had already reached the treeline below where he'd left Rhodri the previous night. He had no idea how the boy felt, or what he could be thinking. The odds were, the lad would turn to his mother for advice, and he'd find her at the top of the cliff face, looking out over the valley.

No telling what the boy would do if approached directly. For pity's sake, he'd just learnt that his father had been responsible for the attacks on the farm and the death of so many sheep. It wasn't outside the realms of possibility for a distraught twelve-year-old to do something drastic. The lad might even decide that life wasn't worth living anymore.

Whatever the boy overheard from Robbie Powell, or thought he'd heard, he needed to know the truth.

Heart pounding, lungs burning, thighs on fire, Kaine drove

himself harder, stretching out his stride length, dodging around trees and hurdling low bushes. He reversed the route he'd taken that morning, checking his footing the whole way.

Kaine slowed, took a chance, and glanced up.

Great Scar stretched out above his head, staring down at him, impassive in its grandeur. Whatever puny human dramas were being played out at its feet, the monolith would endure. It couldn't care less that a twelve-year-old boy might throw himself from its face. Kaine did, though. He really did.

Movement up on the top of the ridge caught Kaine's eye. He skidded to a stop, stood as still as his deep breathing would allow.

Framed by a pale blue sky, a small, round face with a mop of wavy blond hair peeped out over the edge, near the place Kaine had kept lookout. Near the area he'd set the belay, the anchoring point for his rope. The rope he'd used to abseil down the rock face with the boy that morning.

What the hell?

A small arm reached out, grasped the rope, and tugged.

"Rhodri, no!" Kaine yelled, waved his arms. "Keep away from the edge. It's not safe."

The face turned towards Kaine. Wet cheeks glistened in the afternoon sun.

"It's okay," he shouted, the high-pitched, reedy voice barely carrying over the distance and against the slight breeze. "I watched the way you did it."

"Get back."

The boy shook his head. "Dad used to call me a weakling. A coward. Kept saying how I wouldn't amount to anything. I'll show him."

"Rhod, listen to me, please," Kaine called, trying to keep the stress from his words. "It doesn't matter what your father said back then. He was wrong. I know how brave you are. You showed me that last night when we were flying."

"Flying. You mean abseiling, don't you? I looked it up on the internet at school. I know what I'm doing. I'll be safe."

"Only if you're shown how to do it properly. Step by step. In easy stages. Great Scar isn't the right place to start."

The lad leant further over the edge. The wind picked at his hair, whipping it into his face. He reached up a hand and brushed it away from his eyes. A stone moved under his supporting arm, crumbled away from the ledge. It skittered and rattled down the face, hit a jutting rock and bounced out into space, tumbling, spinning.

Kaine dived to one side, barrel-rolled, and sprang to his feet. The stone, little more than a pebble, smashed onto the path where he'd been standing, shattering on impact.

"Sorry, sorry," Rhodri squealed. "Are you okay?"

"Yes," Kaine shouted, waving both arms. "I'm fine, but please back away from the ledge."

The boy eased back a little, but not far enough for safety.

"But I've ruined everything," Rhodri called, his voice little more than a whimper, barely reaching Kaine's ears.

"Sorry? What was that Rhod?"

"Uncle Gwynfor will never forgive me. Never let me keep Night-watch now. I wanted to abseil on my own before he sent me away."

"What do you mean?"

"It was all my fault. All those sheep. If I hadn't done it. If I'd told the truth ..."

The boy pushed out further, dislodging a hail of pebbles. Kaine pressed himself hard against the face, covered his head with his hands and arms, and waited. The stones peppered the earth and rock behind him, falling harmlessly away.

"Mr Sidings! Peter!"

Kaine pushed himself away from the rock face and looked up. Flying dust stung his eyes. He blinked it clear.

Up on the Scar, the boy stared down, face pale, eyes wide and tear-filled.

"I'm okay, Rhod."

"I'm so sorry. Dad always called me a screwup."

Ducky Duckworth had so much to answer for. Such wonderful parenting skills.

"Rhod, will you listen to me?" Kaine called, stepping further away from the cliff face, reaching what he considered a safe zone. "Rhodri?"

"Y-Yes?"

"Are you listening?"

Seventy-odd metres above Kaine, the boy nodded.

"Yes. I'm listening."

"I don't know what you think you've done wrong, but it can't be that bad."

"It is," the lad screamed. "I've ruined everything. It's all my fault! The fire at the stables. All those sheep—"

"That had nothing to do with you, Rhod."

"It did too. If it wasn't for me, Dad wouldn't have done it. The letters. If I hadn't hidden them, none of this would have happened. Uncle Gwynfor will never forgive me!"

The kid had started rambling. No telling where that would lead. Kaine took a gamble.

"Rhodri," he called, "I can't hear you. We need to talk this through like adults. Can I come up there for a chat?"

Rhodri leant back and wiped the tears from his eyes with his fists.

"How?" he called.

"Sorry?"

The lad sniffled. "How are you going to get up here?"

"I'll use the rope. But first, you'll have to back away from the edge. I don't have a safety helmet, and I can't be dodging any more of those stones while I'm climbing. Will you do that for me?"

Rhodri blinked a couple of times before nodding again. "Yes. I will."

Good lad.

"Go on, Rhod. Back well clear of the edge."

"Can we abseil down again afterwards?"

Kaine took his turn to nod. "Yes, okay."

"You promise?"

"Cross my heart."

"Go on then," the lad called. "Cross your heart."

"You drive a hard bargain." Kaine signed an "x" over his chest with his thumb. "Are we cool now, Rhod?"

The lad smiled. "We're cool. Can I watch you climb?"

"Only if you stay well clear of the Scar. Way over there by those bushes." Kaine pointed to a wide patch of bracken and gorse twenty metres from the face, backed by trees.

"Okay." Rhodri pulled away from the lip and hurried to the spot Kaine had indicated.

"You'll stay there while I climb?"

"Yes." Rhodri nodded.

"Promise?"

"Cross my heart."

"Go on then," Kaine said, smiling.

Rhodri copied Kaine's action with his thumb but made the "x" over his right breast. Kaine didn't correct the lad's inaccuracy. It wasn't the time for an anatomy lesson.

Kaine stepped forwards, reached out, and snagged the rope with both hands. His damaged fingers pulsed and complained under the pressure, but he'd put up with it. On such a short climb, he'd manage well enough by favouring his injured hand.

Safety first. He latched on with both hands, found a foothold on the rock, and leant back adding his whole weight to the rope. It held steady and strong. No give. Nothing had changed from the previous evening. Good.

"Climbing now!" he called, hauling on the rope.

"Ready!" Rhodri answered, demonstrating how much of his internet research he'd absorbed.

Ordinarily, using the tethered rope, Kaine could have raced up the face and completed the climb in minutes, but with Rhod watching his every move, he took things slowly. Each time he planted his feet, he tested the placement carefully, checking its position. He gave a running commentary, as though he was a team leader breaking a new climb and instructing his fellow team members.

"Keep looking up. You need to plan your route all the way to the top of the climb. There's a false trail at the foot. It looks good, but it reaches an unstable area at about thirty metres. Unclimbable. If you took that route, you'd have to retrace your steps and traverse to the left."

At ten metres, he paused for a moment and glanced up. Rhodri, blue eyes wide, his expression a picture of concentration, hadn't moved from the bushes. Kaine started climbing again.

"There's an overhang at fifteen metres. Care needed here."

"Loose rock at twenty. Firm and steady to the left. Look for the vertical crevice here. Good hand holds. Wide enough for a thumb lock."

At fifty metres, two-thirds of the way up, Kaine stopped again.

"Footing's solid here. Good place for a rest if you need it."

He looped the rope over his shoulder and tied a figure eight on a bight, attaching it to his belt as a temporary belay. He leant back and away from the face, standing at a near right angle to the cliff face.

"This is a good, safe anchor. I'll show you how to tie some basic knots later."

Kaine pulled on the lead side of the rope, returned to the vertical, and continued the climb. The higher up the rock face he climbed, the easier it became. He found it difficult to maintain the go-slow.

He glanced up again.

A woman—long, dark hair, severe fringe—broke through the treeline, a gun in her right hand.

Oh God!

"Rhod," Kaine yelled. "Get away. Run!"

Rhodri twisted.

The woman reached out and threw an arm around the boy's neck, pinning him tight.

Kaine heaved on the rope, raced up the rocks. Running, pulling, clambering. Hand over hand, hampered by his weakened right arm.

Stones rained down. A large rock missed Kaine's head by millimetres. Another struck him a glancing blow on the back of his right shoulder, further deadening his arm.

"Hold it right there, Captain!" the woman called.

Kaine stopped, looked up. Pins and needles pulsed through his right arm and hand, easing very slowly.

The woman held Rhod in front of her. She'd thrown her left arm over his shoulder. It ran diagonally across his chest, her hand clamped under his right armpit. She stood, yanking the boy off his feet.

"Get off me!" Rhod cried.

He kicked out, arms up, hands scratching at the woman's forearm, attempting to break the hold. All his efforts proved ineffective.

The woman—Maureen Folly, as Mitch Bairstow had described her—smiled. A cruel, victorious smile. Her right arm stretched out and down, the hand gripping a cocked and primed SIG P266. Despite the boy's struggles, she held the gun rock steady and pointed at Kaine's forehead. She'd pushed her index finger through the trigger guard and curled it around the trigger. Ready to shoot.

"That's it, Captain Kaine. Stay right where you are."

Rhod stopped kicking. Stopped struggling. His hands fell away from her forearm. He turned his head, trying to see the face of his captor.

"No, you're wrong," he said, voice faltering. "That's M-Mr Sidings."

Although she never drew her focus from Kaine, the cruel smile stretched out wider. "Sorry, kid. That's the terrorist, Ryan Kaine. I'm here to take him into custody." Folly winked at Kaine, triumphant.

"Liar!" Rhod screamed. "He's not Ryan Kaine. He's not! Ryan Kaine killed my mother."

He slumped against her and hung limp in her arm. Folly released her hold and the boy collapsed to his hands and knees, staring down at Kaine, questioning.

The light of understanding flashed in Folly's dark brown eyes.

"Fucking hell," she crowed, stretching out her gun arm even further. "I get it now. You're here trying to make amends. Currying favour. What a crock. Tell him, Captain. Tell him the truth while you have the chance. Go on. Get it off your chest."

Kaine drew his gaze from the SIG's yawning muzzle and turned it on the lad, who stared at him through tear-filled blue eyes.

Kaine braced his feet more firmly against the rock face and leant out against the rope. His right arm worked better, all but the fingertips fully recovered. He glanced down. One chance. A lightning fall with a perfectly timed rope brake might do it. Even in a marksman's hand, a SIG P226's effective range topped out at less than fifty metres.

If he reached the overhang, he might make it.

But she had the boy. With him under her control, Kaine could do nothing. He hung there, helpless. A fly trapped by a spider.

"Mr Sidings?" Rhod asked, plaintive, pleading.

It hurt Kaine to see the boy suffer.

"It's complicated, Rhod."

Reilly laughed.

"Complicated?" she scoffed. "Complicated? Bollocks. Go on, Captain. Tell him the truth. Tell him before I put a bullet in your head. What? Is the great Ryan Kaine frightened of the truth?"

"Mr Sidings," Rhod cried, "she's lying, isn't she?"

The rope bit into Kaine's fingers. He dangled over the edge of infinity with little chance of survival while the woman had control over the boy.

"No, Rhod," Kaine said, "she's telling the truth. I am Ryan Kaine."

The boy's face collapsed in on itself. His chin trembled, and his eyes streamed.

Not the reaction Kaine expected or wanted.

"No! It's not true. Why are you lying?"

"I'm sorry, Rhod. I really am."

"'I'm sorry'," Folly mocked. "Is that it? Pitiful, Captain. So damned pitiful. Think I'm going to puke."

"You killed my mother?" Rhod jumped to his feet.

More stones tumbled over the edge. Too far away to worry about.

"Rhod, I—"

"You killed my mother!" he repeated, this time screaming at the top of his voice. "I hate you! I hate you!"

He turned, ran. Disappeared into the bushes.

Maureen Folly laughed. Her finger tightened on the trigger.

Now! Go!

Kaine straightened his knees, pushed away from the rock face, released the temporary belay, and plummeted.

A crack. A gunshot. The boom echoed through the valley. He waited for the impact. Nothing.

Kaine fell, letting the rope slide through his loosened fists.

Wait, Kaine. Wait.

The minimal friction of rope sliding loosely on skin scorched his palms. Not enough to let go, but it stared to burn.

Another shot followed a moment after the first.

Kaine felt nothing but the rope sliding through his hands. Flaying his skin.

She missed?

The overhang raced towards him.

A woman screamed.

Now!

He grasped the rope. Gripped tight. Pain flared. Flames burned his hands. Shoulders wrenched. Elbows snapped to full extension. He crashed against the rock wall. Bounced. Crashed again. The powerful forces trying to break his grip.

A shadow flew past him. It thudded into the rocks fifteen metres below.

Kaine bounced against the rock wall once more and stopped. Shoulder scraped rock. Clung on. His boots found a foothold. Fighting the need to release his grip on the rope, hands aflame, Kaine descended fast. Without the lad as an audience, he didn't need to provide a commentary.

He reached flat ground. Planted his feet and tore his hands from the rope. Two lines of torn skin at the tips and along the palms burned. Blood seeped. Red raw. He blew on the scorched, raging tissue. It didn't help.

Folly lay beside him on the rocky ground, face canted away. The back of her head a crushed mess, blood and brains seeping out of the gash. Arms and legs crumpled. Unmoving. Lifeless.

"What happened?" Kaine asked, standing over the corpse. "Lean too far out?"

Rustling. To his right, in the rocks.

Kaine stiffened.

Twenty-five metres away, a man with a round, ordinary face, thinning grey hair, average height, average build, stepped out from behind a rock. He carried a Remington CSR at port arms, the muzzle pointing to the sky, away from the Great Scar.

"Nope," he said, stretching his thin lips into a smile. "I shot her."

Kaine, hands already held up and out, spun to face the newcomer.

CHAPTER 42

Kaine relaxed. Relief flushed through him.

"Hi there, Will," he said, almost light-headed with delight. "Long time, no see."

He'd have leapt forwards to clap Stacy's back, but that wouldn't have done much good to his molten hands.

"Afternoon, Captain," Stacy said, smiling—a rare thing for the man. "I'd shake your hand, but ... ouch. They look painful. Such a daft bugger. A typical Ryan Kaine move. Trying to fly?"

Kaine shrugged. "Couldn't think of anything better to do."

Stacy rushed to close the gap between them. He released his right hand from the rifle's grip and threw it around Kaine's back, pulling him into a hug.

"God, man. It's great to see you."

"What on earth are you doing here? I take it you're the DS Sykes who put the pressure on Mitch Bairstow?"

"Got it in one. And I'm here to save your arse again. Seems I'm making a habit of pulling your chestnuts out of the fire," he said, breaking his hold and stepping back.

Kaine twisted his head to the side and narrowed his eyes into slits. "A habit?"

"The firefight in Fallujah, and the bar fight in Germany."

"Uh-uh," Kaine countered. "From memory, I was the one who saved *you* in Fallujah. Twice. As for Germany, that was Danny, and he only took care of my new jacket."

Mentioning Danny threw a dampener over the unexpected reunion. Kaine dropped his smile and allowed his shoulders to relax.

"Didn't I tell you? I convinced the barman not to call the *Bundespolizei*. Saved you a night in lock-up and a shedload of paperwork. Not to mention a probable demotion for bringing the service into disrepute."

"You did?"

"Yep. And talking of Danny, how is the youngster?"

Kaine lowered his eyes and shook his head.

Stacy straightened his face. "Danny's gone?"

"Yeah."

"Christ on a bike. How? When?"

"He stepped in front of a bullet to save my life, a couple of ... weeks back."

God, was it only weeks?

No wonder being reminded of Danny's loss still had the power to rip his guts open and spew his innards over the ground.

"Hell. Sorry to hear it. What happened?"

"Long story, but can it wait for later? I have a young boy to find —again."

Stacy glanced up towards the top of Great Scar. "That won't take you long, mate. He's up there hiding in the bushes, crying his little eyes out."

"He is?"

"Yep. Didn't go far after bolting from Mo. Just as well he skipped out, too. With him standing so close, I didn't have a shot."

"Getting him to run was part of the plan."

Stacy fixed a dead stare on Kaine. "You knew I was here?"

"No, not at all, but I had to get the lad clear before taking the high dive. Couldn't risk her using him to flush me out." Kaine blew on his hands once more. It still didn't help. "Hope he stays where he is. I'll have to go the long way around. Won't be doing any rope work for a while."

Stacy screwed up his face and looked up. "Why don't you let me go fetch him? After what he learnt from Mo, he's likely to take one look at you and scarper."

Kaine winced.

"Good point. Can you convince him to come with you? The kid's a sharp cookie. He's also defensive."

Stacy patted the back pocket of his overly baggy trousers. "I'm carrying a police warrant card for this ... op. Should be enough to convince the lad I'm one of the good guys."

Kaine grinned. Will Stacy, one of the good guys? Never a truer word said. The man would risk his life for any just and honourable cause.

"Thanks, Will. When you reach him, it would be best if you head to the farm by the long route. Ask Rhod to show you the way. He'll probably beg you to let him abseil down, but we can't let him see that." He shot a sideways glance at the body. "I'll stay here. Wouldn't want any ramblers to stumble over this sight. Might ruin their day. I'll tell Rollo he can call off the search, too."

Gingerly, Kaine dug a hand into his pocket and tugged out his earpiece.

"Rollo's here?"

Kaine nodded, fitting the earpiece, and settling it home with the only undamaged finger on his right hand—the pinkie.

Stacy grinned in recognition. "When Bairstow described the man driving the Audi and called him 'Goliath', I figured it might be Rollo. Not doing a good job keeping you out of trouble, is he."

Kaine thinned his lips. "Poor man does his best in difficult circumstances."

"Maybe he can help you move her?" Stacy tipped his head towards the crumpled body. "My Range Rover's parked in the lane above the farm. You can't miss it." He dipped a hand into his pocket, retrieved a set of car keys, and offered them across.

Kaine winced and showed Stacy his hands. He leant closer and pushed out his hip, Stacy dropped the keys into his jacket pocket.

"By the way," Stacy said, "there's a body bag in the luggage space."

"Of course there is. You always come prepared."

"I try to. The bag was supposed to be for you. At least that was what Reilly thought."

Kaine frowned. "Reilly? That's her name? Not Folly?"

"Yep." Stacy nodded. "Mrs Maureen Reilly."

"Mrs?"

"A widow. No children."

Kaine stared across at the broken form. He simply had to ask. "Answer me this. Did you try to wing her?"

Stacy pursed his lips.

"Nope. I aimed centre mass, and I knew she wasn't wearing a vest. Check out the bullet hole if you like. Although I'm not as skilled as you with a sniper rifle, I usually hit what I'm aiming at. Assuming the shot's not too difficult and the target's not too far away."

"But she was your partner."

"Only for the past few days."

"I'm really sorry you had to kill her."

"I'm not. The woman was a murdering bitch. A basket case. Guard this for me, will you?" Stacy lowered the Remington to the ground, resting it on its biped stand to keep the muzzle free of dirt. "Full debrief after I've delivered the kid and you've cleared up this mess?"

"Sounds like a good idea."

Stacy took hold of the rope and started climbing. He scooted up the cliff face, rising as quickly as Kaine would have done without the injured hands. When he'd negotiated the overhang, he stopped and looked down.

"Ryan," he called softly, "I know you weren't responsible. For what happened to Flight BE1555, I mean."

"Later, Will. We'll discuss it at the debrief."

"Want me to lie to the kid for you? Tell him you really are this Sidings fellow?"

Kaine ached to say, "No. Tell him the truth. I'm sick of all the lies," but if he did that, he wouldn't have been able to look the lad in the eye again.

"Yes, please," he called up. "Staff Sergeant Peter Sidings. Former 2 PARA. You and I can still have met and fought together in Afghanistan. Oh, and right now, Rollo's going by the name Adrian."

"Understood. By the way, her gun fell over there somewhere," Stacy released his left hand from the rope long enough to point towards a patch of scrub behind and to Kaine's right. "You might want to find it before someone stumbles across the bloody thing."

"Thanks. Will do."

Stacy threw Kaine a brief salute and started climbing again. The man made such rapid progress he might as well have been bounding up a flight of stairs.

Kaine headed towards the bushes and the fallen SIG, and double tapped the earpiece. Again, he used his pinkie.

"Alpha One to Alpha Two, are you receiving me? Over."

CHAPTER 43

Stacy flew up the rock face. He hadn't felt so free, or so light, in ages. Six months, in fact. It had been six long months in the planning, but the wait had been worth it. The old cliché, the one about revenge being a dish best served cold, rang true. So bloody true. He didn't consider killing Reilly as murder, more as the fulfilment of a promise to a friend. A justified one at that. Given time, the bloody woman would have killed Ryan as surely as she'd murdered Johnny, six months earlier.

Yep. Justified.

Still, he had some clearing up to do, starting with finding the lad, then covering his tracks.

Stacy clambered over the top of the ridge and stepped well away from its crumbling edge. He pulled up the rope, coiling it with a half-twist on each loop so it wouldn't tangle, and dropped it on the path close to its belay point. Stacy considered releasing the belay and taking the rope with him, but that wasn't his job. Ryan's rope. Ryan's three-point anchoring belay. Ryan's responsibility.

He dusted down his baggy trousers, tugged the creases out of his equally baggy sweater, and marched in the direction he'd last seen the boy. What had Ryan called him? Rod? No, Rhod.

"Rhod? Where are you, lad?"

Stacy stopped at the line, where the trees and bushes crowded in on the narrow animal trail. He pulled out the fake warrant card and held it up in front of him.

"Rhod," he called again, "my name is Will Sykes. Detective Sergeant William Sykes. Please come out. It's perfectly safe now. The woman's gone. She won't hurt you again."

Ten metres away, a blond head popped out of the undergrowth so fast, it could have been on a spring. His cheeks were wet and his eyes puffy behind the wire-rimmed glasses.

"Can I see your ID?" the lad said, sniffling.

Stacy grinned. Ryan was right. The kid had smarts.

Stacy angled the ID card towards him. The boy removed his spectacles, dried his eyes with a tissue pulled from his trouser pocket, and replaced them again. He squinted at the warrant card

"Can't read it from here," he called.

"Well, you'd better come closer. I'm not throwing it to you. We'd never find the blooming thing again, not with all these bushes. Come on, lad. You're not in any trouble. I'm here to take you back to the farm. Staff Sergeant Sidings would have come himself, but he's hurt his hands and can't make the climb."

The lad jutted out his lower lip. "Ryan Kaine, you mean?"

"No, Rhod. The woman who grabbed you was wrong. A case of mistaken identity. She got it all wrong. I've known Staff Sergeant Sidings, Peter, for years."

That's partly true, at least.

"He's a good man, Rhod. I can promise you, he's no terrorist."

Also true.

Despite the way Ryan swerved the response to his statement

about the plane crash, Stacy had no doubt about his innocence. None. He'd seen the evidence.

Rhod stood. The bushes only reached his waist. He'd been crouching.

"Stand back, and I'll come to the path," he called, his voice stronger.

Still smiling, Stacy backed off and waited while the boy weaved his way around the bushes and broke through to the path ten metres to Stacy's left and further away from the cliff face. He'd given himself a possible escape route.

Good lad.

"Hold it up again, please," the boy demanded, leaning slightly forwards, his eyes narrowed.

Stacy did as the kid asked.

"Wh-What happened to the woman? I heard her scream."

Yep. Thought you might have.

He would have had to be deaf not to hear it.

"I'm afraid she slipped and fell. Hurt herself rather badly. Staff Sergeant Sidings ... Peter, is arranging to have her taken to hospital. No need to fret, though. She won't be back. If she survives her injuries, I'll be arresting her."

"Really? What charges?" Excitement gave his voice a higher pitch.

Bloody hell.

Such a sharp kid. What charges indeed?

"Murder, attempted murder, impersonating a police officer. And there will be others. I've been hunting her for the past six months."

Again, true.

"She's a murderer?" The lad gulped and rubbed the reddened area at the side of his neck where Reilly's arm would have chafed.

"You could say that. All she cared about was the reward on Ryan Kaine's head. I followed her here, but she gave me the slip. I'd never have let her near you otherwise. I'm sorry."

"That's okay. What made her think Mr Sidings was Ryan Kaine?"

"No idea. Hopefully, I'll find out when I interview her."

No chance of that ever happening. Not this side of hell.

"So," Stacy continued, "Peter said you'd be able to show me a safe way to the farm."

The boy's face fell. He frowned and his lower lip jutted out again.

"What's wrong?"

"I thought we'd be abseiling down the Scar."

Stacy stuck the warrant card back into his pocket and cut a hand through the air between them.

"Sorry again, Rhod. I can't let that happen, I'm afraid. Health and safety regulations won't allow it. Besides, I'm not all that good with heights."

Oh dear. Shame on you.

He'd just told the kid another lie. Still, he'd done it with the best of intentions. He couldn't let the lad see the earthly remains of Maureen Reilly. They'd give the poor kid nightmares.

Clearly disappointed with the answer, Rhod's frown developed into a full-blown scowl. He spun through a full one-eighty degrees and started marching away. The lad picked a trail that wound through the bushes, heading for a gap in the trees.

"You'd better follow me," he called over his shoulder. "Careful though, it gets steep in a minute. And watch out for the roots. They stick out quite a bit. And there's some loose gravel coming up."

"Thanks, Rhod. I'll be careful."

He followed close to the kid, who hurried along at a decent lick, failing to heed his own advice.

After less than two hundred metres, they broke through the far side of the trees into bright sunlight. As promised, the footing deteriorated, and the lad slowed. He turned and sidestepped his way carefully down a scree-laden slope, steep enough to cause the casual hiker some concerns.

After negotiating a particularly difficult switchback, a hard-panting Rhod stopped so quickly that Stacy almost careened into him.

"What's wrong?"

"A SIG P320, right?" he asked, looking up at Stacy, squinting again.

"What?"

"The woman. She was carrying a SIG P320."

Stacy frowned. "What do you know about handguns?"

Rhod shrugged.

"I play *Call of Duty*," he said, "and I've done a whole heap of internet research. Am I right?"

"No," Stacy said.

Where was the kid heading with this?

"Are you sure? Looked like a SIG P320 to me."

"You're very close." Stacy smiled. "She actually used a P226."

Which Ryan should have found by now.

Rhod's narrow shoulders slumped.

"Heck, I could have sworn it was a P320. It sure sounded like one. The echo from the rocks must have confused me." He paused for a moment before pointing at Stacy's belt. "What are you packing?"

Stacy laughed. "Packing? You mean what weapon have I been issued with?"

The lad dipped his head but didn't take his eyes from the holster clipped to Stacy's belt or the handle of the weapon it held.

"It's a Glock 17."

"Glock 17, huh? Can I see it?"

"Not a chance."

Another frown crumpled the lad's forehead. "Okay, I get it. So, what did you shoot her with?"

"Sorry?"

"I heard two shots, then the scream. The first came from a semi-automatic handgun, the second came from further away, down in the valley. Sounded more like a rifle to me."

Stacy puffed out his cheeks. The kid knew far more than he needed to. What should he do? Tell the truth or bluff it out? Hell of a choice to make.

The truth.

Usually the better alternative. It kept things neat and tidy.

"I used a Remington CSR."

"Wow!"

In his excitement, Rhod jerked upright. He wheeled his arms to restore his balance. Stacy shot out a hand, grabbed him by the front of his jacket, and pulled him closer.

"A sniper rifle," Rhod shouted, oblivious to the dangers of the slope. "One that breaks apart. Collapsible. Where did you leave it? Can I see it? Please."

"Rhod!" Stacy barked. "Calm down."

"Sorry," he said, arms still splayed wide. "But I've always wanted to see a sniper rifle. They are so cool."

"They are not cool, Rhod. Nor are they toys. They're weapons designed to kill from a great distance. And to answer your first question, I left it at the foot of the cliff. Peter's guarding it."

"You shot her? Killed her?"

For pity's sake.

"I had to, Rhod. She was shooting at Peter. If she'd killed him, she'd have turned on you next."

"Really?"

"You were a witness. She'd have had to silence you, and I couldn't let that happen."

Rhod stared deep into Stacy's eyes. His expression thoughtful.

"So," he said, after what seemed like an age, "you saved our lives. Me and Mr Sidings. Yes?"

Stacy narrowed his eyes, scrutinising the kid in detail. No doubt about it. Ryan called it right. The kid had smarts.

"I did."

"Wow, that's so cool. Thanks."

"You're welcome," Stacy said, dismissing the gravity of the kid's self-revelation.

"No, I mean it. Thank you." Rhod shot out a hand.

Stacy took the offered paw, and they shook.

After they'd broken the grip, a thoughtful expression crossed Rhod's young face.

"What happens next?"

"In what respect?"

"Will you need me as a witness? Will I get to go to court?"

"Do you want to?"

"Yes. It would be cool. Wouldn't that be something to talk about at school."

"Let's see how it goes, shall we? The woman might not recover. There might not be a court case. And there are others involved."

"A conspiracy, you mean."

"Exactly. You need to keep quiet about this whole thing. We don't want to alert anyone else who might be involved."

"Um ..."

"Don't tell anyone. Not even your closest friends."

The way Rhod scrunched up his face made him look even younger. "I don't have any friends. 'Cept for Myfanwy. She's my cousin, by the way. In any case, she wouldn't believe me."

Stacy held up his hand.

"A secret? You promise."

"Between you, me, and Mr Sidings?"

"Yes. It'll make things a lot easier for everyone. The shooting, it was justified. You know that, right?"

"Yes. Yes, it was."

"So, if you can keep it to yourself, I'll handle the legal issues and make sure you and your family are kept well out of it. Deal?"

The lad hesitated for the briefest moment before answering.

"Yes. Deal."

Again, they shook hands.

Stacy doubted the lad would be able to hold his tongue for long, but he'd done what he could. Maybe Rhod *would* keep his word. Either way, Ryan and Rollo would be well away from the area by the time the kid's resolve broke down.

"So," Stacy said, "how far to the farm?"

"Not far," Rhod answered, pointing along the track. "Around the next bend there's a trail through the woods, and then we cross the big field."

"Carry on, then. Your family's going to wonder where you've been."

A darkness clouded the boy's face.

"What's wrong?"

"Nothing."

"Another secret?"

Rhod lifted his head in a short up-nod and Stacy let the matter drop. The boy had been through more than enough for one day.

THEY BROKE THROUGH THE TREELINE INTO BRIGHT SUNLIGHT. STACY stopped to absorb the view. Rhod carried on for a few steps before he, too, stopped. The lad hadn't exaggerated. A huge field stretched out below them, hemmed on three sides by neatly trimmed hedgerows. Knee-high grass swayed under the gentle force of a gusting breeze. Beyond the field lay the farm, white walls, tiled roofs. As typical as any he'd seen in that part of Wales.

"Wow. Stunning," Stacy said, and meaning it.

"Yeah," Rhod said. "S'pose it is. Quiet, though."

"It must be."

Stacy waited for the boy to carry on walking, but he didn't seem inclined to move.

"What's up?"

"I've done something wrong."

Uh-oh. Here we go.

"Is that why you ran off in the first place?"

The boy nodded.

"Can you tell me about it?"

"No," he said. "You wouldn't understand."

"Is it a police matter?"

"No. I ... don't think so."

"Good," Stacy said, his expression serious. "You can't just run away. You've seen what can happen. It's a dangerous world. Can't you tell your parents?" Stacy nodded towards the farm.

"They're not my parents," Rhod snapped. "They're my aunt and uncle. My mother ... died. And my dad ... my dad's ... He went away."

Rhod swallowed hard, his lower lip trembled, and he blinked rapidly, fighting to hold back the tears.

Realisation hit Stacy with the force of a punch to the gut. He finally knew what Ryan was doing in Wales. He'd come to help the boy.

"Rhod, I shouldn't have asked. Forgive me."

"It's ... okay. I just don't like talking about it."

"I understand. I really do. Whatever you've done, perhaps you could explain it to your uncle?"

"No, he'd kill me."

"I doubt that. I doubt that very much. But what about Peter? Could you explain it to him? He's a good listener, and he'd probably understand. Might even act as mediator between you and your uncle. What do you say?"

Rhod clamped his jaws together. He shook his head with such violence, his blond curls flopped around his face.

Stacy scratched an annoying itch on the tip of his nose. Tree pollen?

"Well, Rhod. Think of it like this. The three of us have a secret. You, me, and Peter, right?"

"Right."

"So, what's another secret between friends? You never know, Peter really might be able to help. Will you at least consider telling him?"

"Um ... okay," Rhod said, looking a little happier. "I'll think about it."

"Good lad. Now, what's the fastest way to the farm?"

"Straight down the hill and through that gate." Rhod pointed to the first of two gates in a distant hedgerow.

"Fancy making a race of it?"

The boy frowned. "How fair would that be? You're a grown up."

"I'll give you a ten-second head start."

"Make it twenty," he countered, tilting his head to look up.

"Okay, twenty seconds it is."

"Is there a prize?"

"Bragging rights only. Take care, though. Concentrate while

you're running. I don't want to beat you because you looked back and fell over."

Rhod's considered frown turned into a grin. "No chance. I won't look back."

"Okay then. Ready?"

"Ready."

"On your marks ..."

Rhod dropped into the sprinter's starting position. The tall grass grazed his chest.

"...get set ..."

He leant forwards, lifted his left knee off the ground, and took his weight on his skinny arms.

"...go!"

The boy took off fast and hard, bounding over the tall grass. Stacy shouted out the numbers, counting down from twenty. By the time he'd reached eight, the kid had covered thirty-five metres at a very decent pace considering the terrain.

Still counting aloud, Stacy turned and headed back to the treeline.

By now, Ryan and Rollo should have had enough time to reach the Range Rover and stuff Mo's corpse into the body bag. He'd done his part and kept the lad clear. Now it was time tidy up the mess. Time to warn Ryan.

CHAPTER 44

Wednesday 24th May – Afternoon

Cadwallader Farm, Glyn Coes, Powys, South Wales, UK

Kaine and Rollo reached the stable yard via the rear track. Rollo slowed the quad bike enough for Kaine to jump off before pointing it towards the sheds behind the stables. The three of them, Kaine, Rollo, and Will Stacy, had worked out a cover story on the fly. After arranging an RV point for the following day, Stacy left with the body in the bag, and Kaine and Rollo returned to the farm on the quad bike.

Rhod. Everything hinged on a twelve-year-old lad being able to hold his tongue and keep their secret.

Kaine headed towards the back door of the farmhouse, gathering his thoughts.

He rounded a corner. Movement caught his eye. Behind one of the sheds, a scrawny arm beckoned him, an arm attached to a tousle-haired twelve-year-old boy. Without making it obvious, Kaine altered direction and strolled towards the shed. He kicked a stone along the way.

While he approached, the boy backed away, disappearing behind the shed. Kaine followed, stopping when he judged them both hidden from the farmhouse.

The lad looked up at him. Tears spilled from his deep blue eyes. He rushed forwards and wrapped his arms around Kaine's waist.

Kaine didn't have a clue what to do. Should he push the lad away? Would a hug be inappropriate? What would the aunt and uncle think if they stumbled upon a relative stranger embracing their nephew around the back of a shed?

God alive.

He chose the neutral option and stood where he was, holding his arms well away from the lad, allowing him to cry it out. Time stretched out, and the lad kept squeezing with no sign of the tears easing. Kaine hugged the lad briefly, using his forearms only. The pain flaring from the friction burns wouldn't allow him a proper hug.

Eventually, the tortured tears subsided. Rhod unpeeled his arms and stepped away. A crumpled tissue appeared from nowhere. He sniffled and dried his eyes.

Kaine stood still and silent. Waiting. Still clueless.

"Why?" Rhod asked, looking up at him through huge, puffy blue eyes.

"Why what?"

"Why did you pretend to be Ryan Kaine?"

Wow. Good question.

Of all the questions he'd fielded in his head, Kaine hadn't considered that one. He answered, working without notes—off the cuff. Not a solution he preferred.

"The woman, Rhod ... She came out of nowhere. She had wild eyes and the way she waved that gun around—"

"It was a SIG Sauer P226," Rhod interrupted, speaking fast, excited, the words catching in his throat—the aftermath of the crying.

"Was it? I'm no expert on handguns."

Easy, Kaine.

He needed to keep as close to the agreed story as possible.

"Anyway," Kaine continued, "she looked unstable. Ranting. Rambling, you know? I tried talking her down, you heard me, didn't you?" The boy nodded. "But she wasn't listening. I confessed to being Ryan Kaine because I couldn't think of another way to keep you safe. I wanted you to run away. You understand that, right?"

Rhod said nothing. He just stood still, frowning, apparently deep in thought.

"Sorry, Rhod. I really am."

"It's okay," Rhod said, sucking in another shuddering breath. "I understand. You know, when you fell and she fired, I-I thought—"

"You saw that?"

"Yes. Of course. I thought you were going to die. I was so scared."

Kaine sighed. Minimal lies.

"I didn't fall, Rhod. I jumped."

"Really? But ..."

"It's a safety drill called a 'controlled release'. In the service, we practise it regularly. Although we usually do it while wearing a full safety harness and"—he showed the lad his damaged hands—"thick gloves."

Rhod winced and sucked in air between his teeth.

"Ow, they look painful."

Kaine grimaced. "They sting like the blazes. I'm just about to ask Annie to treat them for me. She happens to be a fully trained field medic. Are you coming?" He jerked a damaged thumb over his shoulder, pointing in the direction of the farmhouse.

"I-I can't. I'm too scared."

"Scared of what?"

"Uncle Gwynfor's going to kill me. All those dead sheep. My fault. I ... I messed up. It's all my fault."

"What did you do, Rhod?" Kaine asked, speaking gently, trying to coax it out of the lad.

"One of my chores is to fetch the post in the morning. You know that, yes? Well anyway, a few weeks ago, I saw a letter from my father addressed to Uncle Gwynfor. He ... put his details on the back of the envelope."

"And you stole it?"

The boy nodded. More tears fell. He swiped them away with the tissue.

"What did it say?"

"I-I dunno. Didn't read it. Didn't want anything to do with my dad. I-I was worried he wanted to take me back on account of the money from The Trust ... from the plane crash."

Kaine stiffened. The lad had worked it out for himself. Such a smart kid.

"Is that why you ran away, Rhod? Because of the letter?"

"Letters," Rhod corrected. "There were three altogether."

"And you didn't read any of them?"

"No."

"Where are they now?"

"Gone. I burned them. Threw them in the fire in the kitchen ... when no one was looking."

Once again, tears gathered in the blue eyes. The lad was hurting, and it wasn't fair. Things had gone far enough. Time for some home truths.

"Listen, Rhod. Stealing you uncle's post was wrong. You know it and I know it, and you'll need to own up. Confess. Deep down, you know that don't you?"

The lad sniffled and the breath caught in his throat. He dipped his chin in a nod.

"But before you do that, I need to tell you something. It's not pretty, but you need to know the truth. I think you're old enough and strong enough. Will you listen to the whole thing?"

Rhod's chin still trembled, but the tears had dried. "Y-Yes. I'll listen."

Okay, here goes.

"Last night, that gang we spotted stole about thirty lambs from Ten Acre Field."

"And you let them?"

"Yes, but only because Adrian and I wanted to find out who was organising the raids. So we followed them."

Kaine told the boy everything, including how he found his father at The Red Lion, and what he'd learnt during his phone call to Baker.

"Don't you see, Rhod?" Kaine said, after explaining how he'd banished Ducky Duckworth from Wales under the threat of gruesome reprisals, "the attacks were nothing to do with you intercepting your uncle's mail. Your father would have tried anything to get his hands on The Trust's money. He's not a good man. He really isn't."

"I know," Rhod said, sighing. "He won't come back, will he? You're sure?"

"I'm certain. If he sets foot in Wales again, Mr Baker will ... well, he won't be back. Are you okay with not seeing him again?"

"Yes, he's a horrible man. I'm glad you sent him away. I really am."

Rhod leapt forwards. This time, Kaine braced in readiness for the lad's tight hug. This time, he hugged back, the hell with the way it might look, and the hell with scorched hands. They'd heal. As would the boy.

It took a while, but Rhod eventually broke the embrace.

"C'mon," he said, "Annie ... I mean, Mrs Hallam needs to bandage your hands."

"Hang on a minute, Rhod. We need to talk about what happened up on Great Scar."

"Don't worry. Detective Sykes explained everything. I can keep a secret. I promise."

"No, it's not as straightforward as that. The woman who attacked us has powerful friends. She's protected. Detective Sergeant Sykes is worried about reprisals. They might want to punish anyone involved, and that includes your aunt and uncle and your cousins. No one can know what happened up there." He pointed towards the break in the woods and Great Scar. "You understand, right?"

"Like a vendetta, you mean?"

"Yes, Rhod. That's exactly what I mean."

"Does that mean we have to tell lies?"

"No, we act as though nothing at all happened up there. I like to call it being economical with the truth."

"Okay," Rhod said, nodding. "That sounds a lot better than lying. But ..."

"But?"

"If nothing happened up there, how did you hurt your hands?"

"Good question. What do you think we should tell people?"

Rhodri fell silent for a few seconds, staring at Kaine's hands.

"I know," he said, eyes wide and bright. "We could always say you were climbing the Scar to look for me and you slipped. Burned your hands on the rope. Which is true. Well, nearly true."

"Excellent idea. You're good at this."

"What? Being economical with the truth, you mean?"

Kaine grinned down at the boy. "Exactly."

Rhod reached out and grabbed Kaine's sleeve, taking care to avoid his injured hands. "Let's go."

Kaine allowed the boy to drag him towards the farmhouse. Some salve for his rope burns wouldn't go amiss.

CHAPTER 45

Thursday 25th May – Will Stacy

Top Brownies Café, Catherine Street, Swindon, UK

The slim young woman in the smart grey waitress uniform smiled down at Ryan. She ignored Will Stacy. No matter. He was used to it.

Same old, same old.

So what if he did have one of those instantly forgettable faces? It worked well in his game.

"Will that be all, sir?" she asked, speaking up above the background hubbub of the café.

"Yes, thanks," Ryan answered, looking up from his carefully chosen seat, back to the wall, facing the room and its heaving throng of customers. "It looks lovely."

Stacy had taken a seat at right angles to him for the same reason.

Ryan spoke quietly. His accent, a flat Midlands twang, sounded accurate enough, and totally different from his natural south-west of England drawl.

"Enjoy," she said, turning her back on Will and maintaining eye contact with Ryan until he glanced down at his nut 'n' chocolate brownie and black coffee.

"I see you still have it, Ryan," Stacy whispered, trying not to sound upset.

"Have what?"

He sighed and shook his head. "Never mind."

Stacy took the sachet of brown sugar from his saucer. He ripped off the top, sprinkled the granules into his Americano, and stirred. He lifted the cup, blew gently across the top, and sipped. Rich and strong. Very decent.

In all that time, Ryan never stopped scanning the room. On guard. On the lookout. Watching for anything out of place. Anything untoward. Being hunted did that to a man. A fugitive could never truly relax, never fully drop his guard. Will had started to feel the same way. He'd grow accustomed to it after a while.

What a shitty way to live.

"So," Stacy opened, "what happened at the farm after I left?"

Ryan pushed his untouched brownie away and raised his cup, hiding his mouth behind the rim.

"Nothing much. Rhod fessed up to stealing some letters from his father. His punishment? Extra chores in the stables, looking after a new foal."

"I bet he was upset."

"Nope, the lad was delighted." He looked at Stacy, the brown eyes twinkling with amusement. "Don't ask."

"Okay, I won't. Did he keep our secret?"

Ryan nodded. "So far, so good. The vendetta ruse hit the mark. As far as the family is concerned, nothing happened up on Great Scar apart from me slipping off the rock and burning my hands."

"As if you would ever fall off a cliff." Stacy smiled. "And Bairstow. What happened with him?"

"He's none the wiser. As far as he's concerned, he warned me about a 'clear and present danger', and I thanked him for not giving me up to two creeps pretending to be cops from The Smoke."

"Creeps?" Stacy winced. "Ouch. Where is he now?"

"Still on the farm."

"Really?" Stacy took another sip of the rather nice coffee and joined in with Ryan's scan of the café.

Already, it's started. Get used to it, son.

"Yep," Ryan said. "After all the fuss had died down, we introduced him as a former colleague who'd fallen on hard times. In the spirit of Christian compassion, Becky, that's Rhod's aunt, took him under her wing. She showed him to a guest room in one of the empty cottages and invited him to join us for dinner—after he'd had a shower and a change of clothes, of course. For his part, Mitch insisted on paying for his keep by lending a hand in the stables."

Ryan's eyes lost focus for the briefest moment, reliving a memory.

"Turns out that our one-legged veteran is a bit of a four-legged beast whisperer. He has a real gift with the nags and spending a few hours in the stables seemed to do him some good. When I left, he was happy. More relaxed. Calmer. By the way, I have something for you."

Ryan dipped a lightly taped hand into his jacket pocket and pulled out a buff-coloured envelope. A small lump distorted its bottom corner. He handed it across, keeping it under the table, out of sight.

Stacy took the envelope and slid it into his pocket, unopened. He never opened envelopes in public. Especially when he didn't know what they contained. Not even envelopes from trusted friends. Ingrained habits were difficult to break.

"What is it?"

"The bug you planted on Mitch. I, er, reclaimed it when Mitch was in the shower. Figured you'd want it back."

"Thanks. Those puppies are expensive and hard to come by."

"Thought they might be."

Stacy took another pull on his cooling Americano, taking the opportunity to scan the crowd again. Nothing amiss. No one taking an undue interest in two old friends sharing a coffee break.

"By the way, where's Rollo? I expected you to bring him along today."

"He's on his way back to France. I sent him home for some well-earned R&R ... with his new wife."

Little in life surprised Stacy, but this nugget of news nearly made him spit out his coffee.

"Bloody hell. Rollo's married? Never saw that coming."

"Neither did he."

Ryan laughed and did it quietly. Ryan Kaine did everything quietly. Well, most things.

"I'd like to meet the woman who tamed Big Rollo Rollason."

"One day, I might introduce you. Marie-Odile's a lovely woman. A fine cook, too."

"Don't tell me Rollo's driving all the way to France in that old heap of an Astra?"

Ryan snorted.

"Not likely. We gifted that rust bucket to Myfanwy. She'll be picking up her provisional driving licence in a couple of months. Connor, one of my ... contacts, arrived with a shiny new Škoda Yeti. He arrived too late for the party, but I paid him well enough for his time."

"You're not short of a bob or two, are you."

Ryan shrugged. "I get by."

They fell quiet for a moment. Stacy broke the silence between them with a question he'd been keen to ask from the moment Ryan walked through the door.

"Talking about lovely women," he said, "who was that looker I saw you talking to when you arrived at the farm with Bairstow. You seemed pretty close. She wasn't Aunt Becky, by any chance?"

A darkness crossed behind Ryan's eyes. He shook his head.

Uh-oh. A sore point?

"No," he said, "she's ... Lara. A friend of mine."

"A good friend?"

"Yes."

Ryan turned his attention towards a middle-aged couple who'd just pushed through the café's open entrance. Neither aroused any of his inner defences, and he returned his attention to his half-empty cup.

"How good?" Stacy asked, pushing his old mate for an answer.

"Very good."

"Where is she now?"

Ryan lifted his gaze from his cup, his eyes distant, almost misty.

Christ on a bike.

Ryan cared for this Lara woman. He really cared. With all he'd been through since shooting BE1555 out of the skies, he'd fallen for someone? How special must she be?

Dear me. Poor guy.

"She ... decided to stay on at the farm for a while," he said. "Turns out that she has every bit as much of an affinity for horses as Mitch Bairstow."

"Sorry to hear it."

Ryan scrunched up a shoulder.

"Don't be," he mumbled behind the cup. "It's for the best. And it doesn't have to be forever. Once I rip this monkey from my back ..."

He allowed the sentiment to trail off, gulped down the rest of his drink, and set the empty cup down on its saucer.

"Okay, enough of the gossip," Ryan said, drawing a definite line under the topic. "What's the story with Maureen Reilly? How are you going to explain her demise?"

Stacy allowed himself a half smile. He didn't smile often, and it felt strange to exercise seldom-used muscles.

"I'm not going to explain anything. Reilly and I will simply disappear into the ether."

"You'll do what?"

"Yeah. I've been planning to hang up my spurs for a while. Built up a fairly decent retirement package over the years. I have a nice villa in ... let's say Portugal. There is one thing though." Stacy paused before offering Ryan a sad smile. "I'm afraid you'll be blamed for our disappearance, old friend."

"No worries. My rep's in the toilet anyway, and it won't be the first time I'm blamed for ... Well, you know." Ryan fixed Stacy with one of his dark stares. "You don't have any qualms about Reilly's death?"

"None. She deserved it."

"Care to explain?"

"Don't see why not." Stacy allowed himself a tight shrug. "Maureen Reilly killed her husband for playing away from home and discovered a liking for it."

"She told you that?"

"No, Johnny O'Dowd told me. In a roundabout way."

"Johnny O'Dowd?"

"Yes. Johnny was one of my oldest friends. We met at school and joined the army together. Reilly killed him. Cracked him over the head with a brick. Twice. Claimed she acted in self-defence when Johnny tried to rape her. Bloody woman got away with it, too."

"How?"

Stacy grunted.

"Look at it from the CPS's point of view. He's a squaddie on leave, and he has a gutful of booze in his system. She's an Authorised Firearms Officer with a solid record. Bloody case didn't even reach court. Johnny had no family. His only friends were squaddies. Talk about a lack of credibility. It was a stich-up, Ryan. The bloody woman got away with cold-blooded murder."

Ryan stared at him, impassive, silent.

"Yeah, yeah. I know what you're thinking. Johnny's my friend, and I'm blinded by loyalty. But you'd be wrong. He was one of the most honest and honourable men I've ever known. Yourself included. No matter how heavily he'd been drinking, Johnny O'Dowd would no more attack a woman than deliberately poke himself in the eye with a pointed stick. No bloody way."

"Did you report your concerns to anyone? The police?"

Stacy shook his head. "Couldn't. I was ... indisposed. You know, after Fallujah, I transferred into Military Intelligence, right?"

Still scanning the café, Ryan dipped his head in a sharp nod.

"I had heard something along those lines."

"Anyway," Stacy continued, "I was in the field. Out of contact. First time I heard about the case was when I returned to England. By which time, Johnny was already in the ground."

Stacy tightened his grip on the coffee cup. His knuckles clicked. "What did you do?"

"What I always do. I looked into her background on the quiet."

"And you found?"

"Quite a trail. Her husband, Reed Reilly, disappeared a little over three years ago. Completely vanished. Again, he had no family, few friends. There was no one to ask questions or cause a fuss. The real kicker hit me when I caught sight of Reed's photo. The bloke could have passed for Johnny's older brother. Same sandy hair. Same colour eyes. Same smile."

Stacy ground his teeth and looked away from Ryan's cool and calculating gaze.

"Then I gained access to her police personnel file," he said, forcing his jaws to relax.

"How'd you manage that?"

"I was in MI6, for pity's sake. It was simply a matter of hitting a few keys on a desktop computer."

"What did you discover?"

"On duty, she killed three people in the space of two years. The first shooting happened during an armed siege, the second during a drugs raid, and the third when she was out on a routine patrol. Do you know the odds of an AFO killing three civilians in their whole career, let alone over two years?"

"Nope."

"Neither do I," Stacy said, "but they're bloody long. It's never happened before."

"Don't tell me," Ryan said, keeping his voice barely audible. "All three were men who looked like her husband and your friend?"

Stacy touched his nose with the tip of his index finger. "Got it in one, old buddy."

"And the killings were deemed justified?"

"The first two were, but the third ... Well, the third turned out to be one death too many even for the Met."

"What happened?"

"As usual, the brass swept their dirty rubbish under the nearest rug. Maureen Reilly, and I quote, 'Left the force voluntarily and with her terms and conditions intact'. After that, she moved into the private sector."

"The private sector," Ryan said, nodding slowly.

"Yep," Stacy said. "She was employed by an up-and-coming firm owned and run by one Guy Gordon, *GG Cleaning Systems Ltd*. Which is when I resigned from the service and also moved into the private sector. It didn't take long for GG to come calling. I only had to put out a few feelers. Like I said, it's a growing company, making a serious name for itself."

"Your intention being?"

"To take the bitch down the moment I had the opportunity. I hoped to do it legally, but she rather forced my hand up there on that cliff."

"Great Scar," Ryan said, helpfully.

"Is that what the rock's called?" Stacy mused. "Yeah, I can see why. Nice one. Anyway, I managed to convince Gordon to partner me with Reilly. I'm afraid it took beating up a rather large Geordie to do it, but needs must, eh?"

"So, you and Reilly were sent on a little field trip?"

"Yes, we were. But let's be clear about this, mate. I wouldn't have let Reilly within a hundred miles of you if I didn't need her to help me get close to Mitch Bairstow. Her police background made it easier. And I needed Bairstow's help to find you."

"Why did you need to find me?"

"I had to tell you about the Grey Notice on your head. I couldn't think of another way."

Ryan flinched.

"A Grey Notice," he said slowly. "Official?"

Stacy tilted his head in a half-shrug. "As official as they ever get."

"Who signed it? It can't be anyone at the Home Office. They know I was set up by the SAMS Chairman, Sir Malcolm Sampson."

"Yep, I know. I've seen the video. Can't say it was easy watching his minion work you over in that weird chair."

"Pinocchio, you mean," Ryan said. A wry smile worked its way onto his bearded face.

"Pinocchio? Ah yes, you bit off his nose, didn't you. Nice one, by the way. Well played." Stacy allowed himself another grin. His face hadn't been given such a serious workout in years.

"So, the Grey Notice," Ryan said. "What can you give me?"

"Nothing much so far. Two names. Gregory Enderby and Ernest Hartington. All I can tell you is they're pretty high up in the NCTA. That's the National Counter Terrorism Agency."

"Yes, I know," Ryan said. "What are your plans now?"

"Well, now I've dealt with Maureen Reilly ... Oh, by the way, I dropped her body into a deep hole." Stacy allowed yet another smile to form. "You'd be surprised how many deep holes they have in this part of Wales."

"No, I wouldn't."

"No, I suppose you wouldn't. Anyway, as I said before, after closing the Reilly 'case', I had planned to retire into oblivion."

"But now?"

"Now, my friend," Stacy said. "My plans are fluid. I imagine you're going to visit a couple of members of the NCTA in the not-too-distant future. Is that right?"

"It might be."

"Things could get messy."

"They could indeed."

"You'll likely be going up against some skilled individuals. Individuals with full government support."

"So, what's new?"

"Fancy a little backup?"

Ryan nodded and a determined expression settled on his face.

"Yes, please."

The last time Stacy had seen the same steel-eyed look had been in Fallujah on the eve of combat. Ryan Kaine sat in his seat, preparing for battle, and like in Fallujah, God help anyone who stood in his way.

THE END

THE RYAN KAINE SERIES

On The Run: Book 1 in the Ryan Kaine Series

On The Rocks: Book 2 in the Ryan Kaine Series

On The Defensive: Book 3 in the Ryan Kaine Series

On The Attack: Book 4 in the Ryan Kaine series

On The Money: Book 5 in the Ryan Kaine series

On The Edge: Book 6 in the Ryan Kaine series

On The Wing: Book 7 in the Ryan Kaine series

On The Hunt: Book 8 in the Ryan Kaine series

On The Outside: Book 9 in the Ryan Kaine series

For a free Ryan Kaine origins novella, go to

fusebooks.com/ryankaine

AFTERWORD

PLEASE LEAVE A REVIEW

If you enjoyed On the Lookout, it would mean a lot to Kerry if you were able to leave a review. Reviews are an important way for books to find new readers. Thank you.

ABOUT KERRY J. DONOVAN

#1 International Best-seller with *Ryan Kaine: On the Run*, Kerry was born in Dublin. He currently lives with Margaret in a bungalow in Nottinghamshire. He has three children and four grandchildren.

Kerry earned a first-class honours degree in Human Biology and has a PhD in Sport and Exercise Sciences. A former scientific advisor to The Office of the Deputy Prime Minister, he helped UK emergency first-responders prepare for chemical attacks in the wake of 9/11. He is also a former furniture designer/maker.

http://kerryjdonovan.com/

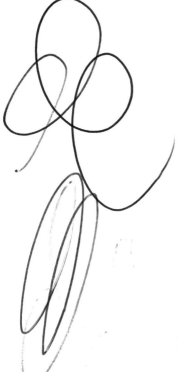

Printed in Great Britain
by Amazon